These rugg...
wor...

PRINCES OF THE OUTBACK

Fan-favourite Bronwyn Jameson brings you
three compelling, classic romances!

PRINCES OF THE OUTBACK

BRONWYN JAMESON

PRINCES OF THE OUTBACK © Harlequin Books S.A. 2010

First published in Great Britain 2010
Harlequin Mills & Boon Limited,
Eton House, 18-24 Paradise Road, Richmond, Surrey TW9 1SR

The publisher acknowledges the copyright holders of the individual works, which
have already been published in the UK:

The Rugged Loner © Bronwyn Turner 2005
The Rich Stranger © Bronwyn Turner 2005
The Ruthless Groom © Bronwyn Turner 2005

ISBN: 978 0 263 88037 3

64-0510

Printed and bound in Spain
by Litografia Rosés S.A., Barcelona

Bronwyn Jameson spent much of her childhood with her head buried in a book. As a teenager, she discovered romance novels and it was only a matter of time before she turned her love of reading them into a love of writing them. Bronwyn shares an idyllic piece of the Australian farming heartland with her husband and three sons, a thousand sheep, a dozen horses, assorted wildlife and one kelpie dog. She still chooses to spend her limited downtime with a good book. Bronwyn loves to hear from readers. Write to her at bronwyn@bronwynjameson. com.

THE RUGGED LONER

Prologue

Charles Carlisle knew he was dying. His family denied it. The herd of medical specialists they'd employed kept skirting around the flanks of the truth like a team of well-trained cattle dogs, but Chas knew his number had come up.

If the tumor mushrooming inside his brain didn't finish him off, the intense radiation therapy he was about to commence would. The only other soul willing to accept the truth was his good mate Jack Konrads. Not surprising since as an estate lawyer Jack dealt with human mortality every day of his working life.

Chas supposed his lawyer friend got to deal with plenty of unusual will clauses, too, because his face remained impressively deadpan as he digested the changes just requested by Chas. Carefully he set the single sheet of paper aside. "I assume you've discussed this with your sons?"

"So they can make my last months a living hell?" Chas snorted. "They'll find out once I'm six feet under!"

"You don't think they deserve some forewarning? Twelve months is precious little time to produce a baby from scratch—even if any one of them was already married and planning to start a family."

"You suggest I should give them time to wiggle out of this?" They were clever enough, his sons. Too clever at times for their own good. "Alex and Rafe are past thirty. They need a decent shove or they'll never settle down."

Brow furrowed with a deep frown, Jack perused his written instructions again. "This wording doesn't seem to exclude Tomas…."

"No exclusions. It's the same for all of them."

"You don't have to prove anything to those boys," Jack said slowly, still frowning. "They know you don't play favorites. You've always treated them as if they're all your sons by birth. They've grown into fine men, Chas."

Yes, they were sons to make any father proud, but in recent years they'd grown apart, each wrapped up in his own world, too busy, too self-involved. This clause would fix that. It would rekindle the spirit of kinship he'd watched grow with the boys as they raced their ponies over the flat grasslands of their outback station. Later they'd roped cleanskin bulls and corporate competitors with the same ruthless determination. He was counting on that get-it-done attribute when it came time to execute this will clause.

"It has to be the same for all three," he repeated resolutely. He couldn't exclude Tomas—didn't want to exclude Tomas.

"It's been barely two years since Brooke was killed."

"And the longer he stays buried in grief, the harder the task of digging his way out." Jaw set, Chas leaned forward and met his friend's eyes. "That, I know."

If *his* father hadn't forced his hand—tough love, he'd called it—Chas would have buried himself in the outback after his first wife's death. He wouldn't have been forced overseas to manage his father's British interests and he wouldn't have met a wild Irish-born beauty named Maura Keane and her two young sons.

He wouldn't have fallen completely and utterly in love.

He wouldn't have married her and completed his family with their own son, Tomas. Their son whose grief over *his* young wife's death was turning him as hard and remote as his outback home. Tomas needed some mighty tough love before it was too late.

"Does Maura know about this?" Jack asked carefully.

"No, and that's the way I want it to stay. You know she won't approve."

For a long moment Jack regarded him over the top of his glasses. "Hell of a way to take all their minds off grieving for you."

Chas scowled. "That's not what this is about. It'll get them working together to find the best solution. My family needs a shake-up, Tomas most of all."

"And what if your plan backfires? What if the boys reject this clause and walk away from their inheritance? Do you want the Carlisle assets split up and sold off?"

"That won't happen."

"They won't like this—"

"They don't have to like it. I suspect I'll hear their objections from beyond the pearly gates, but they'll do it. Not for the inheritance—" Chas fixed his friend with his trademark gaze, steel-hard and unwavering. "They'll do it for their mother."

And that was the biggest, strongest motivation for this added clause to the last will and testament of Charles Tomas

McLachlan Carlisle. He wanted more than his sons working together. He didn't only want to see them take a chance at settled, family happiness. This was for Maura. A grandchild, born within twelve months of his death, to bring a smile to her sad eyes, to break her growing isolation.

He wanted, in death, to achieve what he'd never been able to do in life: to make his adored wife happy.

"This is my legacy to Maura, Jack."

And the only thing out of a multibillion-dollar empire that would be worth an Irish damn to her.

One

Six months later

Angelina Mori didn't mean to eavesdrop. If, at the last minute, she hadn't remembered the solemnity of the occasion she would have charged into the room in her usual forthright fashion and she wouldn't have heard a thing.

But she did remember the occasion—this morning's burial, this afternoon's reading of the will, the ensuing meeting between Charles Carlisle's heirs—and she paused and steadied herself to make a decorous entrance into the Kameruka Downs library.

Which is how she came to overhear the three deep, male voices. Three voices as familiar to Angie's ear as those of her own two brothers.

"You heard what Konrads said. We don't all have to do

this." Alex, the eldest, sounded as calm and composed as ever. "It's my responsibility."

"News flash." Rafe's mocking drawl hadn't changed a bit in the time she'd been gone. "Your advanced age doesn't make you the expert or the one in charge of this. How about we toss a coin. Heads, you—"

"The hell you say. We're in this together. One in, all in." Tomas's face, she knew, would be as hard and expressionless as his voice. Heartbreakingly different to the man she remembered from… Was it only five years ago? It seemed so much longer, almost another lifetime.

"A nice sentiment, little bro', but aren't you forgetting something?" Rafe asked. "It takes two to make a baby."

Angie didn't drop the tray of sandwiches she held, but it was a near thing. Heart hammering, she pulled the tray tight against her waist and steadied it with a white-knuckled grip. The rattling plates quieted; the pounding of her heart didn't.

And despite what she'd overheard—or maybe because of it—she didn't slink away.

With both hands occupied, she couldn't knock on the half-closed door. Instead she nudged it open with one knee and cleared her throat. Loudly. Twice. Because now the voices were raised in strident debate on who was going to do this—*get married? have a baby? in order to inherit?*—and how.

Holy Henry Moses.

Angie cleared her throat a third time, and three pairs of intensely irritated, blue eyes turned her way. The Carlisle brothers. "Princes of the Outback" according to this week's headlines, but only because some hack had once dubbed their father's extensive holdings in the Australian outback "Carlisle's Kingdom."

Angie had grown up by their rough-and-tumble side. They might look like the tabloid press's idea of Australian royalty, but they didn't fool her for a second.

Princes? Ha!

"What?" at least two *princes* barked now.

"Sorry to intrude, but you've been holed up in here for yonks. I thought you might need some sustenance." She deposited her tray in the center of the big oak desk and her hip on its edge. Then she reached for the bottle of forty-year-old Glenfiddich—pilfered from their father's secret stash—and swirled the rich, amber contents in the light. More than half-full. Amazing. "I thought you'd have made a bigger dent in this."

Alex squinted at the glass in his hand as if he'd forgotten its existence. Rafe winked and held his out for a refill. Broad back to the room, hands shoved deep into the pockets of his black dress trousers, Tomas acknowledged neither the whisky nor her arrival.

And no one so much as glanced at the sandwiches. They didn't want sustenance. They wanted her to leave so they could continue their discussion.

Tough.

She slid her backside further onto the desk, took her time selecting a corn beef and pickle triangle, then arched a brow at the room in general. "So, what's this about a baby?"

Tomas's shoulders tensed. Alex and Rafe exchanged a look.

"It's no use pretending nothing's going on," she said around her first bite. "I overheard you talking."

For a long moment she thought they'd pull the old boys' club number, buttoning up in front of the girl. Except this girl had spent her whole childhood tearing around Kameruka Downs in the dust of these three males and her two brothers. Sadly outnumbered, she'd learned to chase hard and to never give up. She glanced sideways at Tomas's back. At least not until she was completely beaten.

"Well?" she prompted.

Rafe, bless his heart, relented. "What do you think, Ange? Would you—"

"This is supposed to be private," Alex said pointedly.

"You don't think Ange's opinion is valuable? She's a woman."

"Thank you for noticing," Angie murmured. From the corner of her eye she watched Tomas who had never noticed, while she fought two equally strong, conflicting urges. One part of her ached to slide off the desk and wrap him and his tightly held pain in a big old-fashioned hug. The other wanted to slug him one for ignoring her.

"Would you have somebody's baby…for money?"

What? Her attention swung from the still and silent figure by the window and back to Rafe. She swallowed. "Somebody's?"

"Yeah." Rafe cocked a brow. "Take our little brother, the hermit, for example. He says he'd pay and since that's—"

"Enough," Alex cut in.

Unnecessarily, as it happened, because a second later— so quick, Angie didn't see it coming—Tomas held Rafe by the shirtfront. The two harsh flat syllables he uttered would never have emanated from any prince's mouth.

Alex separated them, but Tomas only stayed long enough for a final curt directive to his brothers. "You do this your way, I'll do it mine. I don't need your approval."

He didn't slam the door on his way out, and it occurred to Angie that that would have shown too much passion, too much heat, for the cold, remote stranger the youngest Carlisle had become.

"I guess my opinion is beside the point now," she said carefully.

Rafe coughed out a laugh. "Only if you think Mr. Congeniality can find himself a woman."

Angie's heart thumped against her ribs. Oh, he could. She had no doubts about that. Tomas Carlisle might have forgotten how to smile, but he could take his big, hard body and I've-been-hurt-bad attitude into any bar and choose from the top shelf. Without any mention of the Carlisle billions.

A chill shivered through her skin as she put down the remains of her sandwich. "He won't do anything stupid, will he?"

"Not if we stop him."

Alex shook his head. "Leave him be, Rafe."

"Do you really think he's in any mood to make a discriminating choice?" Rafe made an impatient sound, not quite a laugh, not quite a snort. "What the hell was Dad thinking anyway? He should have left Tomas right out of this!"

"Maybe he wanted to give him a shake-up," Alex said slowly.

"The kind that sends him out looking to cut a deal with the first bar-bunny he happens upon?"

Angie stood so swiftly, her head spun. Whoa. Breathing deeply, she leaned against the desk. It was okay. Kameruka Downs was two hours of black dust and corrugated roads from the nearest bar. Even if Tomas did decide to hightail it into Koomah Crossing, he wouldn't make closing time.

She exhaled slowly and settled back on the desk. "Confession time, guys. I really only overheard one slice of your earlier discussion, so who'd like to fill me in on the whole story?"

* * *

Once, on a bet, Angie had raced Tomas and her brother Carlo from the homestead to the waterhole, blindfolded. Remembering that experience fifteen years ago made tonight's steep descent a veritable walk in the park. A three-quarter moon rode high in the sky, casting enough light for Angie to pick a surefooted path through the scrub. Behind a bandanna blindfold there'd been nothing but intense black, yet she'd closed her eyes and run.

Anything to prove herself less of a girl.

You're part feral goat, the boys had spat in disgust as they handed over her winnings, and it had taken Angie years to realize that comparison wasn't exactly flattering.

Her smile, wry and reminiscent, faded as she neared her destination. *Moment of truth, sister.* She rubbed warming hands up and down her goose-bumped arms. She would bet the vintage silk-georgette dress she'd vainly not changed out of—despite the chill night and a setting more suited to jeans—that Tomas had retreated to his usual lair.

And when you find him, you say your piece and you make sure he listens. You don't let him turn his back.

She'd seen Tomas several times since her return from Italy a week earlier. At the hospital before his father passed away, at the memorial service held largely for his city business associates, at Alex's Sydney home afterward. Yet he'd managed to evade anything beyond a quick consoling hug and a few token words of sympathy.

So she'd stayed on at Kameruka Downs after the private funeral, begging a lift back to Sydney on the corporate jet with Alex and Rafe, instead of returning on the afternoon charter arranged for other mourners. She had to talk to Tomas, one on one. She had to set things straight between them.

This had nothing to do with the disturbing clause in Charles's will that she'd just learned about in the library. This was about guilt and regret and failing to be the kind of friend she wanted to be. It was about closure, too, and moving on with her life.

And it promised to be damn-near the toughest thing she'd ever done. Tougher even than the night she'd confronted Tomas with her opinion on his upcoming marriage…and that had been Tough with a capital T!

It wasn't that she hadn't liked Brooke. They'd been close friends at school. Tomas had met his future wife at Angie's eighteenth birthday party, on a night when *she'd* dressed and preened and set herself on being noticed as a woman instead of his wild-child pseudosister.

Instead—the supreme irony—he'd fallen into complete blinker-eyed besottedness with her petite and delicate friend. And eighteen months later he hadn't wanted to hear Angie's opinion on Brooke's suitability to life in the outback. He loved Brooke. He married Brooke.

And *that* had been one tough challenge Angie couldn't face.

Instead of accepting the bridesmaid's gig, she'd taken off on a backpacking jaunt to Europe. Her grand adventure had started as an impulsive escape from pain and envy, from her fear that she wouldn't make it through "does anyone have just cause" without jumping to her feet and yelling, "You bet I do! He's supposed to be mine!"

She'd missed the wedding and, worse, she'd missed Brooke's funeral. But now she was back, needing to make peace with her conscience. She doubted she could make peace with the flint-hard stranger Tomas had become, but she had to try.

"Moment of truth," she muttered, out loud this time,

as she ducked under a branch into the clearing beside the waterhole.

Slowly she scanned the darkness and the empty shadows, before hauling herself up onto a rock overhang. On sure feet she climbed higher to the secret cave. Peered inside.

Backed-up breath huffed from her lungs.

Nothing. *Damn.*

Disappointment expanded, tightening her chest as she slowly descended to the ground. She'd made a deal with herself, a deal about finding him and getting this over with tonight. How could she do that when he wasn't here?

Swearing softly, she turned to leave.

Or perhaps he simply didn't want to be found....

Her eyes narrowed. Perhaps Tomas hadn't changed completely. Perhaps now, as in the past, he wasn't completely alone down here.

Angie allowed herself a small smile before she lifted both pinkies to her pursed lips and whistled.

Tomas figured someone—most likely Angie—would come looking for him. He'd counted on the night hiding his secluded location. He hadn't counted on her whistling his dog.

Ajay responded with a high-pitched whine of suspicion. Rough translation: *You can whistle—point in your favor—but I'm no pushover. I'm a red heeler; I protect my boss. You better proceed with caution.*

Angie didn't.

The quick tread of her approach was as incisive and uninhibited as her personality. Loose gravel dislodged by her climbing feet splished into the water below, and Tomas saw the hair rise along Ajay's spine. Under his restraining hand he felt a warning growl vibrate through the dog's tense body. It was a measure of his own snarled mood that he actually considered letting the heeler loose.

He didn't.

His muttered "Stay" was probably for the dog—God knows Angie wouldn't take a lick of notice!

As if to prove his point, she appeared out of the darkness and used his shoulder to steady herself as she dropped down at his side. The floaty skirt of her dress settled around her legs where they dangled over the rock ledge, a flutter of feminine contrast to the rugged setting and the worn denim stretched over his thighs alongside.

"Did you consider I might want to be alone?" he asked, surprising himself with the even tone of his voice. Ever since Jack Konrads read out that newly added will clause, tension had snarled through his blood and his flesh. An anger that had whipped the hollow numbness of grief and loss into something hot and taut and hazardous.

"Yes," she said simply, with a quick flash of smile.

Although that could have been for Ajay, because on the heels of the smile came a softly crooned note of surprise. Her hand slid from his shoulder down his arm—from rolled-up shirtsleeve to skin—as she leaned around him to take a better look. "While I was clambering up here, I kinda thought you mightn't have Sergeant anymore."

"He died."

For the tiniest hint of time, she stilled. Then the pressure of her hand on his forearm changed, a tactile expression of her next words. "I'm sorry to hear that."

"He got old."

"As we all do." She leaned forward. "Well, aren't you handsome." And started to reach—

"Best you don't do that."

"I'm only saying hello."

And wouldn't you know it? His wary-natured heeler didn't take a piece out of her hand. Tomas breathed a tad easier…but only a tad. He was still struggling to reconcile the Angie he knew—the annoying, exasperating, teenage tomboy—with this exotic, alien creature who'd returned from Europe.

She wore dresses, for pity's sake. She'd straightened her unruly curls into one of those city-girl do's, all sleek and dark and glossy. And every time she moved he heard the delicate tinkle of the jewelry she wore on her wrists and ankle.

Hell, she even had some kind of rings on her toes. And as for the perfume…

"What's with the perfume?"

"Excuse me?"

Yeah, excuse him. He hadn't meant to say it, the question that blared in his brain every time he breathed around her. Ever since that first day he saw her again—*hell, was that only last week?*—when she'd rushed down the hallway of the hospital to throw her arms around him, to hug him and hold him and leak tears and words and more tears into his shirt.

Except instead of feeling comforted, he'd dragged in air rich with this perfume and he'd felt her curves against his body and he'd tensed. His hands had set her aside, this woman who no longer felt anything like Angie should.

She'd changed when all he wanted was someone— something—to stay the same. To anchor him to the past that fate kept wrenching away.

"You smell…different," he accused now. She smelled different, she looked different, and right now in the dark he swore she was looking at him different, too. "You've changed, Dash."

His use of her childhood nickname surprised a laugh from her full lips. With a clink of bracelets, her hand slid away from his arm, thank God, and into her lap. "Wow. There's a blast from the past. No one's called me Dash in…forever."

Yeah, forever about summed it up.

Forever since the last time she'd followed him down here, bent on telling him how the outback and Brooke would never see eye to eye. Like he hadn't known. And like he'd not been young enough and cocky enough to think it wouldn't make a difference.

"It's only been five years, but you're right. I've changed, you've changed, everything's changed," she said softly, and suddenly the darkness seemed more intense. Suffocatingly so. "I'm sorry about your father, that he got so sick and had to suffer and that the last weeks were so hard on you all. I'm sorry I wasn't here, and I hope—"

"You didn't have to come down here to tell me that. I've heard it more than enough times this last week."

"Yeah, well, you haven't heard it from me. At least not without cutting me off midsentence and walking away." She angled her chin in that determined way she had. "I have more to say, actually, and this time I want you to stay put until I finish."

Something about her tone and the sympathetic darkness of her eyes alerted him to what might be on her mind, and he started to move, to get the hell out of the conversation. But she put her hand on his knee, stopping him. It was the Angie-of-old, exasperating and annoying and not letting him get away without first saying her piece.

"Did you get my letter?" she asked.

Yeah, he'd gotten the letter she'd written after Brooke

was killed. What did she expect him to say? Thank you for your kind thoughts? They really helped me cope when my heart had been ripped bleeding from my chest.

"I hated that a lousy letter was all I could send," she continued. "I wish I could have been here. I wish I could have found better words."

"It wouldn't have made any difference."

"It would have to me." She moved her hand—had she always been such a toucher, or had that changed, too?—this time covering his fist where it sat clenched on this thigh. She squeezed his tense knuckles. "I wasn't here for you when it mattered, when I should have been. What kind of friend does that make me?"

Was he supposed to answer that? Or just sit here like some priest in an outdoors confessional and let her talk so she'd feel better about herself?

He hoped she wasn't after absolution, because that sure wasn't anything he was qualified to give!

"Your friendship matters to me. Are we still friends, T.J.?"

His childhood nickname, but it sounded all wrong on her lips because she'd leaned closer, her arm pressed warm and soft against his, her perfume a sensuous drift of woman in his nostrils. And then she did that squeezing thing again, probably meaning to reassure him but only screwing his tension up another notch.

He wrested his hand away, put hers back in her lap. "If it makes you feel better, why the hell not?"

"Yeesh, Tomas!" She let her breath go sharply, exasperated. "Can't you at least pretend to accept sympathy from a friend? Would that hurt so very much?"

When he didn't answer, she shook her head slowly. The slippery ends of her hair skimmed against his bare forearm as if coolly mocking one of the reasons he didn't feel like she was his friend. This strange awareness that he didn't want or like or need.

The disturbing notion that little Angie had grown up into a woman…and his man's body wouldn't stop noticing.

"That's all I came down here to say," she said abruptly. "Accept it or don't. I'll leave you to enjoy your pity party alone."

She'd already started to rise, not using his shoulder for leverage this time, and Tomas should have let her go. Shouldn't have felt the irrational need to ask, "That's it? That's all you came down here to say?"

"Oh, boy." Beside him she stilled, then her laughter rumbled, as soft and husky-dark as the night. "I really want to say, yes, that's it. I really, *really* know I should."

"But?"

"But you wouldn't have baited me to stay unless you needed to talk." She sank back down and he felt her gaze on his face, felt it turn serious. "It's that will clause, isn't it?"

"You don't think that's worth throwing a pity party over?"

She didn't answer that question, not directly. Instead she sighed and shook her head. "It's worth worrying about, sure. But wouldn't you be better off back at the homestead talking it through with your brothers?"

Tomas snorted. "What's there to talk through?"

"For a start, there's some worry about how you'll choose a mother for this baby you think you have to produce."

"There's no 'think' about it."

"My understanding is that only one of you needs do this. One baby between the three of you."

"You think I'd leave it up to my brothers? When I stand to lose all this?" He gestured around him, indicating the land that was more than a family legacy. Kameruka Downs was the only place he'd ever wanted to live and all he had left since the plane crash that took his wife's life, his happiness, his future.

"Your brothers know this place is everything to you," Angie said softly.

Wrong. It wasn't everything; it was the only thing.

"Alex says he's going to marry Susannah."

"Yeah, right. When they both can schedule a free hour between meetings. And as for Rafe…" He made a scoffing noise that said it all.

"Yeah," Angie agreed, and in the ensuing silence—as they both contemplated the unlikely image of Rafe, the consummate playboy, choosing one woman for the job—it almost felt like the old Angie sitting at his side, driving him bonkers one minute, completely in accord the next. "Why do you think he made this stipulation? Your father, I mean."

"For Mau."

She contemplated that for a moment. "He knows you guys would do anything for Maura—that's a given—but he had to know she wouldn't want some token grandchild. That she wouldn't be happy unless you all were happy, not forced into it by a clause in his will."

"Yeah, but she's not to know anything about it. That's why Konrads wanted to see us alone."

"Good luck with that!" She cut him a look, part thoughtful, part rueful. "Although I do think he was pretty smart. I mean, what surer way to distract you all from mourning him?"

Tomas turned sharply, stared at her for a minute. Trust Angie to come up with that angle.

"Smart?" he wondered out loud, thinking words like contrived and cunning where closer to the truth.

Wasn't it their right to mourn a father who'd done so much for them, been so much to them?

"It worked, didn't it?" she asked.

Hell, yes. They'd barely had time to bury him before Jack Konrads called that meeting in the library and turned their sorrow into anger.

Tomas shook his head, dismissing the whole topic with a gesture of impatience. "His reasoning doesn't change what we have to do."

Angie's silent regard, serious and thoughtful, tugged the bands of frustration in his chest tighter.

"What?" he barked.

"Rafe says you're not…seeing…anyone."

Her midsentence pause was just long enough for Tomas to know his brother had used another doing word. "What the hell would Rafe know about who I'm…*seeing?*"

For possibly the first time in her life, Angie's gaze dropped away from his. Probably because of his brutal emphasis on that verb. Fine. He didn't want to discuss his sex life, with her, with Rafe, with anyone.

Worse, he hated the notion that they'd been discussing it in his absence.

"Okay," she said on an exhalation. "So, do you have any sort of a plan? Other than that crazy idea of paying someone?"

"What's so crazy about it?"

"Yeesh, Tomas, do you really want that kind of woman to mother your child?"

"What kind would that be?"

She rolled her eyes. "The kind who'd do it for money."

"I'm not talking prostitution."

"Really?"

Something about her tone—and the arch of her brows—chafed his simmering frustration. "You got any better ideas? Women aren't about to line up to have my baby."

"You are so without a clue. I mean, look at you!" And

she did. She leaned back and looked at him with a narrow-eyed thoroughness that reminded him all over again how much she'd changed. "Women find that whole rugged loner thing a complete turn-on."

"What a load of bull!"

She made an impatient tsking sound with her tongue. "You get to the city occasionally…or at least you used to. You have to feel women looking you over. You can't *not* know you're like their living, breathing, outback fantasy."

Fantasy? Big deal. What he needed was reality, female and available.

"Name me one of these women," he said roughly. "One who'd have my baby."

She blinked slowly and edged back another inch. Which is when he noticed that he'd gotten right in her face. Close enough that he heard the faint hiss of her indrawn breath. The only sound in the intense silence, until she spoke.

"I would."

Two

Angie listened to those two short, stunning syllables echoing inside her head. *I would.* Where had that come from? Was she insane?

Definitely.

Otherwise she would be laughing, right? Not loopy, they're-coming-to-take-me-away-ha-ha laughter, but a smooth chuckle as she nudged Tomas and said, "Ha, ha. Got you a good one, didn't I?" Or something similarly off-hand and flippant.

Anything to fill the awkward silence and the fact that her heart was thudding so hard it physically hurt, and that she really, really wanted to confess the truth.

Well, here's the thing, Tomas....

I've loved you in some way pretty much all of my life. I've wanted to marry you ever since I was thirteen. Somewhere around fourteen I'd already named our babies—three of them, all boys, all with your baby blues.

Except she couldn't admit that. She wanted to shove the intensity of her teenage crush back in the past where it belonged. She'd come down here to try and *save* their friendship, not to send it on a headlong plummet into disaster.

Angie swallowed, and wished that his gaze hadn't dropped to her throat at that exact second. Her throat felt tight, her smile even tighter. "I've really weirded you out, haven't I?"

"Yup." He shook his head, looked away, then back at her. "Was that your intention?"

"No."

"Then…why?"

She wished she could laugh it off, but she looked into his stunned blue eyes and she couldn't laugh and she couldn't lie. All she could find was some small version of the truth. "Damned if I know, but I have to tell you that your response is not very flattering. I mean, would it be so bad? You and me?"

She felt him staring, felt the puzzlement in his sharp regard take on another flavor. Was he actually contemplating the reality? Him with her, skin to skin, doing what was necessary to make babies? Her heart skipped. The tightness in her throat and her skin took on a new dimension, a new heat.

"You can't have thought about it," he said slowly, "at all!"

Oh, how wrong could one person be. Angie had thought about it—specifically, about her and Tomas doing *it*—ever since her first sex education lesson. "Actually I have thought about it quite a bit," she said slowly. "The sex part, I mean, not the having-a-baby part."

In the midnight quiet his expulsion of breath sounded almost explosive. Apparently the concept of Sex-with-Angie was so appalling that he couldn't even look her in the eye when he told her so. He jumped to his feet and stalked to the sandstone wall at the back of the rock ledge.

Turning on his boot heels, he stared at her, all hard, shocked, affronted male. "Hell, Angie, you can't be serious. You're like…you're…"

"So unappealing you couldn't bring yourself to sleep with me? Even to keep Kameruka Downs?"

"Don't put words in my mouth. You don't know what I'm thinking," he said tightly.

No, she didn't, and between the tricky dark and the distance he'd put between them, she couldn't tell a thing from his expression. And, dammit, she wasn't about to lose her oldest friend, her pride, *and* get a cricked neck out of this.

She stood and brushed the gritty sand from the back of her dress as she closed the distance between them. *Moment of truth, sister.* "Why don't you tell me then? Why has the idea of me offering to have your baby got you so wound up?"

"Christ, Angie, we're not doing some hypothetical here. We're talking about a real situation. I need a baby." Chin jutted, he started down at her, his whole expression carved as hard as the rock at this back. Possibly harder. "A baby the mother would have to raise on her own."

Hands on hips she narrowed her gaze and stared back at him. Surely she'd heard him wrong. "Are you saying you wouldn't want any part in this child's upbringing?"

"You got it."

"But why?" She shook her head. Huffed out a breath and waved her hand at their surroundings. "You have this fabulous place for a child to grow up, and—"

"Not everyone thinks it's so fabulous."

"Well, I do! And your father obviously thought so, too, since he chose to bring you all up here. Do you think, when he drafted that clause, that he wanted you to just sire some anonymous—"

"I don't care what he thought."

"Really? Then you *have* changed."

"You've got that right, too!"

For a moment they stood toe to toe glaring at each other, until Angie realized that his expression wasn't so much tight and flat as schooled. To hide his frustration, his anger, his pain? Perhaps even his fear that if he and his brothers failed to satisfy the will stipulation, he would lose this home and career and life that he loved, right on top of losing his wife and his father.

That knowledge caught in her chest, a thick ache of sympathy and shared pain and her own dawning realization: she wasn't anywhere near to closing down this part of her past. Because for all that had changed in him, in her, in both their worlds during the last five years, one thing remained the same.

She still loved this man enough to do just about anything to ease his hurt.

Tears misted her eyes as she lifted a hand to touch the side of his face, blurring his features but not his rejection.

Both hands raised in a stop-right-there gesture, he reared back. "Forget it, Angie. Forget the pity and forget this whole crazy conversation!"

Angie's hand dropped away. Okay. She could do this. She could shrug and pretend indifference while her face and her throat and her heart ached with the effort. Restraint—in words, in actions, in emotions—did not come easily or naturally, but she sensed that now was the time to exercise some self-control.

"I care too much to forget about it," she said, slowly backing away, giving him the space he demanded, "so let's talk this through. What are your alternatives? Say you do find a woman willing to have your baby for money. Unprotected sex with a stranger is a big risk, don't you think?

"Unless you're thinking of artificial insemination, which is worth consideration," she continued, thinking on her feet, literally. "On the plus side, you get all the health checks and no awkward intimacy…I gather that is a plus, right?"

A muscle in his cheek jumped. Which probably meant he neither wanted intimacy nor wanted to talk about it. Tough. He'd stopped her leaving earlier, when she'd been ready to walk away, and now she *was* going to talk this through.

"But that all takes time, the checks and tests and the getting an appointment and such, when you don't have much leeway. Three months to conceive, right?" Angie winced. "That is not a lot of time. Especially since the conception rate would be lower."

"Why lower? A.I. works fine in cattle."

Trust Tomas, the consummate cattleman, to equate this to livestock!

Angie lifted her shoulders and let them drop in an exaggerated shrug. "How would I know? It's not as if I've actually investigated the process. I just read about it somewhere. I was trying to help you work through the possibilities is all."

"You sure you don't want to make the decision for me?"

"You've never once taken my advice on anything, why would you start now?"

"That's never stopped you offering it."

Did he mean her previous advice? About not rushing into marriage with Brooke? She stared back at him, found the answer in the grim blue hostility of his gaze. Yep, that's what he meant all right.

"I thought you wanted to talk this through," she said, finally accepting the futility of the conversation. Same old story, really. "You'd do better talking to the cliff face there. At least it won't tell you anything you don't want to hear!"

He started to say something. Judging by the look in his eyes and the hands-on-hips aggressiveness of his stance it was neither pretty nor appeasing, so Angie cut him off.

"I offered to help you, Tomas. Your answer: 'forget this whole crazy conversation.' Well, perhaps that is the best advice that's been tossed out here tonight!" She lifted a hand, part frustration, part farewell. "I'll say goodbye in the morning. When I'm not feeling so inclined to slug you."

Jaw clenched and silent, Tomas watched her disappear into the darkness from whence she'd come. He hadn't meant to hark back to the last time they'd stood toe to toe at this same waterhole. The last time she'd offered advice that he didn't want to hear.

I know you think you love her, T.J., but don't rush into marriage. Not unless you're very, very certain Brooke can handle living out here.

Yup, he'd ignored that advice and they'd both suffered the consequences, he and Brooke. Through three roller-coaster years of passion and conflict, of separations and loneliness, of stand-up fights and emotional making-up. Three years that ended in the mother of all fights and no chance to make it up, not once Brooke was gone.

He had no interest in finding another woman, but he did need to satisfy the terms of his father's will. For his mother, for Kameruka Downs, for his brothers, for himself. All he had to do was find the woman who'd do it *his* way.

That woman was not Angie. No way. She was too used to dancing to her own wild, unscored tune. Unpredictability was the only predictable thing about her. Even her off-the-cuff "I would" offer to have his baby shouldn't have floored him as it had done.

Angie had been pulling I-didn't-think-this-through stunts all her life.

No, it wasn't so much the offer that had rendered him speechless as the disturbing stuff that went hand-in-hand. She'd thought about having sex with him. *Quite a bit,* she'd said.

Sensations burned through his blood, images burned into his brain, and with a low growl of frustration he flung his body at the path and attacked the climb back to the homestead.

That wasn't going to happen. Not with Angie. He wouldn't allow himself to think of her in those terms. Not naked, not in his bed, not beneath his body.

No, no, absolutely no.

She hadn't meant she would, really, have his baby. Only hypothetically. And even if she had meant it, she would soon change her mind. A woman who couldn't settle in one place—in one job—for longer than a month or three wasn't going to cut it as a mother. Sure, she'd changed. She'd grown up some, but she hadn't yet settled down. He didn't know if her gypsy heart ever would.

Back at the homestead he found Rafe lurking in the shadows by the door. An ambush, he suspected. If he hadn't been so preoccupied by the worrying exchange with Angie, he might have suspected as much and avoided it.

"Alex gone to bed?" he asked, stepping onto the veranda.

"He's on the phone. Business continues."

Even past midnight on the night of his father's funeral. That was Alex.

Rafe lifted his liqueur glass. "Care to join me in a nightcap?"

"Another time."

But when he reached for the door, Rafe sidestepped to block his way. So neatly and pseudo-casually that Tomas knew it was no accident. "Don't suppose you happened across Ange out there in the dark?"

Trick question. Tomas's whole body tensed although he schooled his face into passive indifference. Either Rafe had already seen her coming in—had maybe even talked to her—or she'd snuck under his radar by using the side entrance. "Isn't she inside?"

"She wasn't in her room when I checked a while back."

Tomas crossed his arms. Said nothing, gave away nothing. He suspected Rafe would fill him in on why he was looking for Angie without any prompting on his behalf.

"I had this notion, y'see, about the will." Lips pursed, Rafe swirled the liquid in his glass. Tokay. The same dark amber as Angie's eyes. The same eddying whirlpool as in Tomas's gut as he waited for Rafe to continue. "I think Angie's the answer."

"This isn't her problem," Tomas said tightly. "Leave her out of it."

"She knows the whole story so no tricky explanations are necessary. And Mau loves her like a daughter already."

And there was the problem. Angie and her brothers had grown up like part of the family. Their father had cooked for the Carlisles—he'd moved out to Kameruka Downs after his wife died, head-hunted by Chas because he'd cooked at Maura's favorite Sydney restaurant. The Moris had occupied one of the workers' cottages but the kids had spent as much time in the homestead as their father. The six of them, Carlisles and Moris, had grown up together, played together, been schooled together.

"From where I'm standing," Rafe continued, "Angie's the perfect solution."

"From where I'm standing, she's too much like one of the family."

"You mean like our sister?" Surprise whistled out on Rafe's exhalation. "Can't say I feel the same way, not since she's come back from Italy with the new haircut and that body and the walk." Rafe eyed him a moment. "You did notice the walk?"

The sexy sway of her hips? The gauzy skirt that clung to her legs? The glint of a gold ankle chain against smooth olive skin? "No."

"The sad thing is I believe you." Rafe shook his head, his expression a studied mix of disgust and pity. He sipped from his drink, then narrowed his eyes. "Although this does make things less complicated."

"How's that?"

"No need to toss you for her."

Tomas frowned. "I don't follow…."

"Ange is the perfect solution for one of us. If you're not interested, then I'll ask her."

To sleep with *him,* to have *his* baby? Tomas was shaking his head before the thought finished forming. "You and Angie? No way."

"Why not?"

Tomas forced himself to relax. His fingers, he realized, had curled into fists. His gut felt about the same. "What makes you think she'd be interested in helping either one of us out?"

"She has this thing about owing the family. For Mau looking out for her with all the girl stuff and Dad getting her into the fancy boarding school. For keeping her father on the payroll even after he was too sick to work."

"That's bullshit." Not what the Carlisles had done for Joe Mori and his family—that was all true—but the debt thing. "She doesn't owe us a thing."

"She thinks she does."

"You're not serious. About asking her to…" Tomas couldn't say the words. They stuck in his throat, all wrong.

"There isn't anyone I'd rather ask."

"I thought you didn't give a damn about your inheritance."

"I don't." Rafe swallowed the rest of his drink, then clamped a hand on Tomas's shoulder. Their eyes met and held, his brother's intensely serious for once. "But I know how much you care about yours."

"You're not martyring yourself for me."

"One in, all in. Your words, little brother, and the only way to do this thing. We increase our chance of success and lessen the onus on any one of us. No martyrs here, Tomas, just realists out to get the job done."

"Not with Angie," he said tightly.

"Think about it, bro'. She is just about perfect." And with a last squeeze of his shoulder, Rafe turned and disappeared into the house.

The motionless silhouette of horse and rider etched against the clear blue sky must have been a mirage, because when Angie lifted a hand to shield her eyes from the morning sun, only a single Leichardt pine broke the horizon. She sat forward in the passenger seat and stared harder through the Land Rover's dusty windscreen.

Right the first time—nothing broke the mile-long line of ridge save that tree. The crazy woman not only let fly with impulsive offers in the midnight dark, but now she'd started seeing things! With a rueful half laugh, she sank back into her seat. And heard the driver clear his throat.

"You all right, mate?"

"Fine," she assured Jeremy, the stockman who'd been coopted into driving her to the airstrip. "I thought I saw someone up on the ridge is all."

"Coulda been the boss."

"Oh?" Angie forced herself to sound casual. "He's out riding then?"

"Went out at sunup. Coulda been him up there."

Good to know she wasn't delusional. Not so good to know that Tomas had ridden out at dawn, was likely somewhere beyond the Barakoolie ridge right now, and therefore stood no chance of arriving at the airstrip before they left for Sydney.

Disappointment spiked, quick and sharp, in her chest. She shook her head. What had she expected? A chance to say goodbye or a last second I've-been-thinking-about-what-you-said-last-night turnaround?

Is that what she even wanted?

After a night spent tossing and turning, she'd thought not. Sometime in the hour before dawn she'd managed to talk herself into a rational, sensible acceptance that she had no business offering Tomas anything.

So, okay, she had felt rudderless in the last months, unsure what she wanted to do with her life, where she wanted to live, how she wanted to live. She'd returned to Australia because Charles Carlisle was dying, but now she knew she was home to stay.

But having a baby, even Tomas's baby...

In perfect synchronicity with her heart and stomach, the Land Rover lurched and bounced through a series of potholes.

"That snuck up on me, mate. Sorry."

Jeremy, barely seventeen and a hoon at heart, grinned unapologetically without slowing down. In fact, he applied a tad more gas as he swung the vehicle in a wide circle before skidding to a dusty stop alongside the plane. Angie tsked her disapproval although she'd driven in much the same way growing up here.

As she slid down from the cab her gaze skimmed along the empty horizon one last time. She called the resultant hollow sensation deep inside hunger. After all that tossing and turning and self-debating, she had slept eventually. Right through her alarm.

Meaning Rafe had turfed her out of bed with no time for anything but a hasty shower and a quick farewell to Maura and the household staff. Too late to catch a lift when the boys left to perform their pre-flight checks. Too late for breakfast.

She ferreted a fruit bar from her bag and wrinkled her nose in disgust. "I don't suppose you've got anything less healthy on you?" she asked Jeremy as they walked side by side to the plane.

"Nah. Sorry, mate."

"Too bad." While Jeremy stowed her luggage she finished the breakfast substitute, but the hollow feeling in her stomach only intensified. "Do you suppose they're almost ready for takeoff?"

"Just about."

For some reason Angie wasn't. She'd come up north for the funeral, but also to say farewell to her childhood home and her teenage daydreams. Instead she felt…fretful.

As if she were leaving something behind, unfinished.

"See ya later then, Ange."

With a casual wave, Jeremy started to turn away and ridiculous panicky I'm-not-ready-to-leave tears sprang to Angie's eyes. Before she could stop herself she grabbed hold of the young jackaroo and planted a smacker on his cheek.

So, okay, the kid looked a dozen shades of embarrassed as he sidled away, but *she* felt better. She even managed a big smile as she called after him, "Look after yourself. And drive carefully."

Holy cow. She sounded like a mother!

Was that some kind of a sign? Her destiny sneaking up to answer all the unanswered questions of the night?

Smile fading, she let her hand drop away from its cheerful wave as the ute sped off, dust billowing in its wake. She didn't know if this atypical fragility stemmed from returning home after so long away, the emotional circumstances of her visit, or lack of sleep.

Most likely, all of the above.

With a hitch of one shoulder, she started up the steps of the plane. The engines turned over with a high-pitched whine, and a sudden gust of wind plastered her skirt to her legs and tangled her shoulder-length hair. Pausing to rake the thick tresses back from her face, she felt compelled to take one last look over her shoulder.

Her attention snagged on a distant spurt of movement. Not the rapidly departing Jeremy and not an illusion, either.

A horse and rider loped steadily across the treeless flats, heading straight toward the airstrip.

Three

Angie pressed the palm of one hand flat against her chest. "Steady up there," she cautioned her heart which had taken off at a wild gallop. *Even if it is Tomas, he's likely just coming to see us off or to deliver a last minute message to his brothers.*

Or something.

Rafe called out to her from inside the plane, hurrying her along. Alex, she knew, was already in the pilot's seat. She waved a stalling hand, her eyes fixed on the approaching rider. No one sat a horse quite like Tomas. The familiarity of that sight and the knowledge that she *would* get to say goodbye, soothed the ragged rawness of her emotions. Her pulse, however, continued to race as she watched him dismount and start toward her, not in any hurry yet still eating up the ground with his easy, long-legged stride.

No one wore a pair of Wranglers quite like Tomas.

Those work-worn jeans and the dusty roper boots beneath came to a halt at the foot of the stairs. Two steps up, Angie held a height advantage for the first time in her life and she felt a renewed surge of emotion.

This time it was *good* emotion, as strong and dazzling as the northern sun. Leaning down, she tipped back the tan Akubra that shadowed his face from the bright rays of that morning sun.

"You almost missed us," she said.

"Damn straight he did." Rafe, curse his timing, leaned out the aircraft door and broke their second of eye-meet connection. "Nice of you to drop by and see us off, bro'."

"Wanted to make sure you were leaving, bro'."

Rafe chuckled and Angie couldn't suppress a grin at the dry banter. It was so typical, so familiar, so brotherly. Then Tomas's serious gaze shifted back to hers and froze the amusement on her lips. "And I wanted to see Angie."

"Don't keep her too long," Rafe warned. "Alex is itching to get back to work."

He left them alone then, she and Tomas and the memory of their last conversation stretching tense and awkward in the ensuing silence. Angie's nerves twitched impatiently.

"If this is about what I said last night—"

"I've been thinking about what you said—"

They both spoke at the same time; both stopped at the same time. Their eyes met and locked and Angie felt a curious breathlessness. "You first," she managed to murmur. "Go ahead."

"When you said you would—hypothetically—have this baby, was the offer…exclusive?"

What?

Angie felt her spine snap straight with the implication.

"I hope you're not insinuating I would go around offering to have babies for every Tom, Dick and Harry."

His disconcerted gaze flicked toward the plane and understanding dawned, startling a cough of laughter from Angie's mouth. *Not every Tom, Dick and Harry, just every...*

"Rafe and Alex?"

He shifted his weight from one boot to the other. "Rafe seems to think you'd do this because you owe the family."

"You discussed me with Rafe?" she asked on a rising note of disbelief.

"He brought it up. He seems to think you're the perfect choice."

"And what about you, Tomas? Have you given any thought to *your* choice?"

"I've been thinking about it all night." His eyes narrowed, deepening the creases at their corners. Making those clear blue irises glint like cool water under a summer sky. Making her heart stutter and restart low in her belly. "Will you help me, Angie?"

And there it was, a simple request spoken so quietly and sincerely that it turned her inside out and upside down. Knowing how much fulfilling this will clause meant to Tomas, how could she refuse? "If I can," she said, just as softly. "Yes."

His nostrils flared a fraction. His eyes sparked with... something. "Why?"

Because you need me. Because I love you. "Because I can."

He looked away, huffed out a breath, said something low and indecipherable and probably not meant for her ears. Slowly his gaze came back to hers. "Still as impetuous as ever?"

Angie shrugged. "Apparently."

For a long moment they stood in silence, gazes locked, while Angie's heart screamed at roughly the same decibels as the plane's engines.

What are you doing? it wailed. *What are you saying?*

"What now?" she asked, knowing even as she asked what she wanted. Some sign that this was more real than it felt. That she really had just offered to have his baby. "Do you want me to stay?"

"No," he said quickly. Adamantly. Then he lifted a hand to the brim of his hat, tipping it lower on his brow so his eyes were in shadow. "I'm coming to Sydney next week. I'll make an appointment with a doctor."

"You don't need to…" Her voice trailed off as she remembered what she'd talked about, so glibly, the night before. Then it had been about some hypothetical partner with an unknown sexual history. Now it was about her and Tomas and… She drew a swift breath and lifted her chin. "Yes, we should have the tests, to make sure we're both healthy."

He stared at her a moment. "I meant a fertility center."

"Surely there's no need for that."

"There is. For insemination."

Angie's mouth fell open. "You're kidding, right?"

He wasn't. She could see that in the rigid set of his jaw, in the muscle that flexed and released in his cheek. "It's got to be artificial."

"Got to be?" Angie asked calmly, as if she weren't flailing around trying to get a grasp of something solid. "Because when you asked for my help, when I said yes, I was thinking about doing this the way nature intended."

"No," he said tightly. "That's not going to happen."

Angie fought an irrational urge to laugh or cry or scream—or perhaps not so irrational. The situation, this conversation, the stilted way they kept tiptoeing around straight language, was all too unreal. She couldn't believe how calmly she'd offered to sleep with Tomas, to make love, to try to conceive a baby.

And she couldn't have imagined how much it would hurt, seeing how fiercely he objected.

"Is the idea of sleeping with me so distasteful that you'd prefer doing it on your own? Because most men—"

"Leave it be, Angie!" He muttered a rough word, one that was fairly pertinent to the topic, Angie thought. "It won't work."

"Functionally?" She came down a step so she was right on a level with his face. So she could see the heightened color that traced his cheekbones. See the rigid line of his lips.

Hear the breath he sucked through his teeth. "I meant you and me, any way other than artificial."

"It's only sex," she fired back, her patience so close to snapping she could feel the twitch in her nerves. "Surely you could lie back, close your eyes and think of Kameruka!"

Their gazes clashed, so hot and hostile that neither noticed Rafe's reemergence from the plane until he cleared his throat. "Sorry to interrupt, folks, but we've really got to get moving."

"Two minutes." Angie didn't turn around but she held up a hand. "Just give me two minutes."

She had no clue what she would do with those precious minutes, whether she would sock Tomas one for his stubbornness or take his face between her hands and kiss him one. Just to prove that she was a woman and he was wrong and that this could work if he'd only give her a chance.

Still simmering she leaned a fraction closer, until she could see into the shadow cast by his broad-brimmed hat and beyond the hostility of his stance to the man beneath. And what she saw there sucker-punched her heart.

He looked so torn, so trapped, so tormented.

Ahh, Tomas...

Like butter under the outback sun, her own animosity melted. "I so wish you hadn't been forced into this."

She lifted a hand to touch his face, and for a whisper of time he allowed it. She felt the bristly texture of his unshaven cheek, the warmth of an exhaled breath, the tension that held his whole body straight and erect, and she ached to hold him, to bury her face in that hollow between shoulder and neck, to nuzzle his skin.

And she wanted to kiss him so badly that her lips stung with the wanting, but already she could feel him preparing to pull away. She didn't give him a chance to get any further. Taking his face firmly between both hands, she ducked beneath that broad-brimmed hat and planted her lips on his.

There, Tomas Carlisle, take that.

With her eyes wide-open she saw the shock in his narrowed blue ones, felt the resistance in his stiff lips and the jolt of reaction—in him, in herself—as her mouth opened softly. Then he wrenched her hands away, turning his face so her lips grazed the corner of his mouth and across his whiskery cheek.

She was left kissing nothing but the morning air, left staring into eyes that blazed with blue fire. "You can't stand even a kiss?" she asked.

He thumbed the hat back up his forehead, aggravation etched all over his face. "Dammit, Angie, why are you forcing this? If you're willing to help, then why not my way?"

Because this was her chance—probably her only chance—to have him, and if she could have him and love him and give him the family he needed, then maybe she could also heal his wounded heart. She didn't know if that was possible, but she had to take a chance. One thing she did know for sure and certain—if she told him how she felt, she wouldn't see his Wrangler-wrapped backside for swirling black bulldust.

So she rocked back on her heels, folded her arms across her chest, and shrugged. "If I'm going to sacrifice myself to have this baby, I'm not going to be dudded out of all the fun."

For maybe half a second he went completely still—as if she'd *really* shocked him—and then he shoved his hat low on his forehead and took a slow step backward. Then another. "This is business, Angie, not fun."

"And business can't be fun?"

"Not anymore," he said tightly. And he turned and strode away.

"Nice work, Ange," Rafe drawled from behind her.

She didn't turn around, she was too focused on Tomas's retreat. His broad shoulders were bunched with tension, his long legs moving as if he couldn't get far enough away from her quickly enough.

Nice work?

"Only if my job description was 'lose a good friend,'" she said softly.

Rafe's hand squeezed her shoulder, but the gesture of support and reassurance didn't do much to ease the thickness in her chest and throat. "You gave him plenty to think about for the next week, don't you think?"

She frowned back over her shoulder. "What about next week?"

"We're meeting in Sydney."

"We?"

"Alex, myself, Tomas. We're meeting with Konrads again. About the will."

Angie's gaze slid, helplessly, back to the man who now

sat still and watchful on his horse. Making sure she did leave? "Are you suggesting he might change his mind?"

"With a little help."

"What kind of help?" she asked suspiciously.

"Last night I mentioned asking you to help *me* out. My little brother objected rather strenuously."

"*I* object rather strenuously!"

Rafe winked. "Yeah, but he doesn't need to know that."

"What are you suggesting?"

"A little competition wouldn't harm your cause, babe."

Yes, the Carlisles hated to be outdone, especially by each other. Hadn't Tomas's first words this morning been about her offering herself to the wider Carlisle cause? Angie's gaze shifted back to the motionless rider and her heart skipped a half-beat.

"Between that and what you've given him to think about…"

"What's that?" she asked.

"Close your eyes, lie back, and think of Kameruka." Rafe grinned and shook his head. "Nice work, Ange."

"Have either of you considered other methods?" Tomas felt the impact of his brothers' undivided attention before he looked up from his plate and found them both staring at him, obviously baffled by his out-of-the-blue question.

Around them the late-lunch activity continued in the restaurant of the Sydney Carlisle Grande Hotel. Patrons ate. Waiters waited. Tomas didn't notice.

He didn't recall eating his meal. Didn't recall what they'd discussed while they ate. His attention had been fixed solely on the outcome of their prelunch meeting with Jack Konrads, a week to the day after they'd last met in the Kameruka Downs library.

Long story short: they could fight their father's will. But then they would have to live with the knowledge that they'd disrespected his last wish.

They had to do this. They had to try.

"Other methods—" Rafe rocked back in his chair "—of eating? Meeting?"

"The baby," Tomas elucidated. "Artificial conception. I'm thinking of going to a—" Center? Service? Frowning, he searched for the right term. "What do you call those places?"

"A breeding farm?" Rafe suggested.

"A clinic." Alex put his cutlery down and fixed Tomas with a steely look. The kind he used often in the boardroom to show he meant business. "You don't have to do this— either of you. That message I got before…"

Vaguely Tomas recalled Alex's phone blipping just as their meals arrived.

"Susannah has agreed to marry me."

There was a moment of shocked silence, broken when a waiter arrived to remove their plates. Rafe recovered first and gestured toward the phone. "Are you saying Susannah agreed to marry you by *text message?*"

"She knows we're on a short timeline. I told her I wanted to know as soon as she reached a decision."

Rafe shook his head sadly. "And they say romance is dead."

For once Tomas was in complete agreement with Rafe. Sure, his eldest brother kept a brutal work schedule. Susannah, too, ran her own business. But, still…

"Aren't you going to congratulate me?" Alex asked.

"Only if you can manage to look slightly happy about it," Rafe replied at the same time as Tomas said, "You're only marrying because of the will."

And in his opinion, that just sucked cane toads. A marriage wasn't a business transaction. It was about love and partnership and commitment.

Till death us do part.

"Ah, hell." He didn't realize he'd been screwing up his napkin until he threw the tightly wadded missile onto the table and rolled the crystal salt shaker. "You don't have to marry her, Alex."

"Yes. I do." Alex folded his napkin in half and half again. Placed it neatly on the table. "That's the only way I'll do this."

"When's the wedding?" Rafe asked.

"There's the mandatory thirty-day wait, but as soon as possible. We haven't decided where."

"Not at home?" Rafe asked "Mau will want to be there." By home he meant Kameruka Downs, where they'd all grown up and where Tomas still lived. Their mother, too, in her own place built after his marriage. She rarely left her remote outback home these days. Since intense media scrutiny had led to a breakdown after she'd lost her fourth child to SIDS, she despised the city, crowds, photographers.

"We're negotiating," Alex said. "Susannah has family interstate."

"Not wanting to get personal," Rafe said carefully. "But does Susannah know she's expected to, um, produce an heir right off the bat?"

"She knows." Alex checked his watch, frowned. "I have a meeting to get to, but I wanted you both to know I've got this covered."

Rafe and Tomas exchanged a look.

"You've got your part of the deal covered," Rafe corrected.

"We'll look after ours," Tomas added. "One in, all in." He got to his feet at the same time as his brothers, and offered his hand. "Congratulations, Alex. I hope it works out for you."

There was a moment, a connection that extended far beyond the firm handshake, the quick slap on the back, even the strong meeting of sky-blue eyes. It was the bond of brothers, the knowledge that a pact made would never be broken. They were all in this together, and, come hell or high water, they would make it work.

Then Alex was striding off between the tables with his trademark sense of purpose. Standing side by side, his brothers watched him out the door before Rafe shook his head. "Do you suppose he proposed by text or e-mail or intercompany memo?"

"Wondered the same thing myself." Tomas scrubbed a hand over his face. "It's not that I don't like Susannah, it's just that she's…Susannah."

Not Susie, like Angelina was Angie, but always the whole three syllables. Always so formal and cool and dispassionate. So absolutely unlike Angie.

"The whole deal's too cold-blooded and impersonal," he said, and he felt Rafe's gaze switch and focus on his face.

"As cold-blooded and impersonal as artificial conception?"

"That's different."

"I won't dignify that with a response." Rafe shook his head and indicated the door. "You ready to go?"

Nothing more was said—and that surprised the hell out of Tomas—until they were out in the lobby and about to part ways. "Did you know Ange is working here?" Rafe asked conversationally.

Tomas tensed, then covered quickly by casting a casual glance back at the restaurant. "Waitressing?"

"I meant here as in the Carlisle Grande, in my office.

She asked if I had any jobs going last week, flying home from your place, after—"

Rafe made an expansive gesture and Tomas thought, *Yeah, after.* That about summed it up.

"I gather you're not even considering her offer?"

No longer casual, Tomas's gaze cut back to his brother's face. "She told you about that?"

"We talked some. I've seen a fair bit of Ange this last week."

What the hell did "talked some" mean? And "seen a fair bit of"? Was that in the office or out of hours?

Tomas forced his fingers to unfurl out of fists. Forced himself to ask some other question, any other question. "What are you going to do about the baby?"

"I have some prospects."

"Angie?" he asked before he could stop himself.

"She's one." Lips pursed, Rafe studied him narrowly. "That won't be a problem, now you've decided to go elsewhere?"

"If it's a problem," Tomas said shortly, "it's not mine."

What else could he say? How could he object? He shook hands and watched Rafe walk away. His own decision was made and it involved a clinic and a nameless faceless woman he had to somehow find. It didn't involve any kind of passion or emotion or commitment. It sure as hell didn't involve Angie's boldly stated way of doing things!

Close your eyes, lie back, and think of Kameruka.

How many times had he closed his eyes this last week, lying back in the restless tangle of his sheets, and thought about Angie? Her soft lips grazing his skin, her exotic perfume adrift in his blood, her dark eyes filled with the wild promise of passion as she came to him in the dark.

It's only sex.

If only he could believe that. If only he could get past the disturbing notion of the action and cut straight to the result. Because he could imagine Angie with a baby, in a wildly sensuous earth-mother way.

But Rafe's baby?

The notion burned his gut like battery acid, the wrongness and the certainty that if his brother asked, Angie would say yes. Women didn't say no to Rafe. Ever.

Ah, hell.

Instead of heading out to the street on a quest for cold and impersonal, he found himself in an elevator going up to the executive floor of the Carlisle Grande Hotel. And his gut burned worse than ever.

Four

He found her office empty, yet Tomas had no doubt that this was Angie's workspace. Less than two days on the job—not enough time to even change the name-plate on the door—and already she'd stamped her personality all over the place. Some—Alex came to mind—would call her desk a disaster. She would shrug and call it work in progress.

Knowing Angie, that would mean at least a dozen pieces of work in simultaneous progress.

Amid all the open folders and scattered paperwork sat a bright blue coffee mug which he knew wouldn't be empty. Angie rarely finished anything in one sitting. Relaxing a notch, he strolled over to the desk and checked. Yup, the mug was still half full.

Wry amusement twitched at the corners of his mouth as he straightened. His nose twitched at the scent of her per-

fume…or perhaps that was the bunch flowers shoved hig-
gledy-piggledy into a red glass jar. She had a framed col-
lage of pictures, too. One of her parents smiling into each
other's eyes on their wedding day, a more recent picture
of her father gaunt with the illness that took his life, and a
candid shot of the three Mori kids goofing off at the Kameruka Downs waterhole.

He'd probably been there that day—for all he knew, he
could have taken the picture. There'd been so many days
like that back then.

But what about now?

Tomas put the frame back, next to the coffee mug,
amid the chaos that was Angie's workspace. She'd taken
a convenient job here with Rafe, but how long did she intend staying? Was she ready to settle down? Enough to
raise a baby?

His mood had turned grim long before his thumb
brushed over the rim of the mug, smudging the glossy imprint of her lipstick.

This was the Angie of now, the woman he didn't know.

The one who stained her lips the color of mocha, whose
lips had imprinted his with the fleeting taste of temptation.
The one whose velvet-brown eyes spoke of another wildness, a different type of passion to the laughing girl in the
waterhole picture. *This* was the woman who'd stood on the
steps of the plane and calmly suggested that sex between
them could be fun.

With a silent oath he jerked away from the desk, his action so abrupt he almost upset the mug. He righted it
quickly, pushing aside papers to make some space. And
that's when he found the book.

Babies Made Easy.

He was still staring at the cover, bemused by her choice

of reading material and the irony of that title, when Angie returned.

He heard the quick approach of footsteps in the corridor and sensed her hesitation in the doorway, her presence licking through him like the memory of her kiss—a sweet suggestion of heat and anticipation, chased away by instant hostility. Not toward Angie herself, but toward the unwanted response of his body. He didn't know how to handle this new awareness, the strange tug in his gut, the tight dryness in his throat.

Because she was standing there watching him, eating him up with those big brown eyes.

"I didn't expect to find you here." She came into the room then, smiling with a warmth that made him think she didn't mind the surprise. "How did the meeting go?"

Of course she knew they'd been meeting with the lawyer. Rafe would have told her. They talked a lot, after all. "A waste of everyone's time," he said curtly, irritated that the thought of her and Rafe doing anything together completely wiped away the effect of her smile.

"There's no way out of the clause?"

"None we're prepared to take."

"So, you have to make a baby." Not a question but a matter-of-fact statement as she leaned her hips against the desk at his side. She looked like a candidate for Ms. Hotel Management, in her crisp white shirt and knee-length black skirt, her hair sleek and neat, her only jewelry a fine gold neck-chain bearing the letter A.

At least she was smiling her usual Angie smile, warm and relaxed and spiced with a dash of wryness.

Then she noticed the book in his hand and her smile faltered. His appreciation of that smile nosedived right alongside. He tapped a finger against the book's cover, right under the title. "Interesting choice of reading, Angie."

"I thought I'd research the topic, in case I needed to help any friends out."

"Friends like Rafe?"

"Like Rafe or Alex or Tomas," she corrected without hesitation. "It's fascinating reading…although I have to say the title is very misleading."

No kidding.

"Did you know there's only a seventeen percent chance of conceiving each month? With odds like that, you need to get started. You all do!"

"That's why I'm here."

Their eyes met and held for a second, and he sensed a stillness in her, a new intensity beneath her aura of casual confidence, as if he'd surprised the breath right out of her. Hell, he'd surprised himself even though the words had come out of his mouth!

"Have you changed your mind?" she asked.

"Have you?" he countered.

"About making a baby in some sterile clinic?" With a glancing brush of fingers, she took the book from him and tossed it onto the desk. "Absolutely not."

"I meant about helping me."

"Does it matter? Since we don't see eye to eye on the method, my offer of help is moot."

"Maybe we can compromise. About the method."

"Really?" Eyebrows arched, she regarded him steadily for a drawn-out second. "How would that work, do you suppose?"

Tomas shifted uncomfortably. He didn't have an answer. Until this last minute he hadn't fixed on what he'd hoped to achieve by coming up here. Making sure she didn't get tangled with his hound of a brother, yeah, but as for how—

"Yeesh, Tomas." She interrupted his thoughts with obvious irritation. "You don't know why you're here, do you? Nothing's changed from last week."

"You don't know that."

"I know that you couldn't even stand me kissing you, so why chance anything more intimate?" She blew out a short, impatient breath, and when she started to turn away Tomas reacted instinctively, stopping her retreat with a hand on her arm. For a long moment she just stood there gazing up at him, her eyes widened with surprise.

Good.

He'd caught her on the back foot for a change, and with subtle emphasis he shifted his grip on her arm, not exactly tightening but...adjusting. Just so she knew he meant to keep her there until he was done. Whatever he had to say, whyever he'd changed his mind and come upstairs, he had to put into words. Now. "You caught me by surprise last week."

"So—" she lifted her chin "—if I'd given you more notice you wouldn't have minded me kissing you?"

"I don't know."

"You don't know," she repeated softly, her gaze narrowing and darkening. "Do you want to find out? Or do you want to let go of my arm so I can get back to work?"

The challenge gleamed hot in her eyes, daring him to make that choice. *It's only a kiss,* he told himself, but that phrasing didn't help. Not when her words from last week twined sinuously through his consciousness.

It's only sex.

And this was a test. If he could kiss her, if he could just bend his head to hers and go through the motions, then maybe he could do the sex part, too. Maybe.

He heard the huff of her exasperated breath, felt her start to pull away and blocked her escape with his body. Their eyes met and held. An awareness of what they were about to do charged the air between them, but a breath away from her lips, he paused, too charged with tension to breach that final inch of space.

"Go ahead," she said softly. "I won't bite…unless you want me to."

His head reared back, dumbfounded when he should have expected no less. This was Angie, after all. Angie who was shaking her head with renewed exasperation.

"I was kidding. A joke, you know. Humor."

Yeah, he knew, he just wasn't in a kidding mood, not by a long shot.

And that she must had read on his face because she sighed, a soft relenting whisper, as she leaned forward and touched her thumb to his chin. Then she shocked the hell out of him by reaching up and kissing him there. He felt the softness of her lips, the moist warmth of her tongue and then her retreat.

A small smile hovered on her lips as she whispered, "Sorry."

Sorry for the joke? Or for striking him dumb with that one swift touch of her tongue. Tomas tried to wrap his astonishment into words, to ask what she meant, but she took his face between her hands—the same as she'd done at the plane—and looked right into his eyes, her gaze dark and steady and serious.

"That was your notice." She stretched to kiss one corner of his mouth and then the other. "I'm going to kiss you now, okay?"

Before he could begin to recover his equilibrium, she moved her lips against his with soft restraint, as if she was expecting his withdrawal…or waiting for him to take a more active role. A raw, male part of him itched to take over, but a stronger, harsher voice hammered away in resistance. It wouldn't let him forget that this was Angie, and he had no business wanting to close his eyes and immerse himself in the lush temptation of her lips.

"Relax," she whispered, her breath a shiver of sensation on his skin and in his blood. Her thumbs stroked his cheeks, down to the corners of his mouth. "It's only a kiss."

And then she kissed him the same way she tackled everything—with the same energy and heat and wholehearted passion. She kissed and she willed him to open up, to unwind, to let go. She made a sound low in her throat, a kind of smoky humming that rolled through him in one long, hot wave of desire that caught him totally unprepared, completely at a loss. All he could do was close his eyes and thread his hands into the thick softness of her hair and kiss her back.

Lord, how he kissed her back. With a hunger he couldn't control, with a thoroughness he no longer wanted to control, with a yearning for all the intimacies he'd missed in the last years.

Since Brooke died.

That thought stalled his senses, slammed at his conscience, dragged him out of the drugging depths of that hot, wet contact. Intimacy was not what he wanted. No way. This was only a trial, proof that he could close his eyes and forget himself for long enough to do what had to be done. A means to an end and that was all.

He hauled himself back into his own space and switched his expression to deadpan. Not difficult—he'd had a lot of practice in recent years. Angie had slumped back against the desk. She shook her head as if to clear it and her eyes looked a little dazed. Her hair was a wild tumble, her lips kissed naked and pliant, and when she crossed her arms under her breasts, he couldn't help but notice the outline of her nipples right through her respectable white shirt.

Heat tightened his skin, itched in his hands, swelled in his flesh. He looked away, forced himself to focus on the next step, now he'd conquered the first.

"So," she said on a breathy exhalation. "That didn't seem to go too badly."

His eyes met hers, held, didn't let go. "Do you still want to help me?"

For a long second she didn't react, and he wondered if she hadn't cottoned on to his meaning, if he needed to spell out what he was asking. Again. Then her hand drifted to her throat, and she twisted the fine chain around her index finger. Her throat moved, as if she'd swallowed. "My way?"

"Yes."

"Wow." She eyed him a moment, her expression circumspect. "That's a big step up from a kiss."

"I know that."

"And you think you can take your clothes off and climb into bed with me? That you can do—"

"I don't know, okay?" And he sure as hell didn't need her talking him through every step. He could feel the heat in his face, the tightness in his jaw, in other places he didn't want to acknowledge, and he shifted his weight from one foot to the other, rearranging his weight and the tightness and the jumble of words in his brain. "I don't know, but I want to try."

"Because you want a baby?"

"Because I *need* a baby."

"Right."

There was a sting in her tone, a darkness in her eyes,

and Tomas knew he'd blown it. He knew but he didn't have the words or the sentiment to save the situation. What could he say? He had nothing to offer, no incentive, no promises, no smooth lines. None of the weapons a man like Rafe might use. And he could no more spin her lies than he could beg for her help.

"I don't expect you to commit to this right off," he said. "Not without a trial."

"Trial sex? Is that what you're suggesting?"

"One night without any commitment. If it works, then we can talk about—" He gestured toward the discarded book on top of her desk.

"Making a baby?" She stared back at him a moment, her expression inscrutable. "All right."

All right? Tomas swallowed and stared into her eyes. She meant it. For a panicky second his world tilted and spun, as if someone had hauled the rug out from under his feet. But then she was talking, planning, asking questions, and he forced himself to focus.

"Do you want me to come home with you?" he heard through the roaring in his ears. "I could—"

"No!" Not in his home, not in his bed. "No," he repeated less stridently. "That's not necessary."

"Well, I can't invite you home to my place because I don't have a place. I'm staying with Carlo."

Her brother, his friend. God, no! "I think we should keep this quiet, just between us."

"In case it's a humiliating disaster and we can't look each other in the eye again?"

"In case it doesn't work out," he said, meeting her eyes and refusing to think about such dire consequences. "Neutral territory would be best."

"I suppose a hotel room shouldn't be too hard to organize, given your family owns a whole chain." Despite that wry observation, her eyes remained dark and serious. Slowly she moistened her lips. "When do you want to conduct this...trial?"

"I'm not sure when I can get away."

"You're away now," she pointed out, crossing her arms under her breasts again. Tomas forced himself to concentrate on her words. Not her body. Not the disquieting notion that he'd never seen her naked, but soon would. And he felt the rug start to shift beneath his feet again.

"The kiss worked here and now, with only a little notice," she said with the same matter-of-fact logic. "Why not this, too?"

With a long slow stroke of her hands down her thighs, she straightened her skirt and walked around her desk. "I guess you'd planned to stay overnight?"

Tomas nodded and she picked up the phone and started dialing.

"With Alex or do you have a room booked?"

"A room. Here," he managed. His throat was tight, his mouth dry, and that damn rug was moving way too fast.

"Hello, reception?" She greeted the voice on the end of the phone with a smile. "Hi, Lisa, it's Angelina Mori in Mr. Carlisle's office. You have a booking for his brother, Mr. Tomas Carlisle, for tonight? Yes? I'm looking for an upgrade if you have a suite available."

Tomas stiffened. "That's not necessary."

"The Boronia Suite is perfect," she said into the phone, ignoring both his spoken objection and the adamant shake of his head. "Yes, Lisa, only the one night. That's all Mr. Carlisle requires." Her eyes lifted to meet his, steady and direct and daring him to make something of it. "For now, at least."

* * *

Two hours later Angie was still shaking her head over how she'd hijacked the arrangements so coolly and proficiently. She hadn't let Tomas interrupt and she'd handled his objections with the same aplomb as the room upgrade.

"I've never been in a position to reserve a suite before," she told him. "If I'm going to do this, why not with style?"

And then she'd settled behind her desk, telephone receiver anchored between shoulder and ear, and mentioned how much work she needed to get done before she could meet him upstairs. A very nice ploy, beautifully stage-managed, with no room for objection. Especially when Rafe arrived at her door, his curiosity diverted by his brother's presence.

Tomas left. She shrugged off Rafe's nosiness by pretending huge interest in a bogus phone call. Really, based on the whole scene in her office from start to finish, she should have been an actress. Her talents were much wasted. Who'd have known that her heart was racing, her insides churning, her bones quivering with nervous tension?

Now, two and a bit hours later, she smiled and made small talk with a Japanese couple as the Carlisle Grande's high-speed elevator propelled her toward the upper-floor suites and her future. All in all, she felt remarkably calm. Considering she was about to have Tomas Carlisle.

Holy Henry Moses.

After she said goodbye to the couple on floor fifteen, Angie pressed an unsteady hand against her stomach, drew a deep breath, and willed everything to stop spinning. Although she hadn't decided how, she knew she could go through with this. She knew because of the kiss that still burned strong and fierce in every cell of her blood, a kiss edged with darkness and barely leashed desperation.

He didn't want her, but he *needed* her.

And if all went well, she might not only have Tomas Carlisle this once but she might get to keep him. To live with him as she grew big with his baby, to ease the haunted shadows in his eyes, make him laugh and smile and live again. To be more than a helpmate to secure his inheritance—to be his wife and his partner.

And if it didn't work out? If this turned into the disaster she'd alluded to in her office? Then perhaps that wouldn't be all bad if it meant closure and a signal to move on.

Perhaps she might even silence the incessant heart-whisper that had stopped her committing to any other relationship, to a career or even to a place to live. The insistent whisper that she hold back a chunk of herself, to save it for this one man, this one home, this one life. Deep down she'd always hoped…and now those hopes were about to be realized.

If he hadn't changed his mind all over again.

Outside the door to his suite—*their* suite—Angie hesitated only long enough to draw a deep breath before knocking. But then she couldn't stand the waiting, the not knowing if he was inside or not. Fumbling, swearing softly at the tremor in her hand, she managed to swipe her security card through the lock. Red light. Swearing softly she tried again, her hand more steady this time.

Green light, hallelujah.

She pushed the door open and three slow paces into the entry vestibule her heart and stomach did the same free-fall as in the swiftly ascending elevator. Still, she went through the motions of checking the huge marble bathroom, the bedroom and huge closet, but nope. The whole suite stretched before her, quiet and pristine and empty.

He wasn't here.

* * *

Angie didn't assume she'd been stood up, at least not after she'd circled the whole suite several times and given his absence considerable thought. He may have changed a lot in recent years, but she couldn't picture any version of Tomas hanging around a hotel room cooling his boot heels. He'd never done inactivity well.

She checked with reception, in case he'd left a message. Then she checked every horizontal surface—a five-star suite, she discovered, had many—and came up with no sign of a note. In fact there was no indication he'd even been here, but that was no reason to get her knickers knotted.

No, really, it wasn't.

Most likely he had business to do, seeing as he came to the city so rarely these days. Or he could be downstairs in one of the hotel bars getting well and truly drunk. The Tomas she remembered didn't need Dutch courage to tackle a wild bull or a woman, but this present one—well, she just didn't know.

Cooling heels wasn't big with Angie, either, but what else could she do but wait? Tracking Tomas down wasn't an option, not when he wanted to keep this meeting (encounter? rendezvous? one-night stand?) secret. Yeesh, but she hated not knowing what to expect or even what to call whatever-this-was she'd agreed upon. Not knowing how long she might be waiting made her even more skittish, and determined to find some way of relaxing.

If she could expend some of this pent-up emotional energy then maybe she stood a chance of loosening up Tomas. That, she knew, was essential if this night was going to work out.

She ordered up a bottle of merlot. Then, on a whim, changed her order to the kind of French champagne she'd only tasted once before, at her heartbreaker of an eighteenth birthday party. Courtesy of the Carlisles, as it happened. If Tomas Carlisle was going to make her wait, then he could pay for the luxury of unwinding her nerves!

While she waited for room service to deliver her Dom Pérignon, she filled the spa and added a liberal dash of bath-oil from the complimentary basket labeled "Body Bliss." Then she stacked the stereo with music designed for relaxation. The spa occupied roughly the same space as Carlo's whole bathroom, so she figured if the music didn't work she could use up some stray nervous energy swimming laps of the monster-tub.

Midway through the champagne and chin-deep in richly scented water, Angie felt a sudden sense of…no longer being alone. Her skin tingled, lifting hairs on the back of her neck and over her forearms. Startled, she jackknifed upright and waited, perfectly still but for the wild pounding of her heart. The music masked any sound, but when the bathroom door didn't move from its half ajar position her heart rate slowly subsided.

So much for the relaxing, luxuriating experience.

She'd started to rise from the water, to reach for a bath sheet, when the music volume dipped noticeably. Instantly her pulse skipped, her exposed nipples tightened, anticipation fizzed in her blood—as happened pretty much any time Tomas Carlisle came into the picture. Not that he was exactly in the picture, but he was close enough that her body knew; her heart knew.

And as she slid back into the water's warm embrace, she wondered if her patience could hold out until he came looking for her.

Five

How long, he wondered, could a woman stay in a bath?

Teeth gritted, Tomas attempted to block out another slush of water, another image of slick olive skin, another rush of heat to his loins. For the past two or ten or twenty minutes— God knows, it felt like an eternity!—he'd wished back that second when he'd turned down the music. Her selected volume (raucous) would have shut out the constant reminders that Angie was two open doors away, wet and naked.

Yet he couldn't bring himself to cross to the bedroom, and then to the bathroom, to do what he'd come up here to do. He didn't know what he would say. He didn't know how to begin.

Hell.

He focused hard on the view beyond the window, the lights of a city not yet ready for sleep, the traffic inching toward the bridge, late workers heading home from their jobs the same as every other evening. Everything normal, routine, unchanged in their worlds while his was spinning into some unknown dimension.

And then he caught a flutter of movement, a reflection in the glass before him, and his shoulders bunched in instant reaction. She'd exited the bedroom wearing one of the hotel's white robes, and he tracked her path across the room, saw her stop, heard the rattle of ice as she lifted the bottle.

"Can I get you a glass of champagne?" she asked. "Or would you prefer something else? I imagine there's anything you want here…."

Plus a whole lot he didn't want to want, either, he thought grimly as he turned to face her. All wrapped up in a fluffy bathrobe, dark hair gathered in a tousled ponytail on top of her head, brows arched in silent query, she stood waiting for his response.

Tomas shook his head. He'd had enough to drink downstairs. Just enough to numb the edges of his fear, but not enough to lose sight of what tonight was about.

Apparently Angie had no such reservations. He watched her pour a glass from the near-empty bottle, felt himself tense even more as she padded toward him, her bare feet noiseless on the plush claret carpet. Fine gold glinted at one ankle, and as she bent to adjust the stereo volume the chain at her neck swung forward in a slow-motion arc, then back again to settle between her breasts. *A for abundant.*

"Do you mind?" she asked.

Frowning, he forced his attention away from the deep vee of her robe. Away from the exposed slope of one breast, from the disorienting speed of blood rushing south and to the swirl of classical piano notes that seemed such an unlikely Angie-choice. "I don't mind, although that doesn't sound like your kind of music."

"Relaxation therapy, along with this—" she lifted her glass in a silent salute "—and the spa. Which, I must say, was a treat and a half."

"You needed to relax?"

"A little." The corners of her mouth quirked. "Okay, more than a little. Although I figure I now have the advantage over you, in the relaxation stakes."

"That's not saying much," Tomas admitted, and their eyes met and held in a moment of shared honesty. This wasn't going to be easy—they both knew it, they both acknowledged it.

And being Angie, she also had to try to find a way to fix it. "Are you sure you don't want a drink? Or the bathroom's free and I can really, really recommend the spa. No?"

She must have gleaned that answer from his expression, because he hadn't said a word or moved a muscle. He'd just stood there, growing more tense and rigid while she strolled right up to him. Was it his imagination or did her eyes glint with wicked purpose?

"Okay, then take off your shirt."

What?

She pushed her glass into his hand and somehow wrapped his stiff fingers around the stem. Apparently because she needed to flex her fingers, then shake them, as if limbering up. *To do what?* All that southward-rushing blood congregated in very unlimber anticipation of those fingers reaching, touching, closing around him.

"If you don't want to bother with the spa—" Angie wriggled those damn fingers some more "—then how about I give you a massage?"

"That's not necessary."

"Rubbish! You look tense enough to snap and I've been told I have magic hands." Turning to leave, she cut him a trust-me look across her shoulder. "I'll just go fetch some oil from the bathroom and then—"

"No."

"No oil?"

No oil, no magic hands stroking his shoulders, no naked thighs straddling his back. "No massage. No spa. No drinks." With subtle emphasis he placed her glass on the sill at his back, right out of her reach. "That's not why we're here."

"No, but—"

"No buts."

Their eyes met, held, locked, the air charged with the knowledge of why they were here. Sex. Not for pleasure, but for a purpose. A trial. Angie's throat moved as she swallowed, and he noticed that one hand had come up to twist at the chain at her throat. "I had this notion that we might...I don't know...sit around and talk for a bit to ease the awkwardness. Maybe order up dinner and a bottle of wine."

"Are you hungry?"

"Not really."

"Then why order dinner? This isn't a date, Angie."

Her gaze darkened, maybe hurt, maybe a little shocked at the harshness of his tone. But, in typical Angie fashion, she lifted her chin and fired right back at him. "That's it then? You just want to do it?"

"Yes." That's exactly what he wanted—to do it. No fancy trimmings, no window-dressing, no talk. And, dammit, he shouldn't feel bad about wanting what they'd both agreed on, just because she was doing him the favor. Just because she was standing there twisting that chain, looking for all the world like—

"Are you nervous?"

Probably he shouldn't have barked the question, but he

couldn't contain the surly flanks of his mood. And it seemed so unlikely that confident, unflappable, in-your-face Angie could be suffering a case of the jitters.

"Of course I'm nervous," she answered. "Aren't you?"

"Why 'of course'? You said it was 'only sex.'"

Shaking her head, she released a soft breath of laughter. "Trust you to remember that!"

"You didn't mean it?"

"Of course I didn't mean it. Saying 'it's only sex' is like saying this is only a hotel room, and Dom Pérignon is only a sparkling wine, and this—" she tugged at her lapel "—is only a bathrobe."

He could have asked why in blue blazes women didn't say what they meant, but that would be like asking why the wet season followed the dry. It simply was. But Angie? He'd always thought her a straight-shooter, and what her heated words implied sent a paradoxical chill through his blood.

"Why are you here? Why did you agree to do this?"

"I told you—because I can."

"The truth, Angie." He met her eyes, held her gaze. "No bull."

Angie stared back at him, taking in the uncompromising set of his jaw, the icy chill in eyes she'd always thought of as hot summer-blue, and her stomach swam with anxiety. Everything rested on her answer…yet if she told him her expectations, her belief that she could heal his wounded heart if he only gave her the chance, she wouldn't see him for dust.

Yet she couldn't lie. Not to him and not to herself.

"Well, there is the fact I've always wanted to sleep with you," she said slowly. Truthfully. "Oh, don't look so shocked. I told you that last week, at the waterhole. When I first suggested having your baby."

"That was hypothetical."

"Maybe you thought so. I didn't. I had a crush on you as a teenager, not that you noticed, but that's the truth. Do you remember my eighteenth?"

"The party at Shardays?"

Stupid question. Of course he remembered, since he'd met Brooke that night. But he'd asked for the truth and, painful topic or not, she couldn't stop midstory. "I remember going shopping and picking out the sexiest dress I could find for that party. It was white, this real slippery fabric that clung in all the right places." She shaped her hands over her body as she talked, remembering how excited she'd been to see herself in that dress, how keen her anticipation when she walked into the nightclub. She'd been humming with it, buzzing, singing. "I picked it out thinking about you, Tomas. I had this fantasy going that you'd see me in it and that would be it."

"You had a boyfriend."

"Yes, but he was a boy." She shrugged. "You were a man."

He made a rough sound, of disbelief or rejection or both. "That was seven years ago."

"And I've always wondered what it would be like, you and me."

"You mean you and me scr—"

"Yes." She spoke over the top of him, blocking out the harsh word he'd chosen. Deliberately, she knew, to shock her.

"Because that's all it can be," he said tightly, as if he needed to drive the point home. "Only sex."

"I hear you, although I think you should know for me it's never 'only sex,' not with any man. I'm a woman, in case I need to point that out."

"You don't."

For a long moment she stared back at him, her annoyance at his stubborn stance yielding to those two little words. He'd noticed her as a woman. And he could talk until he was blue-faced about "only sex" but her heart swelled with the knowledge that it would be so much more. If he would only give her the chance. The chance she may have blown with the honesty of her confession.

Moistening her dry lips, she concentrated on what mattered to Tomas—the reason he'd agreed to "only sex" in the first place.

"You know that book I've been reading?" She waited for his nod of acknowledgment, for him to remember the title and make the mental switch from sex-with-Angie to the end result. "Well, I've read all about fertility and conception and, frankly, you couldn't get a better candidate if you advertised. My cycle is regular as a twenty-eight-day clock, which the book says is pretty rare. I've never had any gyno problems. I'm strong and I'm healthy and I'm at my prime."

"You've thought about this. You really want to have a baby?"

"Several, eventually. All perfect angels who don't cry or give their mother a minute's grief."

She smiled. He didn't. And she sensed that she'd taken this one step too far. That perhaps she should never have admitted to nerves and thus diverted his focus back at "just do it." But, with all that had been said in the interim, how could she get back to that point?

Perhaps she did need to remind him about being a woman…a naked woman who'd agreed to have sex with him.

Slowly she closed the space between them, releasing her hair so it tumbled down past her shoulders. As she came up beside him she raked a hand through the thick tresses, no longer slick and straight but rendered thick and curly by the bathroom steam. She leaned down to recover her glass from the windowsill and her arm brushed against his in a slow heated slide. And again as she straightened.

"Have to enjoy this while I can," she said, taking a long sip of champagne. Their gazes connected over the rim of her glass. "If I do fall pregnant, I'll not have the opportunity much longer."

Something shifted in his eyes, sharpening their focus to a hard glitter for a split second before he turned abruptly to stare out the window. "There'll be a lot you have to give up."

"There'll be a lot to gain."

"What about your job?"

"It's only temporary. I'm replacing somebody on maternity leave. There's a certain irony in that, don't you think?"

He didn't answer, and Angie's confidence gave a nervy little jitter. She didn't think it possible that he could look any tenser than when she'd first come out of the bathroom, but he did. Because it was time to get down to it, to just do it, and that was easier said than done.

She took another sip of champagne but all she tasted was her own anxiety. "Awkward, huh?" she said into the lengthening silence. "This. Us. Standing here wondering what to do next."

A muscle jumped in his jaw.

"How about we go into the bedroom? At least that's a first step." When he didn't answer, she turned and started to walk in that direction.

"Angie."

She whipped back around, caught him watching her in a way that made her heart thunder like a bronco let loose on the northern plains. *Heat and fear; fear and heat.*

"Don't expect too much," he said stiffly.

"I never do."

* * *

That was a straight-out lie. Seven years she'd been waiting, wondering, ever since her coming-of-age party. Tonight she had expectations, and Tomas had no one to blame but himself.

He'd asked about her nerves. He'd insisted on the truth. No bull, he'd said, and wasn't that a load of it!

Disgusted in himself, he dragged a hand through his hair. She even remembered the damn dress, when all he remembered about that night was meeting Brooke. The only woman he'd ever loved; the only woman he *would* ever love. The only woman he'd ever taken to bed.

How the hell was he going to do this? How was he going to walk through that door and take off his clothes and lay down with another woman? What in blue blazes had made him think that doing it with Angie would be easier than with a nameless, faceless stranger?

And if he wanted honest, no-bull truth between them, why hadn't he told her about his lack of sexual experience?

Jaw set, he fought to contain the icy spread of fear through his tense body. Struggled to take the first steps toward the bedroom door, left open like an invitation to sin.

Only sex, he reminded himself. Sex with a lush, sensual woman who kissed like she loved everything about the whole man-woman intimacy thing. He imagined she wouldn't be too shy to use that mouth in all manner of ways. He imagined she wouldn't be afraid to take the initiative once he walked through that door. Maybe he should just take her advice: *Lie back, close your eyes and think of Kameruka.*

How hard could that be?

About as hard as the pounding of his pulse, he thought ruefully. And like a nagging toothache it would only get worse the longer he stood here thinking about it. Better to suck up the fear and dread of the dentist's chair and march right in there and get it over with.

If he didn't think about the intimacy, if he just concentrated on the mechanics of undoing buttons and stripping off clothes, if he focused on the part of him that cried out for a woman's slick warmth in the dead of night, the part of him that was sick of his hand providing its only satisfaction, then he could do this.

As long as she didn't expect too much.

On the threshold he paused, eyes fixed on the king-size bed that half-filled the room, covers turned back to reveal an expanse of pure white sheets. Twin bedside lamps cast a pale glow that did nothing to warm the starkness of that bed or to prevent the breakout of sweat, cold and sudden on his skin.

And Angie? His gaze swept beyond the bed and found her standing in front of the dresser, stalled in the act of brushing her hair. Their eyes locked in the mirror, as she slowly lowered her arms and put down the brush. The soft clunk sounded preternaturally loud in the stillness and he realized that her music had stopped. That the silence was so intense he could hear the thick thud of his heartbeat. Too loud, too hard.

"Damn moisture," she said, turning to face him. "Once it gets a sniff of steam, I can't do a thing to contain it."

Her hair. She meant her hair. But stupidly it took him a moment to get past the reference to moisture and steam and containing it.

"I like your hair like that." His voice sounded gruff and rusty, his compliment about as stiff as his body. "The other way, this afternoon, it was too…sleek."

"Really?" She paused in smoothing the thick mass behind her ears—a pointless task since the curls sprang free as soon as her hand dropped away. "You don't think sleek is a good look?"

"Hell, no."

"You prefer the wild look then?"

"On you," he said simply and her lips tilted at the corners in the tiniest hint of a smile. That probably would have relaxed him a notch, that connection, if her gaze hadn't drifted off to the bed—that endless stretch of cold, clinical white—before slowly returning to meet his.

"I intended taking off the robe and being all laid out on the bed waiting," she said softly. "But I couldn't do it."

"You could have left the robe on."

"I could have, if being naked was a problem." Three slow steps, three thick pulses of blood in his lower body, and she stopped in front of him. "Being naked alone was."

"You want me to get undressed?"

Dark and luminous eyes lifted from his chest to his eyes. She moistened her lips. "Do you mind if I do it?"

Not if you do it real quick.

That answer lodged in his throat when her silky female knuckles grazed his abdomen. When he sucked in hard, she got a firmer grip on his shirt and pulled it free of his trousers. Before he could think *holymotherofmercy* she'd unthreaded every button and pushed the sides of his shirt apart.

Maybe it was his vision, his thoughts, his whole body that trembled…or maybe it was her hands as they slowly traversed his bare chest, grazing his nipples, fingering the thick growth of hair, tracing the line of his collarbone. With growing confidence, her palms slid over his shoulders and down his biceps in a long, slow caress that peeled his shirt away until it dropped to the floor at their feet.

"Undo my robe," she whispered, so close that her breath

sloughed over his skin and seeped into his blood. He watched her lean forward and kiss his chest. Watched her eyelids flutter shut and that sight—soft and engrossed and sensual—brought on a surge of lust so intense his knees all but buckled.

He needed something to hold on to, to ground him against the dizzying roar of heat, and he found her robe, her sash, and a simple knot that came apart in his hands. She made a husky sound of approval as the thick toweling fell open. He made a rough sound of unscripted awe as her breasts came into view.

Full, luscious female things of beauty, with wide tawny aureoles and tips that seemed to tighten and darken as he watched—and, hell, he couldn't stop watching until he feared his mouth was watering, until he had to swallow to stop from drowning. Behind his fly, his body pulsed with an ache to reach for her, to drop to his knees and draw those distended nipples into his mouth, to take her down onto the bed and bury himself without preliminary.

Except he'd be lucky to last a minute and he owed Angie better than that. Only sex, he told himself, didn't mean it had to be bad sex.

The hands that itched to shape her body lifted instead to cup her face and he leaned down to take her lips, closing his eyes to shut out the lush appeal of her body. Their thighs brushed and her nipples grazed his chest as she came up onto her toes to meet his kiss. Restless, impatient, her hands shimmied over his ribs and sides before settling against his back and drawing their bodies into perfect alignment.

Heat billowed, a furnace of desire in his chest and his thighs and everywhere in between. Especially in between. In a slow, deep sweep his tongue stroked over hers and retreated. Her complaint was a rough sound that vibrated low in her throat and her hands tightened their grip on his back, forcing him to take notice, driving him past the edge of his control.

He kissed her harder, tasting her lips, drawing on her tongue, forcing himself to ease off when he wanted to devour. *Only sex,* he told himself, *only lust,* and that was okay. It had been so long, too long, since he'd indulged his male nature. It was understandable that he should feel so primitive, so carnal, so desperate.

Especially when she met him kiss for kiss, biting at his chin when he drew back for breath, sliding her hard-tipped breasts down his chest as she dipped lower and reached for his trousers. He sucked in another quick ragged breath but that oxygen didn't make a lick of difference when she undid the waist button and started on his fly.

The accidental brush of her fingers against his erection completely zapped his synapses, and before the red-fire haze cleared she was ducking lower, her hair a dark whisper of sensation across his stomach. For one gasp of a moment he thought she was going to take him into her mouth, and in his explosive state that would have been too much, too soon.

Thinking about that hot, moist suction was damn near enough to bring him to embarrassment.

He backed away abruptly, and sat on the edge of the bed.

"Sorry." In the low light her eyes gleamed dark and hot. "I was just helping with your trousers."

The way she was looking at him didn't help a bit. Especially with his trousers. Finally he managed to extricate himself from the rest of his clothing, and she was still watching him with a powerful hungry intensity.

"I bought condoms," he managed to say, amazed that he remembered the earlier shopping expedition. "I'll get them."

Something in her eyes darkened, as if with a sense of purpose, and through the shimmering haze of lust Tomas felt a pang of misgiving.

"You could," she said, her gaze not leaving his. "Or we could leave them right where they are and try to make a baby."

Six

"**A**ccording to the book, this is my prime conception time." Sure and steady and dark as the night, Angie's eyes held his. "Do you really want to waste this chance?"

Deep inside Tomas felt a keening cry of resistance. No, he couldn't do this wholly naked. *He* needed protection, a barrier in any shape or form, some sense that he could hold himself apart from the intimacy of their bodies joining.

And how will you make a baby then? How will you keep Kameruka Downs?

His heart raced erratically, sweat sheened cold on his skin, and without a word he stood and stalked from the bedroom. Halfway across the sitting room he stopped suddenly, and for one numb second he couldn't think what he was doing or why he'd come out here.

The condoms.

His gaze closed on the box he'd tossed onto the bureau

earlier, when he'd come through the door and heard the music and realized that she was here. When it really struck home that sex with Angie was going to happen.

Do you need birth control? Do you really need this bed-room session as a trial?

Obviously he wasn't going to have any trouble function-ally. Obviously Angie had made up her mind about hav-ing a baby. He could get this over with now. If luck was on his side he wouldn't have to go through this feverish or-deal of wanting and not-wanting-to-want ever again.

All you have to do is go back in that bedroom, shut down your mind and follow the lead of your body. It knows what it wants. It's not having any problem with intimacy. It wants inside Angie, naked, now.

With a grim grunt of determination, he turned and fol-lowed where that leading part of his body pointed.

Several things hit him right in the face when he walked back into the bedroom. The shapeless form of her dis-carded robe, stark against the wine-red carpet. How the white sheets no longer looked cold and clinical, not with Angie's darkly sensual beauty spread across them. And the fact that no amount of rubber or latex or reinforced steel could have protected him from the impact of her lying there naked.

Sucker-punched, he watched her roll up onto her knees, all tumbled black hair and perfect smooth skin and wildly generous curves. Her gaze had fixed on the highly func-tional and grossly underprotected body part that had lead him right back to her. He felt it thicken and pulse. Saw her moisten her lips and then move on to study his empty hands.

"You couldn't find the condoms?"

"I found them." Slowly he walked to the bed. Her eyes

arrowed back for another up-close look, probably to see what he was wearing. Or not. "I left them where they were."

Heavy-lidded eyes slid up to his. Something flickered in their dark chocolate depths. "Are you sure?"

"That I left them there? Yes. That I should have? No," he admitted, honest for once.

"If that's because we haven't talked about STDs and such…I want you to know that I'm good. I had tests done when I last gave blood, and I haven't been with anyone since."

He swallowed the spontaneous question—*how long since someone else?*—and looked away. *Irrelevant. Too personal. None of your business.* And in his mind that justified not telling how long he'd been without. Instead he just nodded and said, "I'm clean."

There was an uncomfortable moment as their gazes connected and a measure of the unasked personal and intimate shivered between them. She made a rueful sound, half sigh, half laughter. "Okay, and now we're back at the awkward stage."

"Us, standing here wondering what to do next."

She smiled, appreciating his recall of their earlier conversation. "Except this time we're already in the bedroom."

"Naked."

"All over."

To illustrate her meaning Angie's gaze dipped, and the mood took on a new sultriness, as if a blanket of heat billowed high before descending to settle heavily over their bodies. One silken finger traced the length of his nakedness. Her breathing hitched. His, more so, as she cupped and stroked him more firmly.

Nope, he wouldn't be having any trouble functionally. Not if he made it inside her body before embarrassing

himself. And if she kept touching him like that, and looking at him with her eyes kinda hazed and her lips softly
parted, then that was quite on the cards.

"Enough," he bit out sharply. Then to take the edge off
he tried a laugh, a laugh that came out all raw and strained.
"It's been a while."

She let him go and for a long silent moment she watched
him with unsettling intensity, as if she was delving inside
and grabbing hold of his fears and laying them out for
open examination. *Oh, no. No, no, no.* Reflexively he
slammed down the shutters on the tiny window of vulnerability he'd unintentionally revealed.

No more private stuff, no expectations, no emotions.

Something of the unspoken must have shown on his
face, because her expression slowly transformed from I-
have-questions intensity to now-where-were-we? teasing.
Settling back on her heels, she pointed at an erection that
didn't need any pointing out. "I thought you told me not
to expect too much."

Okay, so this was better. This he could play along with.
Frowning, he pretended to inspect himself. "Too much?"

"Guess there's only one way to find out."

Despite the sexy banter, there were no smiles and her
eyes flared with dark heat as their gazes connected. "I
guess so."

Slowly she reached out and touched his forearm in a
barely there caress, then her hand slid down to link fingers,
and slowly, inexorably she tugged him down onto the bed.

They came together in an unchoreographed duel for position. It wasn't elegant, but it was so hot Tomas swore he
heard the slow sizzle as their limbs parried for optimum
sensual contact. One of his thighs settled between hers, and
he couldn't stop himself pressing into her heat.

She responded with a deep hum of satisfaction.

For a second their gazes collided and he felt such a jolt—a left-right combination punch of need and fear and dread and desire—that he immediately ducked down to her mouth. They met with lips and tongues, with teeth and passion, and Tomas closed his eyes against the onslaught.

He closed his eyes and thought, *yes!* I can shut it all out. I can dive into the carnal delight of French kissing, I can shape my hands over these curves and immerse myself in the pleasure of all the scents and textures of a woman's body. I can absorb the throaty sounds of a woman's enjoyment and I can stand the roar of need in my ears.

I can handle the rush of lust because that's all it is. Only sex.

His hand shaped one breast, his thumb rasped across the nipple and she sucked a breath from his mouth, an act so intimate he felt its effect raw and deep in his gut. He jammed his eyes closed tighter and breathed more deeply, until the indelibly delicious scent of her skin filled his lungs and his veins.

"What the hell did you bathe in?" he breathed huskily near her ear.

"Cinnamon and honey-milk."

And he gave a half-grunt of laughter because that's what he'd been about to ask. Honey-milk. She tasted so sweet, her skin was so soft and pliant. Unthinking he opened his eyes and saw her roll her head back against the sheets, her dark curls a wild and wanton spread against the white.

"That's what the bottle said." She blinked slowly. "Do you want to taste me?"

"Later," he growled because even the thought of going down on her damn near brought him undone. He could feel a rawness gathering inside, a desperation he didn't want to contain.

Her mouth tilted into a sultry smile. "I can hardly wait."

"Right now," he said, repositioning himself to settle thickly between her thighs, "It's this way."

"Okay," she whispered on a broken murmur of breath.

Okay. That's all this would be, he told himself as he deliberately drew out that initial slide of entry. This would be okay. Not wonderful. Not wild and untamed. Not earth-shattering or mind-altering. Just okay. All he had to do was take it easy, maintain control, keep his focus on the wall or the pillows or on visualizing the twisted thread of his restraint. He wouldn't look into her eyes, he wouldn't indulge in sweet words or tender kisses, and he wouldn't think about the incredible moist pleasure of her body molding to accommodate his penetration.

Slowly. Take it slowly.

Sweat broke out along his back and on his forehead as he stopped himself giving in to what his body craved. To just plunge into her, hard, fast, wild. He sucked in air through his teeth, stared harder at the beige wall, and then he felt the tremulous touch of her hand on his face.

"If you're worrying about the 'too much' comment, then don't."

For a moment he forgot himself and looked down, right into her eyes. Not teasing like her husky-voiced comment, but serious, intent, burning. He drew back slightly and then let himself go in one long hard drive that took him all the way inside and he couldn't contain the long, deep sound of satisfaction that rose from his throat.

Sweet, oh God she was sweet.

Tomas couldn't stand it—not the enraptured look on her face or the softening of her lips or the do-that-again challenge in her eyes. He had to look away, refocus. To remind himself that *she* wasn't sweet. Sex was sweet. Being enclosed in that velvet female sheathing, the silky slide as he withdrew and drove back again, the hot friction of flesh against flesh, of male against female. This sex was so sweet because it had been so long and he'd almost forgotten the intensity of the pleasure. It was okay to enjoy it, to let himself go a little, to ease back so he could touch her breasts and flatten his hand against her belly and imagine that this was about making a child.

Only sex. And if it succeeded, never again.

Conversely his mind railed and bucked against that possibility. This was so good he wanted to do it again and again and again. Abruptly he pulled back, almost all the way out, then thrust himself in to the hilt. Too good to contemplate never doing again and that was all right, too, he justified, because tonight he could do it again and again. He could because it was necessary to make the child he needed.

It wasn't about this rapidly escalating rapture, not about the gut-wrenching explosion of pleasure when his hand slid lower and thumbed her slick plump heart until she came apart in a shuddering cry that kept on going and going as he changed angles and drove into her until his own climax roared through him like a cyclone, rough and whirling and eddying through his rigid frame with uncontrollable force.

He could justify that he couldn't disconnect immediately, not while his heart thundered and his blood roared and his mind clamored with the image of his seed spilling deeply into her fertile core.

For a minute his whole being succumbed to the intensity of that image and he slumped forward, his nose buried in that sweet hot spot where her neck joined with her shoulder. Their heartbeats raced one against the other and he knew he should move but he couldn't, not until she took a slow, shuddering breath that echoed right through him.

They were that close.

Too close, and when her mouth touched the side of his face with the kind of tender intimacy he'd vowed to avoid, he suddenly found his strength. He was on his feet and into the bathroom before her kiss had cooled on his cheek. Shower controls turned to maximum, he stepped under the torrent and let the cold water savage him for a count of ten. Then he spread his legs and planted his arms against the cold tiles and let the water pound out the torpor of sexual satiation.

Somewhere at the back of his mind he imagined it might also pound away a nagging sense of dissatisfaction. Not with the sex—jeez, but that had been unbelievably satisfying. No, it was something deeper, probably tied up with those earlier chills of fear, but even after ten minutes or so of water-torture he couldn't put a finger on the cause.

And he couldn't stand here any longer, not without turning blue. Adjusting the temperature mix, he rolled back his head and let the warmth hit him full in the face. Then he raked his wet hair back from his face, turned off the taps and reached for a towel.

Bare-assed, he padded back to the bedroom, his muscles tightening reflexively with every step. She'd turned the lights out, he realized, but enough light filtered in from the city outside for him to make out the figure curled up on the bed. Motionless. Asleep.

He exhaled a long, audible breath. No need for postcoital conversation or cuddling. She'd left plenty of the bed for him, enough of a buffer zone that he could crawl in under the covers and spread out in his usual fashion without any contact. That didn't help him relax. As the minutes passed he grew tenser, more wide-awake and so attuned to the silence that he swore he could hear each ticking minute on the noiseless bedside clock.

Possibly because he was concentrating so hard on anything besides the soft sound of Angie's breathing.

Damn her, how could she be so relaxed? Had what they'd done been so exhausting…or so meaningless that she could roll over and go to sleep within minutes? He turned restlessly and shucked off the eiderdown quilt. So, okay, he'd been gone more than a few minutes, but still….

Did she think that was it? One time lucky? And what about her earlier invitation. *Do you want to taste me?*

His body reacted instantly, extravagantly, as if she'd whispered the incendiary words into his ear right then. Turning impatiently on his side didn't help. Not when he could see the rise and fall of her breasts under the pure white sheet. *I can hardly wait,* she'd said.

Well, hell, he'd waited long enough. They only had this one night. What a waste to spend it watching her sleep when he was obviously up for making certain.

It was okay to smooth her hair away from her throat and taste her there, he figured. It was okay to kiss his way over her shoulder and whisper "wake up, Angie" when she stirred restlessly and rolled onto her side. Fine to kiss his way down the length of her naked spine and to learn the multitude of curves and valleys that made up her generous body. And when she stretched sleepily and pressed back into him with a lazy sigh, how could he not reach around to cup her breasts and rub her nipples and wake her by stroking her slick, wet heat?

When she rocked hard against him and murmured "already?" he took her like that, in a long, lazy joining, and again in the predawn quiet when the pace was slow and

sensuous with enough time to recognize his earlier bout of
fear for what it was.

Not performance anxiety or any sense of disloyalty to
the wife he still loved, but fear that he would enjoy this—
enjoy *her*—so much that he would never want it to end.
That he'd want to twist his fingers into her chain and drag
her mouth down to his, to swallow her cries of release
whole and absorb them into his body.

That he would want this to go on and on and never end.

Angie woke to the glare of morning sun streaming
through the window and the low sound of conversation.
Frowning slightly, she pushed up on her elbows and
strained her ears. Not the TV she realized, shoving her hair
back from her face, but real voices in the adjoining room.
Before she had a chance to identify words out of the indis-
tinguishable drone, her attention diverted to the scent of
food and her nose twitched and her stomach growled. Between no dinner and the…um…strenuous night, she was
famished.

As she swung her legs out of bed she stretched her arms
and back. And winced. Oh, yes, it had, indeed, been a most
strenuous night. Satisfying in many ways, promising in
many ways, even if she hated the many times he'd refused
to meet her gaze, the times he'd chosen the darkness of
closed eyes over the emotional connection of their joining.

Even if the notion that he'd needed to wash the scent
of their lovemaking from his body still rubbed raw against
her heart.

Slowly she started for the same bathroom. Vaguely she
realized that the voices had stopped, and when she heard
the thump of a door closing, she stopped dead. Surely he
wouldn't just leave? Surely. But her heart shifted with un-

comfortable doubt as she resumed her trip toward the bath-room. Just shy of the door, a sixth sense made her swing her gaze back…and there he was, standing in the doorway between bedroom and sitting-room, watching her.

He, she noticed immediately, was dressed. Unlike her. Ridiculous, after all they'd done in the night, to feel so ex-posed. He'd seen pretty much everything, from much closer than the width of a hotel bedroom.

"I ordered breakfast," he said evenly.

A good start, she thought. Excellent really, since she would have bet on much awkwardness this morning.

"I'm famished, but I just need a quick shower before I eat." She smiled broadly, in appreciation of him ordering breakfast, *and* still being here to share it. "Will you save me something?"

"I've already eaten. With Rafe."

Angie stiffened. That explained the other voice. Yet… "You invited your brother to breakfast?"

"He invited himself."

Aah, now *that* made more sense. And explained the closing door.

"Does he know…?" She gestured between them, indi-cating the meaning she couldn't put into words. *That I'm here, in your bedroom, naked?*

"No, and that's the way I'd prefer we kept it." He shifted his weight from one booted foot to the other. "Look, I just rang the airport. My pilot's ready to go. I have to get moving."

"Well, I'll have my shower and breakfast and go straight down to work, I expect." She managed a carefree shrug, but since she was standing naked in the full morning light, she couldn't quite bring herself to stroll over and casually kiss him goodbye. Which is the comeback she would have liked, to prove that though her heart had just taken a plummeting nosedive, she could handle this. He'd told her not to expect too much. She knew this would be a long haul, this getting past his hurt and distance to the man inside.

Last night she'd taken the first step, and that was only the start.

Despite his gotta-go message, he still hadn't moved from the doorway, however, and Angie discerned he had more to say. Ever helpful, she raised her eyebrows, inviting him to spit it out.

"Call me," he said, "as soon as you know something."

"You'll be the first to know."

He nodded stiffly.

And Angie couldn't help herself, the words just kind of bubbled out. "Do you think I will have to call? Do you think last night was a success?"

Which, in retrospect, was a ridiculous thing to ask. She'd read the literature. Even at the right time of month, with all the planets in alignment and karma beaming down from the stars, a certain percentage of women didn't conceive. It wasn't as if she'd ever tried before. She didn't know, for sure, that she was the perfect candidate she'd promoted herself as the night before.

And her ridiculous questions had obviously made Tomas as uncomfortable as a ringer with a burr in his swag, because now he couldn't meet her eyes. He stared toward the window and beyond, his expression so tricky and unreadable that she longed to climb inside his head.

"If you are—" his gaze shifted back to her face "—will you want to keep working?"

"I told you. My job here is temporary."

"You know Rafe will give you another job at the drop of a hat. Alex, too."

"And what about you? Do you have a job for me on Kameruka Downs?"

His eyes narrowed. "You're joking."

"Why would you think that?"

"Because I wouldn't—" He stopped abruptly, lips a tight line.

"Because you don't want me around?"

"Because there's no job for you there."

The pain she felt was, no doubt, her heart bottoming out of that slow-fall plummet with a sickening crash. "I'll let you know the result, once I know," she said, painfully aware that she was still standing here, having this momentous conversation, stark naked.

Tomas started to turn, paused. "Angie…thank you."

For being such a sport? For not pushing the job issue? For not making this morning-after a train wreck?

It was her turn to nod tightly. "You're welcome."

And then he was gone, probably bolting as fast as his boots would take him, to the airport and the company plane that would transport him back to his territory.

Kameruka Downs, where she was no longer welcome.

Seven

For two weeks Angie hummed through life in a cheerful glow of hopefulness. When she closed the door on that hotel suite—after an indulgently long shower and an extravagantly big breakfast—she closed the door on all doubts and despondency. She left them there in the dark, shut away from the shining light of her optimism.

Only sex? Bull! She'd felt the connection, the specialness, the rightness of their lovemaking.

As for Tomas…well, she could make allowances. He'd been even more nervous than Angie, and he didn't have the crutch of a lifetime of fantasies for support. She'd seriously unsettled him with that revelation, and she'd unnerved him more with the emotion she couldn't completely contain when they'd finally come together.

Plus, in his own words, it had been a while.

Her mind had drifted back to that comment with vexing regularity. A while, as in, not since Brooke? Could he have been celibate that long?

Knowing Tomas…yes. Because that's how he would honor his vows, yet that thought caused a churning storm of conflict in Angie. The very qualities that drew her to this man—his steadfastness, his loyalty, his constancy and conviction—could also be the downfall of any hope of a future with him.

He loved Brooke. He probably believed he would never love again. Yet Angie knew deep in her heart that she was his woman, and she used that confidence to staunch the rebellious doubts as she worked through two weeks without any calls from or contact with Kameruka Downs. He was busy, she reminded herself. This was his busiest time of year with the cattle business. Besides, *she* was to call *him*, she reassured herself, whenever her hungry gaze drifted to the phone late at night.

Then her hand would cradle her belly and her heart would skitter with a mix of nerves and excitement as she contemplated the prospect of Tomas's baby growing there. And she would fall asleep with a smile on her lips and optimism warm in her heart.

This morning, when she visited the bathroom, fate and the female cycle rudely snuffed out that light.

Naturally it was Monday and she couldn't slink back to bed. Predictably it was a stinking grey Monday, the kind that decides to dump its wet load of misery on a woman's shoulders when she's running to catch the bus. And because she was in no mood for company, Rafe came to wander aimlessly around her workspace as soon as he arrived at the office.

That happened to be about five minutes after she'd tossed her rose-colored glasses in the bin beside her desk, along with the pregnancy-test kit she'd bought ahead of time and stored in the back of her filing cabinet. She knew the second Rafe's miss-nothing eyes settled on the discarded box.

Why had she given in to that silly fit of hormonal pique? Why hadn't she just left the kit where it was? She hadn't needed to trash the damn thing!

A small frown lined her boss's forehead. "Is that what I think it is?"

"That's none of your business."

His gaze lifted at her sharp tone. "It appears to be unopened."

"How observant." It was hard not to sound snarky when Rafe—dammit—was pushing aside papers to perch on the edge of her desk.

"Do I take it this is bad news?"

She clicked her mouse and stared hard at the computer screen.

"Because I always thought it was bad news when the lines turned pink."

Eyes narrowed in irritation, she swung back to face him. "In your situation, that would be good news...or have you forgotten the baby you're supposed—"

"So, you did do it."

"What?"

"You and Tomas. That night in the suite. I wondered."

Yet he hadn't said a word. *She* wondered—

"I didn't say anything in case nothing came of it," he said, finishing her thought. He glanced back at her bin. "Is that what the unopened test means?"

"I'm not pregnant, if that's what you're asking."

And because she couldn't stand the sharp perceptiveness of his gaze—or the flicker of sympathy in his eyes—

she turned back to her computer. Tapped at a couple of keys before she realized she hadn't opened a document. The computer beeped back at her, something that sounded like *you dolt.* And she was the stupid, idiotic queen of dolts for imagining she could do this, for thinking that one night would instantly provide a baby, and for wanting it so much. Dammit, and now she had to put up with her boss sitting there looking at her with pity and—

"What are you going to do about it?" he asked, and she whirled on him in a flash of fury.

"What are *you* doing about it? You, also being part of this pact. Why should it be up to me? And how about Alex—has he set a date yet?"

"Last I heard, he and Susannah are still in negotiation."

Which meant no date, no marriage, no baby, since Alex had decided that marriage had to come first. "And you?"

"I'm still considering my options."

"Too much choice?"

Instead of grinning or winking or chipping in with the usual Rafe-line, he looked at her steadily. "Or maybe I can't find the right woman to make a baby with."

The right woman, the right mother, the perfect candidate. Angie's heartbeat sounded thick and loud in the sudden quiet. "Do you think Tomas found the right woman?"

"Do you?"

Yeesh, but she hated questions tossed back in her face. Twelve hours ago she knew the answer, unequivocally, but now? Had so much changed? Or was this only a wet-day hormone funk? She stared at the blankness of her computer screen a moment, and the only answer she found was the truth. "I want to make more than a baby with him. I want to make him live and laugh and love again."

Rafe grinned. And winked. "Attagirl."

Angie scowled back at him, but somewhere inside she felt the tiny flicker of hope. "Fat lot of good it will do me."

"My brother needs someone like you. Someone with the balls—"

"Thank you very much!"

"—to keep pushing and prodding so he doesn't hole up in his shell like a hermit crab. He needs someone who loves him enough to not give up."

"You think?"

"He needs you more than he needs this baby, Ange."

Holy Henry, she hoped so. Yet, if Rafe believed it—if he could sit there and recite with such conviction the belief engraved deep in her heart… "Do you suppose your father thought the same thing?" she asked slowly. "That he was using the will clause to push Tomas to find someone else?"

"Maybe." In silence, they both considered this a minute. Then Rafe shook his head. "Nah, there's too many things that could have gone wrong, the way he worded the clause."

"I guess."

"What matters is making sure everything goes right from here on in. You need to be in his face, Ange, showing him what he's missing."

"What do you suggest? That I turn up on his doorstep and chirp, 'Honey, I'm home'?"

Rafe grinned. "You're reading my mind."

It took Angie a moment to realize he wasn't joking. She wet her lips nervously. "What, exactly, are you thinking?"

"Two weeks, right? Until you can next make babies?"

Angie nodded.

"What if I fly you out there a bit earlier…?" Not really a question, since he didn't wait for an answer. He picked up her desk calendar and studied it. When he looked up his eyes held a wicked glitter. "You know what this Saturday is?"

"Um…the twentieth?"

"The Ruby Creek Races."

Angie frowned. The Ruby Creek weekend was an out-back institution, more about socializing than horse-racing, but what did it have to do with her situation? "You want to go? You think I should go? Do you think Tomas will be going?"

"Unlikely. He doesn't get out much these days. No, what I'm thinking is all the staff will be going and he'll be home alone."

Until she arrived. Angie's pulse fluttered. "He won't like it."

"Does that matter?"

She smiled slowly and the glow of hope spread strong and rosy through her whole body. "No. I don't suppose that it does."

Tomas recognized the sound of the Carlisle Company plane coming in low over the Barakoolie ridge without lift-ing his gaze from the weaners he was tailing. He figured it was Alex or Rafe dropping in to visit with their mother. A wasted trip, since Maura had flown down to another of their stations to supervise the muster after the manager broke his leg. Tomas would have gone himself except…

His chest tightened as he recalled the plea in his moth-er's pained eyes—a look that had cow-kicked him right where he lived. He knew what she couldn't say. *I'm lost and I'm hurting. I need to be busy, occupied, working as hard as my body can take. It's the only way to live through this grief.*

Oh, yeah, he knew better than anyone the benefits of physical exhaustion. Not a cure, but a salve to deaden the acute pain and a bandage dressing for the soul-deep lone-

liness. A means to fill the days and a way to find the salvation of sleep in a marriage bed suddenly left half-empty.
So, yeah, he'd let Mau go with his blessing, and if either
of his brothers gave him grief over it… After several weeks
of fourteen- and fifteen-hour days he felt brutal enough to
knock them both on their Armani-clad asses.

Thinking about that outcome gave him a grim satisfaction
as he watched the King Air bank and turn before coming in
low on its final approach to the airstrip. The young colt he
was training jigged and danced beneath him. And if his pulse
skipped in time with his fractious mount, that wasn't because
some rogue part of him remembered the last time one of company planes had sat on the Kameruka airstrip.

*The way she'd tried to kiss him. The day she'd sowed
the idea of only-sex in his brain.*

"Easy boy," he soothed. "It's just a big old noisy bird."
With a big old noisy pilot.

He identified Rafe as the pilot by the way he approached
his landing. Not sure and steady like Alex, but in a flam-
boyant rush.

The colt tossed his head, and with knees and thighs
Tomas directed his attention back to the cattle. "We have a
job to do, Ace," he murmured. "Keep your eye on the prize."

He didn't turn back toward the strip. He would see his
brother soon enough, whether he wanted to or not. And even
though this was officially a holiday weekend on Kameruka,
with all his staff away at the races or visiting friends or simply sitting it out at the local bar, his time off was this: training a young colt to tail cattle. Later he'd fly a bore check in
the station Cessna. And there was a gate hinge to weld on the
Boolah round-yard. All the stock horses and dogs to be fed.

Only when he was good and ready, would he return
home to his visitor.

* * *

The sun had started its descent behind the rugged western cliffs of Killarney Gorge before Tomas returned to the homestead. His narrowed gaze scanned the deepening shadows of the veranda and, sure enough, found Rafe. He didn't care. He was resigned to enduring his brother's smart-ass company this evening. In fact, he was looking forward to crossing words if not swords—either would suit his mood. But first, he was looking forward to a long cold beer and a longer hot shower.

"Rafe," he said in greeting, as he hit the veranda and kept moving.

"Pleased to see you, too. I was getting bored with my own company."

"No kidding." He paused with the door half-open. "I'd have saved you the tedium if you'd rung first."

"You'd have laid on hot and cold running housemaids?"

"I'd have told you Ruby Creek was on."

Rafe chuckled softly. "I knew that. I'm heading out there in the morning, but I thought I'd spend the night with Mau first. I'm surprised she's not home yet."

"She's over at Killarney, mustering."

"Better that she's keeping busy." No surprise, no censure, barely a pause to digest the news. "I'll fly down tomorrow and see her."

"Only if you've got a couple of days free. She'll be out in the back country by now." And they both knew that no one—not even Rafe—could land a twin-engine there.

"How's she doing?"

Tomas let the door swing shut and tipped his hat back. "She's coping."

For a quiet minute they were in accord, everything else forgotten in shared concern for their mother. Worry that she may sink back into the same depression as after she lost her baby daughter—their sister—so many years ago. Rafe made a scoffing noise and shook his head. "Why didn't he just leave her one of the stations to run? That would have made more sense than this grandchild thing."

"Is that why you think he did it? For Mau?"

"Don't you?"

Tomas let his breath go in a long sigh. "Yup, I do."

"Do you reckon it'll make any difference? That she'll buy we're doing this because we want to?"

"Does it matter in the end? If she gets the grandchild to dote on?"

"Point." Rafe expelled a long, audible breath. "I'll fly out next weekend to see her."

Tomas nodded, but he could see there was more going on in Rafe's head than the fact he'd wasted a trip. He looked almost…pained.

"What are you doing about the baby?" Tomas asked, taking a stab at what bothered his brother's usual carefree attitude. "Have you decided on a mother yet?"

"There's someone I'm hoping to bump into at Ruby Creek tomorrow."

Hence the look of a man headed for the gallows. If he didn't feel a barrowload of empathy, Tomas would have found his brother's situation funny—the last of the great playboys forced to choose one woman. He didn't ask for the lucky lady's name because the look on his brother's face reminded him of his own circumstances. Of Angie, who Rafe would have seen as recently as yesterday. It had been over two weeks. She'd said she'd call as soon as she knew. She should have called.

He scowled down at his boots, tried to find the words he needed down there. *How's Angie? Two simple words, one question. How hard was that?* Instead he found himself asking, "How's the hotel business?"

"Booming." Rafe stared at him a moment. "Can't say you've ever expressed an interest before. Is there a reason? Anything specific you wanted to know?"

Tomas gritted his teeth. Okay, all he had to do was ask. He took off his hat, slapped it against his thigh. "How's Angie?"

"Why don't you ask her yourself?"

Call her? His gut clenched and fisted. "Yeah, I guess I could phone her."

"I meant you should ask her. In person."

Tomas frowned. "In Sydney?"

"Inside." Rafe hitched a shoulder in that direction. "I think she mentioned something about taking a bath. She liked the look of that new spa you put in."

In *his* bathroom? Like hell!

Tomas barreled down the long hallway and shouldered through the half-open door. Yes, she'd taken a bath. In his bathroom. Wisps of steam wafted toward the open louver windows, and the moist sweet fragrance of honeyed bath oil still hung in the air.

The house had a half-dozen bathrooms and she'd had to use his? Dammit to hell and back...

He slapped his hand against the doorjamb, whipped around and his eyes narrowed in cold fury. His bedroom door lay open. Oh, no. No, no, no. *No.* A dozen long strides and he came to a grinding halt, everything locked up by the sight that greeted him through that open doorway.

Angie was bent over his bed, ratting through an open suitcase. Not that he took much notice of the suitcase, since she wore nothing but a towel. For a long minute his anger dissipated, swamped by the heated rush of a body remembering. The soft pliancy of her thighs. The full curves of her buttocks. The sheer carnal pleasure of sliding inside.

She stilled suddenly and turned, as if she'd heard the groan of his lust or the snarl of his restraint, and her eyes widened in surprise. Vaguely he was aware of something—hell, it could have been the crown jewels for all he noticed—drop from her fingers as she straightened.

"Hi."

The husky note of her greeting stroked his aroused glands like a velvet fist, and in that spun-out moment she had only to smile and unwrap her towel and he'd have forgotten every grievance. But she didn't smile. And she clutched the front of the towel with an edginess that reminded him of everything wrong with this picture.

Her body, in his towel, in his bedroom. Uninvited.

"What are you doing here?" he growled, low and mean.

"Looking for clothes. I was about to get dressed." Gathering her usual assurance, she let go the towel and leaned back into her luggage. "If I can just find my—"

"Dammit, Angie, you know that's not what I asked!"

She knew it and she had to know how much was revealed when she leaned over like that, but it didn't stop her dragging out the moment. Deliberately? Was she trying to provoke him? Entice him? Seduce him?

Tomas ground his teeth and forced his attention to her busy hands. They rummaged some more then paused, holding up a piece of ivory satin underwear that dangled from her fingertips like some blatant stroke-me invitation. Oh, yeah, this was deliberate, unsubtle and doomed for failure.

"Forget getting dressed," he barked. "We need to talk."

Her gaze skittered with the same edginess she'd displayed earlier. Good. This was his home, his territory, and he was calling the shots. She had cause to look nervous.

"Why didn't you call?"

"That's why I'm here," she said quietly. And as if her legs lost strength, she kind of flopped down onto the edge of his bed. "Instead of calling."

"You're pregnant?"

The thick ponytail on top of her head wobbled as she shook her head. "No. I'm not."

"Are you sure?"

"Pretty much."

"What does that mean? Did you do a test or not?"

Her backbone stiffened at his harsh tone, and her gaze snapped to his. "I mean," she said clearly, evenly, "that unless I'm one of those women who bleed even when they're pregnant, then I'm not."

Tomas let go an audible breath. Restless, unable to meet the steady darkness of her gaze and unsure how to respond, he paced to the window. Hesitated a second before turning around. "You okay with that?"

"I'm disappointed. What about you?"

How did he feel? Thrown. Rattled. Disgruntled. And, yeah, disappointed that she hadn't let him know. That she'd probably confided in Rafe first—why else would he have brought her out here?

"How long have you known?" he asked tightly.

"Only a day or two."

"You said your cycle was regular as clockwork. I can do the sums, Angie. Either you—"

"Okay." She jumped to her feet in a rush of fluttering towel and creamy skin. "I knew on Monday. Yes, I should have called, but I wanted to surprise you."

What? He scarcely believed his ears. This was supposed

to be a pleasant surprise? *Here I am, in your bedroom, aren't you glad?*

She sucked in a breath, as if preparing to say more, but the action caused the towel-tuck over her breasts to come right undone. Before she could regather the gaping sides, Tomas caught an eyeful of dark nipples and curved belly and feminine curls. His body blistered with instant heat, his groin tightened with instant desire, but he rejected the quickening of lust and fixed her with a hard, cold stare.

"I don't like surprises."

He walked to the dresser and stared for a full twenty seconds before he realized what was wrong. Her hairbrush, a tub of face cream, her neck-chain, were scattered carelessly amidst his neatly arrayed belongings.

Tomas's jaw set so hard he heard his teeth grind.

He didn't want this. He didn't want her here, not in his home, not in his bedroom, not in his days and his nights.

With one fisted hand he scooped up her things and tossed them into her suitcase. In another second he'd gathered up all the gauzy bras and filmy panties that had spilled onto his bed, and jammed the lid shut on it all.

He was fuming that she'd pulled this surprise-him stunt, that she'd thought she could take over his bedroom, that she'd brought all that skimpy underwear with her...for what? They were having sex, not a seduction. He clicked the snaps shut on her case and his icy rage turned to steam.

"I hope you didn't buy all that specially," he said, straightening with the luggage in his hand.

In silence she'd watched him, not objecting, not commenting, although her eyes now flashed with indignation. "You don't like nice lingerie?"

"It's a waste of money if you bought it for me."

"Actually, I bought it for myself. I never thought for a

minute that you'd wear a G-string." She smiled silkily. "Although I do like how satin feels against my skin. Maybe you should feel it sometime."

Tomas refused to let her taunt affect him, refused to picture her wearing a satin G-string and nothing else, refused to imagine his hands skimming over her curves, touching, feeling, caressing. Narrow-eyed he glared back at her. "It looks like I'll have to."

"Are you saying you want to try again?"

"I take it that's why you're here."

"Yes," she answered calmly. "Bad news, I'm not pregnant. Good news, we get to do it all over again. If that's what you want."

Eight

Oh, yeah, he wanted, but this time he was setting the rules—starting with not in his bed. Suitcase in hand, he turned toward the door. "You'll have your own bedroom. That's not negotiable, Angie."

"If you want me out of your bedroom—" her eyes flashed a challenge "—you'll have to carry me."

He only hesitated long enough to think: *dentist, throbbing tooth, get it over with quick.* Eyes fixed on hers, he marched across the room, picked her up like a sack of chaff and tossed her over his shoulder.

She wiggled, she kicked, she punched. Against his shoulder he could feel the soft schmoosh of her breasts but he kept on walking. The towel rode up and his hand ended up cupping her bare backside, but he gritted his teeth and didn't stop until he'd dumped her inside the best of the guest bedrooms. Too bad if Rafe was using it, he was too damn mad to care. "This is your room and when we do it, we do it here. When are you fertile?"

"You did the sums before."

So he did them again, counting off the days on his fingers. "Next weekend."

"How many times?"

He'd turned to leave, had actually taken his first step out into the corridor, but her question stilled him. He could feel her eyes boring into the back of his neck, could feel their dark heat and fierce indignation.

"How many times are we doing it?" she asked again. "The book I read says a woman can conceive if she has intercourse any time up to five days before ovulation and twenty-four hours afterward. Conception isn't an exact science."

"I'm well aware of that." He turned and pinned her in place with an uncompromising look. "The article I read stated the optimum time as two days before and the day of ovulation. And you told me you're a twenty-eight-day clock."

"You're choosing three days of unregulated, unprotected, whenever-you-feel-like-it, however-you-want-it sex over six? Yeesh, Tomas, you're the only man I know who'd prefer that option!"

"Not whenever, however. Once a night, missionary position, in your bed." The exasperated sound she choked out turned his voice even colder while heat of every hue pumped through his blood. "This isn't personal preference. This is to preserve sperm count and let gravity do its bit."

"That's such an old wives' tale!"

"I have a housekeeper," he continued coldly, ignoring her interjection, "and a mother who visits regularly. I don't want either to know about this unless there's a positive result to tell. Either way, they'll both be here long after you've gone."

The expression in her eyes turned from willful to stunned in one blink of her long, dark lashes. Yeah, what he'd said was harsh but he wouldn't back down. If you gave Angie an inch, she always took a hundred miles. If he gave her access to his bed, she would keep on chipping away, wanting more and more of a life he had no intention of sharing, with her or anyone.

He watched her nostrils flare as she sucked in a breath, saw a grim determination replace the hurt in her eyes. "So, if this is going to be all clandestine, how will I know when to lie on my back and expect you?"

Tomas clenched his jaw. "You'll know."

"How is that?" she cocked her head on the side, all fake sweet-voiced curiosity. "Will there be some secret code?"

"You'll know when I turn up in your bed."

Angie hated everything about that hurtful snarky exchange, but she did accept his edict on separate bedrooms. It was his home, after all, and she had arrived uninvited. In retrospect, that hadn't been such a great idea. And if she thought he'd been hostile with her…

Five days later her body still did a kind of internal shudder and wince remembering the unpleasantness of their dinner with Rafe that night.

All her fault.

She should have called and let Tomas know she wasn't pregnant. She should have allowed him—not his brother—a say in what transpired next. Backing a stubborn man into the proverbial corner was not the way to win his cooperation. Lord knows, she came from a household steeped in testosterone. She should have known better.

She should have left his bedroom with better grace and some dignity, too. She shouldn't have let him light a match to her temper. And she definitely should not have kept pushing and provoking until he ground out that line about after-she'd-gone. Mostly she wasn't one to dwell on should-haves and most of that list she'd put well behind her by Thursday—all except the leaving thing and that bothered her deeply.

If he wouldn't let her stay, then how could she prove herself and her love? If he was never home and their paths crossed as rarely as they'd done in the past five days, then how could he see that she'd fitted happily back into station life?

She didn't assume he was avoiding her. It was a hectic time with mustering and branding and weaning and trucking out stock for sale and fattening. Tomas was responsible for managing a hundred thousand head of cattle and fifty employees. He was a busy man. So busy that he'd neglected to tell her he was flying out on a three-day visit to the company's eastern feed-lots.

She simmered and seethed inside for a good twenty-four hours, but what could she do? She could prepare for his return, that's what. She could make sure he *did* notice her seamless integration into his home and station life, and she could do so without another sharp-worded confrontation.

A few casual questions to a head stockman and she had an estimated time for the boss's return. She prepared dinner herself and chose the perfect wine accompaniment from Chas's extensive cellar. She soaked for a good hour in the honey and cinnamon bath-milk she'd bought especially for the trip—the same one she'd used in the hotel that night. "For you, Tomas," she stated with some defiance as she poured a liberal dose into the tub. "Same as all the pretty underwear."

Oh, and she gave the housekeeping staff the night off.

Tonight was the first of her three nights with Tomas, and she intended on making the most of it.

Despite the good food, the wine and the satin she'd chosen to wear next to her bath-softened skin, Angie didn't go for a full-out seduction scene. In the interests of subtlety—and not scaring him off—she scuttled the candles and flowers, and left the stereo turned off. That would help, too, with hearing his incoming plane.

Ready early, she couldn't stand still. She fussed over the lasagna and greens and bread rolls she'd baked earlier. She applied a third coat of Nude Shimmy polish and wandered restlessly around the gardens while her nails dried and the sun clocked off for the day. She even considered straightening her hair, just to fill some time.

But when she looked into the mirror at the mass of curls, she remembered Tomas saying he didn't like sleek. She set down the straightening tool and smiled slowly. "Oh, yeah. I rather like it wild, too."

Except she wasn't thinking about her hair.

She huffed out a breath, hot with memories and keen with anticipation, and eyed her reflection in the mirror. She looked like a woman thinking about sex. Heat traced the line of her cheekbones and glowed dark in her eyes. And when she stood up and braced her shoulders, she felt the sweet tug of arousal in her breasts and satin panties.

Perhaps she should really surprise him and take them off. Perhaps she would after she'd fortified her bravery with a glass of merlot.

Yes, she needed a glass of wine. And to check the meal one more time. She straightened the neckline of her white gypsy top, smoothed the sitting-down wrinkles from her jeans, and set off for the kitchen at the opposite end of the house. With every step she could feel the friction of her clothes against each sensitive peak and fold of her body. Perhaps she should take everything off and *really* surprise him…although that would take a lot more than one glass of bravado!

Smiling at herself, she pushed through the kitchen door and came to a stunned standstill.

Tomas was home.

Right there in the middle of the kitchen, actually, although he hadn't yet noticed her arrival. He stood in profile, a tall, dark, dusty hunk with a long-neck bottle in his hand. She watched his head tilt back as he raised the beer to his lips. Watched the movement of his throat as he drank…and she drank in his almost sybaritic enjoyment of that first long, slow pull from the cold bottle.

In that moment he wasn't Tomas Carlisle, heir apparent to Australia's richest cattle empire. He wasn't any "Prince of the Outback." He was just an ordinary cowboy at the end of a hellishly long working day.

A quiver of pure desire slid through her body, from the tingling in her scalp all the way to the freshly painted tips of her toes. She wanted to walk right up and kiss him on his drink-cooled lips and breathe the commingled scents of horse and leather and Kameruka dust on his skin. But more even than the physical, she longed to share dinner without sniping and harsh words. She wanted to let the evening flow naturally all the way to the moment when they stood in unison and walked hand in hand to bed.

Was that too much to ask?

Suddenly the hand holding the bottle stilled halfway back down from his mouth, and Angie had enough time to answer her own question—*yes, definitely too much*—before his head turned slowly her way. She could feel the

tension in her bones and knew it seeped into the innocent kitchen air. And all she could think to say was,
"You're home."

He grunted—possibly an acknowledgment, possibly
a commentary on the intelligence of her opening remark.

"I didn't hear your plane," she continued, with a sweep-
ing gesture toward the roof.

"I'm not surprised."

Angie frowned. She'd turned off the music so she
wouldn't miss his arrival. "What do you mean?"

"You were in the bath."

What? That was hours ago. And how did he know she—

"You wouldn't have heard me above the music."

*Holy Henry, he must have been in the house earlier.
How could she not have known?* Angie blanched, remembering how she'd belted out whatever lyrics she knew and
improvised the rest. "Why didn't you say something?" she
asked on a note of dismay.

"I only came in to change."

And since he wasn't laughing or looking horrified, perhaps he hadn't heard her singing. Relaxing a smidge, she
now realized the significance of her first impression. He
wasn't dressed for a business trip but for get-down-and-
dirty cattle work, because he'd returned early and come to
the house to change. Her gaze slid over his dusty blue Western shirt and lingered on the Wranglers he wore so well.

"What's going on, Angie?" he asked with a hint of suspicion. And when her gaze flew back to his face she caught
him giving her a similar once-over. "Where is everyone?"

"I gave Manny—" who'd been rostered for kitchen duty
"—the night off."

"Why?"

"I thought it would be easier, given you want to keep this just between us."

He'd started to lift his beer again, but hesitated as the knowledge of what that meant arced between them, hot and sultry and heavy as a summer's night. At least that's how Angie's body felt. Without breaking eye contact he took another long drink, another long swallow. "Is that why you're all dressed up?"

She almost laughed out loud, remembering how many times she'd changed her clothes in an attempt to dress *down*. But, still, she liked that he knew she'd made an effort. She wasn't afraid of letting him know she wanted him.

Slowly she crossed the kitchen floor, closing down the space between them, never losing that hot eye-to-eye connection. She ached to kiss him, to hold him, to have him right here and now. But beyond the surface of his blue-heat eyes she detected a flicker of wariness that held her back. Instead of reaching for the man, she reached for his beer and lifted it to her lips.

As she drank she watched *him* swallow, and desire beat so hard in her veins she swore she could feel its echo in every cell of her body.

"You're why I gave Manny the night off and you're why I'm wearing satin underwear," she said huskily. "But first you're having a shower, and then we're having dinner. I don't know about you, but I'm starving."

While he showered Tomas tried to work up a decent sense of outrage. Without asking she'd used his bathroom again. She'd given *his* staff the night off. He'd let her know, in plain language, how this would happen and she'd gone ahead and set up a seduction scene.

But it was hard to maintain rage in a body tight and hot

with anticipation. *She's waiting out there alone,* it throbbed, *for you. She's wearing satin underwear,* it pulsed, *for you. She's starving,* it thundered, *for you.*

Despite the insistent ache of arousal he forced himself to dress unhurriedly, to arrive slowly, to sit and eat and talk. The wine helped. After one glass he realized he wasn't going to ignite every time their eyes met in an awkward conversational lapse, or each time his gaze was drawn to the erotic caress of her thumb over the rim of her wineglass.

It only felt that way.

He shifted in his chair, surreptitiously rearranging that insistent ache of arousal. He was a sad case. There she was, chatting away about the innocuous and everyday, oblivious to the effect of her unconscious glassware fondling. Lucky he'd worn roomy chinos because sitting down in jeans, in his condition, would have been murder.

"Hello?"

He looked up to find her waving her hands to attract his attention.

"You didn't hear a word of that, did you?"

"I was—" Tomas frowned "—thinking."

"Looks serious."

Yeah, deadly.

She eyed him a second. "About the trip you made to Queensland? Is there a problem?"

His pulse kicked up a notch as he met her eyes across the table and imagined telling her his real problem. *I've been at least half-hard ever since I hauled your naked backside into your bedroom five nights ago. The waiting's killing me, Angie. Let's skip the pretense and—*

"Because I'm all ears. If you need to talk it through."

Abruptly she put down her cutlery and pushed her plate away, and the decisiveness of her action startled the hormone haze from his mind. She thought he was distracted by cattle problems. He was dying for action, and she wanted to talk.

Shaking his head in disbelief, he pushed his plate away, too. "There's no problem with the business."

"Good." She smiled, and damn her, started to play with her glass again. "Yesterday I read that feature article in *The Cattleman,* about how you're now considered the innovator, the market leader. It seems you've made a lot of changes since you took over managing the northern stations."

"Necessary changes."

"And production has increased fifteen percent."

"We've had some good seasons."

"And good management."

Half distracted by the play of her pale-tipped fingers on her wineglass, he didn't answer. Idly he wondered where she was going with this, but mostly he didn't feel any need to answer. She was right. Good management had increased Carlisle's productivity.

"Can I ask you something…about the will clause?"

The idle part of his brain clicked to full alert, driving the lingering heat of arousal from his synapses. Not because of the question, but the hint of non-Angie guardedness in her delivery. Tension straightened his spine as he made a go-ahead gesture.

"Here's the way I understand it—correct me if I'm wrong. If you fail to produce this baby between the three of you, you won't inherit ownership of Kameruka Downs or any of the other cattle stations. The company would keep ownership and the board overall control?"

Tomas nodded. Correct so far.

"So, I can't see the board replacing you as manager or

kicking you out of your home, not when you're making the company money hand over fist."

"It's not the same as ownership. That's what I've worked toward, always." He met her eyes across the table. "More than ever the past couple of years."

"Because of Brooke?"

Yes, because he no longer had Brooke. What else did he have to work toward, to strive for, if not this place?

"Do you want to talk about it?" she asked, and the husky catch to her voice brought his gaze rocketing back to hers. To the undisguised light of emotion in her eyes. "Do you want to talk about—"

"No, I don't," he said curtly.

"Fair enough. That's your prerogative. But any time you change your mind…"

He didn't bother responding. He didn't want to talk about Brooke and he didn't want to debate why. And he sure as hell didn't need her watching him with those serious, solemn eyes that made him want to run a mile…and made him want to lash out at everything wrong about what happened with Brooke. Everything he wouldn't let happen again.

The silence stretched between them another tense minute before he saw her start to stack their plates and set them aside. Her hands with their pale glossy nails spread on the table, providing leverage as she stood. And he looked up to find her watching him, those serious, solemn eyes filled with all kinds of promises of temptation and salvation as she extended her hand toward him.

"Let's go to bed."

Five minutes ago he would have taken that hand and invitation and they probably wouldn't have made it to any bedroom. But now… No, he couldn't touch her. Not in this mood, not with so much emotion and despair and desperate need roiling in his gut.

He couldn't need her like that—he wouldn't allow himself.

"I have to work on the books," he said.

"Okay. I'll pack the dishwasher then I'll come help you."

"No, Angie. You can't help me."

She'd started to gather up the dishes, but paused, her eyes rising slowly to lock on his. "I thought I already was."

"In one way. That's all."

The message hummed between them and for several taut, electric seconds he didn't know that she would accept it. "I don't want to fight about this," he said softly. "I don't want to fight with you, Angie."

"Oh, me, either," she said in a breathy rush. "Those things we said to each other the night I got here—I don't want it to be like that between us. Let me help you, Tomas."

He set his jaw, his resolve, the steel in his heart and his eyes. "Don't ask for what I can't give."

Emotion shimmered in the fathomless depths of her eyes, but she nodded and mouthed one word. Okay. With careful hands she gathered up the pile of dishes, and as she walked from the room he heard one tiny clatter of crockery, as if her hands trembled and then regrouped. At the door, she hesitated and turned. "Will I see you later?"

Tomas nodded. Later when this maelstrom of emotions stopped whipping through his body, when he'd controlled the persistent pounding need to stop her leaving and yell, yes, I want to talk. I want to talk if it eases the pain and the guilt and this bitter knowledge that I could have done better. That I failed my wife.

"Later," he said hoarsely. "Yes."

Nine

Two hours, Tomas told himself, and to prove he was in control of mind and body and emotions he stretched it to two hours twenty. Then he came to her room and quietly closed the door behind him. Head raised and nostrils flared, he waited for his eyes to adjust to the midnight dark.

It wasn't like night in the city. This was outback dark, an intense blackness that amplified the other senses to an acute pitch. He could smell the warm female scent of her body. Could hear the quick in-out whisper of her breathing.

Was she awake? Lying in the dark waiting? Craving the intense pleasure of that first skin to skin contact?

He shed his clothes quickly, felt the night air stroke him like a lover's warm sigh. His skin was as hot and tight as a steer hide stretched to dry in the summer sun. As he stripped off his underwear the fleeting brush of his hand caused his erection to jerk with need.

He sucked in a tense breath, half afraid of the edginess to this lust. Half afraid that the edges were keened with loneliness and need and yearning for more than hot bodies meeting in the darkness. The distant call of a night bird echoed in the dark, a high haunting two-note summons to its mate. Closer he heard the soft stirring of sheets, and his sex quickened in instant response. Its call to mate.

He started toward the bed, and despite the darkness he could make out the slow stretch of her arms above her head. As he stopped by the bed she made a throaty sound of welcome. "You're here."

"I thought you'd be asleep."

She shifted again, rolling onto her side and pushing aside the bedclothes. "I was waiting for you."

He sat on the edge of the mattress and her hand glided over his back, a whisper of sensation that reverberated through his body and pulsed in his blood and his sex. So did her scent—the familiar sweet fragrance of skin steeped in honey and cinnamon milk. The same as the day she'd arrived. The same as in Sydney when he'd yearned to taste her.

Tonight he would.

Then it wouldn't matter if he lasted or not, if first he gave her pleasure.

"Was there really paperwork?" she asked as he settled beside her.

He didn't answer, except to groan a deep thankful note as her arms and her legs wrapped around to draw him flush with her body. He didn't answer because he forgot the question when she rocked against him, breast to chest, groin to groin, soft to hard. Unerringly he found her lips in the dark and kissed her deeply, a long, wet play of tongues and mouths and throaty murmurings that seemed to hang suspended in the heavy curtain of night. He didn't close his eyes. He didn't have to hide in the darkness, didn't have to fear what he might see in her eyes or what she might learn from his.

Slowly he kissed his way down her body, drinking in the soft taste of her skin and the husky rasp of her breathing and the strong arch of her back when he took each nipple into his mouth. When he palmed the curve of her belly and slid lower to part her thighs, she sucked in a ragged breath.

"You don't have to do that."

"Yeah, I do."

And he did. With tongue and lips, with a hunger long repressed, and when she tensed and cried out, when he felt her press down hard and start to come, he knew he had to be there. Now.

"Ready?" he asked, and for answer she arched her back and welcomed him inside with a low guttural sound that echoed through his chest and gut, all the way to the organ that drove down hard inside her.

Staggered by the power of his pleasure, he held himself still and rigid as he fought the urgent desire to keep on driving to an end. He was deep, all the way inside her climaxing body and her legs had wrapped around him, holding him tight against her.

"I'm always ready for you."

God, but that undid him. The thickness of her turned-on voice, the taste of her on his lips, the intensity he felt in her stillness as she watched him start to move. The way she rose to meet the drive of his body, thrust for thrust, flesh meeting flesh. The gentle caress of her fingers on his face and throat, and the not-so-gentle bite of her teeth when she came again without any warning. Against the heat of his skin, where chest and breast met and brushed and drove into hard contact again, he felt the cool brush of her necklace and his fingers twined around the chain and held on while the beast of desire swallowed him whole.

Head back, he took the last uncontrollable plunge and roared over the edge into completion.

Somehow Tomas managed to rouse himself before the lure of taking Angie again or letting her sleep in his arms took hold. And when he sat on the side of her bed and rubbed a hand over his face to clear the last traces of temptation from his consciousness, he realized that he held her A-letter necklace in his hand. In the last minutes of that wild ride he must have gripped her chain so hard that he broke a link.

He rubbed his thumb over the tiny charm and put it down on the bedside table. *A for aftermath, afterward, awkward.* The time to leave before he got comfortable in the lush folds of her sated body. *A,* he thought as he scooped up his clothes and retreated to his own bed, *for another night, another time, another chance at conception.*

Two more times and that was it. Done.

Then she was going home.

Angie heard the drone of a plane coming in from the west and her heart banked and rolled. In fact her whole body revved to instant Tomas-is-home, here-look-at-me! attention a good thirty seconds before logic kicked in. He hadn't said anything about flying anywhere...but then that didn't mean anything...more often than not he didn't say... and with so much acreage to get around, flying was an everyday feature of station life.

But she couldn't deny the punchy anticipation low in her stomach, the heaviness in her breasts, the tightness of her nipples. A little early, but Tomas was definitely home...al-

most. She shoved the last of the flowers she was arranging—until now, artfully—into the table centerpiece and
dashed for the bathroom. No time for soaking in milky
baths tonight. If he drove straight from the airstrip, no
stops in-between, she had a maximum of ten minutes.

Hurry, hurry, hurry.

Shedding clothes along the way, she hit the shower running…then ducked straight back out for a shower-cap. No
time for drying hair—she needed every precious minute for
essentials. The red wine should be opened to breathe. Veg-
etables peeled. Cream whipped. For a wet, soapy second
she rued letting the staff off early, again, so she could savor
every detail of preparing and serving this special dinner.

An intense wave of nervous tension gripped her body.
Ovulation day, she'd joked at breakfast this morning. *I'll
make a celebratory dinner. Don't be late.*

It was a measure of the progress they'd made in twenty-
four hours that she could joke about such a thing, even if
neither of them had laughed. Even if his eyes had darkened
and flared with unnamed emotion as they fastened on hers
across the breakfast table.

Yes, they'd eaten breakfast together. The previous night
they'd eaten dinner together, too, and he'd relaxed a tiny bit
more, talking, smiling, even laughing at one of her anecdotes
about Stink, the mechanic. For the second consecutive night
he refused her offer to help with whatever office-work compelled his devotion, and she went to bed alone.

Around midnight he came to her room and made love
with the same fierce power as the night before. Just once,
damn him, and again he'd left her in the cooling sheets of
her bed, hoping and wishing and praying that the next
night might be different.

Well, Angie, the next night is about to begin.

Angie held her face tilted up for a last cool rinse and switched off the taps. *Last night, last chance.* She'd joked about this dinner but underneath, deep inside where her stomach was knotted with trepidation, she'd fastened her determination to make it special. A lot had changed in twenty-four hours, but not her conviction.

What had transpired between them in her bed the last two nights was too real, too huge, too intense, to cast aside as a purely physical joining. So many times she'd had to bite her tongue—or his shoulder—to stop herself blurting out what filled her heart. She'd curbed her natural inclination to tell it all, to lay it on the line, to charge ahead too fast.

She'd reined herself in and she would continue to do so.

Even when he asked her to go back to Sydney until she knew the result of this round of baby-sex—which she knew he would, probably tonight—she would keep it together. While preparing dinner, she'd also prepared her argument for staying and coached herself on delivering it with cool, direct logic.

If she failed, if he wouldn't listen to her reasoning, then at least she would get to experience something approximating a date. Tonight she wouldn't allow him to retreat to his work. Tonight they would walk hand in hand to bed. Tonight the light stayed on.

He owed her that much.

The dress she'd decided on earlier lay waiting on her bed. She traced one of the bright pink flowers and fingered the silky georgette material in momentary indecision. Too much? Probably, but in that second she heard the solitary bark of Tomas's heeler a second before the whole kennel joined in. A vehicle was coming.

Swallowing her hesitancy whole, she pulled the dress

over her head and wriggled until the satin lining shimmied its way over her hips and down to her knees.

"Hurry, hurry, hurry," she muttered. And of course the zipper stuck. She left it half-undone to shove her feet into white mules, to grab her brush and drag it through her moisture-messed hair…a task made easier when she remembered to take out her ponytail scrunchie. She slapped on some tinted moisturizer, glossed her lips, traced her eyes with kohl and smudged the lines.

Done!

She sucked in a quick breath…and realized she should be wearing a bra. If this were a real restaurant date, with other people present, she would take the extra minute to find one, to make some effort to disguise the hard jut of her nipples. But there were no other people…just her and Tomas and the fact that she couldn't think about him without this obvious result. Why hide that truth?

As she rushed to the living end of the house, she struggled to free the stuck zipper and strained her ears for the sound of his vehicle pulling up outside. She wanted to greet him at the door, to smile and say, "Hi, I missed you." To hand him his beer and, if she caught him really on the hop, surprise him with a kiss.

The canine chorus rose to a second crescendo as she entered the kitchen, then quieted immediately as if in response to a slash of the conductor's baton. Or a one-word command from their master. In the same instant—perhaps in response to the excited jump of her hand—the zipper released and glided effortlessly all the way to the top. That had to be a good omen, Angie decided.

She collected his beer and walked calmly to the door. Her heart, naturally, raced at a thousand miles an hour. That, she hoped, didn't show as clearly as her nipples.

Then she heard a vehicle pull up outside and her skin flushed with heat. The ice-cold bottle in her hand was suddenly very enticing. If she rolled it over her forehead, her throat, her breasts…

Tempting, but she didn't. Instead she drew a deep breath and walked out onto the veranda, lifting a hand to shield her eyes from the rays of the sinking sun. A car door slammed, then a second. Voices? The brief murmur was too far away to identify but it sounded like a brief exchange of words.

Lord, but she hoped the second was one of the mechanics who'd bummed a lift back from the airstrip and not a visitor. She cast a nervous glance downward. Yep, there they were. Both the girls still at full *hello-Tomas, boy-are-we-pleased-to-see-you* attention.

Okay, she was definitely going back to change. Except that decision had barely formed before the first figure walked into view—no *strode* into view—and it was not Tomas or any mechanic.

"Maura," she cried, nipples forgotten in a stunned blast of astonishment and joy. Back from the Killarney muster early and unexpected. And here at the homestead, not her own place.

Maura stopped, luckily, because that gave her a chance to brace herself before Angie hit at full speed. She wrapped her arms around Maura's reed-thin body and held on for all she was worth until her bubbles of surprised laughter turned to tears.

How did that happen? And why? Angie didn't burst into tears for no reason. She just…didn't.

A bit stunned, a lot embarrassed, she pulled back and attempted to gather herself.

"What's the matter, child?" Maura was frowning, her

expression a mixture of confusion and concern. "Why are you crying?"

"I don't know." She scrubbed harder at her face. "I think it's just the surprise of seeing you."

"Do I look so bad?"

Angie rolled watery eyes. In her youth Maura Carlisle had been a world-renowned model. In her mid-fifties, even her bad days couldn't hide that beauty. But before Angie could voice that opinion she glimpsed movement beyond Maura and her body stiffened reflexively.

Oh, no. She did not want to be caught crying. She was the strong, outback woman who would sail through the toughest days at his side.

But it wasn't Tomas who walked into her blurry wet-eyed field of vision, but Rafe. Her eyes widened…so did his, as they took in her dress, the bottle in her hand, the smudged kohl under her eyes.

"You're crying," he pointed out.

"I know that."

And if both Carlisles would stop looking at her so oddly she might be able to get some control over herself. Emotions and hormones and surprises and tears. Holy Henry Moses, she had to get a grip. She sucked in a breath, waved a hand in front of her face, and finally managed to halt the waterworks.

Rafe and his mother were still looking at her oddly.

"Nice dress," Rafe said.

"Is there a special occasion?" Maura asked. Then she turned on Rafe. "Did you know Angie was here?"

Oh, dear. Angie inhaled and wet her lips. "I just—"

"And when did you start drinking beer?"

"It's, um, not mine, actually."

"Speaking of which—" amusement, rich and redolent, colored Rafe's voice "—where is the man of the house?"

She flashed him a warning glance. "I wasn't expecting you. Either of you."

"Obviously."

Maura looked at him narrowly, then back at Angie. "Rafe flew out to visit me at Killarney. I had him bring me straight home when I heard the news."

Angie stiffened. "What news?"

"Alex has set a wedding date."

"In two weeks." Maura's lips came together in a disapproving line. "Civil vows in Melbourne! Why are they in such a rush? Alex fobbed me off with some cock-and-bull story about their busy lives. Rafe knows something and won't tell me. Do *you* know what's going on?"

Fixed with those straight blue eyes, Angie started to squirm.

Maura didn't miss that reaction. Her gaze narrowed. "Is Susannah pregnant? Is that what you're all trying to keep from me? "

"I don't know," Angie answered honestly, her gaze sliding away to Rafe's in silent appeal.

"Oh, for land's sake, will you two stop treating me like a fool! I know there's something going on with you all, not just Alex. I've been too wrapped up in myself since…" Her eyes sharpened, as if with remembered pain, but she drew a deep breath and continued. "Does this have anything to do with your father's will?"

Rafe rubbed at the back of his neck. Angie studied the bottle in her hand. Maura clicked her tongue in disapproval.

"I won't accept that. One of you is going to tell me the whole story and—"

"What story?"

Tomas? They all turned as one, three sets of eyes fixed on the new arrival. Angie felt her stomach drop as if a high-speed elevator had taken off and left her a nanosecond behind. Where had he arrived from? And why couldn't he have done so five minutes earlier?

His gaze slid from one to the other before settling on Angie. "What's going on?"

Ten

The dinner didn't unfold as it had done in Angie's imagination. While she attempted to stretch a meal-for-two four ways—she shouldn't have bothered, since no one had much of an appetite—Tomas and Rafe had drawn Maura a pretty thin sketch of the will clause. Angie knew it was sketchy by the questions Maura continued to ask after they'd all sat down for dinner.

They'd discussed Alex and Susannah and their no frills wedding. Maura, who'd given up all pretence of eating, supposed she wouldn't be able to do a thing to change her eldest son's mind. Silently Angie sympathized. Tomas was equally stubborn, when he made up his mind. And as for Rafe…

"What are you doing about this clause, Rafferty?"

Uh-oh. Maura used her sons' full names rarely. The up-shot was always trouble. Angie put down her cutlery and started to collect plates—escaping to the kitchen and washing dishes suddenly looked very attractive.

"I'm still considering my options," Rafe said carefully.

"Of course you are." Maura's tone hovered between disgust and anger. "And what about you?" Her gaze speared Tomas. "Please tell me that's not why Angie's here."

The crockery in Angie's hands rattled its own answer, even after she gripped hard to stop the telltale clatter. She could feel Maura's eyes on her face, could feel the heat rising from her chest through her throat and into her cheeks. First tears and now she was blushing. What could she possibly do for a grand finale?

She knew what she wanted to do. She wanted to look this woman she loved like a mother right in the eye and tell her the truth. But she couldn't; she'd promised Tomas. Seated beside him at the table she could feel his tension even though he answered Maura's question with enviable composure. "I'll talk to you later, Mau. After we've—"

"Don't be ridiculous. We all know what's going on." Maura looked from one to the other, daring them to disagree. "Don't we?"

"It's no one's business but mine and Angie's. I'm not discussing it at this table."

For a long second the silence was chillingly complete, then Maura exhaled through her nose in a sound of pure exasperation. "If I'm reading your lack of denial and outrage correctly, you two are sleeping together to make a baby. Because Charles thinks—*thought*—he could make up for something that happened twenty-six years ago."

Angie put the stack of plates down with a loud clatter. Is that why Charles added this clause? To replace the baby his wife lost at childbirth? To make up for the devastation of that loss?

"We don't know that," Rafe said.

"No one knows why he attached that clause," Tomas added.

"I do," Maura said with more conviction than either of her sons. "I always wanted more children but after Cathy died, I couldn't, physically or mentally. Charles vowed he would make that up to me, that he'd make me happy again."

She shook her head slowly, sadly, and for the first time that night tears misted her vivid blue eyes. She hadn't been happy in a long, long time, Angie knew, but usually she maintained a stoic facade.

"You, child—" Maura pointed across the table at Angie. "You made me happy when you came to live here. You were such a wild, joyous little thing. So full of life and so eager to give these boys a kick in their arrogance."

"It was an easy target."

Maura's smile couldn't disguise the lingering sadness in her eyes. "And now you're making a baby with my son. Have you planned a wedding I know nothing about, too?"

"We're not getting married," Tomas answered, and his voice was about as tight as the constriction in Angie's chest.

"Even if a baby comes of this?"

"That's right."

Maura stared at her son a second longer, then shifted her attention one place to the left. "And is that all right with you, Angie?"

"Tomas was very straight with me," she said carefully, "about not wanting to marry again. I offered to have this baby, regardless."

Maura nodded once, accepting that answer even though she obviously didn't like it. Her disapproval and disappointment fisted hard around Angie's heart and squeezed with all its might. She longed to blurt out the truth, to say she wanted the marriage, the together, the forever, and she would probably keep on wanting it until the day she died. If she couldn't change the stubborn man's mind in the meantime.

"I'm not going to tell you how to live your life, Angie, that's not my place. But you know I was a single mother, twice over. I was lucky Charles came along and gave us all his love and this life and a complete family. I know which option I preferred, and that's all I have to say to you."

That's *all?* Lucky there was no more because Angie's poor heart would have caved. And the damn tears prickled the back of her throat so she couldn't even look Maura in the eye and say she knew what she was doing. Then she felt Tomas's hand on her knee, not a prolonged caress, but a single moment of pressure that expressed support and comfort and solidarity even.

It also made the battling-tears thing much, much worse.

"If you want to talk to me, Angelina," Maura said, pushing back her chair and getting up from the table, "you know where to find me."

"Thank you," Angie managed.

"Angie won't be staying much longer," Tomas said at the same time.

Maura paused, her gaze flicking from one to the other and obviously reading Angie's reaction correctly. "Charles and I told you a long time ago that this is your home," she said. "You stay as long as you want."

"I thought you were going to Wyndham today."

Angie's voice cut cleanly through the chill pre-dawn, catching Tomas midway through saddling his horse. His hands froze for a full second while his mind processed the facts. Angie. Out of bed. This early. At the barn. Carefully

he finished cinching the girth before he turned to acknowledge her greeting. "I am."

"It's a long way on horseback."

Another time, after more sleep, he might have smiled
at that comeback. Wyndham was a bloody long way by any
transport other than plane. "I don't have to leave till eight.
I'm riding out to Boolah first."

"Feel like some company?"

He hesitated—not to consider her request, but to decide
how to put her off without a prolonged debate. After Maura's return and last night's dinner he knew they needed to
talk, but not here, not yet. He hadn't slept more than an
hour and as for Angie…

"You look like you should still be in bed."

"At this hour of the morning, *everyone* should still be
in bed."

"Funny."

Except he didn't smile, not when she shifted her weight
from one foot to the other and drew his attention to what
she was wearing and not wearing. Like shoes. In fact, she
looked like she'd rolled out of bed, tossed a denim jacket
over her pajamas and raced from the house. And if her elevated breathing was anything to go by, she'd not only raced
but sprinted the hundred yards from bedroom to barnside.

He gestured at the bare feet she was busy shuffling between. "Aren't you afraid you'll step in something fresh?"

"Funny." And she did manage a smile. "I heard you
walk by my room and I was in a hurry to catch you before
you left. For Wyndham. Since I thought that's where you
were going." Her explanation started off jaunty and bright
and then trailed off, as if she'd suddenly noticed his flat expression. At least that's what he was striving for. Flat, forbidding, go-back-to-bed-Angie.

"Sorry I woke you," he said, turning back to his horse and trying to recall where he'd left off with the saddle.

"Oh, you didn't. I was awake. Still."

"Yeah, well, after last night I don't imagine any of us slept well."

He heard her shift feet again, heard the soft exhale of her breath, and when he walked around his horse to check the offside he noticed that she'd started twisting her chain—the one he'd fixed for her yesterday—around her fingers. *A for aftermath.*

"It wasn't only what Maura said. I lay awake thinking you might come."

To her room? As he'd done the previous two nights?

Across his saddle their eyes met and held, sparking sudden heat into the chill morning air. For a long moment there was nothing between them but that heat and her honesty, and Tomas found he couldn't lie. "I thought about it," he said, moving back to his horse's head, gathering his reins. "Most of the night."

"But you didn't...because of what Maura said?"

His hands tensed on the reins and Ace tossed his head in protest. With a few soothing words, he rubbed the green colt's nose and promised to do better. For the horse, for his mother, for Angie who deserved much better than his recent treatment.

"I'm sorry she found out like that."

"Not as sorry as I am."

"It wasn't your fault," she said softly, and he sensed her coming closer, felt the way his body responded. "The will clause stated she wasn't to know."

"That doesn't make any of us feel a whole lot better."

"I know."

They stood in silence for several seconds, still but for the stroke of her hand on his horse's neck. That he could see from the corner of his eye, a long, slow, absent caress that made his own skin tighten. That made it remember every touch in the dark, every slow caress, every driving stroke of passion.

"I'm sorry, Angie," he found himself saying. "That first night in Sydney, you told me about the teenage crush. I knew you expected more from me than what I was prepared to give, but I didn't let it stop me. I should have. I'm sorry I've let you down."

"You haven't."

"Don't bullshit me. I know you wanted more these last nights."

Her hand stopped the idle stroking, and his horse whinnied a protest. Tomas sympathized. She had that effect, with her soft hands and warm eyes and easy touch. "It wasn't all bad," she said. "In fact some of it was pretty good. And I had plans for a spectacular last night."

"I noticed the dinner, the flowers, the candles. The dress." Especially the dress and the fact she'd not been wearing a bra. Same as now. When she lifted her hands to twist at her chain or rub at her arms—as she was doing now—he could see the dark outline of her nipples through the thin material of her pajama top.

"You liked the dress?"

Tomas swallowed. "Yeah." He liked.

A small smile touched her lips, a sweet and innocent contrast to the sultry heat in her eyes. "Maybe it's not too late. If you wanted to give this ride a miss and, well, you said you don't have to leave till eight."

Two hours. One last time. And it would be all about her, about what she liked, about her fulfillment. *A for atonement.* His body thickened in readiness; the air thickened with anticipation. And somewhere in the world beyond, a ringer whistled tunelessly as he approached the barn and the start of his working day.

"Mornin', boss," he said. Then, "Bit early for you, eh, Ange?"

He continued on his way, but his interruption hurtled Tomas back into the real world. *His* real world. "I think it best if we leave things as they are."

The hand at her throat stopped twisting the chain. "Do you mean altogether? Not try again at all, even if this time didn't work?"

"Yes. I do mean altogether," he said stiffly. He gave the girth one final check and excused himself so she stepped out of the way.

"Because Maura doesn't approve?"

He put his boot into the stirrup and looked her right in the eye. "Because Maura was right not to approve."

"But what about the inheritance?" She waved her arms wide. "What about all this? What about the ownership you've worked so hard for?"

"I've tried. It's up to Alex and Rafe now."

"Alex isn't married yet, and Rafe said he's still considering."

He swung into the saddle, adjusted his weight. "He's made up his mind…he's not telling Mau is all."

As intended, that news sidetracked her attention. She huffed out a breath. "Really?"

"Apparently he's going to ask her tomorrow night." He held up a hand, anticipating her next question. "Don't ask me. Ask him."

"I will, but I still won't believe it until I see it. I mean, Rafe as a father?"

"He never backs down from a challenge."

Her abstracted expression tightened and she looked up

at him sharply. "Is that what this is between you three? A challenge?"

"Not to me. Not to Alex. But to Rafe…probably. A challenge is the only thing that drives him." He gathered up his reins. "He's flying back to Sydney today."

"And you think I should go with him?"

"That's not my decision to make."

"I'm not staying if you want me gone," she said simply. "So it is your decision."

And what could he say? *Go, because I'm afraid to have you here. Go, before I can't walk past your door at night. Go, because I'm afraid of what you expect of me, afraid of what I can't give.*

"Stay until you know if you're pregnant. Then we'll both know."

"Well, Charlie, here we are then." Angie coaxed the elderly stock horse right up to the fence and sucked in a deep, dusty breath. "Wish me luck."

Being of the seen-it-all-before persuasion, Charlie didn't wish her anything that she could detect. In fact she thought the old darling might have nodded off around the three-mile mark and sleepwalked the rest of the trip. But he'd got her here, albeit slowly, and that was the main thing.

"Here" was the stockyards at Spinifex Bore, where Maura suggested she might find Tomas. And as she gathered up her reins and prepared to dismount, she cast her eyes over the cattleyard activity and zeroed in on his broad shoulders and tan hat instantly. Angie climbed from her saddle to the top rail without shifting her gaze from that tall, powerful figure standing right in the middle of the bellowing melee of cattle and dust and ringers. As always the

sight of him turned her breathless, tight, hot in a dozen separate places, but as she watched him work the desire softened like candle wax before reshaping into a fuller, richer
craving.

This was a man in his element, doing what he loved,
what he was born for. This was her man, and this was the
life she longed to live with him. Even through the pall of
dust raised by a thousand milling hooves, nothing could
have been clearer in Angie's eyes or mind.

It bolstered her resolve and reaffirmed her reason for
riding out to see him today.

The notion had been simmering around in her brain for
the five days since Maura's return, since the morning at the
barn when he terminated their arrangement. In that time
she'd caught occasional glimpses of the old Tomas, and the
more she saw, the more she wanted that man back. Over
and over she'd recalled her conversation with Rafe about
coming out here.

*He needs you more than he needs this baby, Ange. He
needs you so he doesn't hole up in his shell like a hermit
crab.* That's why she'd come out here, and she was determined to do whatever she could with the little time remaining—not to get him back in her bed, but to remind him of
the life he'd cut himself off from.

This morning Maura, unknowingly, handed her the perfect first step.

A slow smile spread across her face as she remembered
her excitement as the plan took shape in her mind. As she
recalled turning Maura's initial horrified, "Oh, no, child,
no thank you," to nervous consent.

If Tomas approved.

Her smile wavered momentarily, but she forced it wider
and lifted her chin. He would approve. She had her argu-

ment all worked out, an answer for every permutation of *no* she'd anticipated on the long, slow ride out here.

It was, simply, a flawless plan…and she'd been unable to sit around all day and wait.

"Moment of truth, sister," she muttered, and started to climb down into the action.

Tomas didn't see her arrival. What he saw was a jackaroo's distraction and a bullock charging at the draft. In one swift motion, he managed to push the kid aside and grab control of the gate.

"Shee-oot." The youngster dusted off his backside and cast a sheepish glance in Tomas's direction. "That was a close one."

"Unless you like hospitals, you don't even blink when you're working the draft. Understood?"

"Yes, boss."

Tomas nodded and handed control of the gate to the head stockman on this camp. "Watch him, Riley. I don't want any accidents."

"Then you better get the girl out of here."

Shee-oot.

He swung around and instantly saw the reason for, not one, but pretty much every ringer's distraction. Angie, wearing jeans that molded every inch of her backside, climbing into the yards. And smiling widely at every man who tipped his head and said "G'day, Ange." And paying scant regard or respect to the beasts in the yard.

What in the blue blazes did she think she was doing?

Jaw set in a heated mix of fury and fright for her safety, he strode in her direction. A few curt words set the men back on task. A few deep breaths brought his seething response under control.

Her smile faltered and dimmed when he caught her by the arm and swung her back into the relative protection of a corner. "What are you doing?" she asked, when he kept turning her until he was happy he could see both her and the cattle.

"I'm making sure you don't step into the path of half a ton of beef."

"I know what I'm doing." Eyes narrowed with indignation, she waved her free arm toward the activity. "I've been around cattle ten times as long as some of these kids."

"Then you should know this is the most dangerous place on the station. You shouldn't be distracting those kids."

She blinked slowly, and her gaze turned contrite. "You're right. I guess I should have waited up on the rail until you were done."

Tomas shook his head. Did she really think that sight wouldn't have distracted any red-blooded male? Her perched up there in her pretty pink shirt and tight jeans and Cuban heeled boots? His gaze narrowed on the footwear and then on the roping gloves that protected her hands. His gut tightened with a new and different fear. "Did you ride out here?"

"Of course I did. Why?"

He swore softly. Shoved his hat back from his brow. "What if you're pregnant?"

"I rode Charlie, not one of these bulls. I don't see how that could hurt." She looked perplexed, as if she didn't understand his concern. Hell, he didn't understand it completely. Not the almost irrational rush of terror when he imagined her galloping down here at the bone-rattling speed she'd favored in her youth.

"Charlie, huh." Readjusting his hat, he exhaled a long, slow draft of remnant fear. Charlie was a safer conveyance than anything on wheels. He'd overreacted, big time. "I can't imagine you enjoyed that much."

"He has two speeds—slow and slower. I swear that snails overtook us on the way out here." She smiled, but the softening of her expression kind of hitched in the middle when their eyes met and held. Still smiling, she reached out and touched his arm but her eyes were serious, dark, solemn. "I'll be careful, okay?"

That expression, that touch caught at his throat. He knew he'd have to clear it to speak, if he had anything to say, so he just nodded. And his gaze slid down to the warm pressure of her hand on his arm, not so much arousing as…unsettling. Because he wasn't thinking about those kid-gloved fingers stroking his bare skin. He wasn't thinking about them sliding down inside his jeans and folding around him. He huffed out a breath. He was thinking about them sliding down and folding around his hand and, hell, that's what he didn't understand.

And she must have misunderstood his intense interest in her touch, because she suddenly withdrew her hand and tucked it into the front pocket of her jeans. He had the weird feeling that she'd taken something from him and tucked it away.

Unsettling? Holy hell, yeah.

There was an uncomfortable passage of silence before Angie tipped the brim of her white hat and cleared her throat. "So," she said brightly, "do you want to hear why I put up with the slow ride all the way out here?"

Yeah, he did. But not here at the yards where she'd managed to turn him inside out with protective concern. With emotions he didn't want, didn't need, didn't understand. "You can tell me while I drive you back to the homestead."

"What about Charlie?"

"Riley can bring him home.

Her eyes narrowed with a frown, but Tomas didn't give her a chance to object. Yeah, he knew Charlie was old and slow and safe. But he also knew he couldn't go back to work knowing she was out there on horseback. Or still here at the yards with cattle milling around. Remnants of his earlier fear still twisted tight in his gut and sweated on his backbone. "This isn't debatable, Angie. I need to know you get home safely. You're riding in my ute."

Eleven

Angie was enjoying this protective concern of Tomas's a little too much, especially since she knew in her heart it was all about the baby—a baby she might not have conceived. And she really had wanted to spend some time at the yards, maybe even working the cattle alongside the ringers, as she'd done so many times in her teens. Another day, she promised herself. Today she had a more important agenda.

"So." Tomas glanced across at her from the driver's seat. "What's so important it couldn't wait until tonight?"

"Alex rang this morning. He and Susannah are coming out next weekend, to visit with your mother." A compromise, seeing as Maura—in fact, all of the family—would not be at their wedding. That's the way they wanted it, apparently. No fuss, low key, over and done. "Anyway, I was thinking it would be nice to invite a few neighbors over on Saturday night. The ones who've been here while you all grew up. Alex's friends."

"A party?"

"A very small one. Hardly a party at all, really, because Maura wouldn't come if there were too many people." Silently she apologized to Maura for using her obsessive dislike of crowds so shamelessly. "I thought it would be good for her, too, to see a few friends in a nonintimidating environment."

He made a sound that might have been agreement…or might not have. She snuck a quick peek at his face for reaction. None. Did he realize she was thinking that *he* needed to see a few people? To start mixing with *his* friends again?

"And in the interests of killing a few more birds with the one stone, I'd get to catch up with them, too. Before I leave." Deliberately she'd left that point till last. Since she rather thought the point about her leaving would score high points. She crossed all her fingers, metaphorically. "So, what do you think?"

"I think Mau won't have a bar of it."

"Well, you'd be wrong. She agreed…if you did."

He was silent for several long moments, his profile set in that obdurate fashion she knew so well.

"You won't have to do anything," she pressed. "Nor Maura. I'll do all the work."

"Bored with living out here already?" he asked.

The question sounded casual, like one of those by-the-way observations that can catch a person completely off guard. He didn't turn and look at her. His profile remained stern, hard, serious. And Angie's heart gave a warning bump. This was an important issue. She knew without knowing why…or perhaps she did know why.

Had Brooke grown tired of the outback life? Had she ever accepted the isolation? The absence of social stimulation, of shopping?

Not that she could ask, not when he'd cut her off so categorically the last time.

"Bored?" She laughed softly and shook her head. "I've never been bored out here. You know how keen I was to get back every school holiday."

"School was a long time ago. You've changed."

"Have I?" she asked, turning to face him, curious. "Because when I put on these jeans and boots I feel the same as I did back then."

"They're only clothes, Angie. Anyone can look the part."

"True, but I'm not playing a part, Tomas. I'm just me. The same old Angie."

"You're not the same, Angie. No more than I am."

"It's true that some things change or are colored by our experiences, but we're still the same here—" she tapped her chest, over her heart "—where it matters."

They'd pulled up outside the homestead and she knew she had to get out of the ute before she said too much about what was in her heart where it mattered, and how little had changed.

"Can you think about the party?" she asked as she opened her door. "Because I won't go ahead without your permission. Just think about it and let me know tonight, okay?"

In the dry season Tomas spent almost as much time away from home as at Kameruka Downs. That came with the Carlisle Cattle Company's growth and acquisition of stations and feedlots right across the north of Australia. He accepted the travel along with the management challenges, and compensated with as much hands-on cattle work as he could fit into his time on home territory.

This time he'd been gone three days and nights, a standard excursion to the Queensland fattening properties, nothing out of the ordinary. Yet as his plane dipped into its final approach to the Kameruka strip he felt much more than the usual dose of homecoming satisfaction. There was nothing standard about the powerful mixture of anticipation and anxiety that tightened his chest and gut.

That response owed nothing to the half-dozen station Cessnas parked alongside the strip, or the company plane that signified Alex's presence. Rafe was in America, allegedly on business—although Tomas suspected there was a woman involved. With Rafe there usually was.

No, Angie's party didn't excite him; seeing Angie again did. Too tired to muster the usual denial, he accepted the truth much the same as he'd accepted the done-deal with tonight's party.

How could he have said no to Angie's arguments? It might be his home, but this was a party for Alex and Susannah, for Maura, and for Angie.

As for Tomas...well, he had considered not turning up. It would have been easy to make a last-minute excuse so he could escape the speculation and covert looks and awkward pauses after someone spoke Brooke's name in a less-than-hushed tone. He hated all that. It was easier to avoid social functions—easier for him and easier for them.

As he taxied in he identified the various parked craft by their owners. All longtime neighbors and friends, so he'd have to be civil and spend at least a couple of hours in their company.

And after he hangared the plane and climbed into his ute, it struck him that their presence might actually have an up side. Already they were curbing an urgency in his blood, an impulse to flatten his foot and drive helter-skelter for home. If she were there alone—if she were waiting in the garden wearing a killer dress and a welcoming smile—he might do something stupid and foolhardy and ill advised.

A house full of visitors would curb those crazy-man homecoming urges. Alex's solid presence would remind him of the benefits of self-control. And Angie's presence... His heart pulsed hard in his chest with a sudden raw swell of nervous emotion.

Angie's presence would remind him of the date and the fact that today, tomorrow, the next day—one day very soon—they would know if she was pregnant or not.

The night was going about as well as Tomas had imagined. He went through the motions, talking to whichever of the guests cared to seek him out in his corner of the courtyard garden. Mostly they wanted to thank him for the invitation—apparently, *he'd* invited them!—and to congratulate him for handing the organization over to Angie.

Apparently she was a sensational hostess.

Ginger Hanrahan raved about her barbecue marinades. Di Lambert gushed about the fairy lights and asked if she could borrow them for her husband's surprise fortieth. "Surprise?" her husband muttered. "The only surprise is that none of you Carlisles has snapped up Angie. Are you all blind?"

No, Tomas wasn't blind. He could see that Angie wore the same dress as the night of their aborted dinner...except tonight she wore a bra. The tiny ivory one he'd scooped up from his bed the day she arrived, he discerned, since every time she leaned over the buffet table he caught a glimpse of one delicate satin strap.

It was driving him mad, the dress and the peekaboo strap and the fact that he couldn't stop watching her.

"Knockout dress," Alex said at his side.

Tomas scowled, not because Alex had noticed The Dress—who hadn't?—but because he'd noticed Tomas noticing The Dress. Continuously. He had to stop staring.

"Enjoying your party?" he asked his brother.

"Tolerably."

Tomas lifted a curious brow at that answer.

"We only agreed to come for Mau's sake," Alex said. "We didn't need a party."

Tomas's silence was empathetic, since he didn't need a party, either. His gaze scanned the several small groups, found Angie, of course, but not Alex's fiancée. "Where's Susannah?"

"Gone to bed."

"Already?"

"Headache."

Which explained why she'd looked so pale and tense, he supposed, although to his mind Susannah never looked anything else. His gaze slid back to Angie, Susannah's vibrant, strong antithesis. She was talking to David Bryant, her head tilted as she listened intently, and in the muted garden light she practically glowed. For a second he was struck breathless by her sultry beauty, and then by his unconscious description.

His heart thudded hard in his chest. Was that the pregnancy thing they talked about? That inner glow?

At two weeks? Yeah, right. More likely it was the reflection off her party lights and the heady excitement of mixing with other people, new people, party people like herself.

He turned his head and looked away, and when Alex wandered off to check on Susannah, he found a shadowy corner where he couldn't see Angie. She could talk till she was blue in the face about loving this place and this life, but what she loved was people. Lots of people and stimulation and conversation. She wouldn't be any happier living here than Brooke, not once the honeymoon was over.

That word choice settled hard in his gut. What was he doing comparing Angie with Brooke? And talking about honeymoons? He'd definitely had too long a day; he needed sleep. But as he stood glowering in the shadows, wondering how quickly he could execute a round of farewells, music started up in the great-room that opened onto the courtyard.

A few couples took to an arbitrary dance floor and he knew he'd missed his moment for a quick leave-taking. He watched the dancers, drawn by the image of coupledom and unable to look away. He watched their hands connect and their bodies brush, saw their shared smiles and moments of eye-meet, and felt a restless emotion swell inside him, a pain he didn't want to name or know. A loneliness he thought he'd learned to control.

Abruptly he turned to leave, and swung right into Angie.

"Hey, I've been looking for you." And she had, for most of the night. Covertly watching, noticing how he always stood a little apart, how he never seemed to relax or laugh or embrace the party spirit. How at times he watched her with a quiet intensity. How at others he looked as remote and inaccessible as his Territory home.

Now she looked up into his darkly shadowed face and realized that his expression wasn't flat and remote. At close quarters his eyes burned with a harsh blue light, a wildly ambiguous mix of yearning and heat and restraint that reached inside and fisted around her heart. Had she actually thought that throwing a party and forcing him to mix with a few old friends would somehow ease his inner torment? She was such an idiot. Such a Pollyannaish, rosy-glass-wearing fool.

"I'm sorry," she breathed, a hoarse whisper that sounded as dark and intense as the moment.

"Sorry? For what?"

How could she say for everything? All the things she longed to change and for not knowing how or where to start? She huffed out a breath, jerked her head toward the partygoers. "For making you endure this. It hasn't been much fun, has it?"

"I've never been much for parties," he said. "Don't judge this one's success by me. You did a great job."

Yes, right, and she knew that. She knew the party had been a big success for the neighbors who still danced and talked and laughed, and a milder success for Alex and Susannah and Maura. But she'd wanted so much more from this evening. More of the impossible, she supposed, as always seemed to be the case with Tomas.

She looked away, off at the dancers who were moving in sinuous rhythm to a slow, torchy soul number. She'd deliberately chosen this song for tonight's mix, thinking to get him on the dance floor. Thinking to wind her arms around his neck and to nestle against his shoulder and to brush knees and thighs and bodies. It was a song for lovers to dance to, to undress to, to make love to with the same sizzling beat.

So, sister, why are you standing here dying with wanting? Why don't you take his hand and coax him onto the dance floor? Isn't that why you sought him out?

"So." He cleared his throat, and turned at the same time as Angie. Their hands collided in a brush of heat that singed the words on her tongue. For a moment they stood staring at each other, all burning eyes and dark heat and electric want. She didn't imagine it. It was there, blue fire in his eyes, the only impetus she needed.

She tilted her head toward the music. "Do you realize we've never danced together?"

Heat flickered in his eyes, heat and a note of restraint. "I don't dance, Angie."

"Never? Or just with me?"

He didn't answer.

"Come on, Tomas, humor me. I chose this music specially and I—"

"Leave it alone, Angie," he said harshly. "I'm not dancing with you."

"Because you don't want to touch me? Or because you do want to?"

Acknowledgment, hot, strong, direct, charged the air as their gazes met and held. Angie's whole body swelled with the unspoken but conceded knowledge—he wanted her. He might not like it, he might deny it tomorrow, but tonight he wanted her. She watched his nostrils flare slightly, watched the almost visible pull of restraint as he gathered himself, as he prepared to speak.

To tell her it made no difference. To call it sex, desire, lust. To say—

"Either of you care to join me for a nightcap?"

Alex. Angie sucked in a breath and prepared to tell him that, for an organizational genius, his timing sucked. But Tomas was already accepting the invitation to escape. Angie let her breath go and shook her head. "No, not me."

When Alex headed back in search of a decent port, Tomas hesitated a moment. "I'll see you tomorrow. At breakfast."

Angie sensed this was more than a casual comment, but she was riding too fine a line between frustration and annoyance to pay more heed. "Sooner," she said shortly. "In all probability."

He tensed in a most satisfying way. "Sooner than breakfast?"

"I'm going to need to use your bathroom at some point. If that's all right."

"Come on, Angie, stop playing games." A muscle ticked in his jaw, and she couldn't tell if that was about tension or fear or just plain annoyance. "Tell me what the hell you're talking about."

"It's a long story, but—"

"Give me the short version."

Yes, he was definitely annoyed. And for some reason Angie felt her own irritation diminish exponentially. With a soft, relenting sigh, she gave him the short version of her one organizational blunder. "I miscounted overnight guests and came up one bed short, so I'm sleeping on the sofa in your office. Your bathroom's closest and will be least congested."

He stared at her. The muscle in his jaw clenched and released again. "Have my bedroom. I'll take the office."

"Oh, no, you can't do that." Angie shook her head with some determination. "The sofa's not that long."

"By the time I get there, I'll be ready to sleep anywhere."

She saw that now, the tiredness in his eyes and posture. She heard the weariness in his voice, and both combined to steal the last of her irritation. "If you're tired enough to sleep anywhere, why not your bed?"

"I told you—it's yours."

"It's a big bed," she said evenly. "Why don't we just share it?"

Twelve

Good going, Angie. You didn't provide the fun, relaxing meet-with-friends that would change Tomas's attitude to life and love and laughter. You didn't get your slow dance in his arms. You didn't even get close to a hand-in-hand walk to his bedroom. And—to end the night on a perfect note—you chased him from his bed.

For about the fiftieth time since she climbed into that bed, Angie rolled over and checked the bedside clock. Three o'clock. He couldn't still be nightcapping with Alex, surely. She pictured his six-foot frame curled up and hellishly uncomfortable on the five-foot sofa and growled with frustration.

She should be the one tossing and turning on the sofa, not in his king-size bed. That's what she'd intended all along. Sure, she'd started the whole who-sleeps-where exchange in provocative fashion. But only because he'd grabbed such a quick hold of Alex's convenient escape hatch.

Nightcap, Tomas? Does this mean I get out of answering Angie's question about why I won't dance with her? Oh, yeah, I'm there!

"Because you do want to touch me," she murmured. "Why is that so damnably bad?"

With another prolonged growl, she covered her face with her hands and remembered the heat, the knowledge, the breathless pounding swell of certainty. And for a second she thought the growl continued, like a deep echo of the frustrated wanting that reverberated through her. But, no, it was voices in the hallway outside, and her whole body tensed in silent, hopeful wait.

The door opened, and in the slice of light from the hallway she saw his silhouette, tall and dark and hesitant. Should she feign sleep? Would that make up his mind?

"I'm not asleep," she said, too wound-up to fake anything for long. "You can turn on the light if you want."

He didn't, but at least he came the rest of the way into the room and shut the door behind him. Angie closed her eyes briefly and murmured a quiet thank you. "I'd decided you must have crashed on the sofa, and I was lying here thinking—"

"Go to sleep, Angie."

The mattress dipped as he sat on the far side of the bed, a long, long way from Angie. She rolled onto her side and propped herself up on one elbow. It took a second for her eyes to adjust, to find his outline in the dark, to identify the movements of his arms as he tugged off his tie. Unbuttoned his shirt. Stripped it off.

Angie swallowed. Cleared her throat. Tried to think of something to say, an excuse to be sitting here watching him undress. "I can't go to sleep. Not until I'm sure you don't think this is some kind of setup."

"A setup?"

"A ploy to get into your bed."

"Alex told me what happened with the Hanrahans bringing that extra couple." He leaned over, she imagined to take off his shoes. "You don't have to explain."

"So we're good with this—with sharing the bed?"

He'd gone still, the set of his shoulders tense and Angie thought he might have shaken his head. Just one small, disbelieving movement before he answered. "Yes, we're good. Can we leave it?"

Not waiting for her answer, he stood abruptly, undid his trousers, kicked them off. Desire speared through Angie, a strong, sweet ache that came of knowing he stood so close in nothing but his underwear. Would he climb into bed now? Would she be able to stand to lie here, to not reach out and touch?

But he started to walk away and struck by momentary panic, she bolted upright. "Where are you going? I thought you were good with sharing."

He stopped and his sigh sounded unnaturally heavy in the darkness. "I'm not that good with it, okay? I'm taking a shower and I could be a while, so just go to sleep."

He was gone longer than Angie would classify as "a while," but how could she sleep? Through the bathroom door she could hear the sounds of his shower, and when she shut her eyes she saw him in that split second before he closed the door. Illuminated by the bathroom light, in tall, tense, erect profile.

Was that why he said he would be a while? Did he need to take care of that hardness? Did he mean to cure it with a cold-water blast or ease it with a warm, soapy hand?

Heat washed through her, heat and a dangerously alluring temptation. What would he do if she walked into the bathroom and into the relentless wet pounding of that shower? Would he welcome her initiative, her hand, her body?

Hot and restless, she kicked the sheet from her body but the still bedroom air felt no less sultry. Even her silky little nightdress felt too much against her overheated skin. She sat up. Stared at the door. Started to peel the straps from her arms.

I don't like surprises.

Life was so much easier as an impulsive, straight-forward, do-what-comes-naturally gal. Before he filled her mind with doubts and insecurities and cause for caution. She hated diffidence. She loathed this whole game of patience. She despised hiding her feelings, her wants, her heart's desire.

"Aargh." Arms and legs akimbo, she flung herself back onto the bed, kicked the sheet further away, pummeled the pillow. And about a second after she jammed her eyes shut, she heard the blessed silence of a shut-down shower. Probably she took a number of breaths in the ensuing minute or two. That seemed likely since she didn't pass out from oxygen deprivation. But Angie didn't remember doing anything other than lying in heart-thumping stillness.

Waiting.

He came out of the bathroom naked, but not to the bed. After he walked out of her line of vision she heard the soft shush of a drawer rolling open, and she wondered what he was pulling on. The fitted briefs he wore so well. Sleepshorts. Full body armor.

Too tense for amusement at that last image, she closed her eyes and smoothed her nightdress down over her body. He didn't like surprises. And despite the eyes shut and his silent barefoot approach, she knew exactly when he arrived at the bed. She knew he stood looking down at her.

"It's okay," she said, a husky sliver of sound in the dark. "I won't bite."

Ah, but she did. The heat of her voice. The shimmer of her nightdress. The line of her legs against his pale sheets. They all bit great ravaging holes in Tomas's willpower, in everything he'd convinced himself to avoid in that shower. And while he stood there with all his blood and willpower and logic racing south, she stretched out her arm and ran a hand across the sheet.

"See...I can't even reach your side."

Apparently that was a demonstration of his safety. Laughable, really, given the perilous snarling state of his body. She might as well have reached over and ran that hand over his butt. He sat that part of his anatomy down on the edge of the mattress and considered the alternatives. Sheet or no sheet? Tent or no tent?

"Did the shower help?" she asked.

And this time he did laugh, a caustic, rough-edged sound that had little to do with amusement and a lot to do with the timing of her question. "Not my immediate problem, no." However, he was very, very clean.

"Hot or cold?"

What? He swung his legs onto the bed, kept them bent, pulled up the sheet hip-high.

"The unhelpful shower," she persisted. "Was it hot or cold?"

He rolled his head a little on the pillow, enjoying the cool imprint of his wet hair. It was the only hint of coolness in his burning body. "Do you really expect me to answer that?"

"It would stop me wondering."

Yeah, well, maybe it would. And just maybe it would shock her into silence. "I tried both. Neither worked."

"Does it usually?" Her silence had lasted all of ten seconds. And she didn't sound very shocked…just curious. "The cold method, I mean. I'm well aware that the, um, hot alternative does its job."

"You know this from experience?"

"More from reading than firsthand." She huffed out a little sound of amusement. "No pun intended."

"None taken."

He heard her move, a silky frisson of movement as she turned or shifted positions. And, hell, he could feel her watching him. Intently. Which didn't exactly help the problem they were discussing.

"You still haven't answered my question."

Shee-sus. "If you want to know how I get off, why don't you just ask instead of beating around the bush."

"Interesting phrasing," she said after the briefest pause. "But that wasn't really my question. I asked if cold showers help."

"Sometimes. Other times, you need a release."

She didn't say anything for a long while, so long that he thought he'd finally satisfied her curiosity. Long enough that he turned his head on the pillow to check. He wished he hadn't. She lay on her side, closer to the middle of the bed than he would have liked, just watching him with a quiet intensity that grabbed him in more places than under the carefully draped sheet.

"Is that satisfying?"

He made a strangled sound, part disbelief, part laughter. "Jeez, Angie. Can't you just read about this in a magazine?"

"I'm asking *you,* Tomas. I want to know if there's a difference between that kind of release and making love with a woman."

"Of course it's better with a woman."

"With any woman? Like one you pick up in a bar or something?"

"I wouldn't know."

Angie was so involved in her side of the conversation, in choosing her careful words to keep him talking, sharing, giving, that his answer took a moment to sink in. She frowned. "What do you mean?"

"I mean, I haven't slept with a lot of women."

"I didn't think that you had, actually."

"My inexperience showed?"

"No." Surprised by his question—by its tone—she lifted up on her elbow, better to see his face. "Why on earth would you say that?"

"Two, okay? You and Brooke. Is that what you wanted to know?"

"I…" God, what could she say? Angie wet her dry mouth but that didn't help when she had no words.

"Have I finally managed to shock you?"

Not shocked, she realized as the impact of his honesty took hold, but blown away that he'd told her. "It doesn't surprise me," she said slowly. "Knowing the kind of man you are… No, I'm not shocked."

"You don't know me, Angie."

"I've known you most of my life, Tomas. I know what matters to you. I know that you never looked at another woman once you met Brooke. I know this whole deal with me and the baby has been incredibly difficult because you still love her—and because you could never treat sex casually."

She could feel his tension radiating across the space that separated them in the big bed, could sense the barriers going up, but Angie couldn't stop. He'd shared something incredibly personal, and she wanted—no, *needed*—to do the same.

"If your inexperience showed, then I wouldn't have noticed. Every time I slept with you, every time you came to my bed and every time you came in my body, was completely amazing. Completely."

There. She'd said it. And as much as the words, she heard the resonance of her heartfelt passion filling the heavy silence of afterward, perhaps because her heart and her body were so jam-packed with love and need and wanting that she could no longer contain it all.

"Do you know yet?" he asked.

Instantly, with absolute certainty, she knew what he meant. Her heart bumped hard against her ribs and she felt its beat low in her body, deep in her womb. "I don't have my period yet, but that doesn't mean anything necessarily. Not yet."

"When?"

"Maybe tomorrow, although…"

When her voice trailed off he turned his head sharply, his eyes piercingly intense in the dark. "Although?"

"I don't feel PMSy, either." She laughed, a soft nervous bubble of sound, because he'd forced her to think about the forbidden. Every thought and connection she'd disallowed herself these past few days. "No chocolate cravings. No bloated tummy. I feel…"

She pressed the palm of one hand against her stomach, and felt an overpowering surge of emotion, part awe, part excitement, part nerves. Was she pregnant? Was there a minute speck of life already dividing and growing beneath her hand?

"How do you feel?" he asked, his voice low and gruff.

How did she feel? As if she hovered on the brink of something momentous. As if the night and their tenuous connection rested on her answer and his response. Her heart thudded so hard she felt constricted and breathless, and the arm holding her weight suddenly wobbled and wavered.

Before it collapsed her gracelessly, she sank down onto the bed and rolled onto her back. And she could find only one word to sum up that crushing wave of emotion. "Terrified."

"Of having the baby?"

"I'm more terrified that I'm overreacting and overreading these tiny little signs."

Slowly she turned her head and saw his eyes slide down her body. Everywhere they touched she felt an acute need, a cry from deep in her heart, and when they came to rest on her stomach, she could take no more.

"I'm more terrified," she said huskily, reaching for his hand and drawing it to her, "that there is no baby here." She pressed his hand against the curve of her belly. "I'm afraid that if I'm not pregnant I will leave here next week and that will be it. Over between us."

She stroked her fingers between his, linking them, letting him know with her eyes and the arch of her body how much she craved his touch. "One more night," she whispered. "One more time."

"That won't help anything, Angie." Their gazes locked in a clash of heat and resistance, as he dragged his hand free and back to his side of the bed.

Angie followed. Slowly, inexorably, she peeled the sheet from his body and she touched him with only her fingertips, a teasing stroke as soft as he was hard. Breath held, she waited, knowing the night's outcome hovered on the brink of this second.

He didn't move. He didn't turn. He didn't run. And when she pressed her palm against him, when she molded her fingers to his thick heat, his whole body shuddered in response.

"I can help you with what the shower couldn't," she whispered. "Let me."

His eyes burned into hers as she leaned in to kiss his mouth, and when their tongues came together in a slow, wet slide of heat the last threads of his resistance gave. She saw the flames leap, felt them spark and take hold in her body. She kissed him and caressed him until their breathing grew ragged and then she slid down his body, kissing him in a dozen quick places as she went.

She paused below his waist and told him she'd wondered.

"About what?"

"What you put on." From hip to hip, she traced the wide black band at the top of his fitted boxers. "When you came out of the shower."

"Would you like me to take them off?"

"No." She dipped her hand into the waistband. "I would like to take them off."

He helped her by lifting his hips. She didn't help him by scraping her nails down his thighs. Or by dipping down and pressing her lips to the satiny tip of his erection. Then she eased back and took him in her hand.

"I was thinking about this, all the time you were in that shower."

"So was I." His voice was a low, hoarse rip of breath.

"I wanted to touch you, here—" she slowly stroked the full slick length "—and here."

She moved lower and cupped his heavy weight, squeezed gently until he groaned in a mixture of pleasure and protest.

"And not only with my hand."

His eyes flashed with dark heat. "No."

"You don't want me to make love to you?" She shifted closer, until her hair settled in a dark cloud over his tight belly, then she turned her head and rubbed her cheek against him, a soft sensual caress that filled her with a shivery tension.

She touched him with her tongue and his stomach muscles clenched as he sucked in quick air. And when she took him into her mouth and tasted him with slow, moist pressure he swore softly and profoundly and it wasn't in protest. His hands fisted in her hair, stroked her face, touched her lips where they touched him, and his whole body jolted.

"Not like this," he said, as tight and hard and strained as his body. "Inside you."

Fingers fisted in her satin slip, he dragged her up to his mouth and kissed her deep, fierce, long. In the whisper of a moment he stripped her bare, but when he started to ease her onto her back Angie resisted.

"Not like that." Hands planted on his shoulders, she forced him back down. "This time, I'm making love to you."

When she came up on her knees and straddled him, hot hands spanned her waist and stroked around and over her bottom. In a hard roll of flexed muscles, he rose up from his waist to lick across her nipples, one after the over. To draw at her breasts until she cried out with a greedy need for more, for now, for him in her body.

"Now?" Raw, guttural, hot. "Here?"

And he parted her, stroked her there, found her wet and wanting. His eyes burned with the same blue fire that lit her blood as she lowered her hips and took him inside, and her heart all but exploded with the immensity of joyful hope.

This was different. This wasn't a quick, purposeful joining in the dark. This wasn't about making babies.

In this position there was no hiding. Their eyes locked and held with a connection more intimate than the slow, luscious slide of her body on his. More intense than the fire that licked at her control as he lifted and thrust hard. Fiercer than the heat whirling and spiraling through her blood as she rode him harder and faster until the climax exploded in a searing incandescent flash.

And tonight he wasn't leaving afterward. Angie collapsed in his arms and listened to the strong race of his heartbeat against her cheek until sleep claimed her.

Angie woke alone, but that didn't dim her memory of the night or of sleeping in her lover's arms. Her lover, her man, her love. A goofy big smile spread across her face as she smoothed a hand over the tangled sheets. Cool, but that didn't faze her blissful state.

Tomas always woke early, Sunday or not. Usually he rode, although some days he spent the early hours in his office. Today he'd been awake before dawn, when she'd needed the bathroom. Awake but not yet up, and when she'd returned to the bed he'd drawn her into his body, spoonlike, and cradled her belly with a protective tenderness that had twined her heart even faster to his.

Her hand crept now to that same spot, and a thrill of nervous excitement shivered through her body. She had to be pregnant. She felt too changed to be anything but. Not different physically—she palmed the rounded curve that was her normal shape—but different as a woman. Hormonally, she thought, and she smiled even wider, amused with herself.

Could she really recognize the different mix of hormones at play? Could she know without knowing?

Slowly she turned her head on the pillow and her eyes fastened on the bag sitting by the bathroom door. The bag she'd hastily packed with what she might need overnight and what she didn't want visitors to unwittingly find in her room. Things such as the half-dozen pregnancy test kits she'd brought with her from Sydney.

Her heart thumped hard in her chest. Too early? Maybe, maybe not. The instructions said the test was accurate from the time of a missed period, but was she missing a period yet? Maybe, maybe not.

She swung her legs over the side of the bed and slowly padded toward the bag.

Thirteen

Tomas's early morning ride wasn't an easy lope to check water or the recently weaned herd, but a testing session with his young colt. Ace was ready to step up his training and as for Tomas—well, he needed an activity that required concentration, something to ground him in his world, to settle the niggling sense that giving in to Angie last night had changed everything.

It hadn't. A weak moment and consensual sex without promises altered nothing. If anything had changed, then it was down to his visits to her bed two weeks before.

If.

The little word wormed its disturbing way into his composure as he strode back to the homestead. If she was pregnant. If she decided she wanted to stay. If he couldn't convince her he had nothing more than his body to give.

He circled around the back, avoiding the living area

where the overnight guests would be gathering for break-fast. He would do his duty and join them, but first he needed to shower and change. Outside his bedroom door he hesi-tated a moment. His pulse hiked, and he hated that uncon-trolled response as much as he hated his indecisiveness.

And all for nothing, because he opened the door to an empty room. The bed was made, her overnight bag gone, and he fought an illogical sense of letdown. He'd dreaded this morning meeting and what she would say, what she might expect of him, the questions she hadn't asked in the night that he knew she wouldn't let lie.

God, had he really told her he'd only ever been with one woman, his wife?

Shaking his head, he crossed toward the bathroom, un-doing his shirt as he went. He'd started to reach for the doorknob when he heard a sound beyond and stopped short.

The door opened and Angie made a soft noise of sur-prise and took a quick step back. She looked caught-out, and that made no sense at all. Nor did her husky-voiced apology.

Tomas frowned. "Sorry for what?"

"For…" Her brows drew together and her hand came up to fidget with her chain. *A for anxious.* "Because I'm still here. Using your bathroom."

"You asked if you could use it last night."

"And I should have been gone by now, with the guests and breakfast and all."

She was dressed, clinging to her bag with a white-knuc-kled grip, not quite meeting his eyes. There was something wrong—completely wrong—with this picture. He glanced beyond her for clues, and it struck him with sudden clarity.

The bathroom.

"Have you got your period?"

Her eyes widened and, to his horror, filled with moisture. Damn, but he'd rather face a ton of enraged cleanskin
bull than a woman in tears. Especially a woman like Angie,
whose tears always meant something.

Out of his depth, floundering with what to do, what to
say, he took the bag from her hand and put it down outside
the door. "Hey," he said gently, awkwardly. "It's okay."

"Don't." She sucked in a shaky breath, thick with those
brimming tears. "You're only making it worse."

"Making what worse?"

"This. Tears. Bloody hormones." She made a low
growly sound in her throat, a sound of struggle and exasperation that kicked him hard in the gut like that ton of
cleanskin bull. And when he reached for her, when his
hands closed over her shoulders, she walked into his chest
and buried her face under his chin.

Being Angie, she didn't just let go and cry. Her breath
rasped hard as she struggled for control. Her shoulders
were stiff with her inner battle and he smoothed his hands
over them, rubbed her back, stroked her hair and shifted
his feet because he was uncomfortable in too many ways.
She sniffed a wet apology, then rubbed at the moisture with
the flat of her hand.

"If that's supposed to be a mop up," he murmured, "it's
not helping."

"A shirt would have helped."

With one hand he shrugged out of his undone shirt and
shoved it into her hand. "There you go."

A laugh hiccupped through her tears, but she took it and
used it to mop at his chest. For too long. His body's response was completely inappropriate, entirely male, irra-
tionally intense. And the only way he could deal with it was
by remembering what had started this.

"You ready to answer my question yet?"

Her gaze snapped to his, wide-eyed and still bright from the tear-storm. She swallowed, moistened her lips, but then answered with a quick shake of her head.

"No, you're not ready or no, you haven't?"

Her gaze fell away, down to where her fingers clutched tightly at the balled-up shirt in her hands. Probably answer enough, but Tomas needed to be sure. With a finger under her chin, he tipped her face back up.

"Tell me, Angie."

"No, I haven't," she said, and something uncoiled deep in his gut. He didn't want to call it relief, didn't want to call it anything but concern for her and whatever had caused this outburst of emotion. "Then what was all this about?"

"I did a test this morning." She straightened her shoulders and met his eyes. "It was negative."

"Isn't it too early to be accurate?"

"I should have left it a couple more days, to be sure, but I couldn't."

"Impatient as ever?"

"I wanted to know."

Yeah, he could see that in her glistening eyes. He could hear it in the wobble in her voice. She wanted to know and she wanted the result to be positive.

Looking at her face now, he remembered in the night when she'd placed his hand on her belly, remembered the sensations roaring through his body, too many, too fast, too intense. Remembered fighting his way out of that drowning sensation and his relief when she'd reached out and touched him. When his responses turned primal, sexual, elemental. That he could understand and deal with, but not the undertow of emotion he saw in her eyes now. Reaching out, dragging him down to a place he never wanted to go again.

"I so wanted—"

He touched her mouth with his thumb. "Be patient, Angie. You said yourself it might be too early. Do you have another test kit?"

"Several."

"But you'll wait two days before you do another?"

She sighed softly. "Two days. Okay. I will."

When Tomas had to leave the next day on an overnight trip to his western-most station, he almost invited Angie along. A distraction, he'd thought, so she wouldn't run through those several test kits one after the other. He thought about her traveling beside him in the plane, thought about her sharing his bed, thought about her company and the interest she was taking in his business.

Thought about being with her when she read that test result, when her eyes looked up at his, all dark and luminous with—

No. He shut the gate on that thought-track with brutal speed. And he flew west alone, the way he was used to, the way he liked it, the way it would always be.

Thirty-six hours later he returned the same way.

By now she would know. He didn't let himself imagine one outcome or the other, didn't allow himself anything other than an urgency to find her and to know the result. By the time he tracked her down at the waterhole, his edginess had escalated to an acute tension that held his backbone and shoulder muscles rigidly straight.

"Mau said I'd find you here." A fitting location, the waterhole, seeing as this is where it all started. Where she'd looked him in the eye and said she would have his baby.

Today, however, her eyes were fixed on the surface of the water that glistened gold in the late-afternoon sun.

"Did she tell you about Rafe?"

"Getting married? Yup." He hadn't wanted to talk about his brother's out-of-nowhere Vegas wedding with Mau, and he sure as hell didn't want to discuss it now.

He squatted down beside her, intent on telling her so until she slanted him a guarded look across her shoulder. "The pressure's off then. With Alex's wedding next week and now Rafe doing his bit."

Tomas went completely still. "What are you saying, Angie? Yes or no?"

"I don't know. I still don't have my period, but the second test was negative." Tomas swore softly, and she huffed out a breath. "My sentiment exactly."

"Are these home tests reliable?"

"I don't know. I've never had cause to use one before."

He stared at her a moment, unsure what to make of her frame of mind. "What now?" he asked.

"I suppose I'll have to see a doctor."

"You don't sound very happy about the prospect." In fact she sounded downright reluctant, and that rubbed the rough edges of his mood. "What if there's something wrong? You said yourself your cycle is regular—" his eyes narrowed "—or was that a stretch of the truth?"

"Is that what you think?"

"No." He let his breath go on a relenting sigh. "No, I don't. You sounded so…reluctant."

And he sounded so worried that Angie's umbrage turned to instant mush. "I'm fine. Really, I am."

"Is there a doctor in Sydney you'd prefer to see?" he asked, obviously unconvinced.

"Not really, but—"

"I'll ring Alex tonight. He'll know someone."

"You think Alex sees a gyno?"

Not the right time for making jokes, Angie decided as she watched his mouth set in a tight line. But she'd felt the need to grasp at something, anything—including bad humor—before the decision about her immediate future and everything she longed for slipped away.

Okay. No more jokes, no more evading. Moment of truth, sister.

Drawing a deep breath, she slowly turned her head and looked into his eyes. Flat, hard, unyielding. Her heart skipped. "I'm not reluctant about seeing a doctor. I do want to know what's going on. I want to *know.*"

"What is the problem then?"

"I don't know that I'm ready to leave here."

"That's what we agreed, Angie."

And if she was leaving, if this was over, then why hold back? She had nothing to lose in laying everything bare, everything she'd struggled to hold inside these last weeks. Everything that brimmed in her heart.

"That's what we agreed—" she said softly "—before we made love the other night."

Something flared in his eyes for a split second before he set his jaw in that stubborn, uncompromising line. But that minute reaction was enough to set Angie's resolve to match. *Oh, no, Tomas Carlisle. It's time to stop hiding. It's time to find out what you really think.*

"At least that's what I did. I made love to you, with my body and my heart and my soul." Resistance, strong and hard flattened his expression and she leaned closer, placed her hand on his arm. "I'm sorry if you don't want to hear this, but I need to tell you. I can't *not* tell you."

"I didn't promise you anything," he said tightly.

"Oh, I know that. You never promised me anything way back when I fell in love with you, either, but that didn't stop me."

"You were a kid."

"I was eighteen and grown up enough to know what I wanted. That's never changed, Tomas. I've loved you a long time—probably forever—but it really hit hard after you met Brooke."

That muscle ticked in his jaw again, but now she'd started there was no way she would stop, not until she'd told him everything.

"Even then, I thought it might be an envy thing—my friend getting what I wanted so badly. And then I wondered if it was more about losing you as a friend, because the way I felt I couldn't talk to you any more. "

"I didn't ever cut you off, Angie."

"I know you didn't, not deliberately, but *I* felt cut off." Smiling sadly, she shook her head. "You were so besotted and always flying off to the city to see her, and when I did see you together I felt like my heart was being ripped out. I was afraid what I might say to you or Brooke."

"From memory, you did have your say."

"Down here? Yeah, I guess I did have a bit to say that night." She huffed out a breath, remembering. "It was a long time coming, though, because I kept questioning my motivation. What right did I have to caution you about marrying another woman when I wanted you for myself? Not that it stopped me."

She expected his agreement, some wry comment on her always saying her piece, but instead he looked steadily into her eyes and asked, "Is that why you didn't come to our wedding?"

"I couldn't," she said, and her voice shook with emotion. "I couldn't watch you together. I couldn't smile and play happy bridesmaid and catch the bouquet and pretend. The way I felt, Lord knows what I might have yelled out when the minister asked if anyone could show just cause."

Neither of them smiled. The atmosphere felt too intense, too grave, at complete odds with the perfect spring evening with its promise of a magical outback sunset.

"That's why you went away?" he asked.

She nodded. "And that's why I stayed away and why I didn't come home for Brooke's funeral. I felt too much of a hypocrite. I know that doesn't say much for me as a person or as a friend, but that's the truth."

He didn't say a word for a long, long while and despite the warmth of the sun, Angie rubbed her hands up and down her arms to ward off the sudden chill of his silence. She didn't have a clue what he was thinking. He picked up several pebbles from the ground at his feet and ran them through his fingers, and despite the intensity of the moment she couldn't stop watching the play of his hand, the slow stroke of his thumb.

"I can't give you what you're asking for, Angie." His voice, low and taut, shivered over her skin.

"Because of Brooke?"

"Yes." He studied the pebbles another second, then tossed them into the water. Angie watched the disturbance of their entry ripple across the water in ever-increasing rings until they disappeared altogether. And when he looked up again, Tomas's eyes were as mirror flat as that silver-blue surface. "You were right, Angie, what you said down here that night."

It took a moment for his meaning to gel, it was so unexpected. Angie swallowed hard—she had to in order to speak. "About Brooke fitting in?"

"She tried," he said after a beat of pause. "But she hated the time I spent away. Hated being alone, the isolation. The lack."

He didn't need to elucidate on that. Brooke had been a city girl through and through, slightly spoiled, not used to a lack of anything.

"You couldn't find some compromise?" she asked carefully. "A job she could do from—"

"She got a job," he said curtly. "In Broome. She'd applied, interviewed, without telling me. A done deal."

A surprise, Angie guessed, and why he didn't much like them.

"She told me the day she died." He looked up, and although his voice was flat, even, controlled, the look in his eyes was raw. "I can't go through that again, Angie. I don't have anything left to give."

"I'm not asking for anything."

"You are, Angie. I see it in your eyes and I hear it in your voice."

"No." Adamant, needing him to understand, to see into her heart, she leaned forward and made him look at her. "I only want you."

He stared back at her a moment. "Tell me you don't want to be my wife."

"I can't," she breathed, and in that moment she knew that her honesty would cost. Knew it would be her undoing.

"I can't marry you, Angie."

"I'm not asking for that commitment. I just want to stay, to live here with you." Her voice shook with the depth of her emotion. "I know about the isolation, I know how hard you work, and none of that fazes me. Give me a chance, Tomas, a chance to prove that this is the only place I want to be. Give me a chance to love you, that's all I want."

"I can't love you, Angie, and you deserve better than that."

Tomas made an appointment for her to see a doctor recommended by Alex—or Alex's secretary—the following week. Not a good time for him to be away, but he rearranged his schedule so he could go with her. She argued about whether that was necessary, but he stood his ground.

"It's my baby, too. I'm going to be there."

"Are you going to be there when he first starts to move? When she kicks? When he's born? Her first day—"

She'd made her point and he walked away. He wouldn't fight with her—what could be gained? The next day he flew to Brisbane to meet with some Japanese buyers, and when he returned three days later she was gone. He picked up the note she'd left in the middle of his bed, and scanned the words again.

I know you don't like surprises, so I am leaving this note. I want to see the doctor alone—if that's the way it will be in the future, then that's the way it should be now. I'll let you know when I have any news, either before or after the appointment. Love always, Angie.

He tried not to notice the quietness of a house without her vibrant presence, the loneliness of his dinner table, the skip of his pulse when he walked in the door half expecting to see her before he remembered…

She was gone, and wasn't that what he'd wanted all along?

Fourteen

The e-mail arrived the day before the doctor's appointment he'd made on her behalf, catching Tomas completely unprepared. He stared at the screen for five, ten, fifteen seconds while a herd of wild emotions stampeded through his system. When the thunder of his heartbeat receded to a bearable level he clicked on her name and opened the message.

It was short and to the point: she wasn't pregnant. She was very sorry she hadn't been able to help him, in any way. She wished him all the best.

No explanation of how she knew; no hint of how she'd taken the news; no sign that she felt anything like the hollow clenching disappointment in his gut.

Did she really think that a cold, unemotional e-mail was all he wanted from her? Hell, she hadn't even tempered the tone with a personal salutation. He stared at the signature line. *Angelina Mori, Corporate Conference Center, Carlisle Grande Hotel.*

She hadn't wasted any time asking Rafe for a new job. So much for her passionate I-love-the-outback vows. Evidently she'd slotted right back into the city. Clearly she didn't have time to call and tell him the news person to person. Obviously she had no idea how mad that would make him...or how worried because of all she hadn't said.

He didn't bother closing the e-mail or turning off the computer. He had a trip to plan.

By the time he arrived at the Carlisle Grande late that afternoon, Tomas had built up a full head of resentment, all of it justified. He was also tired, cranky, and edgy as a bullock in a branding race. It didn't help that Angie wasn't in her office, that he'd been led on a merry goose-chase through three levels of hotel facilities in an attempt to track her down. It didn't cross his mind to stay put and send a message. Sitting down was not an option.

He was a man on a mission, and when he stepped off the elevator—the fifth time—and caught sight of her at the far end of the ballroom he was in no mood for niceties.

The staff member who stepped into his path obviously was. "May I be of assistance, sir?"

"I'm here to see Angie," he said shortly.

"Do you mean Ms. Mori?"

Tomas ground his teeth. "Forget it, I'll go tell her myself."

"Is she expecting you?"

"I doubt it."

She was wearing the Ms. Hotel Management outfit, he noticed as he strode toward her, and looking all city-sleek and so damn beautiful that he had to work overtime to maintain his rage. Luckily it was a huge room. Luckily she was engrossed in conversation with a small cluster of pink-suited women and didn't notice his approach.

Then he heard the soft chuckle of her laughter and the impact of that sound caught thick in his chest. She was laughing? He'd dropped everything and rushed here because he was afraid for her emotional state after that terse un-Angie-like e-mail and *she was laughing?*

His temper seethed on the brink of control as he came to a halt several yards away, his gaze fixed on her smiling profile. He saw her stiffen slightly a second before she turned his way. Whatever she'd been saying froze on her lips and so did her smile. He was vaguely aware of the other women turning too, of all the chatter gradually fading into an intense, electric silence.

Only vaguely, though, because so much of his attention was focused on her face, on her full lips as they silently mouthed his name, on the surge of emotion that rocketed through his body. On stopping himself from walking over there, picking her up as he'd done that day in his bedroom, and carrying her off someplace private where he could rail and yell and then kiss her senseless.

Visibly she gathered herself and turned to murmur something to her group. Then she walked briskly off to the side and waited for him to catch up. "I'm busy," she said without preliminary. "If you could come back—"

"No, I couldn't."

She met his eyes for the first time, and he realized that she was working on her own head of steam. "I can't talk to you now. I'm working."

"I would be, too, if I wasn't here."

"Which brings us to why you are here," she said. "Didn't you get my e-mail?"

"Perhaps you could have called to check."

Her eyes narrowed. "You expected me to call? To what—discuss how many more ways you can tell me to get lost?"

"So I could ask how you are, how you're coping with the news. Whether there are any problems, healthwise."

"As you can see I'm fine," she said shortly and she started to turn away.

With a hand on her arm, he turned her back. "Are you, Angie? Are you fine?"

She drew a breath, released it on a sigh. "Yes, and I really do have work to do. I can't do this now, Tomas. Really, I can't."

He cast an irritated glance beyond her shoulder and caught a curious bunch of faces watching them intently. "How long will you be?"

"Twenty minutes but, frankly, I don't know what else there is to say…unless something has changed since last time we talked."

And there it was, the perfect opening. His chance to say…what? Had anything changed? Other than he'd recognized the fact that he missed her?

She made an impatient sound. "Does this visit have anything to do with Alex's wedding falling through? Or Rafe's new bride going AWOL?"

"No. I needed to know you're all right. With the pregnancy thing."

"We've established that I am," she said curtly, "because there is no pregnancy."

The cold impact of those words caught him unprepared, and he missed the cue by a mile. She turned out of his hold and started walking away, each tap of her heels on the timber floor a brisk note of finality. A sick, scary feeling settled in Tomas's gut. He'd been here before and got it all wrong, was he going to do the same again? Was he going to let the woman he loved walk away because he was too stubborn and too scared and too tongue-tied to say what needed to be said?

"It's not only about the pregnancy," he called out after her, and he sensed a dozen eyes fix onto his face. Not one of them was dark and luminous and fired with passion or seething with anger. The only eyes that mattered remained steadfastly turned away and she kept on walking.

"Unless you want me to shout the rest of what I have to say across the room, Angie, you better stop walking away."

A thousand emotions pounded through Angie's blood as she heard and barely dared to believe what she'd heard. She stopped, drew a deep breath. "This had better be good, Tomas Carlisle, and it better not cost me my job."

"You want to keep this job?" he asked.

Slowly she turned and met his eyes. Her heart kicked hard in her chest. "It's not my first choice."

"The commute would be tough."

"If I were living…?"

"With me." He took the first steps, as slow and steady and deliberate as the blue eyes that held hers, and her heart started singing with joy. "We miss you, Angie."

"We?"

"Manny and Rae miss you giving them nights off. Stink says you're the only one who listens to his stories. Charlie misses the long walks."

"And you?"

He stopped in front of her. "More than anyone."

"What are you saying, Tomas Carlisle?"

"I want you to come home, Angie." He touched her face with one hand. "I want to take that chance you offered me."

"You said I deserve better."

"I said a lot of things that day. Most of them I thought I meant, some of them I even believed." He swallowed, shifted his feet, frowned. "I'm not good with expressing how I feel, especially with an audience—" he cast a glowering glance at the small gallery of spectators and she heard a murmur of voices and a shuffling of high heels "—but I want to be that better man you deserve."

For a moment she was too overwhelmed by his words to speak, so she turned her face into his hand and kissed the palm. *You are that man,* she thought, *you are.* And just when she thought she might find her voice, to tell him so, he traced her lower lip with his thumb and said, "I love you, Angie."

Not so bad, she decided when she could think again, for a man short on words to express himself. And she told him so before he kissed her, and after he kissed her she told him that she loved him, that she always had, that she always would.

"Are you sorry about the baby?" Tomas asked.

"We still have time to try again, to make sure we keep Kameruka." He didn't miss the *we.* He liked the way that sounded. Their home, their future, as partners. "Third time is supposed to be lucky."

"No," he said, smiling into her eyes. "I'm lucky."

Twenty-five minutes later, after she'd dispersed her Pink Ladies and finished her working day, they walked hand in hand to the best suite in the hotel and as soon as he closed the door she walked into his arms and he got very, very lucky.

* * * * *

THE RICH
STRANGER

This one is dedicated to all the friends I've made
through the eHarlequin community, especially the
Brainstorming Desireables, the Aussie Hour chatters
and the wonderful hosties. Thank you for the support,
the feedback, the laughter and for bringing
the whole world to my little corner.

One

No new mail.

Catriona McConnell stared at the message on her computer screen, not surprised, not even disappointed so much as numb. She resisted the urge to hit the Receive Mail button again, just in case her e-mail program magically retrieved the message she needed to see—the one it hadn't found on the last three attempts—from somewhere deep inside the bowels of the World Wide Web. But Drew hadn't responded to any of the messages she'd left over the past week, via every contact point she could dig up, so why would he respond to her latest desperate e-mail?

Because he's your friend, your one-time lover. He grew up next door. He should care.

"Because neighbors care? Yeah, right!"

No longer numb, Cat turned off the computer and shoved her chair back from the time-battered table she called a desk.

A churning mix of anger and disillusionment and what-the-blazes-will-I-do-now anxiety roared low in her ears, in perfect pitch with the rumble of distant thunder.

Halfway to the door she paused, listening as the noise gathered enough strength to vibrate through the roof and into the solid mud-brick walls. Not despair, not thunder ahead of the forecast evening storms, but the roar of a plane. A plane flying so low over Cat's Australian outback homestead that she instinctively ducked.

Then she got moving.

Before the screen door had slapped shut in her wake, she'd hurdled the veranda rail onto the lawn...or the semidead patch of grass that used to be lawn. Eyes peeled upward, she whipped around in a half circle until she found the plane, a bright slash of white against the darkening sky.

Drew?

Heart pounding with recharged hope, she followed the low dip of one wing as the aircraft banked off to the west. And wouldn't that be just like him? Ignore her flurry of messages, give no advance warning, go for the big dramatic entrance. She guessed he'd deliberately buzzed her home and now he would swoop off to land at his father's airstrip, ten miles to the northwest.

Cat started for her truck without thinking, then drew up short. She didn't want to visit with Gordon Samuels, the snake, but if the unexpected fly-in visitor *was* Drew, she needed to be there. She needed to know what the hell had gone down between father and son regarding the money she'd borrowed.

The whole future of Corroboree, the station that had been in the McConnell family for six generations, depended on the answer. Her whole future depended on the answer. And the way she felt about Drew Samuels right now, *his* life might also depend upon it!

Jamming her stockman's hat low on her forehead, Cat stalked the last yards to her Landcruiser. But before opening the door, she glanced skyward again, and her heart jumped and jammed in her throat. The plane hadn't banked to fly northwest. It had turned a full 180 degrees and now hung low against the horizon, an insignificant-looking dot against the angry billow of storm clouds.

"Oh, no," she breathed. Chill apprehension shivered through her bones. "You aren't. You wouldn't."

Drew knew the locale too well to attempt a landing on her ungraded, out-of-use, pathetic excuse for an airstrip. Surely her last message hadn't sounded so desperate that he'd pull such a crazy stunt. Heart in mouth she watched the plane dip out of sight behind a stand of coolabah trees, and that jolted her out of immobility and into her truck.

All the way to the strip her pulse pounded in rhythm with the *please no, please no* chant running through her mind. She'd wished Drew to damnation many times these past months, but never literally. Her hands clasped the wheel tightly, holding her speeding vehicle steady against the rutted track and the buffeting crosswind. The storm was coming in much faster than anticipated and it was turning into a real howler.

Almost airborne, her ancient utility truck crested the last rise and landed with a bone-jarring racket of overstretched shocks. Cat paid no heed. Her eyes were fixed on the flat stretch of land ahead and the plane that was shuddering to a drunken listing stop at one end.

She expelled a long gust of backed-up breath. Not only her lungs and chest but her whole body ached with a tension that only eased marginally on seeing the safely grounded plane. Yup, it had landed safely, but no doubt roughly and bouncily.

And that pretty much described the state of her outback station these days—rough, bouncy but still hanging together in one piece.

Less than thirty seconds later she wheeled to a halt beneath the stricken Cessna's wing. Up close she could see the buckled landing gear, which listed the whole craft in a pained forward slump. There was no sign of movement, just an ominous stillness.

As she flung her door open, the wind grabbed hold, yanking it from her hand and slamming it back on its hinges. A bolt of lightning cut a jagged path between sky and earth. Thunder boomed loud on its heels.

Cat grimaced as she clambered up to reach the pilot's door. "Please, don't rain yet. Just give me a few minutes." Both her plea to the heavens and her favorite Akubra were wrenched away by the wind's fury, but her aggravation at losing the hat faded when she opened that door.

The plane's sole occupant sat slumped against his restraining seat belt, motionless. A shock of dark hair fell over his forehead, obscuring his eyes but not the bottom half of his face. Cat stared in bewilderment.

She'd been so fixed on Drew that she hadn't considered finding someone else strapped in the pilot's seat. An olive-skinned someone else with a wide mouth and a sulky fullness to his bottom lip. A stranger, yet Cat felt a vague frisson of recognition as she stared at his dark-whiskered jaw and his strong, squared-off chin.

Another sharp crack of thunder rattled the plane, and Cat shook herself into action. With a firm hand on each shoulder she managed to push his upper body into a more upright position, but he remained out of it.

"You must have conked your head good and hard," she murmured as she removed the radio headset and threaded his hair back behind his ears. His skin, she noticed, was a reassuringly warm contrast to the cool silk of his hair. Gently she probed his head, checked his ears, and found no sign of blood. Reassured, she moved quickly, checking the rest of his body for any sign of broken bones or misaligned joints, for any reaction that might indicate serious injury.

Satisfied he was all in one piece, she rocked back on her heels. Quick-decision time.

Medical help was close to two hours away and if this storm delivered on the fury it promised, the dirt roads might become impassable. Better to get him out of here while she could, get a start toward the hospital, rather than wait around for an ambulance that might not arrive. Moving his large, unconscious form could prove tricky, however, and she lived alone. She ran Corroboree on her own. Calling for a neighbor's help would waste more valuable time.

"Just as well I'm the strapping type," Cat said, mimicking one of her stepmother's kinder descriptions of her sturdy five-foot-eight frame. She preferred to think of herself as a woman equal to the task...whatever that task may be.

She put her hands on her current task's jean-clad knees and shook him gently. When there was no reaction, she took his shoulders in a firmer grip and tried again. "Time to wake up, Sleeping Beauty."

She didn't think that was overstating the facts. His face was a real treat, that mouth nothing short of spectacular. For one crazy second the waking-Sleeping-Beauty scenario flickered through her mind and she considered leaning forward and laying her lips against that beautiful mouth.

Of course she didn't, and not only because, as a rule, she didn't kiss strangers. Even those who looked like Mediterranean gods fallen from the sky. She didn't because his lips started to move, to fashion speech...or at least some unintelligible slurred version of that faculty.

Cat's gaze flew up to meet a pair of surprisingly lucid blue-green eyes, and her pulse began to skitter and race like a startled steer. Because he'd jolted her with his sudden consciousness. Because of all the adrenaline still zapping through her blood from the rush to the strip, from the fear of disaster and the shock of discovery.

And, okay, because he'd come to while she was staring at his mouth and wondering if he would taste as good as he looked.

Then those eyes she'd thought so clear a second before lost focus and glazed over. His complexion looked more wan, almost gray. "Are you okay?" she asked.

He started to nod, then winced as if the movement jarred.

"Head hurts a little, huh?"

"A lot."

"Ah, real words." Cat smiled reassuringly. "Now we've got the tongue figured out, let's see what else we can get working."

Something flickered in those hazy eyes. Humor? Cat rejected the notion. He was not up to wordplay. It was more likely pain.

"I hate to rush you, but I'm afraid we're staring down the barrel of a ripper storm." She reached for the latch on his seat belt. "Ready to rock and roll?"

He winced again, perhaps at the mention of the storm that had no doubt led to his unexpected landing. Perhaps at the prospect of doing anything that involved rocking or rolling. Or perhaps because she wasn't watching what she was doing down there with the seat belt. Her elbows nudged the muscular thighs spread slightly on the seat, her knuckles grazed the hard plane of his abdomen, and suddenly she was all fumbling thumbs until, finally, the catch gave.

Swallowing hard, she got her hands out of harm's way as he started to maneuver himself out of his seat. And, ah, hell, even stooped over she could see that he was taller than she'd imagined, and she didn't know how she would manage getting him down to the ground if—

"Are your legs going to hold you?" she fretted out loud.

Slowly he lifted his head and looked into her eyes. A pained attempt at a smile quirked one corner of his mouth. "Woan collapse on you, babe. Unless you wan' me—"

His slurred voice trailed off, his eyes glazed over, and Cat shook her head. The man could barely stand up and he was flirting? *Give me strength!*

"Okay, hotshot." She reached for his arm. "Let me help."

"I'm okay." He rallied to grip both sides of the doorway. Then he squinted at the view beyond her shoulder. "You're gonna get wet."

Inevitably, since the first fat drops of rain were already soaking into the back of her shirt, but she didn't want to hustle him into slipping and falling. "I'm parked right here, see? Not far to walk in the rain."

Despite her worry, he descended without incident…until his boots hit mother earth and he tilted at the exact same angle as his Cessna. Lightning fast, Cat ducked her shoulder under his arm, taking most of his weight.

"I've got you." She braced her legs when they both threatened to overbalance, and wrapped both arms solidly around his chest.

"Sorry." His mumbled apology was almost lost in an explosion of thunder. "Woozy."

With her face shmooshed up against his ribs, she could hear the solid thud of his heartbeat and feel the vibrant heat of his body right through his butter-soft suede jacket. And with every breath her lungs filled with the scent of hot skin and, well, hot man.

Yup, woozy about summed it up for her, too.

Thankfully, he regained his balance as quickly as before, easing the pressure on her shoulder. Together they shuffled to her truck, and he eased himself gingerly into the passenger seat. Cat had to work to extricate her arm from under his and then, as she dashed around to the driver's side, she filled her lungs with cool, rain-wet air and cleared her head of that giddy reaction.

By the time she'd waited the obligatory tick-tick-tick to warm the diesel engine, the rain was bucketing down. "Lucky," she said, turning to check her passenger as she found first gear and the truck lurched into motion. "We'd have been drenched in no time."

His head was back, propped against the top of the seat, but slowly it rolled toward her. His eyes opened and focused with some effort on her face. "Rafe…Car…lisle."

For a second Cat gazed back into his eyes—she'd never seen the Mediterranean, but her imagination painted it that exact sea-green hue—before it struck her that he was introducing himself. Her heart stuttered a half beat. Of course. That's why she'd felt that niggle of recognition.

No, she hadn't met him, but she'd seen enough pictures plastered through the media to know exactly who Rafe Carlisle was. Middle son of one of Australia's richest and most newsworthy families. The media loved to refer to the Carlisles as Australia's "outback royalty" since they owned so much of the northern cattle country, as well as hotels and property and God knows what else.

But this particular Carlisle brother didn't get his Gucci footwear dirty in outback dust or cattle pats. Rafe Carlisle might hold some fancy executive title in the family's hotel group, but from what she'd read he didn't get too close to anything resembling work. Play was more his thing—playing in nightclubs, playing in casinos, playing with women.

And wasn't that just a measure of the way her luck was hanging? One of the notoriously rich and handsome "princes of the outback" drops out of the sky into her paddock, and it has to be the lightweight glamour boy!

"And you are?" he asked faintly, obviously wanting her side of the introduction.

"Catriona McConnell." *Impoverished, nonnewsworthy, hardworking pastoralist, with not a drop of blue blood to bless myself.*

Except what did it matter which Carlisle had landed in her paddock? He wasn't the answer to her barrage of messages or to her prayers. He wasn't Drew Samuels. He was simply a stranger—albeit a rich stranger—in need of her help. She had to get him medical attention, which meant getting through this deluge to the sealed road before the red dirt track bogged.

She *would* make it unless…

Hardly daring to look, she squinted at the fuel gauge and swore silently at the inaccurate flicker of the needle. How much was in the tank? When had she last filled up? She'd been budgeting, rationing, and she prayed fervently that this latest cutback wasn't about to bite her on the backside.

Rafe woke with a start, dazed and disoriented for the seconds it took to register his surroundings and the woman shaking him by the shoulders. Slowly the pieces came back to him, a series of snapshots that blurred in and out of focus.

He remembered landing the company jet at Bourke Airport, remembered heading out again in the Cessna. The storm he'd thought he could outrace. A hazel-eyed angel of mercy and rain so loud he'd thought it was pounding holes in his skull.

Vaguely he recalled waking at his angel's homestead and the struggle to get him inside. Less vaguely he recalled the cold compress she applied to the side of his head. Such a promising start, spoiled when she insisted he sit still, stay awake and answer the same questions over and over with a persistency that hammered worse than his killer headache.

Realizing she'd succeeded in waking him, Nurse Naggard stopped the shaking and leaned back out of his face. This brought her into clearer focus, and Rafe blinked with surprise. "You showered."

"Only because you kept nagging," she said archly.

He kept nagging? That was rich!

He thought about telling her so, but she shifted again, totally distracting him with the sharp, sweet scent of whatever she'd showered with. And her hair…he hadn't noticed she had so much of it. The mass of damp, brown curls hung almost to her waist. Pity about the twin furrows of worry and annoyance between her brows—they completely ruined the pretty effect.

Rafe started to shake his head with regret, then stopped himself. Any movement caused a rolling wave of nausea, as if his brain hadn't regained its balance after whatever walloping it had taken. She'd told him he'd been out cold for a minute or two, that he must have hit his head during what had been a rough landing.

He didn't remember.

He did remember she'd been wet, right through. Now she wore a green sweater that looked soft and pretty and dry. "You changed," he said. "Good."

"You slept," she countered. "Bad."

Ah, yes, his nagging angel of mercy had a quick mouth. He remembered that now. "I was just resting my eyes."

A lie, but a fair one, given the way she kept trying to blind him. Right on cue she picked up a flashlight and tapped it against the palm of her hand. Her very own instrument of torture.

"No." He held up a hand, keeping her at bay. "Enough is enough. I remember where I am and who I am. I remember my mother's name, my brothers' names, and even my third cousin Jasper's middle name."

The last was an exaggeration, but he'd had it with this routine. Every half hour, her same questions, his same answers, while the beam of light burned a hole clear through his pupil and into his brain.

"Don't be a baby." She picked up his hand and turned it over. Despite the "baby" barb, Rafe let her take his pulse. He liked the cool press of her fingers against his wrist, liked the serious intensity on her face and the infinitesimal movement of her lips as she counted the beats. "Only one more hour, as per the doctor's instructions."

The doctor she'd called when the weather defeated her aim of driving him to the nearest hospital. The instructions involved basic observations and this neuro-responsive BS that he'd endured for at least three hours. And that, he decided, was long enough.

"My pupils are equal and reacting?" he asked.

"Last time I checked, yes, but—"

"Has anything changed in the last half hour?"

"No, but—"

"Fine." Rafe wrested the flashlight from her hand. "No more. I'm going to sleep."

He started to lift his legs, angling himself to lie down, and her voice rose in alarm. "You're not sleeping here. The couch is too short. It's not comfort—"

"It's horizontal." And at the moment that's all Rafe required. To shut his eyes, to stop talking and rest his aching brain—

"There's a bed made up," she relented with a heavy sigh. "But first, are you sure you don't need to call anyone?"

He'd radioed when the storm came up, signaling his intention to land and his location, and she'd since notified authorities. That would suffice for tonight. If he let one of his family members know, he'd end up having to field a barrage of concerned calls. His mother, his big brother, his little brother. His personal assistant. His neighbor. His housekeeper.

What they didn't know wouldn't hurt them. Trying to explain would hurt him. "No calls," he said.

"What about food?"

"Just bed."

He got to his feet. And when his brain took a moment to adjust to the new upright perspective, she helped him steady. He didn't mind the solicitous hand at his elbow, and he liked the sweep of her hair against his shoulder and the scent—peaches, he decided—that drifted from her skin. He enjoyed the brush of her hip against his thigh as she ushered him to a hallway off the living room. And when he started to turn into the first doorway, when she stood her ground and blocked his progress, he *really* enjoyed the soft pressure of her breast against his ribs.

"That's my room," she said, a bit breathless as if she, too, was aware of that unplanned contact. "You're next on the right." She steered him that way. "And it would ease my mind if you could stay awake ten minutes so I can do one more check."

"I'll be asleep in five."

She made an impatient sound, tongue against teeth. "Are you always this difficult?"

"Are you?"

Surprise swung her gaze up to meet his. A pretty mix of gray and green and brown, her eyes, in the muted light of the hallway. "I'm not difficult."

"Huh." Whirring head notwithstanding, he felt an urge to tease—to look into those pretty eyes and ask if that meant she was easy. But she nudged the door to his room open, flicked the light switch, and the sudden brightness knifed through his brain.

A short uncensored curse hissed from his mouth. Muttering a quick apology, she turned the light off, but Rafe had caught a glimpse of the bed. Big, broad, dressed in a mile-thick quilt, it crooned, *Come to Mama*.

"Oh, yeah," Rafe murmured, pushing off the doorjamb to answer that sultry siren's call.

Catriona, apparently, moved too.

Perhaps she thought he needed help negotiating the semi-darkness. Perhaps she was still hand-on-elbow in case her patient fell. Whatever the reason, she was there at his side, fussing about extra blankets and bathroom directions, when he made it bedside.

And when, with a blissful moan, he collapsed into the thick folds of feather-down comforter, she overbalanced and went down with him. He heard the heavy hitch of her surprised breath as the bed came up to greet their fall. Horizontal at last, engulfed in sweet-smelling quilt and sweeter-smelling female, Rafe couldn't bring himself to move.

He should, he mused, at least move his hand—the one resting atop a very sweet curve of breast. And he would, just as soon as he summoned enough energy. Meanwhile his eyes drifted shut and the night he'd planned before leaving Sydney drifted through his dwindling consciousness.

If not for the storm he'd be at his destination now. His unexpected arrival would have shocked the blazes out of his onetime girlfriend, Nikki Bates, but not nearly as much as the reason for his visit. Right about now he'd have been getting to that point. Despite a mountain of reservations and providing he could wring the words from his resistive mind, he'd have been asking Nikki how she felt about having his baby.

Two

Cat woke in her own bed, lost for several seconds in the realm where dream and reality collided. It all came back to her then, and she sat up in a rush of shed bedclothes and remembered anxiety.

Rafe Carlisle. Concussed. In her guest room.

She'd last checked on him—she glanced at her watch and sucked in a quick breath—more than five hours ago. Blast. She hadn't expected to sleep so soundly. She hadn't expected to sleep much at all.

Concern sent her scurrying from her room. Caution sent her back to grab her robe, which she pulled on and secured with a double knot as she paused to listen at his door. The silence was rendered oddly loud by the thick thud of her own heartbeat. She tapped lightly on the door, tucked a mass of sleep-tangled hair behind her ear and pressed that ear flush against the timber.

Not a sound.

Quietly she pushed the door open and realized she'd been holding her breath when it rushed from her lungs in a whoosh. Relief, she told herself, since he was still in bed, asleep, not standing there in some state of undress.

And he had moved since her last check in the early hours after midnight. "Good," she breathed, still holding on to the doorknob, warring with herself over what to do next.

Leave him to sleep? Wake him to ensure he wasn't comatose? Stand here and stare at the highly unusual and hugely stareworthy sight of a naked man in her bed?

Not *my* bed, she corrected quickly. And not quite naked.

She had, after all, done the undressing. After she'd managed to rouse him with a solid elbow to his ribs. After she'd recovered from the shock of finding herself pressed deep into the thick eiderdown by his relaxed weight.

Heat tingled through her skin as she eyed that same relaxed weight in the yellow-tinged light of early morning. The long stretch of his legs outlined beneath the loosened bedclothes. The bare olive skin of his back, exposed all the way down to the dip below his waist. Broad shoulders and nicely muscled arms spread high and looped around his pillow.

His head was turned away, his face hidden by the dark sweep of his hair. Not sleep mussed like hers—she lifted a hand to the tangled curls—but as long and sleek and smooth as the rest of him. Her hand stilled mid tidying-comb, her gaze riveted on his hand, on the long fingers that loosely gripped one corner of his pillow.

The same fingers she'd felt, last night, flex ever so slightly against her breast.

Awareness tingled warm in her skin, thick in her belly, heavy in her breasts, as she remembered the heat of his body against hers, the heavy slough of his breath, the low moan that had sounded almost sybaritic. Because he was lying down and a matter of seconds away from sleep, not because he'd landed facedown on top of her!

Cat shook her head and huffed a disdainful breath at herself, much the same as she'd done last night right before she elbowed him aside. Then, when he'd looked like falling asleep where he rested, she'd pulled back the bedclothes and made him comfortable.

Starting with the shirt, ending with the jeans, she'd stripped him. Right down to a pair of white cotton boxers. The snug-fitting variety.

Cat's fingers tightened on the doorknob. She closed her eyes a second, warm from the core right out to her skin, with the force of *not* remembering his outline in the semidarkness, the brush of her fingers against hot skin, against hair-rough legs, against the smooth cotton of his underwear.

Crikey.

She started to turn, to leave, then stiffened at the sound of life from the bed. A muffled movement of sheets…or of a body moving against sheets. Her eyes rocketed back to the bed.

Rafe Carlisle was stirring.

His lazy stretch started with a tensing in his shoulders and eased down his backbone, lifting the tight arc of his backside and kicking one leg free of the bedclothes. Cat held her breath in a tense mix of anticipation and apprehension, but he didn't turn his head. He settled in a reverse ripple of muscles, all olive-skinned, languid beauty against her snowy white sheets.

Still asleep, she deduced after another minute, and she suddenly felt uncomfortable standing there watching him. It wasn't as if he knew, but nonetheless she felt as if she was taking advantage. And standing around watching was not at all like her.

Galvanized into action, she hurried back to her room where she dressed, plaited her hair and splashed her face with cold water. In practical clothes and ready to face her working day, Cat felt much more like herself. Her first task was to check for storm damage and assess the state of the roads so she could work out the quickest way to get Rafe Carlisle out of here.

Alone again, with nothing to worry about but her own set of troubles, she would truly feel like herself again.

After the previous night, the thought of getting outside and doing something more active than checking her patient's pulse rate and pupil reaction beckoned as brightly as the spring after-storm sunshine. Cat hit the back veranda at such a pace she almost tripped over the red-and-tan Kelpie waiting on the welcome mat.

The startled dog jumped to attention, tail wagging, instantly alert. A smile curved Cat's mouth as she dropped to her haunches and scratched his neck. This was the only male she was used to seeing first thing in the morning.

"And a mighty handsome male you are, too."

Bach only put up with the petting to humor her, then he gave a let's-go yip and trotted down the steps where he waited, rocking from side to side, eager to start work.

"Okay, I'm coming, I'm coming." She pulled on her boots, still smiling at Bach as she straightened…until she caught sight of the branch that had collapsed across her fence. "Blast."

On closer inspection the branch turned out to be half a tree—a lot more than one strapping woman could shift on her own. It would have to wait. What worried her more than her flattened fence was the merry havoc such a strong wind might have wrought on a light plane.

"That," she told Bach, "is where we're heading first, mate."

Halfway to the airstrip, she heard her call sign over the UHF radio and recognized the laconic voice of her neighbor's foreman. Bob Porter was a good man, despite working for the king of reptilian life forms, Gordon Samuels. A good friend of her father's, Bob made a point of looking out for her, especially since she'd been living on her own and running Corroboree without any permanent help.

They swapped greetings and rainfall measurements before she asked about the state of Samuels's airstrip.

"You expecting a visitor?" Bob asked.

"I have one already." She explained, long-story-short, about the man asleep in her guest room. "I imagine he could have a plane out here to collect him in a matter of hours."

"Well, it ain't landing anywhere around here," Bob drawled. "Not today or tomorrow."

Blast. "I'll have to take him into Bourke then."

"You in a hurry to get rid of this bloke for any reason?"

Yes, he's a distraction. "No, except he's concussed and should see a doctor."

"Hang on a sec."

In less than that second, his wife was on the radio. "I'm going in to town later, Cat. I wouldn't mind a passenger if that helps you out."

"You bet it does." Cat didn't know if she had enough fuel to make the trip herself, and she sure couldn't book anything else up. Not when she hadn't paid her last bill. Not when she didn't know when she would have the money to pay it. "Call me when you're leaving, Jen, and I'll meet you at the cross-roads."

Ninety minutes later Cat shifted the designer overnight bag she'd found in the Cessna from right hand to left, squared her shoulders and knocked on her guest room door. This time she *would* wake him. He'd slept long enough and she needed to know he was all right. She needed him dressed, fed and ready to go when Jennifer Porter called.

Again, no answer.

She edged the door open and found the bedclothes flung back, the bed empty. Her attention flew straight to the bathroom door. She couldn't hear any sound of activity from beyond—no hiss of the shower, no running water, no telltale clank of pipes.

What if he'd done the wonky thing again? What if he'd passed out in there? What if he'd knocked his head falling?

"What if you get your butt over there and find out?" Cat muttered. It was the logical thing to do, the sensible thing to do, the practical thing to do…which all added up to the Cat thing to do.

And she would do it, right after she put his bag down. And neatened the bed. Not that she was procrastinating. Much.

She was smoothing the bottom sheet and pretending not to notice the lingering warmth from his body when she sensed or heard…something. Slowly she straightened and turned and there he was. Standing in the bathroom doorway, watching her. Wearing nothing but the gleam of residual moisture from his shower.

Cat didn't think about looking away. He was, after all, something to behold. And she was, after all, completely beholden. Then he cleared his throat and she realized how long she'd been staring and gave an apologetic caught-out shrug.

"I brought your luggage." She moistened her dry lips and gestured behind her, to where she'd left his bag. "From the plane. I thought you might appreciate some, ah, clothes."

Despite that rather pointed comment, he took his own sweet time reaching for a towel and wrapping it around his hips. He seemed as comfortable in the altogether as she was in her Wranglers. That, she supposed, came with the territory when one possessed the body of a Greek god.

"Thanks." His big smile matched the body. Perfectly. "For bringing my bag."

She probably murmured, "You're welcome," or something equally asinine.

Or she might not have, since she'd become totally involved in watching him rake his hair back from his face as he strolled out of the bathroom. He came right up to the bed, to her side, and her mind went completely blank for a second or three. She forced herself to focus, to think. She couldn't just stand there staring at the dark finger tracks in his shiny wet hair.

Or pretending not to stare.

"You're looking good," she said. Then silently cringed at how that could be taken. Ugh. "In comparison to last night," she added quickly.

He looked as if he knew exactly why she'd felt the need to clarify. The knowledge glinted in his eyes, in the teasing quirk at the corners of his mouth. "What a difference a night makes. I slept like a baby."

No, Cat thought, not a baby. There was something altogether too wicked, too knowing, completely not innocent, about this man for any baby analogy to stick. "For ten hours straight," she said.

"That long? Why didn't you wake me?" Slowly, reflectively, he rubbed his stubbled jaw. "The Sleeping Beauty way would have been nice."

"Excuse me?"

"While I was in the shower I remembered you calling me that in the plane." His gaze drifted to her mouth. "Isn't there supposed to be a kiss involved? Or am I muddling my fairy tales?"

"You were conscious?" *Oh, man, what else did I say? And where did I have my hands at the time?*

Damn his smooth, knowing hide, he grinned at her. "Must have been something about your magic touch."

"I should have left you there!"

"Nah. You enjoyed playing nurse too much."

"Let me think about that…." Cat tapped a finger against her chin. "Did I enjoy your whining? Nope. Prying your eyes open so I could test your pupils? Nope. Getting crushed when you fell on top of me? Nope again."

"I fell on you?"

The man remembered one murmured line while coming out of unconsciousness but he didn't remember lying thigh to thigh, hip to hip, hand to breast with her? Cat shook her head. "I was trying to get you into bed."

"I gather you succeeded?"

"Eventually."

One dark brow arched skeptically—as if he didn't quite believe he'd have put up a fight—and then he gestured toward his clothes, the ones she'd folded and placed on the bedside table. "And you undressed me?"

"Eventually."

He shook his head slowly, almost solemnly. "Sorry I missed that."

Oh, he was good. The deep note of sincerity, the way he looked into her eyes. Cat looked right back and wondered how many women had fallen into those sea-green depths and drowned. Not her. She might live in the arid outback, but she wasn't so parched that she'd swim with sharks.

"I'm not," she said, smiling a little, letting him know she had his measure. "It was…interesting. With you all but unconscious."

He laughed, a rich two-note sound of surprise that ended on a slight wince.

Cat's enjoyment of the moment, the bantering, his laughter, sobered instantly. "How does your head feel?"

"Like it got hit by a plane. Here," he invited. "Feel for yourself."

The instant he ducked his head, the mood dipped, too, slowing and swelling with sensuality. She breathed the scent of his nearness—her soap, her shampoo, but all different on his skin, in his hair. And she was suddenly aware, all over again, that he wore only a towel and that his skin was bare and warm, and that he was waiting for her to touch him.

His head, silly. He only invited you to feel the bump on his head.

Gingerly she palpated the lump, breath held, concern for his injury overriding her preoccupation with the slippery wet strands of his hair, with those damn tracks her own fingers itched to trace. With his sudden stillness and the sense of a new tension in the air.

"Well?" he asked, straightening slowly.

"Does it still ache?"

His eyes narrowed with suspicion. "That depends."

"On?"

"Whether a yes gets me more of your tender loving touch—" Rafe picked up her hand and ran his thumb lightly across her fingertips before releasing it "—or more of that light in my eyes."

"Testing your responses was on doctor's order. If I could have gotten you to hospital, they'd have done the same."

"Except with significantly less wattage."

She opened her mouth, then shut it, as his point about the flashlight's power sunk in. "That's my only torch. And it doesn't appear to have done you any harm. Anyone else would have had a corker of a black eye."

"The cold compress helped."

"I guess." Her gaze softened a little, relenting, relaxing. "What about the rest of you? You're not stiff or sore anywhere else?"

Oh, yeah, she realized how *that* could be taken about a second after the words left her lips. And it wasn't in Rafe's nature to let such a choice opportunity slide. He cocked a brow. "Would you like to check?"

"I'm going to pretend I didn't hear that."

Rafe shrugged. "You can't blame a guy for trying."

She gave him a look that said she could. "It was a godawful line. You should be ashamed."

"Harsh."

"But honest."

Conceding her point, he tapped two fingers against his temple. "Can we blame it on damage to my head?"

She smiled, but there was a worried edge to the gaze that followed his gesture. A knowledge that while he joked about head damage, it had been a very real concern to her in those long hours of the night.

"I haven't thanked you," he said, watching her turn to pick up his bag. She set it on top of the bed.

"For bringing your bag? I think you did that earlier. I'll leave you to get dressed, then." She started to turn, preparing to leave, but Rafe caught her by the arm and waited for her surprised gaze to swing back to his.

"Not only the bag," he said quietly. "Thank you for rescuing me. Thank you for bringing me into your home and continuing with the observations even after I begged you to give it up. Thank you, Catriona."

She shrugged and shifted uneasily within his grip. "Anyone would have done the same."

"I know a lot of women—" she rolled her eyes in an I-bet-you-do way that Rafe ignored "—and most of them wouldn't have known how to get into that plane, let alone thought to get me out." With his thumb he traced a jagged white scar across the back of her hand. Then he smiled to ease the new note of gravity in the mood. "Most of them would have been afraid they'd break a nail."

"I dare say I'm nothing like most of those women you know."

That went without saying. No fawning, no flirting, not even the hint of a come-on. Most of the women he knew would have taken immediate, unsubtle advantage of his state of undress, but not Catriona McConnell. She was, indeed, a novelty. "When I picked your airstrip, I chose well."

She made a scoffing sound and tugged at her hand until he released her. "Any one of my neighbors would have helped you. And *their* strips wouldn't have wrecked your plane!"

"The landing gear malfunctioned. I was never going to land smoothly."

Eyes wide and appalled, she stared up at him. Her face seemed to have paled a shade, so the smattering of freckles across the bridge of her nose stood out starkly. "Your landing gear malfunctioned? You could have crashed? *Badly?*"

"Hey," Rafe said softly, reaching for her. But she was already backing away, hands held up in classic don't-touch mode. "I didn't mean to frighten you. I was never going to crash-land."

"How do you know that?"

"Because I'm too good a pilot."

She huffed out an incredulous breath. "Well, at least we know your ego wasn't damaged."

"Why do I have the feeling it will suffer if I stick around here much longer?"

From the doorway she paused long enough to cut him a look that perfectly illustrated his point. "Lucky for your ego, you won't be."

Three

"**W**hat is it with you guys and that whole macho 'I'm too good a pilot' business?"

Cat paused in ratting through her pantry for ingredients—anything!—to add to her breakfast hodgepodge and glared at the only male present and therefore answerable. Bach, however, had nothing to say in his gender's defense. He merely tilted his broad canine head and looked curious. Or puzzled. Or possibly both.

"Have you any idea how that cavalier attitude bothers other people?" *How it robs their breath and turns their stomachs sick with dread? Even when they're virtual strangers?*

Halfway across her kitchen, hands filled with cans and condiments, she stopped and frowned, disturbed by the extremity of her reaction to the idea that Rafe Carlisle could have crash-landed.

Must have been the timing, she justified. The surprise element. Plus after seeing him in all his glory he just seemed too vital, too larger than life, to imagine damaged and scarred. Or cold and lifeless.

"Too good a pilot?" With an unladylike snort, she dumped her ingredients on the bench top. "Lucky is more like it!"

Up until that disclosure about his landing-gear malfunction, she'd been handling herself so well, too. Hardly turning a hair when she'd caught him in the buff. Holding her own in the ensuing exchange. Then he'd gone and turned all serious with the thank-you speech, as if she'd done something special.

Well, it was no news flash that Cat McConnell didn't do special. She did capable, she did practical, and some people said she could do stubborn better than anyone. But she sure did not do up-close, skin-tingling, hand-holding seriousness with seminude strangers.

No wonder she'd reacted so intensely to the landing-gear shocker. No wonder the breath had caught in her lungs while her stomach roiled with—

The microwave timer pinged, startling her out of her unsettling memories.

Wake up, Cat, you have breakfast to finish. A guest to get on his way. Normalcy to be returned.

But as she crossed the kitchen to check on the concoction of minced beef and sundries she was nuking, her gaze caught on the photo on the fridge. Drew Samuels with his lopsided grin and black Resistol and laidback cowboy charm.

No, not normalcy. She doubted her life would ever feel normal again. Not if her best friend, her only lover, had let her down as badly as she feared.

"Lucky I've got you," she told Bach, "to keep my faith in males from going completely down the gurgler."

Ears pricked, her dog pattered to her side and growled deep in his chest. Not so much in understanding as in hunger, Cat noted, since she'd lifted the lid on the nuked breakfast dish. Steam spiraled to her nose, piquant, aromatic, and she dipped in a spoon and lifted it, cautiously, to her lips. Tasted. Cocked her head in the dog's direction.

"Not too bad, considering." Considering the amount of scrambling she'd done to find anything substantial enough to feed a man who'd eaten nothing the previous night.

Whimpering, Bach touched a paw to her leg and gave her the big doggy-eyed look.

"Oh, please!" She rolled her eyes and saw him out the door. "I'll get you something in a tick, mate. This is for the guest and I doubt there'll be any leftovers."

Since the guest looked like a man of appetite.

Cat expelled a breath, a swift wisp of air that matched the swing of the door closing behind her dog. She rested her shoulders against the door's solid weight for a moment. Closed her eyes. Rafe Carlisle, she mused, looked like a man with all manner of appetites, food being but one of them.

And it struck her, standing there in the very real surrounds of her kitchen, her home, her niche, how surreal this all was. Everything from Gordon Samuels's revelation about the origin of the money she'd borrowed from Drew, through to watching one of the princes of the outback drop out of the sky, and on to this morning when she'd unwittingly eyed his impressive, um, scepter.

To top it all off, here she was making breakfast for him. Rafe Carlisle. One of Australia's highest-profile playboys, a former Bachelor of the Year, a socialite pin-up who dated actresses and swimsuit models. Oh, how she'd love to share *that* tasty tidbit with her stuck-up stepsisters!

Smiling—ruefully, given she tried to avoid seeing those witches whenever possible—she opened her eyes and pushed off the door.

And jolted to startled attention when she realized that she was no longer alone. The former Bachelor of the Year lazed against the doorjamb on the opposite side of the kitchen, looking so languid and comfortable that she wondered how long he'd been there.

"Ready for breakfast?" she asked, refusing to be rankled. She had, after all, watched him sleep. And he was, after all, now fully dressed.

In a smooth unraveling of long limbs and relaxed muscles—Cat fought to suppress a strong visual of those muscles bare-skinned, as she'd seem them earlier, rippling into lazy motion—he straightened and came into the room. Right past the table, which she'd already set, to rest his hips against the bench. To watch her fill the toaster and turn on the kettle and stir the mystery mince.

He leaned close and drew a long, appreciative sniff.

Then—oh, crikey—he rubbed his belly and made the same sound she remembered from the night before, when he'd fallen into the soft folds of her nanna's handmade quilt.

It was a sound that went with croissants or frittata or eggs benedict served on a sun-drenched terrace. The sound of a man who came to breakfast wearing designer jeans and a butter-colored knit that looked soft enough to melt under the strong outback sun. A sound too luxurious, too rich, too sensuous for her utilitarian kitchen and her tossed-together breakfast.

A sound too rich for Cat, which made it easy to dismiss.

"You cook, too?" he asked.

"Save the praise until after you've tasted," she said matter-of-factly. "I've not been shopping in a while, so this is whatever I could find. It's not gourmet cuisine."

Not that she was apologizing. He was bloody lucky she'd found anything.

When he didn't respond, she glanced sideways and found him looking at her—no, not so much looking as giving her the once-over. Lifting her chin, she met his examination head-on but he didn't look the least chagrined. In fact a smile kicked at the corner of his mouth, not apologetic, just caught out and not caring.

The toast popped, distracting them both, but Cat shot him one last raised-eyebrow glance. "If you're finished with the inspection, take a seat and I'll bring you breakfast."

"And if I'm not…?"

"Take a seat, anyway—" she marched past him and deposited the casserole dish in the center of the table "—you can finish while you eat."

"Are you going to join me?"

"In a tick."

He waited, watched, and only sat after Cat had finished making the tea and taking her own seat opposite. Nice manners, she admitted, a trifle grudgingly since that only indicated two things: he'd been brought up well, and he'd shared a lot of breakfasts with a lot of ladies. Most of whom wouldn't have served him minced beef.

There was a moment when he pushed up his sleeves, and her gaze became riveted on the details. The dark hair on his forearms. The silver links of an expensive-looking watch. His long elegant fingers. The remembered warmth of his touch on her arm and stroking the back of her hand.

Then he caught *her* looking, and the moment stretched with a warm awareness that quickly morphed into awkwardness—on Cat's side of the table, at least—as she poured tea and fussed with the food. A stranger sat at her table, long fingers folded around the handle of one of *her* mugs. *Her* cutlery was transporting the food she had prepared to his mouth, touching his lips, his tongue.

The intimacy of it all shivered through her like quicksilver. More intimate even than before, in the bedroom, although perhaps this disquieting sensation was just the whole twenty-four hours catching up with her.

Whatever the reason, she didn't much like it. Whatever the reason, she had to get over it and start acting more like herself again.

"Relax, Catriona." His mouth quirked, amused and reassuring at the same time. "I know I'm starving, but I promise not to bite."

"Easy for you to say."

His fork paused, halfway to his mouth. "About biting?"

"About relaxing. You aren't the one with a strange man sitting at your breakfast table!"

"I should hope not," he drawled. "Strange women are much more my taste."

"I thought you didn't bite."

He laughed at that, the same rich sound of appreciation as earlier in his bedroom. Cat wasn't sure which affected her more—the warm-honey tone of his laughter or the fact that he appreciated her quick retort. Whichever, the man was lethal.

Lethal and obviously as hungry as he'd intimated, given the way he tucked back into his breakfast. And since the short exchange of banter—plus his rather gratifying appetite—had settled her uneasiness, Cat joined him in several minutes of almost companionable eating. She, too, was starving.

"Glad you've gotten over the strange-man thing."

Cat stopped chewing.

"I wondered about that before," he continued, piling his plate with seconds. "When you were in my bedroom."

"Wondered about…what?" she asked slowly, suspiciously.

"If you lived here alone. And if so, why you weren't more concerned about having a strange man in your house."

"I can look after myself."

"Yeah?"

She met his eyes with unflinching directness. "I've lived here on my own for the last four years. So, yeah, I can look after myself."

"You don't find it lonely here, on your own?"

"Sometimes." Her shrug was a bit tight, a bit not so casual, but her direct gaze turned rueful. "Then my stepmother comes to visit and I get over it real quick."

"You have a wicked stepmother?"

"Good guess."

"Any evil stepsisters?"

"Just the two."

Rafe ate in silence for a minute, digesting all she'd said. "And you run this place single-handedly?"

"What," she said, bristling, "you don't think I'm capable?"

Rafe held up his hands—with knife and fork—in mock defensiveness. "Hey, keep your panties on. That's not what I meant."

"Yeah, well, if I had a dollar…"

"For every man who didn't think you capable?"

"Every*body*," she growled. "No cause to be gender specific."

"Well," Rafe started slowly, carefully picking his way around what was obviously a sore spot. "You've got to admit it's not the usual career choice for a young woman."

"It's all I've ever wanted to do, since I was a little girl."

"You didn't want to be a ballerina or a supermodel?"

"Oh, please!" She didn't exactly roll her eyes, but the gesture was implicit as she rocked back in her chair, a mug of tea cradled in her hands. "Do I look like the supermodel type?"

Trick question, Rafe decided. Wisely he let it slide right by. "You must have had some fantasy occupation, though. I was going to be a fighter pilot."

"See *Top Gun* one too many times?"

"Is that possible?" Smiling, he met her eyes across the remains of their breakfast. "Come on, I've shared my boyhood fantasy. Your turn, Catriona."

"Cat," she corrected. "Everyone calls me Cat."

"I'm not everyone."

This time she did roll her eyes. Then she surprised him by admitting, "I did go through a rodeo stage once."

"You wanted to be a cowgirl?" In jeans and check shirt, with her freckled nose and her hair tightly braided, that wasn't a stretch. All she needed was the big hat and boots.

"A cowgirl? Are you kidding?"

"A rodeo clown?"

Over the rim of her mug she grinned at him, genuine amusement lighting her eyes. "A bull rider, actually."

"I should have known." Rafe shook his head, entertained by the notion but not surprised. His gaze drifted away, toward the kitchen and the picture he'd noticed earlier. "Don't suppose that has anything to do with the cowboy on your fridge?"

"Not really."

"Is he your boyfriend?"

A stillness tightened her expression, and Rafe was surprised to feel an echoing tension in his body as he waited for her answer. As she lifted her mug and took a long deliberate sip before lowering it to answer. "He's a...friend."

Ahh. "A friend you'd like as more?"

She snorted. "A friend I thought *was* more!"

The front legs of her chair hit the floor with a sharp rap, and she was halfway to her feet, gathering cutlery and plates before Rafe stopped her with one hand over both of hers. "I didn't mean to hit a nerve."

Her eyes whipped to his. "You didn't."

Oh, yes, he had. "Where is he now, your cowboy?"

Beneath his hands he felt her tension, felt it gather then ease as if by force of will. She slumped back into her chair, exhaled on a relenting sigh. "Drew's my neighbor—*was* my neighbor. We grew up together. We went out for a while. Then he went to America, on the rodeo circuit."

Her flat, just-the-facts delivery didn't fool Rafe. The neighbor, the ex, the cowboy with the big black hat had let her down. Badly.

"You want me to find this Drew, beat him up for you?" he asked, wanting to make her smile again, and rather liking the notion of playing her champion. "I do owe you."

"For coming to your rescue?" She smiled, not the dazzler of before but a smile that held a sharp wry edge. She tugged her hands free and rocked back in her chair. "You want to hear something funny? Yesterday, when I heard your plane, I thought you were Drew."

"You were expecting him?"

She shrugged. "Not so much expecting as hoping."

"Ah, so finding me must have been a huge disappointment."

"It wasn't all bad," she said with that same wry smile. "At least you and your head gave me something else to worry about. I didn't have much time to be disappointed."

"Ouch," he murmured, without a lot of conviction. "I knew you wouldn't be good for my ego."

"I imagine your ego is in as fine shape as the rest of you." And with that matter-of-fact diagnosis, she started packing up their plates and taking them to the kitchen.

Rafe bit his tongue. He didn't need to ask how she knew about his fine shape. She'd seen pretty much all of it in the bathroom earlier. But he did need to ask what she'd meant earlier, before she walked out of his bedroom.

"The last time we were discussing my ego, you said I wouldn't be sticking around long."

"That's right. A neighbor's going in to Bourke today. I've arranged a lift for you."

It was Rafe's turn to rock back in his chair. She sure hadn't wasted any time. "When?"

She looked up from the sink where she was stacking dishes and smiled. "Not too long. I imagine by the time you've finished clearing up the table and washing these, Jen will have called with an exact time."

With thirty years of practice, Rafe had perfected his helpless-male routine. Catriona McConnell wasn't the first woman to see right through it, but she'd done so with a remarkable indifference to his charm. Twenty minutes later Rafe still wore a rueful grin. She really was something else!

When he'd stared cluelessly at the sink and murmured, "Washing dishes, huh? This should be interesting," she didn't

roll her eyes and nudge him aside so she could take over—
which is what he'd been angling for.

He'd tried another tack. "I've never done this before. I
don't suppose you'd care to give some hands-on instruction?"

"Oh, I'm pretty sure you're smart enough to work it out
for yourself."

"What if I break stuff?"

"My stuff is hardly Limoges," she'd flung over her shoulder on her way to the door. "But if it makes you feel any better, I'll add any breakages to your bill."

"That should make me feel better? With this head?"

Hand on door, she'd paused, frowning. "Your head's aching? Perhaps you should go and lie down."

"Will you bring me a cold compress and take my pulse,
Nurse?"

She made an impatient sound, tongue against teeth. "Don't
you ever give up?"

"What?"

"The lines. We both know they're wasted on me."

Rafe shook his head sadly. "You're a hard woman, Catriona McConnell."

She'd smiled and thanked him, as if that were the greatest
of compliments, before closing the door behind her. Ten seconds later it opened again—and, yeah, she caught him still
grinning and shaking his head over that exchange—so she
could remind him about the phone calls he'd been deliberately
forgetting.

"The phone is in my office—" she pointed off to her right
"—through that second doorway over there."

"Will the calls be on my bill?"

"Of course. Knock yourself out."

Rafe had winced at her unfortunate wording, but that was
all for show.

After finishing his phone calls, as he headed out the door
where she'd disappeared earlier, he remembered her words

with a grin of approval. It didn't surprise him that he liked
her—he rarely met a woman he didn't like on some level—
but it surprised him how much this smart-as-a-cardshark
woman tickled his fancy.

On the back porch he paused to look around, seeing her
place for the first time. Seeing what lay beneath and beyond
the debris scattered by last night's storm with another jab of
surprise. The paint peeling from the outside walls. The empty
garden beds. Beyond the back fence, what looked to be the
remains of an orchard, the trees long dead. Catriona's home
wore an air of disrepair like a patched-up coat and he hadn't
expected that. She seemed so on top of everything.

Then he remembered the moment at the breakfast table,
when he'd asked about her cowboy and he'd felt the tension—and her disillusionment—hovering in the kitchen air.
Things weren't any more shipshape in her world than in his,
and it struck him that fate—or his most faithful mistress,
Lady Luck—might have landed him here for a reason. Nine
times out of ten he would have backed himself to outrace a
storm. But yesterday he'd been flying with his mother's words
soft in his memory.

*Take care, Rafe. Please, don't do anything harebrained that
you might come to regret!*

He knew she'd been talking about more than his daredevil
ways with a joystick, yet her message of caution and the accompanying concern—in eyes already pierced with grief from
her husband's recent death—had led him to search out a strip
when the storm billowed quicker and wilder than predicted.

That strip was Catriona McConnell's.

And as he crossed the yard with its random patches of
would-be lawn, as he sidestepped sheets of roofing steel
blown clean off a nearby shed, he decided that fate had put
him here for more than washing her dishes. More, even, than
shifting the uprooted tree that lay crushing her fence.

This trip had a purpose, one he'd resisted for the first month or more since his father's death. Since he and his two brothers learned about the will's clause and the baby they needed to produce. Needed, not wanted. Rafe couldn't see himself in the role of father, which meant he needed to choose very wisely.

More wisely than Nikki Bates. More wisely than any of the women in his past.

Yup, he decided as his narrowed gaze fixed on Catriona down by the kennels. Fate had come to his rescue in the nick of time.

Four

Cat was sitting cross-legged on the concrete stoop outside her kennel enclosure, her lap filled with sleeping puppies, when she heard the distant slap of the kitchen door closing. Blast. She'd hoped that the washing-up and his phone calls would have kept him occupied for longer. Another five minutes enjoying the simple, comforting warmth of the morning sun and her canine company was all she wanted. Five minutes before she faced up to the consequences and cost of last night's storm. Before making the tough decisions on what to do next, how to find Drew, who to believe.

With a heavy sigh, she lifted one chubby tan body close to her face. "Not that I have any idea where to start on that one, little mate." Everything about her dealings with Drew had turned out to be so much less than she'd bargained for.

For some reason that turned her thoughts right back to Rafe Carlisle, who had turned out to be so much more than she'd bargained for. It was one thing to enjoy looking at him, appreciating his beauty the same as she would a sleek Thoroughbred or an exquisitely formed sculpture or some out-of-her-reach trinket in a shop window. It was another entirely to enjoy his company, to sit at the breakfast table trading quips and confidences. To stick her head through the door and see him with sleeves pushed up, hands in her sink, that lethal grin lifting the corners of his exquisitely formed mouth.

Knowing that *she'd* put the grin there.

That memory mingled with the crunch of his footsteps on the gravel approach, and Cat shivered—not in her skin but somewhere deeper. For a wisp of time she buried her nose in the puppy's fur, absorbing its comforting warmth, centering herself so that when she turned and peered up at him none of that unease showed in her expression…despite the way her heart revved up a gear.

From her position down on the ground, it was a perilously long way up to his face. A long traverse past thighs and hips encased in expensively aged denim. Past that buttercream knit that should have made him look soft but—damn it—didn't. And by the time she'd taken that all in, by the time she'd arrived up at his face with all its dark planes and masculine angles, he was ducking down to her level and reaching out to stroke the puppy in her hands.

"So…Cat is a dog person," he said, sea-green eyes awash with amusement.

Cat tried to smile back, but she was transfixed by those eyes and then by the gentle stroke of one large fingertip over the tiny puppy's head. Snared by the magnetic power of his proximity. Even in the bedroom he hadn't been this close, his head almost grazing hers as he bent to study the bundle of puppies in her lap.

"How many have you got there?" he asked, his voice as slow and mesmerizing as that caress.

"Seven, all up."

"Huh. My lucky number."

Probably another line, but she had to admire the finesse of his delivery. The smooth way he had of drawing her in with what appeared to be genuine attentiveness. Why not enjoy it? Any kind of attentiveness was a novelty, and dogs she could talk about until the cows came home!

"Where's their mama?" he asked, and Cat looked around for Sheba.

"She won't be too far away. Especially if she gets a whiff of a stranger lurking near her babies."

"Ah, a warning. Should I step back slowly, hands in the air? Before or after she bares her teeth?"

Cat smiled. "I think the worst you'll suffer is a severe growling."

"From a mother, growling can be scary stuff."

Although he grinned back at her, she sensed a truth in his words. And glimpsed another element she hadn't bargained for—the disquieting element of Rafe Carlisle in family mode. Carefully she settled the puppy from her hand back with its siblings. "Yeah, well, Sheba's growl is much worse than her bite. She's only ever taken a violent dislike to one man."

"Your cowboy?"

"His father, actually." Cat met his eyes and saw a stillness, a seriousness, she hadn't expected. Saw questions she didn't want to answer...and was saved by the distraction of a low canine whimper. The perfect segue. "Speaking of fathers—" she nodded toward his right "—that's the pups' daddy over there."

As expected, Rafe turned to inspect the daddy. Head on paws, Bach treated them to his best put-upon look and another pitiful whine.

"Oh, please!" Cat shook her head at her dog before explaining to Rafe. "I have to lock him up while Sheba goes for a run, otherwise she won't leave her puppies. Bach thinks it's the height of indignity."

"You called your dog Bark?" he asked on a note of disbelief, although a smile lifted the corners of his lips.

"*B-A-C-H*. Like the composer."

"Awful pun."

"Yes, but *Wag*ner would have been worse."

He laughed at that, a rich rumble of amusement that warmed her from her inside out. Oh, yeah, the man knew how to laugh, how to smile, how to charm. "At least my cat has a dignified name."

That laconic admission whipped her attention from his lips to his eyes. "You have a *cat*?"

His eyes narrowed. "Don't tell me you're one of those dog people who look down their noses at cat owners?"

"Not at all. I just didn't picture you with a cat, is all."

Cat didn't want to picture him with a pet any more than being growled at by his mother. She much preferred her pre-conception of Rafe Carlisle as a superficial, self-obsessed rich kid. Entertaining, likable, highly watchable, but essentially lightweight. She really wished she didn't have to ask, "What is your cat's dignified name?"

"Tolstoy."

"Is he a Russian blue?"

"I have no idea."

"Then why did you name him Tolstoy?" she asked, hope stacked upon hope that he didn't enjoy the classics, because that would be too much on top of all his charm and wit and the pet-ownership thing.

"I didn't. He belonged to a woman I knew. I guess she named him."

Cat's heart put in a funny little kick beat as she wondered what, exactly, the word *knew* meant in Rafe-Carlisle-speak. "And she gave her cat to you?"

"She left, and the next day Tolstoy was back." He gave a careless little shrug, like the shift of spare muscle inside his silk sweater. "Apparently he preferred living with me."

"Didn't she?" Cat asked without thinking.

And when his eyes lifted to hers, when their sea-green

depths glowed with a wicked lick of heat, she wished she *had* thought. Wished she'd bitten her tongue and her curiosity.

"Oh, she liked it well enough," he drawled, and Cat believed she knew why. He would be lethal in bed. As lazy and graceful as that shrug; as knowing and sinful as those eyes.

As hot as the wash of curiosity that streamed through Cat's veins.

She struggled to contain both the heat and the curiosity. Struggled against the crazy itch to reach out and touch the silky strands of his hair, the extravagant fullness of his bottom lip, the stubbly regrowth of dark beard along the sharp line of his jaw.

Methodically, one by one, she folded the fingers that itched to touch into her palm, forming a loose fist, which she rubbed along her thigh. And she reminded herself what this exchange really meant about this man and his life and his lifestyle. *Not for you, Catriona McConnell, not even in your wildest midnight imaginings.*

"So you kept her cat," she said.

"His choice."

Cat was saved from remarking on Tolstoy's taste when Sheba trotted back from her short spell of exercise and took immediate exception to Rafe's presence. "It's okay, baby," she soothed while she quietly transferred the puppies to their kennel. "This is Rafe Carlisle and he's not as big and scary as he looks. He has a cat."

Rafe gave a half grunt of laughter. It didn't surprise her that he felt no need to defend himself against the cat-ownership charge. As she'd already noted, his male ego was in excellent shape.

For an oddly comfortable moment they watched the pups jostle for prime positions at their mother's belly. Odd because she'd thought this might have been awkward in its intimacy…and perhaps it could have been if he'd let the moment, silent but for the muffled sound of suckling, stretch.

Instead he smiled and said, "Hungry little beggars."

"Lucky they've got a good mamma."

But when she finished securing the gate on Sheba's pen and turned, ready to get on with her chores, she found him watching her with unexpectedly serious eyes. It jolted her for a second, that expression, the stillness in his big body, the skip of her heart.

But she kept on moving, picking up the hose and turning on the tap, keen to push whatever that moment was about out of her consciousness. "Did you make your phone calls?" she asked.

"Unfortunately."

His dry tone brought her gaze swinging back to his as she filled the water containers. "Alex wasn't happy then?"

"Why do you suppose I rang my brother?" he asked slowly.

Cat shrugged. "You mentioned him enough times yesterday. I gathered he owns the plane in my paddock…although you kept calling it a jet."

"I did?" Uncertainty clouded his expression, bringing his dark brows together in a confused frown.

"After I got you out of the plane," she explained, "when we were driving back here, you kept repeating yourself. You'd tell me something, then forget and tell me again."

"Did I embarrass myself?"

Oh, the temptation to tease him! It hovered in front of her, a great big shining orb of enticement, too bright to resist. "I crashed the jet." She slurred the words, imitating his voice from the previous day. "Alecsh will be pished."

Rafe winced, and she felt a tiny pang of remorse for teasing him over something so serious. But only a tiny one.

"I gather it is your brother's plane?"

"No. I hired it in Bourke. Alex's jet is safe and sound at the airport. I rang and checked." Expression rueful, he rubbed a hand along his jaw. "If I had crashed the Citation, Alex definitely would have been pissed."

"If you'd crashed a jet, you really wouldn't have to worry about your brother!"

A sobering thought, and one Cat didn't want to revisit. She had no business feeling fright or relief or anything on his behalf. No business feeling *anything* for the man. He flew a private jet, for heaven's sake. He hired a light plane the way other mere mortals hired a car or hailed a cab. At the moment Cat would give her eyeteeth for enough cold hard cash to hire a bicycle!

"You hired the Cessna?" she began as she turned off the tap and coiled the hose. She didn't need to know more about him, but she needed to talk, to consolidate who he was, to chase away the whispery traces of uneasiness that coiled through her gut. Straightening, she found him lounging against the mesh gate of Sheba's pen looking askance. "After you flew Alex's jet to Bourke?"

"That's right. I'd been visiting with my mother."

"She lives on a station, right? In the Northern Territory? I remember reading that somewhere."

"Kameruka Downs," he told her. "We grew up there, my brothers and me. Tomas still lives there and runs the cattle business."

"I read an article about him in *The Cattleman*."

"That's the one," Rafe said slowly as their gazes linked. "I guess you've read a bit about my family here and there."

"A bit."

The classic understatement, Rafe knew, especially when there'd been so much to read in the past couple of months. And when her hazel eyes clouded, when their expression softened with sympathy, he knew she'd been reading that press.

"You lost your father recently," she said. "I'm sorry."

Rafe inclined his head in the briefest acknowledgment. Charles Carlisle might not have been his birth father, but he was the only father he'd known.

"How is your mother coping?"

"Barely." Little point in sugarcoating the truth, not when the gossip media had made a meal of Maura's "increasingly hermitlike existence" in the month after her husband's death. As if her choice to live out of the public eye and her decision not to attend his very public and photographed memorial service painted her eccentric. "Although she might have coped better without Dad's interference."

"Interference?"

Rafe hadn't meant to bring this up yet, but since she'd introduced the topic…since she was studying him with such a cute look of befuddlement…why not answer her question? Why not see where it took him? "He had this notion that a grandchild would abbreviate the grieving process."

Her cute puzzlement turned to a deep frown. "I don't understand."

Rafe could appreciate her confusion. Theirs—his and his brothers'—had been considerable. And heated. Their mother's more so when she found out six weeks later. "When he got sick he added a clause to his will. We didn't know anything about it until afterward."

"When the will was read?"

He nodded. "So, we have twelve months to produce a grandchild for Mau."

"Or you lose your inheritance?"

"Yup."

Her face was a picture of astonishment as she digested this information, as she sifted through the pieces and put it all together as a whole. "You and your brothers," she asked slowly, "do you *all* have to have a baby?"

"The clause specifies only one grandchild among us, but given the short time span and the fact we're all starting from scratch, as it were…we're playing the odds."

They'd made a pact, one in, all in, the same way it had always been between them. No other way seemed fair. No other way gave them the best odds of succeeding.

"So." She cleared her throat. "How's that going?"

Rafe laughed dryly. Trust Catriona to cut straight to the chase. "Tomas has a willing lady but he's being a stubborn fool over it. Alex and Susannah—" he shook his head "—are still trying to find a spare hour in their schedules to get married first."

She raised her brows.

"He's a traditionalist."

"And you? Have you any, um, projects in the making?"

"Why? Are you offering to help me out?"

She laughed and shook her head. "Funny."

"Is that what you think?"

Their gazes locked, and the mocking laughter in her eyes darkened, deepened. "Yes, actually. I do think that's pretty funny."

"Which part?"

"The part where *you* can't find a woman to have your baby. I rather thought they'd be queuing up at your bedroom door!"

"Maybe I'm particular."

She snorted. "What about your cat lady?"

"A possibility…although her husband might object."

"Can't you pay someone?"

"There's a thought," he said slowly, consideringly, even though her throwaway line had dripped with sarcasm. "How much would it take, Catriona?"

She stared back at him, her eyes wide and starting to spark with indignation. "I was kidding, you know! Paying a woman to have your baby so you can inherit more money—that's appalling. It's just plain…wrong. What would the child—" She stopped cold. Gave a short, strangled laugh. "You weren't serious, were you?"

"Do you think my mother would want a grandchild from that kind of a union?" he asked.

She wouldn't. But his mother *would* want a woman who considered the idea appalling and just plain wrong. A woman who'd stand up with her eyes sparking and tell him so. A woman who managed everything from a concussed stranger to driving through a savage storm to copping an eyeful of naked man without missing a beat.

A woman who held a tiny puppy cradled in her hand and who crooned soft words to the agitated mother.

And Rafe?

He liked that this same woman seemed unimpressed by who he was or how much he was worth. He liked the idea that she had never wanted to do anything but live in the outback and run her property. An independent woman who would let him do his own thing....

Slowly he closed the space between them. "We're not doing this to inherit more money, Catriona. We want to keep the Carlisle companies in the family, true, but mostly we want to honor our father's last wish by doing what we can to make our mother happy."

"You said before she'd be happier without his interference."

"I said she might have coped better." He stopped in front of her, not close enough to crowd but close enough to see the responsive skip of pulse in her throat. "Instead she's worried sick about us doing something harebrained."

"Harebrained?"

Rafe smiled. "Her word."

"Like having a baby with an unsuitable woman?"

"Precisely." He cocked his head and pretended to inspect her intently. Eyes narrowed and wary, she looked right back. "Now you, Catriona, would be quite suitable."

"Oh, yeah, sure. And will that be just the one baby with you, or one with each of your brothers, too?"

"You don't want to have kids?"

"Eventually." She shrugged but the effort looked tense, far from casual. "But not today, thanks for asking."

"Pity" was all Rafe said, but he smiled at her answer, at her crisp no-nonsense delivery, at the fact that she'd just made up his mind without knowing it. Convincing her would be a challenge, but he loved nothing better than a worthy adversary.

When she tried to step sideways, he moved with her. First left, then right. She exhaled an exasperated breath, stood her ground, and when her eyes met his, they flashed green with annoyance. "What now?" she asked.

"That tree in your yard…"

It only took a second for her to catch up with his abrupt change in topic. "I assume you mean the one that's not supposed to be in my yard?"

"That's the one. If you point me in the direction of your chainsaw I'll take care of it."

She started shaking her head round about "chainsaw" and was speaking over the top before he finished. "You think I'll let you loose with a dangerous power tool?"

"You let me loose with a dangerous dish mop."

"Funny."

"Come on, Catriona, you can't shift that monster on your own. Your friend will be here soon to take me away. Why not put me to work while you can? Come on," he cajoled, leaning closer, smiling into her eyes. Letting his voice drop a half, silky note. "You know you want to.…"

Cat refused to think about what she wanted to do with Rafe Carlisle and his wickedly unsettling suggestions. Since he insisted, she did put him to work, although not with the chainsaw and not without another confrontation. "You were concussed. You should be taking it easy, not doing physical work, let alone with a chainsaw screaming in your ears."

"Don't you have any of those Princess Leia ear muffs for protection?"

Yes, but… "You can't work in those clothes. You'll snag your pretty sweater."

He obliged by taking it off. "Better?"

How much longer did she have to put up with him driving

her crazy? Less than an hour, she told herself as he stood there before her, all fake innocence and bare-chested beauty.

"What if you scratch yourself on the branches?"

"I'm counting on it." He grinned wolfishly. "So you can play nurse again."

Exasperated, she stomped inside and fetched him an old work shirt and insisted he put it on. He did, except the buttons wouldn't do up, and then he ripped both underarm seams hauling away one of the branches she'd lopped.

"Add it to my bill," he said after he tore out the sleeves to give himself more room.

He fashioned one into a bandanna, which, combined with the too-small shirt and the ear-muffs, should have looked silly. Not on Rafe. He looked as if he'd walked right out of a diet cola ad. Cat sighed and went back to work with the chain-saw. At least the tree would soon be gone…and so would he. Gone with his smooth-skinned beauty and his nefarious grins and his way of making her laugh and talk and remember what it was to enjoy company.

Making her forget for hours at a time that she had little to smile about.

A pleasant diversion, she told herself. Extremely pleasant to look at and to talk to…up until he started on the baby thing. That whole exchange had left her feeling weird, unsettled, as if she'd stepped off a roller coaster and hadn't regained her balance. She sneaked a look at him over the decimated remains of the gum tree and felt the same swamping wave churn through her body.

This had nothing to do with muscles that flexed and curved and gleamed with the makings of sweat. This was about the love in his eyes when he talked about his mother, the way he wanted to satisfy his father's last wish, the obvious bond with his brothers. This was about the dreams for her future that had slipped away with Drew—dreams of the babies she would have to make her own family. This was about all she didn't have and all she'd thought she'd got past missing and wanting.

Blast.

She turned off the saw and sat back on her haunches to take a breath. To gather herself because she realized she was shaking. Not tremors on the outside, but that same shivery feeling deep inside she'd felt earlier, only more so. Not good with a chainsaw in one's hands! She pulled her ear protection down around her neck and swiped the back of one hand across her sweaty forehead.

Then she sat up straight, eyes fixed on the vehicle thundering up her drive. Behind her she sensed Rafe's stillness, as if he, too, had stopped work to watch the four-wheel-drive as it bounced across the last cattle grid and disappeared behind the house.

"That must be Jen," she said, even though the Porters drove a crew-cab and Jen hadn't called to say she was on her way. Even though she and her sinking stomach both knew who drove that exact model of Landcruiser. It reappeared, swinging around the back of the house, and she and her sinking stomach both recognized the big bullheaded shape in the driver's seat.

And so did Bach. He appeared out of nowhere in a rush of snarling outrage, intent on chasing the vehicle to a standstill. Carefully Cat stood, chainsaw in her hands. The idea of greeting her visitor, thus armed, held huge appeal.

"Is his name really Jen?" Rafe asked at her side.

"No, his name is Gordon Samuels. He's Jen's boss and my neighbor."

"The cowboy's father," Rafe muttered, obviously clued in by the sight of Bach, teeth bared, three inches from the driver's door. Which explained why that door hadn't yet opened. "I gather you weren't expecting him."

"No," she said with a tight smile. "But if I were a betting woman, I'd lay my last dollar on why he's graced us with his company."

"Us?"

Cat's laugh was short and caustic and had nothing to do with mirth. "You're right. This isn't about us. This is about *you*."

"I've never met the man."

"I dare say he found out you were here from Bob Porter. And now he's here to drive you into Bourke because, well, you are a Carlisle."

Side by side they watched Samuels's motionless silhouette inside the truck for another crawling minute. "Are you going to call your dog off?" Rafe asked.

"I haven't decided."

"I guess it's a pickle of a choice for you."

"How's that?"

"You let your neighbor out and get rid of me. Or you leave him to fester in his own juices and you get to keep me." Eyes glittering with a dangerous light swung slowly to meet hers. "What's it going to be, Catriona? Do I go or do I get to stay?"

Five

Catriona met his gaze with steady directness while she appeared to give that choice due consideration. "Tempting," she murmured, "But…"

Rafe sighed. "There's always a *but,* isn't there?"

"Sadly…yes."

She called her dog off, and after a couple of minutes in her neighbor's company, Rafe wished she hadn't. He'd met a thousand patronizing, self-important, butt-kissing Gordon Samuelses in his time and that was about a thousand too many.

Only too happy to help out a neighbor in need. Would have been here earlier if I'd known Catriona was going to put you to work. Good grief, girl, don't you know who the Carlisles are? Etc, etc, etc.

Apparently, getting one's hands dirty and riding with the hired help was beneath a Carlisle's station in life. Who knew? Still, Rafe accepted his offer of a lift into Bourke in Jennifer Porter's stead, but only so he could put the man's toadying to good use. He had questions to ask; he expected to find Samuels bursting with ready answers.

After a quick shower—he'd have preferred leisurely, but he'd left Catriona and her chainsaw alone with Samuels—there wasn't anything left to do but say goodbye.

Oh, and kiss her.

Distracted by whatever had gone down between her and Samuels while he showered—whatever had made her eyes churn in a dark and angry storm—she didn't see the kiss coming until his head was bending down to hers. By then his hand cupped the back of her head and his fingers were dipping into the thick sections of her braid, and she couldn't escape.

His lips found hers just as her mouth opened to object. Perfect timing, he decided, smiling against her lips. Tasting her tiny gasp of surprise while he stroked his thumb over her sun-warmed hair. It was a short kiss, a sweet kiss, with no body contact but a whole world of connection when their eyes met and held. Rafe felt a jolt of pleasure, not savage, not fierce, not even unexpected.

He knew he'd enjoy kissing his angel of mercy. Knew she'd taste as warm and earthy as she looked and that her eyes would shimmer with a thousand pleasurable possibilities. He wanted to tell her to think about every one—to think about him—when she was alone in her bed, but Samuels cleared his throat and reminded him they weren't alone right now. Which started Bach growling like a turboprop before takeoff.

Catriona made an impatient sound in her throat. "I know, I know," she told her dog. "But he's about to leave, I promise."

Rafe knew she was talking about Samuels and grinned at the edgy snarl to her voice. He fished a card from his pocket and jotted down his contact details. "I'll call you when I get back to Sydney, but these are my numbers, home and office, in case—"

"There's no need."

"Oh, but there is." He folded her fingers around the card she seemed reluctant to take and focused on the solid practicalities instead of the ethereal promise of that kiss. "There's the small matter of the plane I landed in your paddock and then there's the not-so-small matter of my bill."

"I was joking."

"And I'm not. Whether you want or not, I'm going to repay your hospitality, Catriona. You might want to start thinking about how and when."

Restitution was only the first of Rafe's goals for Catriona. During the next sixty minutes, he intended to learn all he could about her—anything to stack the odds in his favor for when he got to the main one. As expected, Gordon Samuels fell all over himself to help.

He learned that she'd inherited the debt-ridden Corroboree from her father while she was still at school. Samuels had managed the station and her stepmother the trust account while she completed her education. Significant, Rafe thought, that she now seemed to hold both parties in extreme contempt.

Samuels told him that since Catriona took over management, she'd struggled to keep her head above water. "I threw her a life buoy but once she sets her mind on something, the girl's as tough to shift as a barnacle."

Catriona might well be stubborn, but she didn't strike him as a fool. Obviously, she needed help badly, so why had she refused to grab ahold of that buoy? There was something going on between her and the Samuelses, more that he needed to discover—more that he would discover—in order to find out what kind of rescue raft she would climb aboard.

Unfortunately, he didn't have much time to launch that raft. Two months and the clock was ticking.

He cut a sideways glance at Gordon Samuels, at the man's tough profile shaded beneath a big western hat, and he remembered the picture on Catriona's fridge. And his certainty that the cowboy had let her down, badly.

The same conviction snared him now. The knowledge that the key to Catriona rested with Drew Samuels.

"So, Gordon," he commenced casually. "Catriona tells me you have a son in America. A bullrider…?"

Cat heard her phone ringing as she stepped out of the shower, and the certainty of who was calling buzzed through her at roughly the same frequency as that strident bell. She wished she could ignore it. Or at least take the time to dry herself instead of bolting, towel in hand, for her office.

Unfortunately, she couldn't. Nor could she stop the tremble in her hand as she picked up the receiver, although she put a choke hold on her unruly anticipation and took a deep breath before attempting to speak.

All this just because the man had dropped in a cursory thank-you-and-goodbye kiss!

"Hello," she said, sounding quite calm, considering.

"You really should get a message bank, Catriona." No hello, no other preliminary—not that Rafe needed to identify himself. Who else drew her name out over all four syllables in that thoroughly extravagant way?

"You've been trying to call?"

"I told you I would." She heard the smile in his voice, pictured those full lips quirked at the corners. Remembered their pressure against hers with a flutter of heat somewhere deep inside. "You must have started early this morning."

"Sixish," she confirmed.

"Guess I just missed you then."

"You called at *sixish*? I meant in the morning!"

He laughed, a soft, low sound that vibrated through her like a cat's purring. "I was down at Randwick Racecourse before sunrise, watching Alex's next champion gallop. I called on my way home at sixish. Then again at sevenish. Again over lunch."

Whoa.

"I thought I might catch you in. Don't you ever eat?"

Only when I have food in the house. "Only on odd-numbered days."

"So, you haven't eaten tonight?"

"If I say no, will you buy me dinner?" A safe question, with him five hundred miles away in Sydney. Safe and easy to swap banter with him at the other end of a phone call.

"How long would it take you to get ready?" he asked.

"For a free meal, I'd go as I am."

"And how's that, Catriona?" His deep voice lingered over her name in a way that made her very aware of her nakedness. And of how she'd been daydreaming under the shower about seeing him right out of the shower.

Daydreaming about him using that princely body to pay her back for her hospitality.

An acceptable fantasy, she'd justified sometime during the night when it first slid steamy and alluring into her imagination, since it was only a fantasy. Acceptable, too, because it stopped her thinking about that disturbing conversation out at the kennels. Stopped her daydreaming about things like, oh, having the man's baby.

"What *are* you wearing?" he prompted.

Cat snorted and propped the receiver between ear and shoulder so she could wrap herself in the towel. "Don't tell me you get your jollies from women describing their underwear."

"Usually—" he paused and the sound of movement made her think he was settling back, getting comfortable "—I get my jollies taking off women's underwear."

That predictable response rolled smooth and silky from his tongue—the same way she imagined him rolling underwear from her body. Except he hadn't meant *her* underwear, and the notion of his expert hands on other women's underwear—on other women's bodies—turned her next provocative response to bitter-tasting ashes.

She sat heavily in her desk chair and gripped the front of her towel more firmly. Fun time was over. "Why were you calling all day, anyway?" she asked. "Is there a problem with salvaging the plane?"

"No. They're sending someone out tomorrow…but that's not why I called. I need to settle my bill."

He'd called half a dozen times about that? "You do understand I was joking."

"You do understand I was serious about repaying your hospitality."

"There's no need," she said quickly. Her heart was starting to beat with similar speed. She was getting bad vibes about this. "I don't need any payment."

There was the briefest pause before he asked, "Are you sure about that, Catriona?"

Grimacing, she pinched the bridge of her nose between finger and thumb. *Gordon Samuels and his big mouth. That's where the bad vibes stemmed from!* "You shouldn't believe everything you hear."

"And what is it you think I've heard?"

"It's a long drive into Bourke," she said dryly, "so I expect you heard a lot."

"Samuels told me you were doing it tough. Should I believe that?"

He'd been there. He'd stepped over roofing iron blown from her rundown buildings. Did he really have to ask? "Did my good neighbor tell you why I'm broke?"

"He mentioned drought years after your father's death—"

"That's not what I meant, unless you count the way his drought mismanagement drove Corroboree into the ground!" She inhaled sharply in a last-ditch effort to contain the bitterness that had crept into her tone. "Actually, I meant more recently. Like in the last month."

Silence. She'd thought as much. And although every instinct hammered at her to shut the hell up, she couldn't. Whe knew what crap Samuels had spun during that drive? It shouldn't have mattered what Rafe Carlisle had heard and whether that had influenced his opinion of her, but it did. She'd lost so much over the last several years. Pride was one of the few things she had left.

"I took money from his son. A personal loan, I suppose, although—" She stopped cold, realizing suddenly that she didn't want to share the "although" because that included the part about giving Drew her body and her love and her trust. The part where they'd lain in her bed and talked about running Corroboree together. When he offered her the money, she took it as his commitment to their future, although her pride had insisted she call it a loan.

"Although?" he prompted.

"Last month Samuels told me the money was his. He says he wants it repaid, but what he really wants is Corroboree."

"Is the money his?"

"I don't know." Cat sighed and pinched the bridge of her nose again. Harder. "I've been trying to contact Drew to find out what's going on, but he's not answering my messages. He could be anywhere, competing or on the road. He mightn't have e-mail access, he might have changed his mobile phone number, he mightn't be getting my messages."

Rafe said nothing for a long time, and that pause seemed to resonate with the desperate ring of her words.

Cat squeezed her eyes shut and grimaced. "I'm sorry. I didn't mean to tell you all that. I just wanted to set the record straight, given what Samuels might have told you. I just opened my mouth and out it all came."

"Don't apologize, Catriona. I like that you've taken me into your confidence."

Is that what she'd done? Taken this man—this stranger from another world—into her confidence? Like a friend? She coiled the phone cord around her hand while tendrils of unease coiled around her stomach.

"So, what are you doing to set this straight?"

"What can I do?" She huffed out a ragged little laugh. "Look, Rafe, you don't have to concern—"

"Does Samuels have proof that he loaned you anything?"

Apparently he *did* have to concern himself, and Cat hovered for a second, twisting and untwisting the phone cord, unsure about this confidence thing. Perhaps talking it over with a stranger, an outsider, was a good thing. Perhaps he'd shake loose an angle she'd missed.

"Did you sign anything?"

"No," she admitted, sinking deeper into the chair and closing her eyes. "I took the money from Drew on a handshake agreement, but Samuels says he signed the loan over to him. How could that work?"

"Sounds like you need legal advice."

A fine idea if she had the money to pay for such advice! "What I need is to talk to Drew."

"Have you thought about hiring someone to find him? Or going over there to track him down?"

She laughed without mirth. "If I had a dollar for every time I've thought about getting over there and grabbing him by the shirtfront and shaking the damn truth out of him, I'd be able to afford the airfare."

"What if you had the airfare?" he asked after a tick of pause, and Cat sucked in a breath and straightened her back in bristling denial.

"Oh, no, Rafe. You are not going to pay for a ticket."

"Are you too stubborn to accept help?"

"I can't accept *your* help."

"Yet I had to accept yours."

"That was different," she fired back. "If I ever knock myself out landing a plane, I will accept your help in a heartbeat."

"Do you remember taking me to bed?" he asked softly. Cat swallowed. *In her fantasies, yes.* "You told me you weren't a difficult person."

Oh, *that* taking him to bed. Taking his weight when his balance gave out. Stumbling at the door to her bedroom. Shaking her head when he refused to allow one last check of his responses.

And he'd asked if *she* was always this difficult!

"Let me help you with this, Catriona." His voice changed, as if he'd shifted position again, as if he held the receiver closer to his mouth. As if he were right here, mouth close to her ear, enticing her to let him do all kinds of things for her. To her. With her. Cat shivered. "Let me do this very small thing to repay you. Let me buy you a plane ticket so you can go shake the hell out of this cowboy of yours."

"It's not that easy." She shook her head, hoping to clear the heat that seemed to be hazing her good sense. Why else would she be feeling the insidious tug of temptation? "I don't know where he is."

"An investigator would locate him in a day."

"Maybe, but that'd be—" Underhanded. Over-the-top. "—wrong."

"Scared?"

She bristled at the low-voiced taunt. "Scared of what?"

"I don't know, Catriona," he said in that same low, dangerous voice. "Maybe you're scared of what you'll find out about your cowboy."

"Scared of the truth? No way."

"Then let me—"

"No," she said quickly, adamantly. "If you insist on repayment, you can buy me that dinner sometime."

"Think about it."

"Oh, I'm sure I will think about it." With a rueful half smile, Cat shook her head. She would think about it most every waking hour, and dream about it while she slept. "I'll think about it but I won't change my mind."

After he disconnected, Rafe's smile curled with the thrill of a challenge innocently laid down and not-so-innocently accepted. He didn't know how he would change her mind, only that he'd give it one hell of a shot. And not only because she'd challenged him, not only because his life had become too easy, too predictable, too dissatisfying.

He knew his brothers treated his part in their baby-making pact as a joke. *Rafe as a father? Shoot, he's too irresponsible, too reckless. Too shallow. He hasn't grown up himself.* Not that he blamed them for that opinion, since it amused him to overplay his reputation. Charm, after all, was the one and only thing he excelled at.

But now it was time to show his hand. Time to show his brothers that he was up to the challenge, that he could do something as well as—even better than—them.

For once he could give something back to his family.

He'd found the right woman, but could he find the means to change her mind?

Six

"What made you change your mind?"

Cat sighed, unleashing a fraction of the tight breath she swore had been backing up in her lungs for days. Ever since she left a message on the man at her side's voice mail to say, *I have changed my mind. I would like to accept your offer to help.* The man she'd found already seated when the flight attendant walked her through the curtain into first class on this Sydney to Los Angeles flight.

Clever, clever man. He knew she'd have balked at accepting a first-class ticket and his company, so he'd waited until the last minute to spring both on her.

Shaky already with nerves and an awful sense of what-have-I-gotten-myself-into, he hadn't helped matters by standing and kissing her shell-shocked lips. Nothing explicit, nothing extreme, just a brief taste of mint and a wicked lick of temptation that curled Cat's toes and weakened her knees. So much so that she'd slumped into her seat while he calmly explained about having some business to attend to. Thought he might as well travel with her. Make sure she found her cowboy, who he'd located recovering from injury in Vegas. Two birds with the one stone. Etc, etc.

How could she dispute what sounded too glib and convenient but could be the straight truth? He worked, apparently, as some kind of executive with Carlisle Hotels. He was, reputedly, a gambler. He could, easily, do business in Las Vegas.

With a small elite audience and a hovering flight attendant wanting to make her feel at home—in first class with champagne? not likely!—she couldn't kick up a fuss. And when she did open her mouth to question his motives, Rafe pressed a finger to her lips and suggested she follow the safety demonstration.

As if a whistle and light would do her any good if this big bird went down over the Pacific Ocean!

By then the plane was rolling and he was asking why she'd changed her mind and it was much too late to change it back again.

"My stepmother," she replied. "She changed it for me."

"I'm going to have to meet the wicked stepmother. Find out how she managed the impossible."

She turned her head and found him watching her, his eyes alight with the same smile that laced his voice. Silky and sexy and altogether too satisfied. As if he'd known she would change her mind, which he couldn't possibly have done since she hadn't known herself.

Not until after she'd dialed his number in a furious fit of pique, driven by one phone call from the step-monster. No one had the power to play her emotions like Pamela McConnell Smythe—not even Gordon Samuels, although he came close!

"She manages the impossible by being impossible," she told Rafe. "You do not want to meet her, believe me."

"Okay. But I would like to hear how she influenced your decision."

The jumbo had reached the runway and it lumbered in a slow arc to face east, the ocean, her future. Cat's heart started to thunder like a stampeding steer. Why not tell him? Talking might take her mind off the rising panic that threatened to engulf her—a turbulent anxiety that rivaled the high-pitched whining of jet engines impatient for takeoff.

"Pamela loves to tell me all about her daughters and their brilliantly successful careers." Compared to, say, her own spectacular struggle to survive. "And she can't resist reminding me, in subtle little ways, how much keeping Corroboree in the family meant to my father."

"And has she helped you to do that?"

"She offered once, but…" Cat shrugged instead of finishing the sentence. *But I chose to take Drew's money instead.* At the time it had seemed the better option. Better than accepting help from a woman who didn't think she could do the job, who undermined her confidence at every turn, who made her sweat with guilty, angsty fear over letting down her father.

"But…?" Rafe prompted.

The giant engines roared and he leaned across the console between their seats, ducking his head to wait for her answer. Expecting her to speak that answer close to his ear.

Cat stared. At the smooth curve of hair behind his ear and the bristly texture of his sideburn before it. At the squared edge of his jawbone and the flat plane of his cheek. She swallowed. Her fingers curved reflexively around the ends of the armrests, gripping tight, partly because the plane was accelerating down the tarmac and partly because her senses had been hijacked by wild imaginings.

Pressing her lips to that ear. Touching his skin. Biting the lobe.

His prompting question forgotten, she closed her eyes and held on tighter. Then his hand covered hers, enclosing it in heat and the surprise of his palm's texture. Not silky smooth like the rest of him, but slightly rough and very male.

She couldn't stop the sensual shudder that rose from deep

inside when the pressure of his hand increased, stroking over her knuckles and between her fingers. And when he leaned closer to say, "We'll be up there soon. Just hang on tight," she couldn't help the flare of her nostrils as she breathed deeply and caught the musky note of his scent.

Yes, she was slightly nervous of flying.

Yes, he was helping her overcome it—not with his reassuring words, but by guaranteeing she forgot all about the unlikely physics that kept 350 tons of metal airborne.

Did he know how violently he affected her?

Probably. She imagined all women responded the same way to his sexy sweet-talking appeal. God knows, the gossip magazines insinuated so. Not that Cat read them, as a rule, but in the last week she'd allowed her curiosity to type his name into an internet search engine. She'd allowed that curiosity to start reading from some of the sites unearthed…until she'd realized what she was doing and shut her computer down in self-disgust.

The plane lifted and her stomach took a lifetime to catch up. She eased her grip on the armrest but he didn't take his hand away until she wriggled and tugged. "I'm okay now."

And because he was looking at her too closely, his amazing eyes narrowed and fixed on her face, his expression speculative and ready to call her on that lie, she circled back to their interrupted conversation about her stepmother.

"Pamela withdrew her offer of help. She's just waiting for me to fail."

"Is that why you want to save your station so badly?"

"No, that's for my father and myself." The quiet intensity of her words resonated with the same vibrant power as the climbing jumbo for several seconds. Maybe longer. Then a touch of wryness curved Cat's lips. "Although I wouldn't knock back the chance to do something—just once—to wipe the floor with her patronizing attitude."

"I imagine that goes for Samuels, too."

"Crikey, yes! Doubly."

Settling back in the superwide seat, she allowed herself to image that scenario. For the short time it lasted, my, it was good, but then the raw reality of her situation shoved its ugly head into her fantasy. She had no clue how to resolve her mess. This trip to America was only to answer questions, to close her past with Drew, to arm herself with the truth before facing her future.

"I take it he's not looking after your place then, while you're away?"

Cat pulled a face. "Good guess. Bob and Jen Porter are feeding the animals and keeping an eye on things."

"Good neighbors."

"Yes." Her only good neighbors. Her only support. And not nearly enough in the long run.

Perhaps he saw the change in her expression because he leaned closer, his voice lowered to an intimate, conspiratorial level. "Whatever you're thinking, Shauna will be along in a minute to cure it."

Cat frowned. "Shauna?"

He indicated the flight attendant with a nod and a wink. The latter was for the sleek and beautiful Shauna. Figured that he knew her name already. Figured that he was flirting with her already. What didn't figure was Cat's own fierce reaction.

"How will she cure me?" she asked, testy with herself for what felt like the razor's slice of jealousy. She had no right to those feelings. No right to any feelings for Rafe Carlisle.

He turned her way again, just a slight roll of his head against the soft leather headrest and he was looking right into her eyes. Smiling right into her eyes. "She'll be along with champagne."

"The universal first-class cure-all?"

"I didn't know you were such a cynic."

"I'm a realist, Rafe, and this—" she waggled her hand, in-dicating everything around her in the first-class cabin, including him "—only happens in the movies. It's not real. Not in my life."

He raised a lazy eyebrow. And before she realized his purpose, he twined his fingers through hers and picked up her hand. Mesmerized by the soft stroke of his thumb across the center of her palm, by the unwitting intimacy of their linked fingers, by the flare of heat in her belly, Cat blinked slowly. She sat helplessly entranced while he stroked her knuckles against the soft leather of the seat. While he lifted them to brush his cheek and then to touch the sensual fullness of his bottom lip.

"See—" the warm breath of his word washed against her knuckles "—it is all real."

Crikey, he was lethal.

She was in trouble if he kept this up all the way to L.A.

She tugged her hand, and after a short tussle that brought heat to her cheeks, he let her reclaim it. He touched the back of his hand to her face and she jerked back, furious with herself for overreacting, but also with him for playing his games with her. Surely there had to be better in-flight entertainment.

"This is a long flight." She kept her voice and her gaze even, despite the furious heat in her cheeks. "Let's get a few things straight, so there are no mixed messages."

"I'm listening."

"I'm serious, Rafe. Please."

"So am I," he said, mimicking her stern tone. "What messages are getting mixed, Catriona?"

"I'm not a plaything," she said tightly. "Don't toy with me."

"Toy with you?"

"This...*thing*...you do with women."

"This...thing?"

She clicked her tongue with annoyance. Did he have to repeat everything she said in that pseudo-studious way? "Flirt. Kiss. Touch. The lines, the looks. We both know you don't mean it, so just cut it out!"

For a long moment he eyed her in a way she couldn't fathom. Then, with devastating slowness, he brushed his fingertips down the length of her hair. "I promise I won't toy with you, Catriona. But I can't promise not to touch you."

What was that supposed to mean? Cat's heart beat hard and high in her chest. She had to swallow before she could attempt to speak. "What if I don't want you to touch me?"

"Let's make a deal." His voice was low, lazy, lethal. "Just so there are no mixed messages."

Cat swallowed again.

"I won't touch you if you don't want me to. I won't do anything you don't want me to." He extended his hand. "Do we have a deal?"

Did they? Mouth dry, heart thumping, she stared at his hand a second, two, three, while she mulled over his terms. It sounded too good to be true.

"Well, Catriona?"

"My call? You'll back off whenever I say?"

"Promise."

They shook on that, just as Shauna appeared with the promised champagne. Cat settled back into her cushy seat and rubbed her fingers over the warmth lingering from his handshake while her trepidation remained, unallayed, unrelenting.

After all, hadn't a handshake deal with another charmer gotten her into this mess?

The investigator Rafe employed had found Drew Samuels easily enough, shacked up with a woman named Cherrie. He'd told Catriona about the injury but not about the woman. That's why he'd hung around outside the apartment complex after Catriona disappeared inside. That's why he was waiting when she came out half an hour later, ready to take her back to their hotel for some intensive play time.

Yes, he'd promised not to toy with her, but this wasn't that kind of play. This was about making her laugh and forget the ex and everything he'd done to hurt her. This was about treating her and indulging her and reminding her that she was a desirable woman.

Then he would get serious.

As for their deal…well, like all contracts, the devil was in the detail. As he'd told her on the plane, he couldn't agree to not touching but he could shake on not trying anything she didn't want. And Catriona did want him. He felt the spark when their gazes connected, the heat when their fingers meshed, the soft sexy tension when he brushed his mouth with her knuckles.

She might not have realized it yet, but she would.

Slowing with the traffic as they approached the Strip, he cut her a sideways look and felt the same gut kick of reaction as five minutes before, when she slid into the passenger seat of the rental sports car without a word. At worst he'd expected a short dose of cynicism on men in general; at best a fiery diatribe on the specific worm who'd sold her out without a breath of warning.

He hadn't counted on her looking so pale. So lost. So damn beaten.

He hadn't counted on his own savage response, either. If the bastard had had the common courtesy to walk her outside—hell, she hadn't known he was waiting, she'd told him to go and attend to his business, she'd catch a cab—Rafe would likely have given in to the violent need to grind his face in the dirt. That rocked him almost as much as Cat's silence. He wasn't a violent man. And he didn't even have the full story on Drew Samuels…although he intended to get it once they arrived back at their hotel and he could concentrate only on her, instead of the car and the traffic and the tourists who wandered around in a bright-lights-induced coma. Even though it was only midmorning.

They were half a block from their hotel when he changed his mind and kept on driving. It was a whim, but the kind that sat right in his gut and even righter in his mind the farther he drove without her taking any notice. When he pulled over to dispense with the convertible's roof, she finally sat up straighter and looked about. Behind her dark glasses he couldn't see her eyes, but he knew they roamed the red desert vista with dawning realization.

"Where are we? Where are we going?"

"Nowhere in particular. Just driving."

"For how long?" she asked after a moment.

"As long as it takes," Rafe answered easily as he steered the Jaguar back onto the single-lane road. Divergent currents of warm and cool air eddied through the car, whipping several long tresses around her face. "You might want to tie your hair back."

The powerful engine pleaded for release in a low rumbling purr he couldn't deny. He opened her up for the time it took to hit the speed limit—and a bit more—and she thanked him with a blood rush of sheer speed-induced pleasure. Not as good as sex, not as good as flying or outwitting a sharp opponent at the poker table, but the next best thing.

He glanced at Catriona. She'd given up holding her hair, and it sailed beyond the car's confines in wild cinnamon streamers that obscured her face. He hoped the rush of speed had chased away some of her anxiety, that the sparse landscape with its rich ochre shades and wild, rough edges would feel enough like home to ease her tight expression.

That's what he'd meant by "as long as it takes."

He turned up a dirt trail leading nowhere in particular and eased off the speed. He aimed to find somewhere to pull over, somewhere they wouldn't be disturbed. He hoped she was ready to let all that heartache pour out.

"Don't you need to get back? To your business?"

They'd been stopped out here—wherever that was—for a while. Cat didn't know how long. She'd walked until her sandals started to rub through her numbness and register as imminent blisters. Then she'd returned to the sleek silvery blue sports car and climbed back into her seat.

Rafe didn't move. "I don't have to be anywhere."

But despite the peace of this place and his relaxed immobility in the driver's seat—how could someone slouch so gracefully?—she couldn't sit still. She felt edgy and restless, as if the short walk had freed all her simmering frustrations from their previous frozen numbness.

She turned in her seat, better to face him. "Why did you bring me out here?"

"To walk. To talk if you want. I'm a good listener."

"Talk." She made a tight growling noise in her throat. "That won't help me any!"

"Would it help if you tossed rocks at something? There are some sturdy-looking cacti out here. If you feel so inclined."

No, she didn't feel like throwing things any more than talking. She felt like…like…

"Did you know about Cherrie?" Harsh, almost accusatory, the question exploded from deep inside, deep down where panic and anger and despair roiled in a churning cauldron of contained emotion.

"The girlfriend?"

"The *pregnant* girlfriend," she corrected, and she could see by Rafe's face that that much was news. And it struck her, randomly, inconsequentially, that he wouldn't be the only one stunned by the news. Her laugh came out low and bitter, and she shook her head slowly. "Can you imagine his father's face when he finds out?"

"Samuels doesn't want grandkids?"

"That's not the point. The point is Cherrie. Let's just say Gordon would welcome even *me* with open arms in preference to a Vegas showgirl-slash-waitress!"

She could feel him watching her, silent as the spread of desert landscape, intent as one of the hawks that circled over a distant canyon. "Was that ever an option? Samuels as your father-in-law?"

"I thought so. We lived together for a while, when Drew was home from rodeos. He and his father had a falling out, and we'd always been friends. It became…more. I took his money thinking we'd end up running Corroboree together, that we'd be partners, and the silly handshake I'll-pay-you-back deal was only about my pride." Now she'd started talking, the words simply wouldn't let up. It didn't matter who she was telling or whether he wanted to know, she just had to let it all out. "Why couldn't he have told me about Cherrie and the baby and his busted shoulder? I would have understood him needing the money. I could have done something without him selling me out to his father!"

God knows what, but something! For a start she would have avoided this pointless trip, saved herself the discovery of Drew's failure firsthand, of meeting the beaten flatness of his eyes. Of knowing he'd been too weak to return her calls and tell her the truth.

"I take it his rodeo dream didn't pan out?"

"He says he was doing all right until he got laid up with injury, but who knows? As far as I know he didn't even tell his father that much. Back home I kept hearing how well he was doing on the circuit." She slapped a hand against the console. "I should have known better. I had my doubts when I stopped seeing his name in the results on the Internet."

"You were hoping you were wrong."

With a rueful sigh, she slumped back in her seat. "Yeah. I was hoping."

"Valid," he suggested after a long beat of pause, "since you love him."

That statement, spoken quietly, evenly, stretched through the ensuing silence and wrapped around Cat's conscience. She frowned. Did she love Drew? Present tense…no, she didn't. Past tense…yes, she must have. Why else would she have trusted him? Why else would his betrayal have struck such an acute hurt in her heart?

Because *the result* mattered so deeply. Because, now, she would have to find some way to repay Samuels and she feared that selling at least part of Corroboree was her only option. She feared that Samuels wouldn't stop at part, that he would keep hammering away until he had the whole.

"He's always wanted Corroboree." A simple statement, but her voice ached with all that meant. Failing her father and failing herself. "I don't know what I'm going to do, Rafe."

She'd turned toward him, her arms spread in unconscious appeal, and although he didn't move a muscle, she sensed a change. A new alertness. As if he'd been sitting there waiting for her to get to this point. Waiting for his cue to take over.

"You're not going to do anything, Catriona. Not yet."

"But—"

"You're tired, you're stressed, you're emotional. That's not the time to be making big decisions."

True, but…

Rafe the listener, lounging back in his sports car seat, prompting her to toss her verbal rocks at the abandoned terrain…*that* Rafe she trusted. This intent, take-charge version disturbed her at some elemental level. Having to seek his advice on what to do next disturbed her even more, yet she couldn't help herself. She felt so lost and fretful she might as well have been out there, wandering across the red-tinged vastness of the Nevada landscape, alone and without a compass.

"When will I be ready?"

"Not before tomorrow," he said without pause. "At the earliest."

"And what do you suggest I do in the meantime?"

"You're in Vegas." Slowly he straightened out of his lazy sprawl. "I suggest twenty-four hours of self-indulgence."

Oh, right, sure. "You think I'm going to what…take in the

sights and a show? Check out a few casinos? When my world is falling apart?"

"I think you need to forget about your world for twenty-four hours."

"And experience yours?"

"Not so much mine. I'm talking spas and shopping. Relaxation and retail therapy."

"Not my thing."

"You're a woman." His gaze lingered on her lips. His mouth kicked with a hint of wicked knowledge. "Of course they're your thing."

"They're a waste of money."

"I've got plenty."

Exasperated by his attitude, she threw her hands in the air. "If you're so damn desperate to squander your money, why don't you spend it on something worthwhile?"

For a long second he eyed her silently. Then he smiled. "Oh, I intend to, baby."

Seven

Cat didn't so much give in as give up.

Physically tired, emotionally drained, she put herself into the hands of Bridget—who worked for the hotel in some do-whatever-the-wealthy-guest-wants capacity—because it was easier than convincing Rafe that she didn't go for the conventional female treats. That her idea of self-indulgence was sleeping in an extra hour on the odd Sunday morning and buying fresh peaches instead of canned. That the only spa she'd ever seen was in her stepmother's bathroom. That her idea of retail therapy would be unlimited credit at a stud cattle sale.

Bridget, it turned out, was very good at her job.

She had a way of drawing Cat into conversation and distracting her with an apparent keen interest in Australia and all things outback. Then, midconversation, while they strolled through the hotel's high-rent shopping arcade, she would point out something and get all excited.

"Oh, that would look smashing on you, Catriona! You must try it on!"

Cat's eyes boggled at the designer names—Dior, Chanel, Prada, Armani—and balked at the changing-room doors. Bridget cajoled. Cat gave in. Saleswomen gushed. And against all previous experience and knowledge of herself, she started to enjoy the trying-on, being-gushed-over thing.

The slinky fabrics shimmered against her skin when she moved. The world's cleverest push-'em-up bra produced never-seen-before cleavage. Cunningly shaped dresses defined her waist and skimmed her hips, and in the magical mirrors she looked tall and slender and sexy.

It was a deception, she knew, but a harmless one. A girly game she would soon forget back in the real world, but for now she conceded Rafe's point. Today she needed to forget that world. Just for a little while.

After the shops, she gave herself over to the day spa staff without demur. When they asked which treatments she preferred, she shrugged and smiled. "You decide for me. Just wake me when you're done." Several hours and one body wrap, one oxygenating facial, one hair revival treatment and one full makeup application later, she was done.

Strangely enough she wasn't done in.

On her way up to the top floor of their hotel, her heart hammered fifteen to the dozen with what felt like anticipation. Outside the door to their suite she paused and drew a deep breath and called herself to task for that ridiculous nervous excitement. She didn't even know if Rafe was in. She didn't know if she would see him at all tonight. One still-functioning kernel of her brain cynically suggested that this whole long afternoon of Cat-pampering served another purpose—it had taken her off his hands so he could do whatever he'd come to Vegas to do.

And what if that's you, Catriona? What if he's come to Vegas to—

No! She didn't let that wanton thought go any further. She didn't even know where it had come from, but it could go right back there! He hadn't even mentioned his need of a baby again, not once since that morning at Corroboree. For all she knew, he'd already found someone. For all she knew, he could be off finding someone now.

What if that someone is inside now? In this suite? In his bed?

"Then it's his business," she told herself sternly. Not hers to ponder or judge. Not hers to care about. She'd already made a fool of herself over their sleeping arrangements at check-in.

"A shared suite?" she'd objected. "Oh, no. I'll take an ordinary room."

Rafe's eyes had narrowed. "You expect me to pay for a room of your own? On top of the plane ticket? And the jet?"

He'd meant the private jet waiting in L.A., ready for the early-morning hop to Vegas. Another stunning surprise in a list that went on and on. "I'll pay for my own room," she'd said stiffly. "I'd rather have my own."

"Do you know what that will set you back?"

She'd guessed. He'd laughed. And the literal-minded clerk had corrected her miles-too-low assumption. Afterward, on their way to this penthouse suite, she'd paid more attention to the marble tiles and mother-of-pearl mosaics and intricate old-world furnishings.

"I didn't ask you to pay for my room," she said tightly, feeling gauche and ill equipped to deal with such plush surroundings. Feeling another swamping wave of what-have-I-let-myself-in-for panic.

Rafe had just shrugged with his trademark negligence. "It's a two-bedroom suite. I only need one."

They'd showered, changed, each on their separate side of the huge central living area. And she'd rushed through it all, dealing with her anxiety by focusing on what lay ahead with Drew.

Now, ten hours later, with her heart in her mouth, she forced herself to open the door and walk inside. Instantly she felt the empty silence and contradictory pangs of relief and disappointment.

She was alone.

"And that's okay, Cat," she told herself. She didn't need his company. She was used to alone…although not in such an alien habitat. She kicked off her sandals and prowled a circuit of the parlor. *The parlor. Huh.* That's what the concierge had called it when he'd shown them through. A grand name for a grand room in a grand suite of a grand hotel.

After picking up her sandals, which were making the place look untidy, she padded off to her bedroom. No need to feel abandoned. There was a television with about a zillion cable channels. Her choice of movies. She could get adventurous and order room service, which she would somehow pay for herself, and then—

She stopped short in the doorway to her bedroom.

Mouth open like a startled guppy, she stared at the boxes and bags—*shopping* bags—neatly stacked on the satin chaise beneath the picture window. It was not a small stack. Her stomach went into free fall.

Was it *everything* she'd tried on?

Heart palpitating, she slowly crossed the room. Had Rafe told Bridget to do this? To buy her all these things? Yes, he had plenty of money. He hadn't needed to tell her that. But she'd didn't want him wasting any more on her. She didn't need pretty clothes she would never wear.

Her breath caught as she opened the first box. It held the last dress she'd tried on. An evening dress she would never choose in a million years. White satin, tucked and pleated. Completely impractical.

She jammed the lid back on and kept her hands pressed down hard on the box. Not that she expected the dress to fling itself free like a jack-in-the-box. She didn't trust herself. If she didn't get rid of the thing—all the things!—right away, she might fall for the lure of that exquisitely soft fabric.

The temptation of playing dress-up again could strike her at a weak moment.

But not if she called Bridget—provided she was still on duty—to come and take it all away. She was pretty certain that once she'd eaten and slept and come to grips with the past twenty-four hours, she'd feel guilty enough about the cost of the spa treatments she couldn't give back. The clothes she could.

Pleased with that decision, she looked around for a phone…and heard the outer door to the suite open. Rafe. Her heart skipped and stalled, but for the life of her, she couldn't move. She was standing, frozen, midway between the chaise and the desk with the phone when he appeared in her doorway.

Their gazes met, linked, locked, and for a long moment that was it…no words, no movement, nothing but hot, heavy desire in her blood, in her breasts, in her belly. In the silent, sandalwood-tinted air of her bedroom.

Rafe moved first, his gaze ambling over her face, lingering on the soft-coral curve of her lips, taking in the carefully constructed wildness of her curls…and when he met her eyes again, Cat saw satisfaction and something else in those sea-green depths. Something that wasn't surprise. Something that electrified her sluggish nerves with wanton excitement.

If he'd said, *Take off your clothes,* Cat would have started stripping. It was that kind of look, that kind of response. That potent.

But all he said was, "Nice job," in that low, lazy way he had, and Cat felt a ridiculously sharp stab of disappointment. She hadn't really expected the let's-get-naked demand, but "You look good" would at least have given some credit to her. Instead he'd complimented the stylist.

"You paid them enough," she said. "You should expect better than a nice job."

His eyes narrowed a fraction. "Didn't you enjoy yourself? Don't you like your hair?"

"Do you?"

"Yeah," he said after a long beat of silence. Long enough for Cat to regret her hastily fired retort. Long enough for her heart to start thundering in her chest because his expression had changed, turned tricky and unreadable. "I like it. But then I liked it that night at your house, when you'd washed it and you smelled of peaches. I like it in that long braid that slaps against your spine when you walk. I liked it all mussed when you slept on the plane."

Crikey. She'd been looking for a your-hair-looks-good compliment. And he'd noticed all that!

"Right now you look like one of those Botticelli angels...but that's not the point. This afternoon was for your pleasure, Catriona, not mine."

For her pleasure, and she'd returned the favor by sniping about the cost.

Cat shook her head, a vain attempt to dislodge the scintillating effect of his comments. The knowledge that he'd watched her, noticed her, on all those occasions. A vain attempt to snap her brain into action.

"I did enjoy myself," she assured him finally. "Even the clothes."

A corner of his mouth quirked. "I wasn't sure how that part would go."

"I'm not a big fan of dressing up."

His eyes slid behind her, to the pile of bags and boxes. "Looks like you found something you liked."

"Oh, no. I mean, yes." Confused, she frowned. "Beautiful things, and fun to try on, and, yes, how could I not like them? But I don't want them. I can't keep them."

"Why not?"

"Because they're too expensive and I would never wear them." She lifted her arms and let them drop. "This is me—jeans and shirts. I don't go anywhere to wear flashy clothes."

"What about tonight?" he asked, ever so casually. She hadn't seen him move, but she noticed that he was lazing against the doorjamb. Posture as laidback as always, but those eyes still dangerously alert. Disturbingly sexy.

"What about tonight?" she asked warily.

"To thank me for today, for this afternoon, you're letting me take you to dinner."

Cat stared at him. Did he really think she would buy that excuse? She would have dinner with him…as a thank-you? What was wrong with that picture!

"You must be hungry."

"Yes," she conceded. She'd missed lunch. Breakfast on the plane seemed a lifetime ago. "I'm starving, actually. But I thought I'd just order in some room service and then crash."

"Even better. You want to eat formally at the table, or pizza while we watch a movie?"

The televisions were in the bedrooms and the next question went unasked, but she read it in the heat of his eyes as they flicked to her bed and back to her face.

Your room or mine?

Five minutes ago he'd looked at her and she'd almost started shedding clothes. Now he'd shaken her up enough for her brain to start operating on some subliminal level—enough to know that if she stayed in this suite, if they ordered in food, she would end up naked. She was too tired and too sensually smitten and too emotionally needy to resist.

And tomorrow she would hate herself.

"Well?" he prompted.

"I…I've changed my mind." Decision made, she spoke quickly, convincing that part of her that still wanted to stay in and get naked as much as convincing Rafe. "I'm in Vegas and I'll probably never be here again. I would like to go out— for a little while—to have a meal and see the lights and the famous fire-and-water show. Bridget said I shouldn't miss that! And I have to put at least one coin through the slots."

"You are in Vegas," he agreed, sounding not the least put out by her vacillations.

In fact, he looked a little too pleased with himself as he straightened from the doorjamb and came into her room. Cat stiffened reflexively. "What are you doing?"

"Choosing something for you to wear."

"You can't."

"I am."

He unlidded the top box. And stilled. Slowly, softly, he ran the back of his hand across the white satin, and Cat's skin tingled with heat as if he'd touched her in that same way. As he *had* touched her, on the plane.

When he started to lift the dress from the box, she stopped him with a hand on his arm. On the hard curved muscle of his forearm. "Not that one."

Slowly he lifted his gaze to hers. "Why not this one?"

"It's too formal." She took her hand back. "Too much."

"Are you going to find a complaint with every one of these?" he asked, reaching for a smaller bag.

It was the underwear—the lace and satin and gel cups and g-strings—she just knew it. Fighting the urge to grab and wrestle him for possession, she stood calm and still. "No. There's a green dress I tried on. It's probably in one of these bags. I'll wear that one."

"Green?"

"Sort of green." And sort of flattering, she remembered, the way the sheer layers of fabric draped from the halter neck over her breasts, and flared from the waist to an uneven hemline that played peek-a-boo with her knees.

Sort of sexy in a subtle way.

He smiled in a way that was definitely sexy—no "sort of" about it—as he handed over the underwear. As he told her to wear that dress because, "Sort of green's my favorite color."

Rafe didn't really have a favorite color. Not until he saw Catriona in that dress. It wasn't "sort of" green; it was knock-your-eyes-out, kick-in-the-gut, heart-pumping green.

Although that reaction, when she came out of her room fifteen minutes later, probably had as much to do with the shy heat in her eyes and the nervous jump of her pulse and the certainty that he'd be peeling that green lick of silk from her body in a couple of hours' time.

He'd thought about making that sooner. He was pretty sure he could have talked her into staying in, but then he'd have missed the awed delight in her wide eyes as they watched the water fountains play under golden lights. He'd have missed pouring her a glass of champagne and feeding her her first taste of truffles…and watching her spit them back out again. He'd have missed the quiet intensity of her gaze on his face while he told her about his apartment in Sydney, her husky laughter at his collection of hotel management war stories, the gusty appetite with which she consumed her meal.

And, yeah, he'd have missed *this* moment.

Defeated by her white-chocolate and raspberry dessert, she'd finally laid down spoon and fork and sighed with dreamy completion. And, yeah, he'd been watching her play with the stem of her champagne flute and thinking about another kind of completion, when she'd looked up at him and smiled. "How did you know this is what I needed?"

"Cheesecake?" he'd asked. "Or more champagne?"

"You know what I mean. Tonight. This afternoon. Everything. You've taken my mind off my problems, as you promised, and you've made me laugh when I thought I'd never laugh again. I haven't thanked you."

"I think you just did."

She studied him a moment, her eyes solemn. Her expression serious. "Just saying thank you seems inadequate."

"I'm enjoying your company."

"Me, too." Her smile flashed, soft and sincere. "This morning you said you were a good listener. You're not so bad in the talking field, either."

"I'm not just a pretty face."

"No." Their eyes met and her eyes flamed as if she, too, was thinking of other things. Other areas of expertise.

"You ready to find out what else I'm good at?" he asked slowly.

The pulse in her throat fluttered. Her smile faltered and her laugh sounded brittle and edgy with nerves. "Oh, I don't know that I'll ever be ready for that."

"No? There's an old saying my father liked to use." He stood and held out his hand, daring her to take it. Daring her to trust him. "Fortune favors the brave."

He didn't take her back to their suite, as Cat had anticipated when his fingers wrapped hers in the promise of startling heat and solid purpose. He took her by the hand and led her to the casino—not to one of the high-rollers' rooms with the other rich and famous and beautiful, but to the main floor and the endless raft of slot machines. Indulging her. Then rattling her by standing at her back and offering instruction close to her ear. Resting a casual hand on her shoulder. Engulfing the bare stretch of her back in the heat of his body.

She couldn't concentrate on the mindless roll of symbols and pictures before her eyes. Not when her body wanted nothing else but to turn and press hard against him. To bite his ear and say: *Enough. Let's go back to our room and see what you're really good at.*

It was better when the machine chomped her last credit and they moved to the roulette wheel…although that might have been due to their astonishing run of luck. Excited by the rattle of the wheel and the rush of color and the adrenaline hit when the ball dropped, she didn't even blink when he turned and pressed a kiss to her lips.

When he grinned and said, "Our luck's running hot, baby," she smiled right back.

"Must be the green dress."

"Nah," he drawled. "It's you."

If only it were, she thought, before she could stop herself. Then she excused herself that moment of whimsical dreaming by blaming the champagne and the touch of his hand on her back and the whole fantastical nature of this day.

A day out of time. A day out of reality. A day that would never be repeated.

Their number came up again and she laughed with a giddy lack of restraint at the pile of chips the croupier pushed their way. Except, at the end her laugh evolved into a giant yawn. Rafe, of course, noticed.

"You want to call it a night?" he asked.

Her stomach tightened, her pulse jittered, but she met his gaze with a reckless sense of what will be, will be. "I think I probably should before I pass out and you have to carry me home."

"Now that sounds like fun."

He put his arm around her as if he might actually follow through, and Cat panicked at the inglorious thought of him trying…and stumbling because she weighed more than this sexy green dress let on. "If you're carrying me," she said quickly, breathlessly, "then who's going to carry all our winnings?"

"You won it. You get to carry it."

"Me?" Cat shook her head. "Oh, no, I didn't. This is all yours."

"No," he said easily. "This night's all yours."

Stunned, head spinning faster and louder than the roulette wheel at their back, she stared into his face. He looked serious. He looked like he meant it. "I can't. You can't. No way."

"Think about it, Catriona. It's a lot of money. In your situation—"

"It's *your* money!"

Their eyes connected, clashed, and his flared with some kind of challenge. "Okay," he said softly. "Let's make this interesting."

Everything inside her tensed, stilled, focused on that dangerous glint in his eyes. "Interesting?"

"Let's up the ante."

Cat had to swallow and moisten her Nevada-dry mouth before she could get her throat and mouth to cooperate. "What do you propose?"

"One last spin. Red or black. All or nothing. If you win, you keep all the money. Enough to pay off your debts and some to spare."

"And if I lose?" Cat's voice was barely a whisper.

"You marry me. You have my baby. And I pay off your debts."

Eight

Afterward, Cat couldn't believe that she'd accepted such a crazy fantastical wager. That she'd calmly pushed all their chips onto black, before standing at the center of a hushed crowd watching the wheel spin and the numbers whirl and the colors slow from a gyrating blur to a distinguishable red-black-red-black sequence.

She hadn't thought he meant it. She hadn't believed he would go through with it. But then, she hadn't known that a person—two people, actually—could stroll right into the Marriage License Bureau and fill out the necessary paperwork for a wedding.

Little more than an hour after the fateful ball rattled to its resting place on red seven, she found herself married to the man at her side.

Rafferty Keane Carlisle. She hadn't even known his full name until they applied for that license. He was a virtual stranger, and he was her husband.

Somewhere between the wedding chapel and the hotel lobby, the molasses-thick stupor in Cat's mind stopped swirling long enough to let that detail seep in, along with all its ramifications. At the roulette table tonight, she'd won herself a husband. A rich husband who would pay off her debts so she could keep Corroboree.

A husband who wanted a baby conceived as soon as possible.

That particular ramification ambushed her completely as the elevator doors slid noiselessly shut, and the mirror-lined cubicle commenced its smooth ascent. Earlier she'd thought about sleeping with him, at least a dozen times during dinner alone. She'd decided that this night would probably end in his bed, but that had been part of the whole fantasy twenty-four hours. Part of the makeover, of licking her wounds, of rebounding from the Drew debacle and reasserting herself as a woman. Something to regret in the morning, and to walk away from once she returned to the real world.

But during that adrenaline- and champagne- and lust-fueled casino madness, she'd allowed fantasy and reality to collide. To connect. To join and meld and bond.

A wave of heat shadowed that thought. A rippling montage of bodies joining and melding and bonding in a tangle of Egyptian cotton sheets. She felt the heat in her cheeks and her eyes and the softened fullness of her lips, and she let her head drop a little, away from the telltale evidence in the mirror before her.

From the corner of her eye she could see his right hand tapping a lazy beat against the elevator wall, and she remembered the soft brush of those fingers in a dozen places, a dozen times. She remembered, and her pulse began to drum in time with his fingers.

Unable to watch any longer—not without taking that hand and drawing it to the achy heat of her body—she lifted her head and let it roll back against the cool, mirrored wall. For a second she closed her eyes and attempted to block out that insistent beat of desire with the image of their left hands joined by the celebrant. Left hands wearing the plain gold bands borrowed from the hotel concierge and about as disconnected from reality as this whole surreal night.

But that carefully constructed mental image faded, replaced by another. His hand drawing her into his body. His face blurring in and out of her dazed focus as he bent and pressed his lips to hers. *Go ahead and kiss the bride, now.* Heat washed through her veins, pooled sweet and liquid, low in her body.

She needed to think. They needed to talk before this went any further. Before this sexual energy took total possession of her mind as well as her body.

Restless, she rolled her shoulders. Shifted her feet. Their upper arms bumped and parted in what should have been a casual brush of contact, except it charged Cat with enough power to light up the whole Vegas strip.

Her eyes jolted open. A low, needy sound growled up from her throat. At first she thought it was in her mind, her own silent howl of protest because that one grazing brush of his jacket against her bare skin left her baying for more. But then their eyes met in the mirror with a hot, electric force that rocked her to her toes.

Oh, yes, she had groaned out loud. That knowledge was in his hot stare. It tugged tight in her belly and ached in her breasts.

Oh, yes, she wanted him. But somehow she'd imagined falling into bed with the Rafe from tonight's dinner, from the long conversations during their night on the plane, from the breakfast table at Corroboree. The man who'd lounged naked in her guest-room bathroom without batting an eyelid. The flirt with the knowing smile and the drawled lines that made her laugh or roll her eyes or fire back a cynical retort.

The man in the mirror was not that Rafe.

His eyes burned with a fierce flame. The lines of his classically hewn face were set with an intensity that both thrilled and terrified her.

And it struck her, in that long, drawn-out moment, that he'd barely spoken a word since that fateful moment in the casino. Nothing beyond the necessary instructions, as he took over and swept her along with an efficiency and purpose she'd not seen in him before. Up until now she'd been too dazed, too shocked, too brain-sluggish to work that all out.

Her heart beat slow and heavy in her chest. Pounding with the knowledge that she'd underestimated Rafe Carlisle. Pounding with the fear that she'd bitten off way more than she could chew.

The elevator chimed their floor, a brief rich peal that barely impacted on the tension inside the car. The tension inside Cat. "We're here," she said, surprising herself with the calm clarity of her voice. Yet she couldn't coax her limbs to move or force her gaze to disconnect from his.

"Finally."

And that one quietly uttered word propelled Rafe into action. Before she realized his purpose, he'd turned and ducked one arm under her thighs to swing her into his arms.

Her eyes widened as he carted her out of the elevator. "No, you can't. I'm too—"

"Too what, Mrs. Carlisle?" He stopped and met her startled eyes with a look of grim satisfaction.

Crikey. Mrs. Carlisle. That was her!

That whammy effectively wiped her mind clean of whatever she'd been about to say and a good lot else besides. He started striding toward their suite, and the combination of that motion and the wall of his body hard against hers joggled Cat's senses back to life.

She wrapped her arms around his neck and held on tight.

Her dangling legs brushed his hip and thigh, curling her toes with raw heat. One of her sexy new shoes fell from her arched foot, and she almost told him to leave it be. But he turned and dropped down on his haunches so quickly that her world tilted and spun.

"Put me down. I'm too heavy," she gasped as he came back up again, one delicate, glittery stiletto dangling from his hand. "You don't have to carry me."

"Yeah, I do. I have to carry you over the threshold. It's a tradition."

"I thought you said Alex was the old-fashioned one in your family. Since when have you worried about tradition?"

"Since I decided to marry you."

She huffed out a dubious breath. "So, about an hour, give or take? That hardly makes you an expert."

"An hour? What gives you that impression?" Stopped at the door to their suite, he looked long and hard into her eyes. "I made up my mind about you last week, baby. This wasn't a spur-of-the-moment decision."

Too much information? Admitted too soon?

As he extricated the key card from her itsy little nothing of a purse, Rafe suffered a moment's unease. She'd gone silent again, and he felt the stiffness of her body—a far different kind from his—against his chest and arms. Even through the intense buzz of arousal, he swore he could hear her mind ticking with questions. If he gave her half a chance, she'd launch a debate on the logic of what they'd just done. If he didn't keep her occupied, she might try to wangle another crazy handshake deal with him.

He wasn't about to give her *half* of half a chance. And once he got her inside, he intended to keep her very occupied.

The door swung open and he angled her through, swinging her with enough velocity that she gasped and caught hard at his shoulders and neck. Yeah, he liked the clutch of her fingers. The puff of her breath against his skin. But mostly he'd wanted to distract her from that thinking. From voicing the question he'd seen forming on her lush lips.

"I'm too big for this rubbish," she reprimanded. "You're lucky you haven't done yourself an injury!"

"Yeah, well, I've always considered myself a lucky bastard." He stopped spinning her and looked into her eyes. "And I've been particularly lucky with you."

Her eyes narrowed. "That roulette bet was only even money. A fifty-fifty chance, either way."

"True, but that's not what I meant." Luck had been on his side from the moment that storm sent him Catriona's way, and he'd caught one lucky break after another ever since. Her changing her mind. Finding the cowboy in Vegas. His impulsive challenge to up the ante.

"Then…what? And what did you mean about this not being spur-of-the-moment?"

Ignoring her questions, he started moving again, carrying her through the sitting room toward her bedroom.

"Stop." She pushed at his chest. "Put me down. We have to talk about this."

"Yeah, we do and we will. But not now. This is my wedding night, and the only thing I'm interested in discussing is how we're going to spend it." At the door he stopped and looked into her face. "And where. Is your bedroom okay or would you prefer we went to mine?"

Stunned eyes stared back into his.

"Yours, then." He nudged her door open with his shoulder. "I've been fantasizing about undressing you in this room all night."

He heard the soft explosion of her breath. "You didn't have to marry me to do that!"

Holding her tighter, he looked into her eyes and smiled. "I know. That's not why I married you."

"Then why did you?"

"Because you're going to be the mother of my baby."

The shock of that line registered deep in her eyes and resounded deep in Rafe's gut. The baby he'd only thought about as his mother's grandchild had tonight taken shape and sub-stance. A baby with Catriona's changeling eyes and calm strength and solid values.

"How can you say that?" She began to struggle again, this time with more determination. "I might not be able to get pregnant. I might not be able to carry a baby. Did you think about that?"

"I'm prepared to take my chances."

"Do you even *know* what those chances are?"

"Is there a reason you ask?" He carried her to the bed. Sat with her in his arms. "Something in your history I should know about?"

"No."

"Are you on any form of contraception?"

"No."

"Then why bring it up?"

All uptight and irritated, she clicked her tongue. "To illus-trate why this was such a dumb idea!"

"You get your debts paid off. How is that dumb?"

"From *your* point of view. Marrying me doesn't ensure you get this baby you need." Agitated, she started to wiggle in his lap, trying to extricate herself from his arms. "I don't understand why you had to go and marry me! I would have slept with you without a marriage license. I know that. You know that."

"Do I?" he asked evenly. "Because the way you're trying to get away from me isn't exactly filling me with confidence."

Somehow, in her struggles, she'd managed to wiggle her hip hard against him. She went still, and he watched her ex-pression change from flushed annoyance to flushed knowl-edge. Watched her eyes flash with heat and spirit. "From where I'm sitting you feel pretty damn full of confidence!"

"Him? Yeah, well, he's always confident."

"Yeah, well, I guess he has reason," she fired right back. "With all your talk of wedding night expectations!"

She was really something, his wife. Sharp, smart, straight. And from where he sat, Rafe could see a choice of two options. Kiss her into submission—his first and favorite option. Or give her a better explanation of his motivation... before kissing her into submission.

Readjusting her to a more comfortable—and less distracting—listening position, he sighed resignedly.

"Say we'd walked away from that wheel tonight. Say we'd come back here and I'd got very lucky and talked my way out of that handshake agreement." Her eyes widened as if she'd forgotten about the deal they'd struck on the plane. "Say I'd managed to talk you into letting me touch you, any way I wanted to, every way I wanted to. Say you'd stripped out of that sexy little dress and invited me into your bed and your body."

She swallowed. Rafe's gaze dropped to that convulsive movement and saw the flutter of pulse in her throat. Satisfaction beat hard in his blood as his gaze returned to hers.

"Would you have still felt the same when the champagne wore off? Would you have woken up beside me in the morning? Would you have stuck around long enough to make this baby I need?"

She didn't answer, but then she didn't have to. Rafe knew a one-night stand would not sit right with a woman like Catriona, not the morning after. Nor would the kind of affair that consisted of baby-sex without any commitment.

"That's why I married you, Catriona. To make a baby." Slowly, gently, he palmed the curve of her stomach where that baby might one day grow. Felt the soft shiver of reaction in her flesh and saw it reflected in her eyes. "To do it right."

"You can't know I'm the right woman." That same shiver roughened the edges of her voice. "You don't know me. I don't know you."

"What do you want to know?"

"I don't know. Something. Anything. I didn't even know your full name." Rattled, edgy, her words came out in a rush. "I thought it might be Rafael."

"I'm Rafferty after my Gaelic grandfather—my mother's father. My brother Alex couldn't get the whole mouthful out when he was a tot, so he shortened it to Rafe. It stuck."

"See? I didn't know that. The Gaelic thing, I mean. You look Mediterranean."

"Courtesy of my birth father," he said shortly. He didn't share his background with many people, but Catriona had a right to know. This much at least. "My mother's Irish, though. Her name was Maura Keane."

"Your second name," she said softly. And that was enough, Rafe decided. Time to change the subject. He stroked the length of her arm, up and down, then paused at her shoulder. Touching the fabric of her dress with one fingertip. "My favorite color is green."

Her breath hitched when, with that one fingertip, he traced the draping folds of fabric down to her breast. He stopped. Leaned closer and sniffed the warm scent at her throat.

"My favorite scent is you."

She laughed, a husky sound of surprise that smoked through his blood and settled in his groin. "Whatever I smell like isn't me. It's a fancy day spa. It's lotions and potions."

Nuzzling closer, he inhaled again, then leaned back and met her eyes. "No, that's you...wife."

Her eyes darkened dramatically, and Rafe smiled with a satisfaction just as deep, just as dark, just as dramatic.

"My turn to find out about you," he said. "What's the origin of your name, Catriona?"

"I don't know."

"Okay...so, what's your favorite color?"

"I don't have one."

"Yeah, you do. Come on, own up."

"Sunset," she relented, after a short pause. "Pink and orange and indigo all strung together in a perfect outback sunset."

"Favorite scent?"

"Peaches. Fresh picked, ripe, juicy. We used to—" She

stopped suddenly, gave a dismissive shrug of one shoulder. "Just…peaches."

Rafe pressed his lips to that shoulder. Smooth. Warm. Sweet as a fresh-picked peach. "Come on," he coaxed. "You used to…?"

"We had an orchard. At Corroboree."

He remembered. An orchard that was now a graveyard of gray-timber and naked boughs. "And…?"

"If it didn't rain we didn't get fruit, but when we did…" She sighed, a soft sensual memory as her mouth curved into a smile. "You know when you take that first bite and the juice oozes out between your fingers and sweetness fills your nostrils…? That's my favorite scent."

Rafe kissed her then, while her eyes were soft and dreamy, while her lips were parted and curved with the contemplation of sweet and succulent fruit. Face cupped between his hands, his thumbs stroked the warm silk of her cheeks and along her jaw. He kissed her slowly, thoroughly, savoring the thought of peach juice on her lips, her tongue, her skin.

Gently he nipped at her bottom lip, and she opened to him with a sigh, a yielding that hummed in his throat with satisfaction. He licked into her mouth and felt a tremor run through her body. Hunger gripped his, not raw and primal like in the elevator, but rich and earthy and unexpectedly sweet.

Like the fruit she'd described; like Catriona, the woman. His wife.

Her arms settled heavily on his shoulders; the tips of her fingers traced a slow pattern against the back of his neck. And when he changed the angle of the kiss, she shifted in his lap, angling closer to his body. Pressing more firmly against his arousal while she kissed him back with her eyes fixed on his with drowsy-eyed passion.

And when he eased back slightly, drawing out of that long, lazy, kiss, she followed. Kissing the corners of his mouth. His chin. The line of his jaw. While her hands shaped his face and sifted through his hair.

Rafe laughed softly. Shook his head a little.

"What?" she breathed, hot against his skin. Hot against his thighs and areas in between.

"You."

"What about me?"

"I didn't expect you to be so…" He hesitated over word choice.

"Easy?"

"Willing," he corrected.

"Oh, I think you knew I'd be willing before we left this room tonight. You knew when I first suggested we stay in."

"Yet you decided to go out. Were you being contrary or cautious?"

She smiled, slow, sexy, mysterious. "What do you think?"

"I think I married a phony." Narrow-eyed he looked at her a second and then he gathered up her hair, masses of curls that he fisted in one hand. "I thought I'd have to work extrahard." With his free hand he started to undo the halter neck of her dress. "That I'd have to take this real slow."

"And?"

The question came out on a husk of breath as the last button came undone. As the fabric slipped from Cat's neck.

"And I don't know if slow is going to work." His fingers gathered the material, stroked it over her breasts, briefly teased her taut nipples, then were gone. The dress pooled at her waist. His eyes met hers. Flames licked and burned. "What do you like, wife? Fast or slow?"

Cat's heart beat hard, knocking her ribs with the same deep sultry note as his voice. He demonstrated *slow* with the backs of his fingers, barely grazing her skin as they trailed upward over her ribs. She sucked in a breath, closed her eyes and waited, breath held, waited and willed him to keep going. To touch the breasts that grew tight and heavy with longing.

He didn't.

Those taunting fingers trailed back down to her waist. "That isn't slow," she groaned. "That's torture."

But when she opened her eyes, his were fixed on her breasts, on that artfully created cleavage that fleshed over the half cups of sheer white fabric. Heat traced the line of his cheekbones. Heat burned in the eyes he slowly raised to hers. His hands palmed her ribs, pressed up against the undersides of her aching breasts. "You prefer fast?"

"I prefer…efficiency. I don't like wasting time."

"Some things are meant to take longer." A slow finger traced the line where lace met flesh. "To draw out the pleasure."

Cat wasn't sure how much more drawing out she could stand. Or how much of Rafe Carlisle's expert brand of pleasure. For a hint of a second she revisited that moment in the elevator, that stab of fear, of knowing she'd bitten off more than she could chew.

But then his thumbs stroked over her nipples, and the spear of desire low in her belly and hot between her legs razed everything from her brain. Her breath hitched and caught as his head dipped and he brushed his whisker-rough cheek against the flesh that pushed out of her bra. That same breath rushed from her lungs in a long, low sound of wanting as he turned his head and kissed her sensitized flesh.

With his lips, with his tongue, with his teeth.

He laved her nipple through the sheer material of her bra, and she was so lost in the intensity of sensation, she didn't notice his hands at her back. Didn't register the clever flick of his fingers until the hooks she'd taken minutes to fasten gave effortlessly. Through the sensual pall that expertise vaguely registered. A dull glimmer of unease because he'd undone more kinds of bras that she'd ever seen.

But then his hands palmed her naked breasts and he made a guttural sound of arousal that echoed through her whole body.

With single-minded concentration, he circled each nipple

with his fingertips. Played the aching tips with the pad of his thumb. Then with a soft grunt that was unabashedly male, unashamedly turned on, he lowered his head and sucked her deep into his mouth.

And, oh, man, he was just as skillful with his tongue on her nipples as when he'd kissed her mouth. Just as attentive. Just as big a tease.

She couldn't sit still. She couldn't stand her lack of participation. Fingers twined in his hair, she dragged his head away and up and their mouths met at exactly the right angle, with moist heat and erotic promise. They kissed, strong and hot and bold, and her body took on the rhythm of his mouth, the rhythm of sex.

It wasn't enough.

Without breaking the hot, wet contact of mouths and lips and tongues, she leaned her hands and her weight on his shoulders while she rose from his lap and resettled herself straddling his hard thighs. Their mouths parted but their gazes locked and held as his hands cupped her hips, molded her bottom and rocked her, slowly, deliberately, against the thick bulge of his erection.

"One of us is wearing too many clothes."

He leaned forward and blew warm air over her exposed nipples. "I gather that's not you."

For a second she could do nothing but ride the intense wave of pleasure generated at both breasts and her female core. Then she wiggled back a few inches.

"Quick on the uptake," she murmured, "for one so slow on the uptake."

"Are you complaining?"

"Maybe." With deliberate purpose she shifted her hands from his shoulders to his chest. Started unbuttoning his shirt. "Be warned. I'm all about efficiency."

"You don't want my help, then?"

"No." She finished the buttons, then looked into his eyes

as she tugged the shirt free of his trousers. "You are altogether too slow."

His laugh was thick and turned on. "You are altogether too sexy."

Cat pushed both his jacket and shirt from his shoulders. "You find my efficiency sexy?"

The last word hitched and hissed as he slid his hands under her dress and palmed her thighs. "I'm finding pretty much everything about you sexy, wife."

Oh, she loved how he said that. *Wife*. The word drummed in her blood as his thumbs stroked a sinuous path up her inner thighs. Built to a sweet pressure point of pleasure when he touched her through her panties.

He knew how to scintillate her with a word or a touch. He knew every sweet, delicious secret of a woman's body. He knew every smooth ego-seducing line.

And Cat knew why. He was Rafe Carlisle. Prince of the bedroom.

She held no illusions about what he was doing here on her bed, sliding the dress up her body, urging her to lift her arms so he could pull it all the way free. She was his wife—perhaps because he'd been born of a single mother, perhaps for his mother's sake—but only because it suited him. For as long as it suited him.

He tossed the dress behind her, on the floor, and she felt a sharp frisson of foreboding.

"That's a very expensive dress to treat so carelessly."

"I bought it," he told her. Hands spanning her waist. Head dipping to her breasts again. "I can treat it however I want."

And me? she wanted to ask. *Now you've bought me, will you treat me the same? Discard me as easily?*

But then his mouth closed over her nipple, and her back arched with a pull of desire that obliterated her disquiet. As she took pleasure from his expertise, as he rolled her from his lap onto the bed and slid her panties down her legs, she refused to think about how he'd grown so clever. How he knew exactly how to touch her, how long to tease her, how to use his tongue so ruthlessly.

When that clever tongue brought her to an abrupt, unexpected climax, he smiled with supreme masculine pride. "Nice, but too fast."

"Efficient," she retorted, her voice thick and slumberous, as she sagged back onto the bed. "Sufficient."

"Hardly." He finished undressing himself, and she prolonged her pleasure by watching. He let her. He stood before her, as spectacularly beautiful as she remembered from that morning in her guest room.

More so, with his assets at full look-at-me attention.

"I have condoms if you want."

She rolled her gaze from belly height to his face. Found his eyes narrowed and his eyes glittering with blatant arousal. Cat blinked, trying to gather her wits. "Condoms?"

"Protection. I've always used them. *Always*. But I had tests when this clause came up. For your reassurance."

"You had tests." To reassure *her* about unprotected sex. She frowned. "What about me?"

"Need I worry?"

"I've only had one lover." Drew, who was paranoid about an unexpected pregnancy screwing with his plans to make world champion. Maybe he'd had a premonition of what lay ahead. "He used condoms. He did with me, leastways."

And maybe this wasn't the time to be making cracks about Drew and the baby he clearly hadn't planned on making with his new girlfriend. Not the time to recall how much it had hurt, seeing the man you thought you loved, whom you wanted to spend the rest of your life with, shudder with dread at the thought of getting you pregnant.

Rafe still hadn't moved. His expression was guarded. His voice quiet and deliberate when he asked, "So, Catriona." Not *wife,* but *Catriona.* "Do we start now?"

Cat's stomach lurched as their gazes locked. "Perhaps you should have asked before we signed that marriage license."

"When you signed it," he said, "I took it as your binding word."

Not just that she would marry him, but that she would try to conceive his baby. Her heart thundered. Her world spun on its axis with the enormity of what she had done. And all she hadn't considered.

"Well, Catriona?"

A baby in return for saving Corroboree. Rafe's baby, yes, but also hers. A McConnell to carry on her family tradition, as her father had wanted. As she silently promised him, every time she stood at his grave, every time she stood under the unforgiving western sky and faced another tough season, another year of uncertainty.

She exhaled slowly, and her heart steadied to a dull, thick beat.

"Okay," she said finally. Then stronger, echoing the beat of her heart. "Yes. We start now."

Nine

Rafe knelt on the mattress beside the sexy sprawl of her naked body. "Are you sure, Catriona?"

She took a long time to answer. A long time while he took in the spill of her hair and the loose abandonment of her limbs. A hellishly long time with the scent of her desire in his senses and her eyes fixed low and still on his body.

Impatience growled through his blood, but Rafe waited.

He'd played on her vulnerabilities when he challenged her with the wager. He'd crowded her when she needed time to think, coerced her with the win-win nature of the deal, coaxed her with all she stood to win even if she lost that last spin. And then he'd rushed her to the altar before her head stopped spinning.

Suddenly he couldn't rush her any further. He wanted her willing now and tomorrow and the next day back home in Sydney. He wanted her willing for as long as he wanted her, however long that might be.

"You know there's no going back."

Her lids fluttered for an instant as if his words had scraped a nerve. But her redirected gaze met his with the openness that had attracted him to her from the very start. No coyness, no chicanery, just Catriona about to tell it like it was. "I said yes to not using a condom. That doesn't mean I'll fall pregnant. That's not something you or I can control."

"Is this a good time?"

"We're both naked." Her gaze slid back to the part of him that wasn't used to being naked in this situation. "I'd say that makes it as good a time as any."

Rafe laughed, short and gruff, as he stretched out beside her on the rich cream sheets. His knee brushed against the side of her thigh, accidentally the first time. Deliberately the second. He propped himself on an elbow so he could look down into her face. "I meant a good time in your cycle. For conception."

Her nostrils flared and her eyes darkened and jittered. Rafe felt it, too—the slam of reaction that was more than lust. Unsettling, unusual, uncomfortable.

"I'm not sure. Maybe." She shifted restlessly. One hand lifted, then dropped back against the bed. "I hate talking about this. I feel…"

Her voice trailed off as if she couldn't find the right word. Rafe sympathized. Easy to describe the hard tension in his groin. Not so easy to identify the weight bearing down on his chest.

"Can we forget about the conception part?" Direct as always, but her voice sounded raw and edgy. "Can we just do this?"

Now was the time to grin and tease her. To regain that sexy byplay of before by framing some lazy comeback about how he never "just did it." Except the smile wasn't happening and the line sounded superficial and shallow—the kind he'd drag up in any situation, for any woman.

This wasn't any woman. This was his wife gazing up at him, moistening her lips with apprehension. His wife whose hand shifted nervously against the sheet at his side.

And suddenly, intensely, he wanted those eyes, those lips, those hands on him.

"I think we'll get to that," he said slowly, heart drumming in his ears, desire throbbing in his blood. "But first I'd like you to touch me."

"Where?"

"Wherever you want."

She swallowed. "How?"

"That depends on where." Leaning closer he blew softly against her breast. A shiver of reaction rippled through her skin, traveled the length of her arm until her fingers curled into her palm. "Some places require a whisper." He leaned down and licked the skin at the inside of her elbow. Heard the change in her breathing. "Others demand a kiss." Lower still, he stroked the length of her thigh until her toes curled and her feet flexed. "And some require a firm hand." He continued that long, slow, firm caress all the way back up her body until he was gazing into her eyes.

Dark, turned on, not apprehensive anymore.

Satisfaction, fierce and intense, gripped Rafe where he lived. He watched her ease up onto her elbows to blow a whisper of sultry breath against his lips. Watched her follow him down to the mattress so she could press her tongue to his nipple.

"How am I doing so far?" she asked.

"Very efficient. Very—" Air hissed through his teeth as she stroked her hand down his body, across the tightly held muscles of his abdomen, skimming the hair at its base with her fingertips. Whatever he'd been about to say was gone. Every red blood cell had rushed from his brain as she followed her hand with her mouth, tracing the play of muscles in his belly with her lips and her tongue.

Teasing him for way too long before finally—*finally*—she took his steely length in her hand.

The dark curtain of her hair obstructed his view as it swung and dragged across his taut belly, his flexed thighs and that giant pulsing scream of need in between. She squeezed gently and he jammed his eyes shut. Fisted his fingers in the sheet as her thumb coasted over the head and almost brought him undone. Then she leaned down and breathed, a hot wash of breath against the moisture she'd incited, and the tentative touch of her tongue caused a bolt of sensation that almost lifted him off the mattress.

Her head came up with a start. "Not so good?"

Rafe couldn't stand that flash of uncertainty in her expression, any more than he could stand the torture of her touch.

He slid his hands up the inside of her arms, stretching them over her head, as he rolled her onto her back and followed. Her eyes widened, heat flushed her cheeks as he settled between her legs, as he instantly found the perfect position.

"Too damn good," he growled into her mouth as he kissed her. As she wrapped her legs around his hips and pressed up against him, inviting him into the moist heat of her body. *Too damn good,* he repeated silently, easing his way into that exquisite heat, holding back the urge to go faster. To pull back and just bury himself. Deep. Hard.

That urgency clamored in his blood and tightened in his lungs until he had to end the kiss, to breathe, to press his face into the side of her throat to escape the passionate intensity of her expression.

"That does feel pretty damn good," she whispered and *that* was almost too much. A simple, straight comment that struck him with the same erotic force as the tight clasp of her body closing around him, drawing him deeper, sinking him into her core.

Not just pretty damn good but pretty damn perfect. Pretty damn unforgettable. That's what he wanted for this first time. He wanted to obliterate everything from her sensual memory except him. He wanted momentous where in the past, with every other woman, every other lover, he'd only wanted to satisfy. And for a brief instant of still and silent intensity, their eyes locked and it stunned him how much he wanted…and how much that wanting shook him up.

Sweat beaded on his brow, traced the line of his backbone as he slowly started to move, as he willed himself to set the same torturously slow rhythm he'd used hundreds of times before. He knew how to please a woman, how to drive her wild, how to hit every sweet spot.

How could this time feel infinitely sweeter…more intense…and so damn different?

Because it's only your naked flesh moving in hers, with no barrier and nothing to diminish the pleasure. Because of the expression in her eyes, the soft humming noise in her throat, the grip of her fingers as her hands fluttered under yours.

Because this is Catriona, your wife.

And he couldn't hold back any longer. He released her hands, freed his so he could palm the stretch of her body beneath his, so he could reach between them, between her soft folds to find the supersensitive spot and stroke it with sure pressure.

So he could watch the explosion of heat in her eyes, so he could know that he'd given her the same pleasure that he felt building as he drove harder, deeper, stronger. As he flexed his hips with a last full thrust and let his release come, more powerful than he'd imagined possible, a wild spasm that rocked through his body and reflected in the splintered depths of her eyes as she came again, and he spilled himself deep within her body.

Cat woke slowly. The smile came easily to her lips, the stretch not so easily to her shattered body, and her mind took another ten minutes to get within cooee of cognizance.

Her first random thought was, *Crikey, it's bright!* Eyes squinted against that brightness, she rolled onto her side and checked the bedside clock.

For several ticks, the time displayed made no sense. It couldn't be after ten. She never slept this late, even on holidays.

But she had, and the reason why struck suddenly and with devastating force.

Because of a very late night…a very late *wedding* night.

Her heart thumped loudly in the morning silence. She was alone, she knew, even before she rolled her head on the pillow and inspected the vast stretch of her king-size bed. Even before she lifted up on her elbows and listened to the enveloping quiet that extended beyond her bedroom door.

But she hadn't dreamed up amazing wedding-night sex in her jet-lagged sleep. With her left thumb she touched the gold band on her ring finger. A borrowed wedding band, and that fact chimed, loud and significant, through Cat's sluggish consciousness.

Borrowed because of the whole rushed nature of the event. She barely remembered the moment when he put it on her finger. She barely recalled the vows or where they'd taken them.

How could she be married? How could she have a husband?

How could she have slept so long and so soundly that she didn't even know if he had stayed in her bed or retired to his own? She hadn't heard him leave…but then she didn't recall anything much of afterward. The incredible force of her last climax, the relaxed weight of his body on hers, stroking the cooling sweat over the long planes of his back. Sifting her fingers through his hair and smiling against his throat when he'd murmured something about waking him when she was ready to "just do it" again.

She'd probably fallen asleep with him still there within her arms. Still in her body.

Heat crept through her veins, remembering. Regret stole through her mind, remembering how she hadn't woken him again.

Would he have expected that? Would he have expected

more from her than that once? More times, more variety, more participation? More—

She cut herself off with a sharp mental slap. Rafe Carlisle's critique of her sexual performance didn't matter. Rafe Carlisle as her husband did. She'd married him to regain control of Corroboree, to secure its future in her family. Her hand lifted and paused above her lower abdomen as a whispery flutter of hope stole through her body.

Hope that she could secure that future with a baby…a baby he also needed.

Except they had a lot to work out, to get straight, before any baby came along, and this time Cat would not trust a handshake deal. She'd married Rafe for his money, and he needed to protect his interests as much as she did. With a written contract.

She needed to find him and get this sorted out.

That decision to act sat well with Cat—much better than lying in bed with the morning half-gone. She tossed the bedcovers aside, and—despite the obvious emptiness of the suite—made a quick dash for the closet and the hotel robe inside. The Rafe Carlisles of this world could be as content and arrogant as they liked with their nakedness. The Catriona McConnells needed their robes.

What about the Catriona Carlisles?

That out-of-nowhere thought stopped her short, one hand on the closet door. She sucked in a deep breath—so deep it turned her slightly dizzy. But she gathered herself and shook her head and uttered a grim "No way."

Marrying him didn't include taking his name. She didn't want that kind of link. She didn't want anything beyond what he'd promised in the casino. Not even great, toe-curling, spine-tingling, world-altering sex. She didn't want anything she would miss once he was gone. She wanted—

"Blast."

With a pained grimace she eyed the clothes in the closet—

the ones Bridget had ordered on her behalf after yesterday's shopping extravaganza. She'd forgotten all about returning them; she'd forgotten about everything sensible and practical from the moment he appeared in her doorway.

Well, today was another day, and Bridget could take the clothes back.

Cat slid the robe from its hanger and pulled it on. And when she turned, heading for the bathroom, her eyes snagged on the one dress that wouldn't be going back to the store. The green fabric hung limply from the edge of the chaise, where it must have caught when he tossed it so glibly. A frisson of déjà vu crawled over her skin, a reprisal of that moment in the night when she'd thought about him discarding her.

The morning after, for example.

"Don't be so silly." Impatient with herself, she picked up the dress and flung it into the closet, then jammed the door shut. He'd probably gone to do the business that brought him to Vegas. She didn't expect his attention. She didn't want a big-deal morning after. She was practical, capable, independent Cat McConnell. After her shower, she would find Bridget and arrange to have the clothes returned. The ring, she supposed, would have to go back to the concierge, as well.

Twisting it on her finger, she realized it felt tight. Too tight. She lifted her hand and studied her fingers. They looked a bit swollen. Her feet felt the same, no doubt from the flying and not enough exercise.

Okay, so after her shower, and after she found Bridget, she would go for a long walk. Find a shop that sold cheap and comfortable footwear.

Their flight home from L.A. wasn't until tonight. She had plenty of time, time she would put to good use walking and thinking through what terms to include in their contract.

Rafe had gone downstairs to the jewelers on an impulse. Lying beside her in the bed watching her sleep, fighting the desire to wake her the same way he'd put her into such a sound sleep, he'd caught sight of the ring on her finger. And the beat of desire in his veins changed in nature. Suddenly he'd wanted to wake her with more than a platinum-strength erection. He wanted to surprise her with a ring, her own ring, a symbol of last night's significance.

He hadn't counted on being away long. He hadn't counted on the decision of which stone, which setting, which ring, proving so damn difficult. He'd chosen jewelry for women on countless occasions, but this was different. He wanted it to be special. Unique. A gift she would accept from him without the arguments of yesterday over the clothes.

In the end he couldn't decide, and that sat uneasily on his shoulders as he made the return trip. So did an unfamiliar tension over the gift he *had* bought—a diamond necklace he'd selected because he liked the idea of giving her everything pretty and missing from her hard and frugal life. Because he liked the idea of sliding the cool stones around her neck while she lay naked and sleeping in her bed. Anticipation settled the nervous churn in his belly as he thought about stripping off and slipping into her bed and spending the rest of the day warming them up.

When he opened the door to an empty suite, the swoop of disappointment was intense. But as he walked from room to room looking for a note—a note she apparently hadn't left— his mood shifted from disappointment to discontent. Logic suggested she'd gone for a walk, maybe even looking for him, and that she would be back soon.

He gave her ten minutes.

Then he called the floor concierge and discovered that, yes, she had gone out. But only after searching out Bridget with a request to return the clothes. That rankled. So did her continuing absence past midday, especially when his speculation over her whereabouts turned to Drew Samuels.

Prowling the sitting room, he tossed up whether to call

and ask the cowboy if he'd happened to have seen his wife today. And that turned his mood downright dirty. Not a good time for her to return, but that's when the door opened.

She didn't see him until she'd closed it behind her and crossed the entry foyer. Then she came to an abrupt halt, eyes wide with surprise when they lit on his still figure across the room. If he'd thought the sight of her, home and obviously unharmed, would ease the moody tension in his gut, then he'd been wrong. Dead wrong.

"Bridget said you were looking for me earlier," she said, recovering quickly, "but I thought you'd have gone out again by now."

He could have asked why the hell she'd have thought that, but he was too busy taking in her outfit. *Her* jeans, *her* shirt. A couple of generic plastic bags hung from her hand and slapped softly against her leg as she skirted the dining table into the sitting area.

"You saw Bridget? Was that to check if she'd returned the clothes I bought for you?"

Her eyes narrowed a fraction, probably in response to the frosty tone of his voice. "She saw me by chance, actually. Down in the lobby. Is something the matter?"

Where did he start? Rafe wasn't used to feeling so out of sorts, so close to losing his cool. So rattled by the irrationality of his mood. She was back, right? She'd come to no harm. So, why couldn't he just leave it? Why couldn't he concede that nothing was wrong except his pride over the clothes issue.

And, okay, some justifiable concern over her absence.

"I didn't know where you were," he said tightly. "I've been cooling my heels here, waiting for you to get back."

"I thought you'd be a while dealing with your business."

"My business?"

She paused behind one of the crimson velvet sofas. A wary frown shadowed her eyes as they connected with his. "I assumed that's where you went this morning. To do whatever business brought you here to Vegas."

"I did that last night, Catriona." His gaze dropped to her hand—the *naked* hand—resting on the back of the sofa. He felt every muscle bunch with tension. "Where's your ring?"

"My hands are swollen. I had to take it off."

Rafe couldn't argue with that. He didn't like himself for wanting to argue, for wanting some kind of aggression that was completely foreign and over the top. And he was so caught up in the confusion of his own responses that it took him a long moment to twig to her stillness. To the cooling narrowness of her gaze.

"Was I your business in Vegas, then?" she asked slowly. But she didn't wait for an answer. She gave a slight shake of her head, as if she should have known all along. "All that rubbish about needing to pay me back for getting you out of that plane and taking you in—"

"That wasn't rubbish, Catriona."

"But you brought me here to Vegas meaning to marry me? That was your business?"

"If you put it like that…" Rafe shrugged. "Yes."

"Then don't you think we should have been a little more businesslike? Don't you think we should have ironed a few things out *before* we swapped wedding rings?"

"Things?"

"Terms. Conditions."

"I thought we agreed to our terms last night. I'll pay off your debts. You'll have my baby."

"That's it?" Her voice rose on a note of disbelief. "Don't you think that's a bit sketchy on detail?"

"What do you need to know, Catriona? I'll pay you a monthly allowance, plus wages for a nanny and whatever help you need to run your station."

"Help? What help?"

"A stationhand. Any extra—"

"I don't need a stationhand. I can do my own work. I like it that way!"

"I'm sure you do." Eyes narrowed, Rafe met her mulish expression with unflinching directness. "But what about when you're pregnant? When your belly is way out here, and you can't lift a bale of hay or ride a horse. What about when you're feeding the baby and—"

"Okay, I get your point," she cut in, her voice as tight as hay wire. "But that's a case of *if* I get pregnant. *If* I have a baby."

"That's why I married you."

"In case I'd forgotten?"

Her eyes glittered with more than irritation, more than mulish pride, but in his current mood that's all Rafe wanted to see. "I just wanted to make sure," he drawled, "that we'd got that condition clear."

"Hard not to, given last night."

"Are you complaining?" he asked, deadly soft. "Because I didn't hear you complaining last night. I heard you moaning. I heard—"

"I didn't mean your sexual prowess. I wouldn't be fooling anyone if I complained about that!"

Rafe's gaze narrowed. "Now, why doesn't that sound like a compliment?"

"I'm sure you've heard every compliment I could come up with a hundred times before."

"How do you figure that, Catriona?"

"I figure that because you've likely slept with half the women in Sydney!"

"That many? Just as well I did the blood tests, then!"

Their gazes clashed, blazing with the anger of their exchange and with the knowledge of all they'd shared in the night. "Just as well I'm a sucker," Cat all but hissed after that searing second, "and took your word for it!"

Something glinted hard and sharp in his eyes. Anger? Hurt? Disbelief? Before she could pin it down, he turned and stalked away. He stopped by the piano, the taut lines of his body reflected in the highly polished wood. Then he hit a couple of keys, a delicate tinkling of sound at odds with the stark atmosphere.

At odds with the harsh note of laughter that escaped his throat as he turned back to face her. "Do you really think I'd have lied to you about that?"

Cat shook her head. Expelled a long breath and with it a piece of her white-hot outrage. "I shouldn't have said that. It was uncalled for. I'm sorry if I hurt you."

"You didn't hurt me, Catriona. You disappointed me."

She deserved that. She'd disappointed herself by giving in to the temptation to read up on him on the Internet. And she'd disappointed herself again, just now, by allowing her emotions to derail and overturn a discussion that deserved better.

Inhaling deeply, she concentrated on steadying the churn in her stomach. The uneasy knowledge that she might not be able to get this discussion back on track. But she had to try.

"You mentioned a nanny. For after—*if* I have a baby. Does that mean the baby will live with me?"

"If that's what you want. Yes."

"Of course that's what I want," she said quickly. "But what about you? You're the one who needs the baby. Won't you want to raise your child as a Carlisle? Won't you want to—"

"I'm having this baby because I have to, Catriona, not because I see myself as father material."

"You won't want to be part of his upbringing?" Cat's heart was beating hard. "You don't want custody?"

"While we're married, that won't be an issue."

While they were married—what did he mean by that? Cat moistened her dry mouth. "What kind of marriage are we talking about?"

"The kind where we both keep our independence. That's what you want, right?"

"Yes," she agreed cautiously. "But won't that make it a little hard to have that baby? If I'm living at Corroboree and you're in Sydney?"

"That's the arrangement after we conceive."

Her heart skittered with a panicky sense of foreboding. "And until then…? You can't expect me to live with you in Sydney."

"Why not?"

Why not? *Why not?* "I hate the city. It makes me crazy." Agitated, she lifted her arms, shopping bags and all, then let them drop again. "You didn't mention living in the city when we cut this deal."

"True." Hands in pockets, he leaned negligently against the piano and appeared to consider this. "We need to arrange a compromise."

"What kind of a compromise?"

"You'll stay with me one week a month, act as my wife."

"I don't know how to act as your wife."

Slowly he straightened, eyes glittering with a different kind of heat. "You did fine last night."

"That was sex, Rafe. I don't imagine you want that twenty-four hours a day."

"Don't you?"

Cat's heart danced a tango beat of fear and anticipation as he started to move closer. Blast it. She didn't want to back away. But she didn't trust him, either—him or the heat drifting through her blood and seeping into her skin.

One week a month, in his bed, trying to conceive his baby.

He stopped in front of her, and she forced herself to lift her chin and meet his gaze. To keep this conversation about what mattered. "If I were to stay with you—what else would you expect of me? Do I have to cook? Clean?"

"I have a housekeeper," he said coolly, while his eyes sparked with heat. "I didn't marry you to cook and clean. I married you to be in my bed."

"One week a month, until I conceive. Will that be in the contract?"

"Contract?"

"Yes. I want all the terms and conditions spelled out in a written contract. And there should be something like a pre-nuptial agreement, too."

His eyes narrowed momentarily, then he laughed. Not his usual smooth, silky sound of amusement, not even the earlier harsh sound of disbelief, but a low, edgy sound that snaked through Cat's senses. "What? You don't trust me not to take your station away from you?"

"I mean to protect you. All *your* wealth. When this marriage ends, I don't want anything of yours."

"Anything?" he repeated, dangerously soft.

"Anything other than what we've agreed upon. I don't want anything else from you."

"You've made that abundantly clear, Catriona." Eyes cooler than she'd ever seen them drifted over her, taking in her clothes and lingering on her naked left hand. "Anything else you've failed to drum into me? Anything you think I may have missed?"

No way could she back down from that look of cool disdain. No way could she back away from the challenge in his voice. "There is one thing." She lifted her chin. "I won't sleep with you again until the contract is drawn up and approved."

He stared back at her for a long time while her heart beat hard and high in her throat. A long time while her stomach churned because she could not tell what he was thinking. Too long for her not to point out the deal they'd made on the plane coming to America.

"You promised it would always be my call, Rafe. That you would back off whenever I said so."

"If that's what you want, Catriona." Expression flat, eyes cool, he started to turn away. "I've never imposed myself on any woman. I'm not about to start now."

Ten

A written contract and no sex until it was drawn up, approved and signed.

Not the outcome Rafe wanted for himself or needed for the sake of the will clause. The real bitch of it was how he'd let it get to him for a good two hours after he strolled out of their hotel suite. Yeah, he'd strolled out of there just as coolly as he'd agreed to her terms.

His smarting ego wouldn't let him show how much her lack of trust affected him.

He'd strolled out of the suite and right on down to the hotel casino where he'd done something he hadn't done in close to ten years. He gambled indiscriminately. He lost badly. And he didn't have anyone to blame but his own stupid self.

The money didn't matter. Losing did. He hated the whole concept of loss, and today had to be a landmark day of failure. He'd not only lost at the tables, but he'd lost the exchange of words with Catriona and—worse even than that—he'd lost his cool.

Rafe Carlisle, legend at laidback, king of nonchalant, had got his ego all in a twist because Catriona hadn't played his game his way. Afterward he'd sulked like a kid following a tantrum.

And wasn't that the perfect analogy for his behavior today?

Outside the casino Rafe shook his head in self-disgust. It was his own damn fault for not sorting out the details beforehand. Truth was, he didn't altogether blame Catriona for her stance. She'd been burned in a handshake deal with neighbors she'd known all her life. Friends she'd trusted.

If he'd played his cards right, he would have conceded whatever points she wanted, negotiated a few perks of his own, and parleyed his way right back into her bedroom. Right now she'd be naked except for a cool handful of diamonds around her flushed and sweat-dampened throat.

Rafe patted his jacket pocket where the jewelry box rested. He could go upstairs and present them to her now, along with a bunch of exotic orchids and the world's smoothest apology. But his male pride balked at being set on its bruised backside again today. She could do that, his wife, if he let her. The way she'd done with that crack about other women.

Hell, if he'd slept with a tenth of the women the gossip magazines claimed, there'd be a certain part of him worn-out by now.

No, Rafe wasn't about to present his wife with another chance at putting him down. She wanted a written agreement, and that's what she would get. No pleading, no asking, no cajoling in between.

A contract signed and sealed, and then she would be in his bed. Honoring her side of the deal.

They flew to L.A. late that evening, then met their flight home to Sydney. Over dinner Rafe took the opportunity to talk through Catriona's terms and conditions, making sure they agreed on all the salient points. It was all very cool and civilized, and Rafe hated that fake cordiality almost as much as their earlier confrontation.

Almost.

When they were done eating and conciliating, she politely excused herself, donned headphones and engrossed herself— apparently—in a movie. Rafe swallowed his irritation and muttered, "Don't mind me. I can entertain myself."

But then, watching the nervy flick of her thumbs against middle fingers, he recalled her uneasiness about flying on the trip over and he reached across the dividing console for her hand. She shook her head and mouthed, "No, I'm all right," and he shucked off her rejection with a lazy shrug.

He didn't bother her again.

He made some calls home, checking in with his secretary, booking an early appointment with his lawyer, calling his downstairs neighbor to let her know he'd be back in the morning. Milla had a key so she could look after the cat whenever he was away, and for some reason he didn't like the idea of her bowling in unannounced on Catriona. And since he had the morning meeting with Jack Konrad's law firm, Catriona would be home alone.

It mattered, he discovered with a sharp grab of tension, her first impression of his home. He wanted her to be comfortable. He wanted her to feel as relaxed there as he'd felt at her breakfast table. He wanted her to like it enough that she'd want to extend that one week a month into more.

And he wanted to introduce her into his family. She might not want his fancy clothes or the staff wages he intended to pay on her station, but here was something he could give her free. His family.

That's the call he left until last, but Alex didn't pick up his phone. In the past he'd have gotten a real kick out of irritating his elder sibling with a drawled message on his voice mail. Something like, "Guess what, bro? I got hitched last night in Vegas."

But not today. Not with this news. It was too…hell, he didn't know what. Too serious. Too important. Too—

Frowning, he cut a glance toward the next seat. Found Catriona watching him with a curious intensity. As if she were trying to work something out, too. Something that confused her sleepy hazel eyes, and that unusually soft and vulnerable expression seemed to suck the breath right out of Rafe's lungs.

She blinked slowly and looked away, breaking eye contact and leaving him feeling hollow and, yeah, cheated. Because she hadn't smiled? Because she hadn't maintained her usual direct gaze? Because she'd turned away without a word to explain what was bothering her?

Rafe turned back to his phone with a strange tightness in his chest. A feeling that something had changed right there and then but no one had let him in on the secret. He watched her for another minute, hoping she'd turn back, but she didn't. And suddenly it struck him what had changed.

His attitude.

He wanted more than her, naked and willing, her hands in his hair and eyes linked with his as he came apart deep in her body. He wanted more than great sex, and more than the knowledge that they were each providing the other with something essential.

He wanted more than the essentials. He wanted her respect and her trust. He didn't know how to earn those or even if that was possible, given his reputation and her current attitude. He would try, starting with honoring their handshake deal, keeping his cool, and making her feel comfortable in his home and comfortable with his family.

"I'm on my way home from America," he told Alex's voice mail, after dialing again. "There's someone I'd like you to meet tomorrow. Someone…important. I'll call back in the morning."

Cat completed another aimless circuit of the spacious penthouse, back to where her sole companion watched her with wary circumspection. When she got too close, the Russian blue rose from his perch on a suede window seat and meandered on long, graceful legs to the far end of the living room. A pretty efficient snub, Cat decided, trying not to take it to heart.

"He's shy with strangers," Rafe had explained while he petted the animal's plush silvery coat with long, slow strokes. While fine hairs rose and quivered all over *her* skin. "He'll get used to you."

If I stay long enough.

The words had shimmered through her mind then, and they did again now, three hours later. She wouldn't be able to stand seven days of inactivity. She wouldn't be able to stand feeling this twitchy restiveness, which was almost as bad as the awful awkwardness of the first hour, before Rafe had left for work. Almost as bad as one of the panicky attacks she kept suffering at regular intervals, whenever it struck her that this wasn't all a dream or some Cinderella fantasy.

This was real. This was happening to *her*. She had married this man, and this harborside penthouse apartment was her home, too.

For one week every month.

With a flutter of pulse, her gaze shifted off to the right—to the stairs leading up to the loft-level master bedroom. He hadn't taken her up there during the tour of inspection, but only because she'd demurred. That had been one of the most awful moments of all, when she'd reminded him that she wouldn't be sharing his bed.

"Take whichever bedroom you want," he'd said, apparently unperturbed. "Make yourself at home. I have a meeting to get to but I'll call when I'm finished."

"You don't have to check up on me." Polite, cool, when she was quietly freaking out at being left alone in his too-tidy, too-color-coordinated, too-designer-chic home. "I'll be fine."

"I'm sure you will be, but I'm waiting on a phone call from my brother Alex. We may be meeting him for lunch."

At the elevator he'd turned and looked back at her in an all-encompassing way that made her heart do a silly skittery thing. A really silly skittery thing given his parting comment.

"You might want to change into a dress for lunch. We'll likely be going to Zarta's."

"Whoever Zarta may be," she'd grumbled at the closing elevator doors. "Like I would know!"

Left with a ton of turbulent energy pumping through her veins and a ton of time on her hands, she'd wanted to get out, to walk, but she was afraid she'd mess up the tricky security system or that she'd walk so far she'd end up lost. And she couldn't ask for directions since she didn't even know his address!

Didn't *that* sum up her situation perfectly? She was married to a stranger, installed in his home, the address unknown.

She took her time showering but she hadn't dressed because she couldn't decide how to dress. Wandering around in a bathrobe, she was still working on whether to defiantly show up in jeans or to compliantly choose from one of the Vegas dresses, which never did get returned to their places of purchase. For the past half an hour of wandering, her sole focus had been that decision. Jeans versus dress. Floral sundress versus pink retro number.

"My God," she told the cat, disgusted with herself. "I am turning into my stepmother!"

Brilliant green eyes stared back at her, unblinking. Not so much as a twitch of his regal Russian tail. Looking at her with the same disdain her stepmother always employed, as if she were not only a blight on the aesthetic landscape but a complete disappointment. The big, raw, homely girl with no fashion sense. Best bury her at the back of the family photo.

Cat thought she'd gotten over caring about that.

"I have," she muttered as she paced another restless circuit of the open-plan living area. It was just this apartment, these surroundings, the decor.

The place had monstrously high ceilings for an apartment and a full wall of glass looking out over Sydney Harbour. She shouldn't feel so confined. Turning, she forced herself to still and look around her. And to acknowledge that her restiveness might not be due solely to the apartment or disturbing thoughts of her stepmother or even the claustrophobic sense of being trapped in a deal that was way out of her league.

Perhaps it was also the notion of meeting his brother.

She hardly even knew her husband. How could she meet his family? How could she smile and shake this brother's hand, knowing that he knew what she knew? That she'd married Rafe out of desperation. For money. And that she'd been chosen, too, for a specific purpose. Looked over and procured for breeding purposes.

An overwhelming gust of anxiety swamped her, leaving her feeling clammy and slightly ill. She hadn't even thought ahead to this scenario or how she would handle it. How she would feel to be introduced to his family.

How they might judge her and find her wanting, the same way her father's new wife had done.

The phone rang, an expensive burr of sound that cut through the quiet but not through her jittery nerves. She couldn't force herself to pick it up. She let it ring out, then she sat on the couch, hugged her knees to her chest and despised herself for being a coward.

Rafe pocketed his phone and cut across some heavy pedestrian traffic toward Phillip Street and the quickest route home. He'd actually hailed a cab before logic intervened with a compelling alternate suggestion. *Take a deep breath, my man, and think again.* In Vegas he'd reacted on raw, unfettered emotion, and look what that coughed up.

A wife he couldn't entice into his bedroom for a look-see, let alone anything hands on.

Thinking about Catriona in his home that morning—restrained, awkward, gaze sliding away from any meaningful eye contact—didn't help his state of mind. Nor did thinking about those hours in Vegas when he'd stewed with worry while she was out taking a walk and buying a few necessities at Walgreens.

She'd likely gone for a walk now. That's why she hadn't answered his call. No reason to rush home for round two of marital mess up.

Turning on his heel, he headed back toward Circular Quay and his office at the harborfront Carlisle Grande. He'd spent the last two hours at Jack Konrad's offices, thrashing out wording and details with a trio of contract experts. Lawyers who'd felt compelled to remind him, at every turn, how much he stood to lose.

Lawyers who hadn't seen the proud set of Catriona's chin when she told him she didn't want anything from him beyond the debt repayment.

In the end he'd had to remind them who was paying whom. And that he wanted the contract drawn today. And until his wife approved and signed that document, he figured it best he keep away from any one-on-one encounters, especially at his apartment where his irritation over the bedroom arrangement would not stand another round of testing.

If, in fact, she was still at his apartment.

Worry shadowed his footsteps but he kept on walking.

When he got back to his office, he would call again....

"Catriona?"

"Yes. I'm here."

Breathy, and with the briefest hesitation, but at least she'd answered this time. Rafe shifted from his tense perch on the edge of his desk, slumping into his chair and closing his eyes for a second. A ridiculous intensity of relief wiped his mind clear of everything except instinct, and he said what he'd wanted to say early that morning, when he'd taken her into his home for the first time. "I'm glad you're there."

She was silent for a beat, and then her voice—still husky, still hesitant—came through the line again. "Sorry I didn't answer before. I was…in the bathroom."

"I thought you must have gone out."

"Out…where?"

"For a walk." *Or a drive to, say, the airport.*

"I thought about it."

"But?"

"I wasn't sure about getting back in," she admitted in a rush. "I know you told me about the security, but my mind was so thick from flying and I…I didn't want to end up locked out."

Rafe swore silently. He'd been so busy keeping his instinctive responses in check, so busy thinking ahead to the contract that would set them straight again—that would get her moved upstairs and into his bed tonight—that he'd neglected the basic essentials. Like introducing her to the doorman and ensuring she knew her way around. Making sure she had money. "I'm sorry. I should have—"

"It's not your fault. This morning was…"

Her voice trailed off and Rafe chuckled. He found that lack of description oddly descriptive. "Yeah. It was."

"I didn't want things to be like that between us, because of what I said in Vegas," she said softly. "I'm sorry."

"Me, too." And thinking about all the things he was sorry about chased the earlier amusement from his voice. "I will make it up to you, baby."

Silence followed, a quiet flavored with his fervent hope that she was on the same wavelength when it came to making it up.

"The contract should be ready this afternoon," he told her.

"That quick? Will I get to see a draft?"

"If you want."

"Of course I want," she retorted.

Now that sounded more like the old Catriona! With a soft grunt of satisfaction, Rafe kicked back in his chair. "We can do that after lunch. Give them time to make amendments—" *while I take you shopping for a ring* "—so we can sign before the end of business."

"After lunch…with your brother?"

"Yeah. Do you like seafood?"

A two-note laugh bubbled from the phone.

"Is that a no?"

"No. That was just my nervous commentary on how little we know about each other!"

Not the response he'd expected, but… "Here's your chance to fill in another blank…seafood or Japanese? Or would you rather—"

"I'd rather not go at all."

Rafe frowned. "Is this about meeting Alex? He isn't as scary as he looks, you know. There's even the occasional strange woman who finds him charming."

"It's too soon to be meeting family," she said in a rush. "I need to get used to the notion myself first."

"So this is a postponement?"

Silence.

"I want to introduce you to my family." And he hadn't anticipated her resistance. Nor had he anticipated the primitive cut of emotion that snapped on its heels. "I want to introduce you as my wife. As Catriona Carlisle."

Her sharp intake of breath hissed through the receiver. "Catriona *McConnell* Carlisle."

"If you like." Rafe didn't care what she put in the middle, but he did care about the spark in her comeback. That was the Catriona he knew, not the stiff, polite stranger of this morning. Now all he had to do was figure out a way to get that spirited woman to the restaurant. "So, what have you been doing all morning?"

"Nothing."

"I bet you don't get to kick back nearly enough. Feet up, eyes closed, nothing to do but pass the time—"

"I'm not coming to lunch," she said, obviously seeing right through his ploy. "No matter how bored I am."

"What are you going to do, then?"

"I need to get out, take a walk."

Rafe sighed. Okay, so she wasn't about to relent on the lunch date, but he could at least make sure she found her way back inside after her walk. That she was there when he dropped by after lunch to take her into the city. Those plans he wasn't changing. "I'll get Milla to come up and walk you through the security thing again."

"Who's Milla?"

"Just a friend who lives downstairs. She looks after Tolstoy when I'm away."

For some reason her lack of response felt meaningful, although for the life of him Rafe couldn't figure out why.

"Catriona?"

"This…Milla. She isn't the lady who owned your cat. You know, originally?"

"Hell, no." He laughed softly, tickled with that notion. And with the motivation behind her question. His voice dropped a semitone to ask the question he couldn't resist. "Jealous?"

"Should I be?"

"No, but I like that you are." Yeah, he liked that spark of possessiveness a lot. But he also remembered in Vegas when she'd cut into him about the women in his past. He didn't want her sitting there, alone in his apartment, getting crazy thoughts. "I'll ask Milla to come up," he told her. "And, Catriona…"

"Yes?"

"You know there are women in my past—not as many as you'd like to believe, but enough. They're in my past. They stay in my past. There's only one thing to remember." He paused a beat. "I chose you, Catriona Carlisle. Only you."

* * *

A part of Cat wanted to believe his deep note of sincerity, and for a while after she hung up the phone, she indulged that fanciful place by stretching out on the plush sofa and enjoying the little thrills of he-picked-me delight. She wanted to believe in the fairy tale where the wildly handsome prince chose the plain but plucky heroine as his soul mate and rescued her from her loneliness.

Then the neighbor came visiting and knocked that silly little fantasy right back where it belonged.

Rafe had described Milla as "just a friend who lives downstairs." Cat didn't think she could be described as "just" anything. Not "just" svelte, not "just" stylish, not "just" as darkly exotic as her name. She was stop-and-stare stunning.

Especially when she smiled with what appeared to be genuine warmth as she introduced herself. "Rafe said you needed some company, but please let me know if I'm intruding. He tells me to get lost quite regularly. I expect you to do the same when warranted!"

Cat doubted that any male would ever tell a woman who looked like Milla to get lost. Tolstoy illustrated that point by—after taking a wide and exaggerated path around her to get to their visitor—winding his lithe body around her legs and mewing to be picked up.

With a soft peal of laughter and a few crooned words of greeting, she complied. Tolstoy purred in her arms. Any male would do the same, Cat figured.

And she realized that her silence had stretched too long. "Sorry," she said quickly. "You caught me unawares a bit. I'm Catriona McConnell."

"Hmm. A little bird told me you were Catriona *Carlisle*." Milla wrinkled her perfect nose disarmingly. "It takes a bit of getting used to the change, doesn't it?"

"You're married?"

"I was. Twice, actually. Probably best you don't ask. I'd hate to color your newlywed bliss with my cockeyed cynicism."

Cat didn't know quite how to respond. In the space of a minute her emotions had rocketed all over the universe. From her pleasurable little fantasy after Rafe's phone call to stunned awe at Milla's appearance. From depressed how-can-I-compete to aren't-I-a-goose, she-isn't-competition relief.

Now curiosity licked through her blood, lighting dangerous need-to-know spot fires. About Milla's twice-married state, but mostly about her relationship with Rafe.

"Would you like coffee?" she asked. "Or something to drink?"

"We can do that or would you rather go out somewhere? I don't mind waiting while you get ready."

Cat wondered how long she was prepared to wait, given that her hair was an unbrushed mess from her shower and she didn't have a clue what to wear. Milla wore casual, but her jeans were white and designer smart. Her T-shirt a statement in less is more. Her straight, midnight-dark hair was clipped into one of those artless messes of a ponytail that only suit the sleek and beautiful. On Cat, that style would have attracted nesting birds.

Feeling decidedly overwhelmed and underprepared, she took the easy route. "I'd as soon stay in, if that's all right with you."

"Settled." And with easy confidence Milla headed for the kitchen. "I'm a tea drinker myself—what about you?"

Cat followed slowly. Stood at the edge of the terrazzo tiles watching the downstairs neighbor put her hands on everything she needed as if she'd done the same a hundred times before. All the while Milla chatted—effortlessly—about varieties of tea and the merits of drinking from fine bone china. Elegant and expensive, she fit the decor as smoothly as the black marble countertops and sleek silvery backsplashes.

She fit the apartment and Rafe's lifestyle in a way that Cat never would, no matter how many shopping expeditions or spa visits he treated her to. Her heart did a heavy-handed stop-start maneuver high in her chest as she recalled his words on the phone earlier, his comment about the women in his past and how he had chosen her.

Could she believe him? Did she trust his word? Would she ever fit into his life?

Or was she setting herself up for another failure, a second heartbreak at the hands of a smooth-talking charmer?

Eleven

With Milla leading the way, they took their tea upstairs to a rooftop terrace beyond the master bedroom. Since she hadn't allowed Rafe to take her up those stairs, she didn't know about the terrace...not that she was about to let on. She was, after all, supposed to be enjoying newly wedded bliss. And she should have experienced some of that newly wedded bliss in the big, bold bed that dominated his sparsely furnished bedroom.

As they passed, Cat couldn't help taking a peek. The bed sat on a platform one step up, so that at first glance it appeared to float above the ebony floor. Heat trickled through her senses as she imagined Rafe lazing back on the heaped cushions, his mouth curved in a come-hither smile....

"Great bed, isn't it?"

Like a bucket of cold water, Milla's voice washed down on that warm sensual image. Milla, whose relaxed attitude in this apartment was raising little prickles of alarm along Cat's

nerve endings. The kitchen was one thing. Hopping uninvited to the master bedroom level with "great bed" comments
something else again.

Feeling vastly out of sorts with the whole setup—and with
herself for allowing her visitor to take charge—she took a seat
and pulled the tea tray to her side of the table so she could pour.

Unperturbed, Milla waved an elegant arm at the vista.
"What do you think? It's bloody stunning, isn't it?"

Cat's sound of agreement was probably colored with her
testy mood because her companion slanted her a long, measured look. "Too much?"

"Higher rent than I'm used to."

Milla asked about where she was used to; Cat told her
about Corroboree. A nice, polite, innocuous conversation over
tea that lapsed into silence, neither awkward nor comfortable.
Cat decided that—on her side at least—it was wary.

"I imagine you'll be going to the Wentworth show on Friday night," Milla said eventually.

She would? To hide her cluelessness Cat took a long sip
of her tea. Made a noncommittal sound.

"If you need a hairdresser—" Cat felt the other woman's
gaze drift over her tangled curls "—I can recommend my gal.
And since she's coming here to do me, she might be able to
fit you in, as well."

If she were going to any Friday-night "show"—this had to
mean a society party of some kind—Cat would need help. Big
help. But sharing that help with this woman… "Thank you
for the offer." She put down her cup. "But I'll manage."

"Sure?"

"I haven't even decided if I'm going." Hardly a lie, since
she didn't yet know what Rafe expected of her, socially. "I'm
not so big on parties."

"You know, I don't blame you. Those things can be brutal
at the best of times and you will be the center of attention."

"Because I'm with Rafe?"

Milla laughed. "Because you're *married* to Rafe, sweetie. Everyone is going to want to size up the lucky duck who snagged bachelor number one!"

Despite the balmy spring temperature, Cat felt herself go cold. Why hadn't she thought of that? She'd read the articles, damn it, on the Internet. All that interest in the Carlisle brothers' private lives. All those insinuations she'd sniped at him about in Vegas. She'd been so busy worrying about meeting his family that she hadn't spared a thought for the larger population.

The laughter faded from the other woman's face. She leaned forward a little, her voice gentle. "Hey, I was joking, you know."

"Were you?"

Milla grimaced. "Not about the interest in you, unfortunately. But about snagging Rafe, yes. We both know that happened the other way around!"

That Rafe had snagged her? True, she supposed, in a way. But now she wondered how much Milla knew. How much her husband had shared with this just-a-neighbor he'd sent to keep her company. "Rafe told you how we met?"

"You rescued him from a crashed plane, I believe. How romantic!"

No, it hadn't been romantic. It had been practical. But Cat bit her tongue from making that distinction out loud.

"I'm glad he found you." A surprising sincerity steadied the other woman's exotically dark eyes as she held Cat's gaze across the table. "Rafe is a much better man than he lets on, even to himself. He deserves someone gutsy and real. He deserves better than a bimbo like Nikki!"

Cat's heart began to soar like the gulls over the harbor before them, then dipped and dove on the last word. She had to ask. She couldn't not. "Who is Nikki?"

Slowly Milla put down her cup. Her expression looked pained, caught out, and she took a long time to answer. As if she were choosing her words with deliberate care. "He was flying out to see her…when he met you."

Understanding cannoned through Cat, tightening her chest and her throat. A constriction that squeezed every last remaining drop of her earlier fantasy from her consciousness. "He was flying to see her…to ask her…when the storm put him down? At my place?"

The answer was obvious. Milla didn't have to say a word, although she made a rueful moue. "Rafe has always had the most sensational luck!"

Yes, Cat couldn't help thinking. How lucky to have landed on the doorstep of a sucker. A sucker who hadn't even seen it coming. Even when he'd lazed against her kennel enclosure and joked about paying someone to have his baby. Even when he'd stood in the middle of a Las Vegas casino and offered her one "win-win" spin of the wheel.

Even when he'd said, *I chose you, Catriona. Only you.*

It was another of his lines, another of his sweet-talking, get-his-own-way lines. And she, prize sap number one, had fallen for it body and soul.

Milla left, but her impact remained, as subtle as the lingering scent of her perfume, as pervasive as the hurt centered in Cat's chest. It wasn't her heart, though. It was her pride that hurt, because she'd wanted to believe in those momentary senses of connection. She'd wanted him to have chosen her for something more personal than convenience. She'd wanted it to have been *only you*.

But no, he'd intended to ask someone named Nikki. Then, because of circumstances, luck, fate, the vagaries of weather, he'd landed at her place and transferred his goal onto her. She tried to remember that morning in the guest room, the kitchen, the kennels. Tried to recall if he'd said where he was going before the storm hit. Perhaps she hadn't ever asked.

"Can you believe that?" she murmured, but nobody heard.

Tolstoy had skulked out of the living area after Milla's departure, and that desertion felt like another crushing blow to her pride. Silly, since the cat's only previous communication was via a disdainful stare.

Silly, too, that she should feel this alone in the center of Australia's biggest city.

At Corroboree she'd spent years on her own but she'd never felt this thick choking sense of abandonment. At home her *alone* was filled with the morning call of birds, the background chatter of open radio, the bellow of cows calling to their calves. The creak of old boards shifting with the change of temperature. The sound of the lilac tree scraping against her bedroom window, or Sheba yapping at a possum as it scampered from rooftop to orchard.

Suddenly Cat felt an intense yearning for the familiarity of the outback where she belonged. Sitting on his plush sofa, she closed her eyes and tried to force it aside, to remember that Rafe would be back in an hour or two to take her to check the contract.

The contract that would bind them together, that would make this marriage more real than their Vegas vows.

Her need to escape, to go home to the place where she was herself—the strong and capable Catriona McConnell, a woman she liked—came back at her again in a great big wave that rocked her with its force. She didn't belong here in this expensive world filled with beautiful people and Friday-night "shows" that required hairdressers and promised to put *her* in the spotlight.

Not Catriona McConnell, not even Catriona Carlisle, but Mrs. Rafe Carlisle.

Her mind and her stomach churned. This wasn't real life—not *her* real life. She should never have agreed to live here for a week. She should never have agreed to this marriage as a quick fix for her financial problems or to fill the void of her missing family.

Marrying him was a dumb rebound thing that could only end in heartbreak. A couple of days in his company, one night with him in her bed, and she'd tumbled halfway into love. Or lust. Or something somewhere in between the two.

She shot up from the sofa and started to pace.

Surely they could annul this sham of a marriage. People did that spur-of-the-moment Vegas thing all the time and got out of it.

And what about your debt? What about Corroboree?

Slowly she sank back down onto the sofa and clutched her head in her hands. She couldn't think straight here. She had to get away—except how? She didn't have enough money in her bank account to pay a bus fare, let alone a plane ticket.

Fraught with anxiety she scanned the possibilities and came up with only one.

Was she that desperate?

Did she need to escape to her home that urgently?

Sick with the decision she needed to make, her stomach pitched. But she sucked in a breath and reached for the phone. Waited an agonizing beat of five seconds before her stepmother answered. Before she sucked up her pride and asked her to buy the ticket that would take her home.

"What the hell happened, Catriona?"

When she finally answered her phone, it was after nine that night and Rafe didn't bother with preliminaries or small talk. He'd spent close to seven hours trying to read between the lines in the short message she'd left on his voice mail.

"I'm sorry, Rafe, but I have to go home. I have responsibilities there and I should never have agreed to stay with you in Sydney. I need to think this whole thing through before we go any further. I can't think here. I need to be home."

She—as he'd noted before they went to Vegas—had no facility for leaving messages, so by the time she finally did pick up he was struggling against a wall of simmering emotions. He struggled, too, to contain his impatience while he waited for her response to that straight-to-the-point opening.

"Did you get my message?" she hedged.

"Couldn't you have waited another hour and told me in person?"

"There's only one afternoon flight. I had to leave to make the airport in time."

"Milla said you never mentioned a word to her about leaving. Half an hour later, you're gone. Why?" He paused, slammed a hand through his hair, forced himself to stop pacing. "Is there something wrong at Corroboree? Did you get a phone call?"

"No. I…" She paused and he heard her draw a breath. "This isn't going to work."

"This?"

"Us. This relationship. You should have stuck with Nikki." Rafe went very still. "Nikki?"

"Your first choice. Her name's Nikki, isn't it? You were flying out to see her, to ask her to have your baby, the day the storm forced you down."

"Who told you that?"

"Does it matter?"

No, it didn't. She was right. What mattered was the fact that she was five hundred miles away. That for some reason— maybe it was Nikki, maybe it was more—she'd decided to run away from their deal. "We have an agreement, Catriona. The night you married me in Vegas I told you to be very sure. I said there would be no going back."

"You also said you chose me. Only me."

"I didn't mislead you, Catriona. I decided on you the day after we met. Nothing has happened since to change my mind and I can't think of anything I've done that should have changed yours."

"It's not any one thing—"

"Good," he cut in, not giving her a chance. This wasn't something he would debate over the telephone. "Because the contract is drawn and ready for signing. I promised you a draft, and *I* honor my promises. I'll e-mail the document tonight."

"I won't sign anything until I'm sure I'm doing the right thing."

"If you want to keep Corroboree, you don't have a choice. My lawyer has spoken to Samuels. That part of our deal is already in motion. All you have to do is sign the agreement, Catriona. You have forty-eight hours to request any changes. Otherwise, I'll see you Friday morning."

"You're coming down here?" Her voice rose on a note of anxiety, and Rafe smiled with a perverse sense of satisfaction. She had cause to worry. If he had to chase halfway across the country to make her uphold her end of the deal, then he intended making the trip very worthwhile.

"I'll see you Friday, Mrs. Carlisle," he said, and hung up.

Cat returned the amended draft of their contract because she didn't have any choice. It was up to him now, whether he accepted her changes or not. She didn't expect he would. She did expect another heated phone call, and spent many agitated hours pacing around her office on Wednesday and Thursday nights, waiting for the instrument to ring.

It didn't, and his silence caused her even more misgivings.

She did receive two e-mails. The first reported that he'd installed a message bank on her phone service. The second was a scanned invitation for the Friday-night event Milla had mentioned. The "Wentworth show," apparently, was a fashion fund-raiser for a children's hospital, and the Carlisle Hotel Group was a major sponsor.

Cat stared at the invitation with intense trepidation—she would rather wrestle a pit full of tiger snakes than a room full of fashionistas all eager to size her up—but that quickly morphed into consternation. What did this mean? He'd said he was coming here on Friday—had he changed his mind? He hadn't included any note of explanation. Did he expect her to hurry back to Sydney on the strength of this invitation?

No way. And no way would she give him the satisfaction of calling to find out. Maybe that was stupid and stubborn of her, but she wanted to imagine she could hang on to her pride since he'd taken a grip on too much of her life.

Coming home had not been all she'd imagined while sitting on his plush sofa back in Sydney: she hadn't slept worth a bean; she'd gained little comfort from the hollow emptiness of her home. Only her dogs made it worthwhile with their enthusiastic adoration.

By Friday morning she was completely frazzled and out of sorts. But she got on with her work and she worried about whether he would turn up as she watched the sky for any sign of his plane.

"Not that I know what kind of plane to watch out for," she told Bach. Her worried eyes scanned the eastern horizon yet again.

I should have called. I should have told him to use Gordon's strip. I don't want to hear an engine overhead and go through another rough landing...or worse.

What would her pride be worth then?

"I'll call," she decided. "As soon as we get these cattle yarded, I will call."

With a new sense of urgency she gunned her trail bike around the heifers she was bringing in for drenching. Bach skirted the flanks of the mob, hurrying the stragglers.

They were within a stone's throw of the yards when she saw the plume of dust on her driveway. Her heart skittered.

"Silly," she muttered, although her gaze remained glued on that approaching speck of a vehicle. Her heart continued to skip and skate. "He wouldn't drive."

Even from the airport?

Even from another strip?

A recalcitrant heifer attempted to break, and she forced herself to concentrate on her job, keeping the mob intact as she herded them toward the holding yard. When she looked back toward the road again the vehicle had disappeared. Her lungs felt constricted, tight with anticipation as she waited for its reappearance from behind the homestead.

Ridiculous, but she knew in her bones that it was him. Knew before the white Landcruiser came back into view, heading now for the yards. The air wheezed in her lungs as she sucked in a deep breath and attempted to steady the frantic beat of her heart.

Gordon Samuels's vehicle. Just one figure in the cabin. The silhouette too tall, too refined, too familiar to that wildly beating heart to be anyone but Rafe.

She kicked down the stand on her bike and swung her leg over the seat. *Walk to the yards, Catriona. Shut the gate, secure the chain. Don't forget to breathe.* Simple everyday things she was having trouble remembering.

And when she turned around he was getting out of the vehicle. Long legs in dark trousers. Dark shirt. Dark designer shades. A shiver of heat chased through her veins as his head came up and his shaded gaze fixed on her. He'd never looked more out of place, standing there in the red dust kicked up by a hundred milling cattle, and before Cat could start crossing that space between them she had to remind herself to breathe again.

A dozen emotions pounded Rafe as he watched her approach, all of them expected, most of them tight and tumultuous, none of them evident on his face. He kept his expression schooled, the same as his posture and the lazy cadence of his voice as he asked, "What the hell do you think you're doing?"

A spark of irritation lit her eyes as she lifted her chin and met his gaze from under the broad brim of her stockman's hat. "I'm working. As some of us do. Is that a problem?"

"I told you I was coming today."

"And here you are. Should I have been waiting at the homestead?"

Rafe ignored the sweet sarcasm in that question and allowed a smile to curve his mouth. "That would have made things easier. But that's never on your priority list, is it?"

The sting registered in her eyes, in the tightening of her lips. Good. She needed to know he'd had enough of her contrary behavior and stalling tactics.

"This—" he lifted his chin to indicate the cattle at her back "—looks like a job in progress."

"I'm about to start drenching."

"I assume this won't take long?"

Her gaze narrowed. "Why would you assume that?"

"Because we have business to conclude." Straightening, Rafe tapped a hand against the roof of the Landcruiser. "I gather you recognize this vehicle?"

The dog crouched at her feet growled. Her voice held a similar edge when she said, "Of course I do. I assume you wisely chose to use his airstrip."

"That was convenient. Seeing as I also hand delivered a cheque."

A flinch of emotion crossed her face but her gaze remained fixed and narrow on his. "You paid off my debt with Samuels? But I haven't signed the contract."

"Are you going to?"

"Did you make the alterations?"

"Would you sign if I hadn't?"

She didn't answer. She didn't need to.

Rafe smiled. "I figured as much. That's why I let you have your changes."

"All of them?"

"I expected you'd want to halve every payment or allowance I wanted to give you. That's why I doubled them in the first place."

Shock widened her eyes and widened Rafe's satisfaction as he watched her take that aboard. "What about the clause I crossed out?" she asked, recovering. "The one about spending a week a month in Sydney?"

"I hated approving that one, but I did."

"Why?" Obviously nonplussed she spread her arms, palms up. "Why would you do that? And why would you pay off Samuels without my signature?"

"I was always going to do that, Catriona."

She stared back at him, still and quiet, for a long moment. "And what if I don't sign now?"

"That's your prerogative."

"What if I've decided that this whole marriage is a complete sham and I can't do it anymore? I mean, that's possible isn't it? People annul those quickie Vegas marriages all the time. No one need even know."

"Don't you think it's a little late for that?"

Knowledge flared in her eyes. Knowledge of wedding-night heat, of all they'd shared, of what they may have created.

"Even if you're not pregnant, Catriona—" he let his gaze drift down to where one of her hands hovered near her belly, and he felt a deep and rich stirring in his "—there are others who know we got married."

"Your brother. And your neighbor."

"*Your* neighbor, too."

"You told Samuels? Did you have to?"

Renewed irritation burned in Rafe's belly at her indignant tone. "Why is that such a problem? Would you prefer he spread the word that you'd slept with me in return for that cheque?"

"Isn't that what I did?"

"No, Catriona. You married me." And this time he didn't attempt to hide his irritation or his impatience. "I have a contract in the vehicle that you asked for, with amendments you requested. Sign it or not, that's your choice. What matters to me is the deal we made in Vegas, the vows we exchanged in that chapel and in your bed."

A pulse fluttered in her throat, heat rose in her cheeks. But her voice, when she finally spoke, was clear and even. "And after I sign?"

"I would like you to come back to Sydney with me. For the weekend."

"Because of this charity thing tonight?"

"Yes."

She moistened her lips. "You wouldn't want to take me to something like that. I'd hate it."

"How do you know that?"

"I know, okay?"

But beyond the obstinate answer he saw a glimmer of appeal in her eyes that he couldn't refuse. And, hell, if he could just get her to sign the contract after that panicky talk about annulment he'd be happy.

And afterward…well, afterward he intended to make them both very happy.

"So—" he looked beyond her at the cattle "—how long should it take us to knock this lot over?"

"Us?"

Rafe's gaze rolled back to lock on hers. "I'm going to help you, Catriona. And in return you're going to tell me the whole story about what happened on Tuesday to send you running home."

Cat didn't bother objecting to his help—she could see he meant business—and that help more than halved the time taken. There was no opportunity to talk about her flight from his apartment. With one of them feeding the draft and the other on the drenching gun, they weren't ever working side by side, so their conversation was restricted to shouted instructions and the odd passing remark about the job they were doing.

They returned to the homestead separately and met up

again over a cold drink of water in her kitchen. She thanked him for his help, and he grinned and thanked her for letting him help. "I haven't done any cattle work in years. I enjoyed myself."

"Really?"

He told her how all three brothers learned the ropes at an early age on Kameruka Downs, going out on stock camps during their July and October school holidays.

"I never pictured you as a cowboy," she said.

"There's a lot you don't know about me," he countered.

A frisson of unease skittered through her bones, not because of all she didn't know about him but because of all she did. She suspected the negligent playboy charmer thing was just a clever disguise. When it came down to it, he could do purposeful as well as anyone she'd ever met. And he had such a way of twisting things around to get what he'd wanted all along.

Is this what he'd wanted?

The two of them together in her house, her day's work finished with an afternoon stretching long and lazy before them?

She looked up and found him watching her in a way that chased all thought from her mind and all breath from her lungs. It was the look of a hunter eyeing its prey. A look of intensity and purpose and soul-searing heat.

Cat's heart thundered. She put down her glass, carefully, afraid it might slip through her trembling fingers. Despite the water she'd just finished, her mouth felt thick and dry. "I'd like to take a look at that contract now."

"If you like." He lifted a shoulder, casual, negligent, while his eyes told another story entirely. "I'd like to take a shower…if that's all right."

"Of course. I'll just make sure there's a towel."

Inside the guest bathroom, she slumped against the wall a moment to catch her breath and think. Except, all she could think about was the last time Rafe had used this bathroom…and that he'd soon be naked here again. All she could picture was the look in his eyes across her kitchen, and when she opened her eyes he was there, in the door of the bathroom.

Not yet naked but working on it.

Twelve

"**W**hat do you think you're doing?"

The squeaky rise in her voice and the flush of heat in her cheeks gave Rafe no end of satisfaction. He'd followed her into the bathroom to catch her off guard while she found him a towel, and while her guard was down he intended finding out what had gone wrong in Sydney. Here they wouldn't be working at opposite ends of a cattle draft. Here she would be naked and unable to escape.

He dropped his shirt on the bathroom floor and met the nervous flicker of her eyes as they rose from his bare chest to his face. "I told you I was taking a shower," he said.

"And I said I was making sure you had a—"

Rafe peeled off trousers and underwear in one efficient pass and straightened. "A...towel?"

Her gaze whipped back up to his. "You could have waited until I'd finished in here."

"I could have. But then I remembered how you liked efficiency." Eyes still linked with hers, he reached into the shower enclosure and turned on the taps. "I thought we'd save time by getting two things out of the way at once."

"Two things?"

Her voice was barely audible above the hiss of the shower as he leaned into the water to test the temperature. When he straightened and raked his dripping hair back from his face, she licked a nervous tongue across her lips. Anticipation surged in his body, a solid rush of heat beneath the cool patina of wet skin.

"Two things...or possibly three." Slowly he closed the space between them, smiling as he backed her up against the vanity. "If you ask nicely."

Her eyes flashed, cross, indignant, but the effect was spoiled by her quick intake of breath when he rested his hands on the vanity on either side of her hips. Trapping her inches from the jut of his aroused body.

"What are the first two?" she asked.

"Getting clean." His gaze swept over her dusty face and braided hair. "And having that conversation I mentioned earlier."

Her mouth opened but all that came out was a wheezy gasp as he straightened, wrapped his arms around her and started backing toward the shower. "What are you doing?"

"Let's start with getting clean."

Her eyes widened with shock as he walked them both under the water. He hadn't planned this part, but it seemed to be working out well. He'd definitely caught her off guard. Her hands flapped uselessly, trapped at her side. "My clothes," she spluttered. "They're getting soaked."

"We'd best get them off you, then."

But before he let her down, Rafe turned them a half circle until she was cornered in the small enclosure. Barricading her there with his body, he started unbuttoning her shirt. Of course she protested. Naturally she batted at him with her hands, but he used his elbows to block her arms, and when she tried to duck out of reach he took advantage of her widened stance to press a naked thigh between her jeans-clad ones.

She sucked in a shuddery breath, but her wide eyes snarled in a satisfying way. "You said you'd never imposed yourself on a woman."

"I'm not imposing."

"You're just taking?"

That gave him pause.

His gaze rose swiftly to meet hers, but Cat found it hard to focus on their sea-green complexity. The heels of his hands rested on her breasts, distracting her with their rough-edged heat even through the soaked fabric of her shirt. She attempted to focus instead on the tiny pulse that beat at the corner of his jaw.

"I think you have the wrong idea, wife." Very deliberate, very slow, he leaned closer and she felt the increased pressure of every point of contact. Shock waves of heat pulsed through her breasts and tightened in her nipples. She didn't realize his purpose until he'd rolled back, the bottle of shower wash in his hand. "I'm only washing you. And your clothes, too. Efficient, aren't I?"

He pumped a glob of the creamy wash into the palm of each hand, then smoothed it over her chest, tracing her collarbone and the swell of her breasts above her bra. Then while she was still savoring that delicious touch of sensory pleasure, he efficiently peeled off her shirt and slung it over the glass partition.

"Turn around."

Cat obeyed. She felt his hands at her back, unhooking her bra, sliding the straps down her arms until it, too, was gone.

"Can you hold your plait up, out of the way?"

She did, and he made a soft sound of approval in his throat. A perfect accompaniment to his hands as they slicked the body wash over her shoulders and back.

"We worked well together today, don't you think?"

He expected her to think? With his big hands making those slow, gliding strokes over her back and down her sides. Teasing the outsides of her breasts with each pass. Closer and closer. Slower and slower. With a low groan she slumped forward and pressed her forehead against the cool tiles.

"We work well together in other ways, too."

His voice was close to her ear, a low rumble of heat in her blood as his hands slid around her ribs. As his thumbs stroked the underside of her breasts.

Then retreated.

The breath left her lungs in a hot gust of frustration. But when she tried to turn around he pressed a splayed a hand across her abdomen and held her there. Trapped between the wide spread of those fingers and the wall of hard, wet body at her back. Trapped in a web of wanting that twined through her, as warm and slow and liquid as the gentle wash of water on their bodies. As warm and slow and liquid as his open-mouthed kiss against the side of her throat.

"I'm not taking," he murmured, moving that sensuous mouth up to nip at her earlobe. "I'm giving."

And, finally, his hands closed over her breasts, cupping each with finely textured skin and finely hewn restraint. Cat didn't give a damn who was giving or taking or receiving. Shamelessly turned on, she arched her back and drew a long breathy moan of pleasure at the dual friction of her nipples against his palms and her backside against his erection.

"Can I take off my jeans?" she asked.

"Not yet."

His hands slid from her breasts, down over her abdomen to rest at her hipbones.

She turned her head, frowned at this lessening of contact. "You said you were washing me."

"And your clothes."

"Well, you're taking your time and that isn't efficient!"

He laughed, low and gruff and sexy. "If I take off your jeans, I'm likely to get very inefficient. And I haven't washed your hair, yet."

Cat growled impatiently as he rolled away from her back, but then his hands were in her hair, unbraiding her plait, separating the thick sections and playing them against her skin. Working a thick lather of shampoo, massaging her scalp, turning her weak with the impact of that whole sensual experience.

The brush of wet skin, belly to back, as he leaned past her to reshelve the bottle. His hands smoothing a delicious path from her shoulders down her arms until they closed over her hands and linked their fingers. His face nuzzling her wet hair aside, his mouth at the junction of her shoulder, kissing, biting, sucking.

The press of his body at her back and the sweet ache of hunger in her blood and her body.

"My hair is done," she said, and her voice felt as thick as her blood, as clumsy as the fingers that struggled to unsnap her jeans. "Can you get this blasted thing?"

His laughter rasped over her as he turned her around. As he stroked those wonderful hands over her shoulders and upper arms and kissed her and kissed her and kissed her. Most inefficient, she thought, but then his hands were at her waist and tugging at her jeans and she decided he might just be getting the message.

He released her mouth with a last long stroke of heat, tongue to tongue, a last nip of her bottom lip, and his half-lidded gaze lifted to hers. "We are having that conversation."

Talk? Coherently? Was he serious?

"I want to start by making one thing clear." He lifted his hands and cupped her face, a gentle, cool contrast to the searing intensity of his eyes. "I haven't thought about another woman since I opened my eyes in that Cessna."

Cat blinked. "Why are you telling me this now?"

"In case you need any reassurance."

"I need," she said slowly, "you to take off my jeans."

One corner of his mouth lifted but his hands didn't move from her face. "I'll get to that. After you tell me why you ran away."

"That's blackmail."

"Let's just call it enticement."

He leaned forward and kissed her again. And because of the sweet hunger in that kiss and the straight heat of his gaze and, yes, the enticement of getting his clever hands to soap where her jeans now covered, she met his eyes with complete honesty. "I was homesick. And scared. I panicked."

"Scared of…?"

"Your home…it's so…" How could she explain? How could he expect her to find words with him naked and—

"You don't like my home?"

He sounded stung, and Cat closed her eyes and tried again. "You know it's beautiful, but I didn't feel at home. It's all too much."

"It's just an apartment."

"Like you're just a man?" She laughed softly at the incomprehension in his voice. "You're Rafe Carlisle."

"So?"

Her eyes drifted open when she shook her head. "Do you really think you're no big deal?"

"To you I should be a big deal. I'm your husband."

"Well, there's a problem right there. I have trouble thinking of you as that. There's so much I still don't know about you."

"Then learn me," he rasped. Eyes sparking with what looked like irritation, he took her hand and put it on him, traced it over the hard sculpted muscles of his chest, rested it against the heavy thud of his heart until his heat seeped into her skin and chased through her blood.

Her husband. A mystery, a heartbreaker, a very big deal.

Cat shook her head.

"What?" he growled, leaning closer again, driving the worrying impact of that thought from her mind with the intensity of his expression. She lifted her other hand and traced the sculpted line of his jaw, his cheekbone and the brooding fullness of his mouth. Then she stretched up on her toes and kissed him with all she had to offer in her heart, while her fingers spread over his skin and learned the thick steady beat of his heart.

Her big-deal husband would break her heart when he left. She did not have enough to keep his attention here in the outback and she could not live in his city. He would leave and she would regret, but for now—this time and maybe again tomorrow, maybe a few more weekends—she would take what he had to give.

And she would give back in equal measure.

Easing back from that rich, earthy soul kiss, she touched his lips and asked, "Will you take my jeans off now?"

The corner of his mouth lifted under her fingers. "Are you asking nicely?"

Eyes linked with his, she slipped her other hand down his sleek wet hide until it closed around his sleek wet erection. "Is that nice enough?"

He licked at her bottom lip. "Did you say please?"

She squeezed until he groaned and pushed more fully into her hand. "Pretty please," she said sweetly. "With sugar on top."

He took her jeans off then, although it wasn't an easy task. The wet denim might well have shrunk already. It stuck to her skin and he kept dipping in to lick at each new exposed portion of her body. To nuzzle her thighs with the bristly texture of afternoon whiskers. To pump a new dose of body wash onto his hands and smooth it over her bottom and the backs of her legs.

By the time she kicked the weight of sodden denim aside she was breathing heavily and an inch away from begging. He rose in one smooth movement, and she saw the ripe color of arousal along his cheekbones and in his lust-dark eyes. They locked on hers, and his nostrils flared as she breathed one word.

"Yes."

His hands on her hips lifted her, a long cool slide against the wet tiles and she wrapped her arms around his neck and her legs around his hips. She felt him, hard and hot between her legs and felt a swell of need, unbearably intense.

"Take," she whispered against his mouth, "whatever you want."

His hands cupped her buttocks, held her there wide and open as he plunged, one full thrust of his hips that slid her hard against the tiles and drove the air from her lungs and filled her with heat and sensation and emotion so big it burst from her lips in a wild primal cry. But her eyes remained locked with his, linked in a supercharged arc of connection, lost in the sensual thrall of their sea-green intensity and the awed revelation that he felt the same magnitude, the same power, the same intensity.

He didn't need to touch her anywhere else, didn't need to do anything except drive her with the primitive rhythm of his body and look at her in exactly that way and whisper her name until she came apart in a swell of sensation that rose and rippled and peaked, only to come again as he drove deeper and faster and spilled himself in a spasm that resounded over and over and over in her blood.

She felt the slump of her boneless weight against the slick tiles and muttered something about letting her fall, and his grip on her hips tightened. "I won't let you fall, baby."

"I won't feel a thing if you do."

His laugh was a rasp of sound, and she smiled along with it, feeling marvelous and spent and impossibly invigorated all at once. Then his laughter exploded into a raw curse and rush of movement as he tried to evade the water that beat down on his back.

In the shelter of his body, Cat started to laugh. "I guess the hot water ran out," she gasped between chuckles.

He went very still. "So, my wife thinks that's funny."

"In a laughing *with you* kind of way."

"Huh." His eyes narrowed and gleamed dangerously. "They say marriage is about sharing…"

And she had barely enough time to yelp before he redirected the showerhead and a stream of cold water onto her.

* * *

Rafe turned off the water and warmed his wife's cool skin with a thorough toweling before he carried her from the bathroom.

"Where are you taking me?" she asked when he kept walking past the guest-room bed.

"Your bed." He stopped and looked into her face. "Did you expect I would want my own room?"

"No," she said without hesitation. "But I've been thinking about you in this bed."

"Have you, now."

"Ever since the night of your accident. When I undressed you."

"I will let you do that again one day." He started down the hallway. "Except, this time I'll be conscious."

She smiled and Rafe felt something stir through him and then settle rich and warm in his chest. Contentment. Satisfaction. And a major dose of sexual relief. A man should not have to wait five days to make love to his wife again. Not in the first week of his marriage.

"How many other places have you fantasized about having me?" he asked as he carted her into her bedroom.

"Besides in the guest-room shower?"

A bark of laughter escaped his throat as he sat on the bed and rolled with her until he had her positioned exactly where he wanted. Stretched out, with him on top. "So, Mrs. Carlisle. Did the reality live up to the fantasy?"

"In my fantasy I got to soap you. All over."

"Is that a complaint?"

"More an observation."

"Anything else you observed?"

Mischief gleamed green in her eyes. "My fantasies tend to be low on talking, big on action."

"My action not big enough for you?"

She wiggled her hips and then blinked slowly. "Already?"

"Just adapting to the concept of a long-distance relationship."

Something shifted in her eyes, a touch serious, a tad wary, and Rafe thought how easily he could chase that suspicion away. To sink down into a kiss and then into her body. But no matter what his friend downstairs might be signaling, he had taken the edge off his sexual hunger, and the mental side craved some loving, too.

He rolled onto his side, drawing her with him until they lay facing each other. He knew his expression had turned serious, knew because the wariness in her eyes had deepened. "I assume that's what you want," he said slowly. "Me flying out here on weekends and whenever else I can manage a night away."

"You'd do that?"

"I'll have to put some serious work in on your airstrip so I can land the Citation…but, yes."

Alarm widened her eyes. "You'd fly out here in a jet? Don't you need a—"

"Hey, I was joking." He leaned forward and kissed her. "But only about the jet."

That didn't erase the sharp notes of whatever worried her eyes. She stared at him, intent and silent for several seconds before she asked, "Why me?"

He knew what she meant: Why had he chosen her? He couldn't believe he hadn't told her, at least several times, but he could stretch himself to tell her again. "Originally? Because I liked you right off the bat and I knew you'd make a good mother."

"How can you say that?" A frown pleated her brow. "I'm used to being on my own. I don't mix with families. I don't have any experience with babies."

"Yeah, but the way you looked after me when I was concussed—that's the kind of care a mother should show. And then I saw you with those puppies." He shrugged. "I could picture you with a baby."

The fractiousness in her eyes settled, darkened, as if it turned inward. As if imagining that same picture.

Rafe realized then how quickly, how easily he'd grown used to the notion of a baby—*his* baby—when that thought had terrified the bejesus out of him two weeks ago. Who would have predicted it? An introspective smile played over his lips. "It's a great picture, isn't it?"

She nodded and attempted to return his smile. Hers wobbled a little at the edges. "I hope you're right about the mother call."

"How old were you when your mother died?" he asked, guessing at the cause of her concern.

"Four," she said softly. "I don't even remember her."

Sorry didn't cover something like that so he simply stroked a hand down her arm. "When did the wicked stepmother come into the picture?"

Her lips twitched. "I was twelve."

"And she made your life an instant misery."

"No, I was over-the-moon excited at first. A new mother who was beautiful and sophisticated and who brought me amazing gifts. Plus I was getting two sisters. Life was going to be perfect!"

The quiet shadow of sadness in her voice twisted Rafe's gut. He leaned forward and brushed a soft kiss to her lips, and another and another until he'd chased that unhappy curve away. "What dastardly things did she do?"

"Oh, nothing overt. She didn't make me scrub floors and chop firewood or anything. She just made me feel…less. Like no matter what I did I could never meet her standards. Then she started undermining my relationship with Dad. She even convinced him to send me to boarding school."

"Isn't that necessary?" he asked carefully. "Given your isolation?"

"Maybe, but I hated it from day one. I hated being away from home. I missed my dad and my animals like crazy."

She was silent a long while, but Rafe waited, knowing there was more. Knowing, instinctively, that this was crucial to understanding her and why she wouldn't spend time in the city.

"I was away at school when my father died. He was out mustering and he came off his bike. He broke his back and...other stuff." Her hand fluttered under his, her breath shuddered and hitched and pierced somewhere deep in his chest. "He was alive for close to twenty-four hours but no one found him. He died out there, alone."

"I'm sorry, baby" didn't even come close, but he said it anyway. He said it and he wrapped her in his arms and wished he could absorb all her hurt into his own body. Wished he could say that being there wouldn't have made any difference for her father but he didn't know that. He did know it would have made a hell of a difference to Catriona.

"Tell me about him."

"My dad? Oh, he was tall. Dark."

"And handsome?"

"*Rugged* I think is the right word." Wry and sad, her smile reached in and grabbed him where he lived. "He was built like a rugby second-rower, which was handy since that's the position he played."

"Lucky."

"He had a wicked sense of humor and a laugh that rolled up from his belly. I swear nobody could resist Dad's laugh."

"Sounds like you got a gem."

"Yeah, I did. What about you?" she asked after a beat.

"I got lucky when my mother married Charles Carlisle."

She watched him solemnly for a moment. "Have you ever met your birth father?"

"Once." Rafe played a long tress of her hair through his fingers. Then he shrugged. "I wish I hadn't bothered."

"Why's that?"

"He wasn't worth knowing."

The tenor of her expression changed, a subtle shift in the way she eyed him. Unease swirled in his belly because he knew he'd revealed more than he intended in that one flat statement. Knew that he had to divert her attention before she honed in on the one area of his life he didn't intend sharing.

He propped himself on an elbow and trailed a hand down her body, throat to navel in a drift of knuckles and warm velvet heat. "So, Mrs. Carlisle—"

"Are you trying to distract me?"

"No, I'm trying to keep on subject."

Her eyes narrowed. "Which subject would that be?"

"You asked why I thought you'd make a good mother. I hadn't finished answering." Curiosity flared in her eyes, then heat as he caressed the curve of her belly. "I knew you came from good stock. Strong character, sharp brain, smart mouth." Pausing for effect, he spanned her pelvis with his hand. "Good child-bearing hips."

Naturally she growled and swatted him.

Naturally he wrestled her to her back and pinned her to the bed with the weight of his body.

Naturally he kissed the fire from her lips and looked deep into her eyes and told her he was joking, that mostly he just enjoyed her better than any woman he'd ever met. In and out of bed. And then he let her roll him onto his back so he could enjoy the weight of her body and her eyes smiling into his and then not smiling at all as she took him inside her and consumed him with her heat.

Thirteen

Cat managed to keep him in her bed long enough that the Friday night show became a moot point. But she didn't forget how he'd distracted her from asking more about his birth father, or how much she had revealed in comparison. Over the next two days she tried to entice more from him, but he had a way of deflecting the conversation if he didn't like the topic, and he did so with such finesse that Cat didn't know she'd been stonewalled until afterward. Usually after a couple of orgasms and a nap to recover.

All weekend they worked together, sometimes in surprising harmony, but more often than not arguing about the most efficient method. Rafe might be good at giving, but he was not so good at giving in or at taking orders. He excelled, she discovered, at delegation and negotiation and cutting deals.

He excelled, too, at making her laugh and snarl within the same minute. At keeping her mind entertained and her tongue sharp and her body sated. Constantly she fought the notion that she was getting too used to his company and too comfortable in his company, with him wearing jeans and boots and working alongside her.

Or wearing nothing at all and working alongside, on top of or beneath her.

This time there'd been some of all three, and now Cat lay sprawled beside him in the Sunday twilight quiet. Spent and satisfied but also shadowed in sadness because early in the morning he was returning to Sydney. Back to his job and his apartment and the life she felt no more ready to be a part of than five days earlier.

He'd asked, several times. And she'd tried to explain that she didn't like the person she became in the city. Awkward and ill-at-ease and out of her element. She didn't like spending time there. She didn't want to damage what they'd forged this weekend, either.

Now, on the cooling sheets of her bed, she sensed him watching her again, and she didn't have to ask what he was thinking. "Leave it," she said, before he opened his mouth. "I won't change my mind."

"You said that about Vegas...."

"And look where that got me!"

Her debt paid off, a future for Corroboree, a possibility of family.

Feeling incredibly lucky and humbled and thankful, she turned her head to look at him. To quietly say, "Thank you."

He didn't smile and say, "My pleasure," as she'd anticipated. He didn't say anything for a long, solemn second. "How about you thank me by coming to Kameruka Downs next weekend."

Not the first time he'd broached the subject of taking her to meet his mother, either. She shook her head against the pillow. "No. Not yet."

"You're being stubborn."

"No, I'm being practical. I have responsibilities here. My animals—"

"The Porters looked after them while you were in America. Is there any reason they can't do that again?"

"I can't ask them every weekend."

"I'm not asking—"

"Please, Rafe," she cut in, quiet, intense. "Not yet."

For several strong, hard beats of her heart she didn't think he would let it go. He had that look in his eyes she didn't trust. That intentness and purpose that always set her on edge. But then he rolled onto his back and stared at the ceiling. "I'll come back here, then."

The tight breathlessness in Cat's chest eased. He was coming back. Another weekend, another chance to forge his indelible impression in her home and in her life. In her heart, too, but she was stoically trying to ignore that. "I hope you will."

"Why don't we invite your neighbors over," he asked after another short pause.

"Now?" she asked, rising on her elbow. Indicating their nakedness with an arched eyebrow.

"Next weekend."

"I gather you mean Bob and Jennifer Porter." She eyed him a moment, trying to work out his angle. Suspicious of this seemingly random idea coming hot on the heels of his latest invitation to spend a weekend away. "Are you thinking of using them to persuade me I'm not needed here? Because—"

"I'm thinking they're your closest neighbors and old family friends and you might like to introduce them to your husband."

Taken aback by his tone and the matching snap to his eyes, Cat blinked.

"Unless there's some reason you don't want to," he added.

"What would that be?"

"You tell me. You don't have a problem with having me here, putting me to work, having me in your bed…but you don't want to go anywhere with me. You don't want to meet my family or me to meet your neighbors. I'm starting to wonder if you don't want to be seen with me."

"Don't be ridiculous!"

"Am I?" He asked, low and dangerous. "Who have you told about our marriage, Catriona?"

Her silence was telling.

"Not even your stepmother? You told me last week you'd love to wipe the floor with her patronizing attitude. Aren't I a big enough prize?"

"Is that how you see yourself?" she countered. "Is that how you'd like me to introduce you to my neighbors next weekend? Jen and Bob, meet Rafe Carlisle, my prize husband. I won him on the roulette wheel in Vegas!"

He glared at her a long moment, then he shook his head and expelled a low oath. "I would like you to introduce me as your husband. That's all."

"I can do that," she said softly, relenting. "Saturday night?"

"Saturday night is good."

As always, the heat of their exchange shifted to another kind of heat, and he made love to her with an edgy intensity that set her pulse hammering and her blood roaring. And when he held her on the brink, fire burned in his gaze as he insisted on hearing his name on her lips.

Cat didn't think about that conversation again until after he'd gone. Around midmorning on Monday she was drawing up a working budget—arguably the world's most boring task—when she recalled Milla's words that day on his terrace.

He's a better man than he lets on, even to himself.

Unsettled, she rocked back from her computer spreadsheet and onto her feet. She knew she'd underestimated him from the start, dismissing him as lightweight and a charming diversion. That seemed to come so easily to him—he played on it, she knew—yet there were so many other layers to the man.

Depth and capability and intelligence that he liked to bury beneath the sexy, playboy charm.

Now she wondered why…and Milla's comment and that Sunday evening conversation drifted through her consciousness.

Surely he couldn't have any kind of inferiority thing. Not Rafe Carlisle. Surely he didn't believe that she'd kept their marriage from her friends and distant family because *he* was lacking. That was laughable in an ironic way, seeing as she'd been thinking the exact opposite.

That *she* might be seen as deficient by *his* family and friends.

She knew she lacked nothing here in her environment, in the life she'd chosen as a child riding at her father's side. Here she was herself, she was happy, and that was that. If she fell pregnant, she would have an added link with his family, a bond beyond her marriage.

Then she would travel to Kameruka Downs and meet his mother. Then he could take her to a fancy restaurant to lunch with his brothers, but not before. It would be hard enough saying goodbye to Rafe when he decided to end their marriage.

She did not want to lose her heart to his family, as well.

Cat hated to admit it—even to herself—but all week she'd been like a kid waiting for Christmas. She had enough work to fill her days. She had his phone calls to look forward to each night. It shouldn't have taken so long for Friday to come around. And when it did and she arrived home to a message saying he wouldn't be arriving until Saturday, she should not have felt such a dismal sense of letdown.

It's okay, Cat told herself, since she wasn't a kid waiting for Christmas. She was an adult. Independent and capable of dealing with the first hiccup in their long-distance marriage. He, too, had responsibilities.

Saturday morning she'd intended to wait for Rafe before

starting work, but the early arrival of her period had her wired tight and sharp as a newly strained barb. She couldn't sit around wringing her hands in disappointment because she hadn't fallen pregnant the first time. Now, there was no reason not to yard the cows herself.

Mustering gave her some time to think and to decide she didn't like her happiness hanging on his arrival or nonarrival. Perhaps she should reevaluate their relationship. Perhaps the long distance thing would never work.

And perhaps she shouldn't make any decisions on a day when she felt so funky and out of sorts. Or while working with large, unpredictable animals, she added, when a cow balked suddenly almost knocking the gate from her hands.

She paid more attention then, as she prepared to start drafting off the dry cows. The day was warm already, the air thick with dust churned by racing hooves. She ducked through the railed fence and was unlatching the gate at the end of the draft when she thought she heard the buzz of a plane overhead. Even as she tipped back her hat to scan the sky she called herself silly. The airstrip hadn't been graded. He would fly to the Samuelses' again.

Swinging back, she saw the danger a millisecond too late. A cow hit the gate she held, knocking it from her grip and driving it into her chest. Before she could regain her balance, the whole yard sniffed the open gate and charged full tilt for freedom.

This time the iron bar caught her on the side of the head and she went down for the count.

Rafe had a bad feeling gnawing at him all the way from Sydney. It made him fly cautiously for a change, but once on the ground and behind the wheel of his borrowed vehicle he nearly flew the ten miles to Corroboree. He barely slowed for the cattle grids or the sharp turn by the house. He could see the dust cloud of activity at the cattle yards a mile farther on that confirmed his gut feeling was spot-on.

He'd told her not to start without him. She'd argued that she'd been working cattle on her own since her teens. He pointed out that since he had a vested interest, he'd prefer she didn't do such work on her own again. Not when she could be pregnant.

"And of course you have to do it your way," he ground out as he wheeled to a halt beside the yards.

His hot anger morphed to cold fear the second he slammed the door on the utility. The cattle wheeled around the yards in obvious agitation stirring up a choking cloud of dust, but even through that he should have been able to pick out Cat's figure.

He couldn't. Yet her bike was here. He took the fence at a run, climbing two rails at a time and feeling his heart lurch in his chest when he saw her from the top. Crouched in the corner of the yard, her dog at her feet.

He called her name as he hit the ground, but the croaky sound was swallowed up in the bellowing chaos of the startled herd. *She's all right, she's conscious, she's trying to get to her feet, she's all right,* chanted through his mind as he pushed through the next fence and finally she looked up, her face pale beneath a coating of dust, a smile trembling on her lips.

Her legs started to wobble, and before he could get there she started to sink to the ground. Rafe hunkered down with her, his own limbs felt wonky with fear and shock and relief because at least she was conscious.

"It's okay, baby," he told her. "I'm here now."

Her attempt at a smile was wan. "There's two of you."

"That's a good thing, surely."

"Ish it?" There was a definite slur to her speech. "'Nough trouble handling one…"

Her voice trailed off as she slumped into unconsciousness and Rafe swore silently as he bent to scoop her up.

"You just need more practice."

* * *

Cat couldn't remember anything about the accident or getting to the hospital. Dimly she recalled an altercation over her admission and the objections swirling in her dizzy brain because she didn't want to be hospitalized. She remembered being blindsided by the pain of her head injury and her broken ribs, and the sharp note in Rafe's voice as he demanded a doctor's attention.

Sometime later she'd drifted into consciousness and he was there, sitting beside her bed, holding her hand and murmuring something she couldn't catch through the blur of pain medication. She'd floated back to sleep with a smile on her lips and in her heart, but when she woke again the chair was empty. Perhaps it was the drugs, but that small vignette of the big picture had seemed profoundly significant. He'd been there, looking out for her, making her smile, easing her loneliness, and then he was gone.

On Monday, when she opened her eyes and found him smiling down at her, the sweet ache of joy was almost unbearable. She could have put that down to her injuries—her chest hurt like the devil—but deep inside she acknowledged the inevitable. She wanted the glorious impossibility of Rafe Carlisle's smile whenever she opened her eyes. She wanted him as her real husband, at her side, forever.

In that instant she knew that nothing less than his love would do.

"Nice shiner," he drawled, parking himself on the edge of her mattress. But the kiss he pressed to her lips was tender, the depths of his eyes dark with concern.

"You're here."

"Did you think I'd leave you? All beaten up? In this place?"

"I thought…" Her frown hurt like the blazes, but not as much as the leap of her heart against her bruised and broken ribs. "I thought, maybe, you would need to be at work today."

"I needed to be here today." He lifted her hand and held it against his face for a second. "How are you feeling?"

"Like I was trampled by a herd of beasts."

The low note of his laughter did glorious things to her aching body. So did the brush of his fingers against her cheek. "I brought you some flowers and fruit."

"Thank you."

"And this."

"This" turned out to be diamonds. A diamond necklace, to be precise. Cat blinked in shock. Then—she couldn't help herself—she laughed. Flowers and fruit and, as an aside, diamonds. That was so over-the-top. So Rafe.

And so not her.

The laughter, the warmth, her delight in his presence suddenly turned brittle. She stared at the dazzling stones without touching them. "Where on earth did you get that?"

"In Vegas."

"It's…" *The same as those clothes. Beautiful, expensive, impractical.*

"You don't like it?" With a casual-looking shrug, he snapped the lid of the box shut and tossed it on the bedside table. "No matter."

But it did matter. In all kinds of ways. It mattered that he'd spent all that money on her…and that he didn't seem to care whether she liked the gift or not. Easy come, easy go. He could afford to buy a necklace like that with his lunch money. He was Rafe Carlisle.

It mattered even more over the next few days as he breezed in and out of the hospital, coloring the spare hospital room with his beauty, dazzling the nursing staff with his sexy grin, and entertaining her with his company, with covert kisses, and with news from Corroboree.

At first his interest and involvement in her station pleased her no end. They *did* have common ground. They just might have grounds for a relationship that worked in places other than in bed. Then she learned of the changes he was making, the money he was spending, all communicated in the same negligent tone as he'd delivered the diamonds.

I bought you a new Landcruiser. I've ordered a new hot water system. You need a better kitchen.

It mattered that he was infiltrating her life, her home, her business. Corroboree was *hers,* and she needed to keep control of that one last bastion. Her last remaining link with her parents; her strength; her confidence.

It mattered that when she attempted to explain this to Rafe, he shrugged it off in a way that grated all over nerves stretched taut by her enforced inactivity. "I want to do this for you, baby. I can afford it. Indulge me." Then he'd distracted her with wicked suggestions of how he'd like to indulge her in the new spa bath he'd ordered.

Today it had to end. Everything…including her hospital stay, which she was sure had stretched longer than necessary due to Rafe's influence. She was itching to get back home, to take over her life, but Rafe threw her planned speech right off balance by arriving on the heels of the breakfast cart—at least three hours before official visiting hours—dressed in a suit.

"I'm on my way to the airport," he told her after a soul-stirring kiss. "Board meeting I can't miss."

While she was recovering from his unexpected arrival, from the aftershocks of his kiss, he nabbed a piece of toast from her plate.

"Had to leave too early for breakfast," he said around his first bite. Then, "I saw your doctor outside. He says you'll be all right to go home tomorrow. I'll—"

"Today."

Rafe stopped chewing.

"I'm all right to go home today, if anyone would care to consult with me."

"Look, baby—"

"Oh, no. Don't even start with that."

"What?" he asked, genuinely puzzled.

"'Look, baby. Don't worry, baby. I'm handling everything, baby.'" Apparently, she was mocking his tone, although not very well. She shook her head and continued in her own voice. "I tried to explain this yesterday, and I'm going to try again now. I don't want you handling everything. I want to worry about my business, about my life."

"Okay."

"Okay?"

Alerted by her sharp inflection, by the glint of temper in her eyes, Rafe put down the remains of the toast and brushed the crumbs from his fingers. "Is there something specific I've done to upset you?"

"Everything you've done without asking first upsets me! The new vehicle, the stove, the spa you tossed into the equation."

"They're just things, Catriona. To make your life easier."

"They're things I didn't ask for, things I don't want." Her brows drew together in an uncompromising line. "None of this was part of our deal, Rafe."

"Can't I buy—"

"No. Don't you see? You're buying me all these *things* because you can afford to fling money around, and I have nothing to give back!"

One side of him wanted to say straight out that she didn't need to give anything back but herself, while the other balked at her attitude. At what sounded very much like a rejection of all he'd done for her and his reason for doing so. "You know why I married you, Catriona. I've told you more than once. Can't you accept that I don't need any more from you?"

Something shifted in her expression, almost as if she was gathering herself, preparing herself. "I'm not pregnant."

Rafe stared back at her. She thought he only wanted a baby? Hell, he—

"I don't know why I expected I would be. I just…"

Her voice trailed off, one hand lifted and then dropped to the blanket in a gesture of futility. Without thinking he reached for her—for that hand—but she pulled herself upright, warning him away with her body language and her eyes.

Rafe felt that rejection like a slap. He felt his own gaze narrow and instead of asking if she felt the same kick of disappointment as he did, instead of reassuring her that they could try again next month and the one after that if she wanted, he asked, "How long have you known?"

"Since Saturday."

Four days. At least six separate hospital visits, six opportunities to share the news. "And you didn't think I would want to know before now?"

"It doesn't make any difference," she said. "This isn't something you can go out and buy."

"Is that what you think I would want to do?"

"You bought me to have your baby."

He couldn't dispute that, didn't want to debate it. But he needed to get one thing straight… "That might be how we started out, but a lot has changed in the last two weeks."

"Has it?" she asked after a beat, and the quiet question rocked him back on his heels. Nothing had changed for her, he realized. Nothing.

"You only wanted the money to secure Corroboree? That's the only reason you married me?"

Her gaze met his, honest and unflinching. "I wanted the baby, too."

But not him. Never him.

Oddly the knowledge didn't spark heat or frustration or denial. Instead it turned him cold and numb some place deep inside. Frozen with an understanding that had been too slow coming. She didn't want him buying her things because she didn't want him. He'd made no impression on her heart, so everything he'd done—the things she knew, the ones she'd yet to discover—meant nothing to her except as an affront to her independence.

The very thing that had drawn him to her in the first place. How ironic.

"Tell me one thing, Catriona," he said slowly, coolly. "If

you'd had you choice of a father for this baby, would I have even figured in your selection process?"

For a second her eyes widened, raw with an emotion he couldn't identify, and then she looked away. And that telling silence cut through his numbness, sliced all the way to his soul.

As he'd expected, as he'd feared—he wasn't the man she would have chosen. He wasn't a man she could ever love.

"Rafe, I'm sorry."

And that was the last thing he needed. Her pity, an apology, some tepid justification. "Hey, babe," he drawled, as if it didn't matter a damn to him. "There's no need for you to be sorry. You've got your property back and a few extras into the bargain. Why should you be sorry?"

"I thought you needed this baby."

He gave a shrug. "There's time to try again."

A pulse beat hard in her throat as she slowly shook her head. "I don't think so, Rafe. I think…I think I need some time alone to reconsider."

"Take all the time you want, Catriona. I won't come chasing you again. If you ever change your mind, you know where to find me."

Fourteen

When the hospital discharged her later that day, Bob Porter was waiting to take her home. Bob didn't volunteer how he came to be there and Cat's pride didn't let her ask. She must have nodded off as soon as they hit the road because she woke at home with Bob shaking her arm, and she didn't recall anything of the trip.

Still groggy, she stumbled inside and pulled up short when she found his wife inside. Cleaning.

"You didn't have to do this," Cat said.

"Just getting used to the place."

Cat frowned. Perhaps the rap on the head had affected her more than she'd thought.

The other woman smiled secretly. "He said it would be a nice surprise."

A tight feeling gathered in the center of her chest, like a knot being tugged hard from either side. "He?"

"He, your husband." Jennifer winked conspiratorially. "He headhunted us, you know."

"Headhunted?" Cat's voice sounded as weak and thready as her knees. She needed to sit down. She did. And Jennifer looked concerned. "Are you all right, love?"

"I will be once you stop dragging out the suspense. What are you talking about, Jen?"

"Our new jobs. Bob's your stationhand. I'm the housekeeper. We weren't supposed to start for a couple more weeks, but Gordon didn't take the news of us leaving well. He told us not to bother working our notice. We were going to take a holiday but then your Rafe rang and told us about your accident.... We thought it might be nice to start straight away."

"I'm all right, Jen. Really. I don't need any house help."

Jen ignored that. "Can I make you a cuppa?"

Cat nodded. She needed to sit and digest this a minute. Work through how this had happened…and what she was going to do about it. The knot in her chest tightened several more notches as she thought about that argument in the hospital. The coldness in Rafe's eyes before he walked from the room.

"When did Rafe employ you?" she asked, turning toward the kitchen where Jen was setting down their cups.

"He rang last week. Tuesday—no, it was Monday night. He made us an offer and we asked for some time to think it over."

Last week? And she'd known nothing about it… "Why didn't you ask me what I thought about this?"

"Rafe said he wanted to tell you himself." Jen smiled. "I told him it was the kind of present you would appreciate. You not being one for jewelry and the like."

"What did he say to that?" Cat's throat felt tight, her voice husky with the certainty she'd made the biggest blunder of her life. That she'd done Rafe a serious disservice.

"He said he was working that out. And I have to agree, given his other surprise."

A peach orchard.

Cat's heart stalled when Jen spilled that news, and restarted

with a thick, slow beat that ached through her body. He'd remembered what she'd told him in Vegas about loving the
scent of freshly picked peaches. As soon as Bob rang back accepting the job, Rafe had talked to him about how and when
and where to put the new trees.

All she'd wanted was some sign that he cared, that he
might even love her, and now she had it—a peach orchard,
the perfect sign—and it was too late. She'd sent him away.
She'd let him believe there was nothing between them, that
she wanted nothing between them.

If he didn't care, why would he have chosen something this
personal? This special?

If he didn't care, why would he have told her where to find
him if she reconsidered? Wouldn't he have simply told her to
forget it? To forget him?

Her heart beat so hard it echoed in her ears, drumming with
the clear certainty of what she had to do. She didn't want to
give up. She didn't want to be lonely anymore. She didn't need
to reconsider when the truth beat so strongly in her heart.

Rafe was operating on autopilot. Shaking hands. Dispens-
ing small talk. Smiling and sipping the sponsor's champagne
at yet another charity event and all the while thinking, *How
long until I can get the hell out of here? Until I can go somewhere to snap and snarl the way my gut and my heart and my
head have been doing all night long. All week long.*

Ever since Catriona convinced him he was wasting his
time. That he wasn't the kind of man she would ever choose.

He didn't blame her. This whole scheme had been flawed
from the start. He'd been too clever, thinking he wanted an
independent wife who made no demands upon his heart or his
lifestyle.

That's what he'd wanted; that's what he'd got. How could
he complain?

Surreptitiously he checked his watch again. Eight o'clock.

He'd intended staying another hour, but in his current mood it was wiser to cut and run. Before he snarled at someone important and cost the hotel a big corporate client.

He made his excuses to the head of the charity committee, promised her a donation that wiped the moue of disappointment off her lips and was in a taxi heading home before she stopped gushing her thanks.

In the last week there'd been a lot he didn't like about his apartment—specifically, being alone in it—but one thing he appreciated right now was its location so close to the city. He was walking through the lobby of his building five minutes later. Pressing the elevator button. Rocking on his heels and wondering what the hell better things he had to do upstairs tonight. Alone.

Ah, hell, at least he could smash a glass if he felt like it. Snarl at Tolstoy. Play some tragic opera at full volume and wallow in his misery.

The elevator dinged. Not the one he faced but the one at his back. He turned on his heel as the doors opened and the woman inside looked up and right in to his eyes.

Her coral-painted lips mouthed one word. His name. But she didn't move, and Rafe found himself frozen in place, stunned, wondering if his imagination had conjured her up.

A vision in white satin sent to taunt his lonely night.

Then the elevator doors slid noiselessly shut and propelled him into motion. He dived for the button just as the doors reopened. He met her on her way out and turned her back inside. Closed the doors.

"What are you doing here?" She sounded as incredulous as he felt. Looked even more beautiful up close. And she was real.

"I live here." He met her eyes. Cool. Polite. "You?"

"I…know someone who lives here."

"You were visiting?"

"I came to visit." She lifted her chin a little, and he saw the nervous tick of the pulse in her throat. Watched the nervous flick of her tongue as she moistened her lips. "To stay, actually. But he wasn't home."

Rafe felt something flutter back to life deep inside. "Weren't you going to stick around and wait for this…someone…to come home?"

"I thought about that," she said gravely. "I was going to climb into his bed and wait."

"A sound plan."

"But we have some problems to iron out, and they never seem to be a problem in bed. Out of bed…that's what we need to work on."

He nodded. And he let his eyes drift over her dress. The one he'd opened in that box in Vegas. It looked even better on her body, and the diamonds at her throat were the perfect foil. Slowly his gaze rose to meet hers. "So you decided to go out somewhere?"

"I wasn't sure what to do. My husband didn't know I was coming to town, you see—"

"This man's your husband?"

"He is." Despite her nerves, despite the wild uncertainty of her heartbeat, Cat stood tall and sure. This was her one chance to let him see what he meant to her. "He is my husband who I sent away because I didn't understand how much he had given me or how well he knew me."

"And now you do?"

"Yes, and I want to tell him so. Except I didn't know where he was or how long he would be. So I asked his neighbor and she told me he'd gone to this charity party, an important one for his work, and I decided to go, too. To talk to him."

"About those problems you mentioned before…?"

"That's right." She moistened her lips again, but her eyes never left his. "I have this fear, you see, about getting dressed up like this and going to a fancy party where I'll be looked over and judged by people such as my husband's family and friends and business colleagues. Important people I want to make an impression with, but there's this fear I'll be found wanting."

"Sounds as if you were about to face up to this fear."

"I was. For him." She sucked in a breath that hitched a little before continuing. "Then there's my stubbornness. I'm used to doing things my own way."

"Independence isn't all bad."

"I'm starting to think I overrated it. That it might be nice to have a partner to share life with. Not part-time, and maybe full-time won't be possible, but more of the time."

Rafe felt his nostrils flare. Felt that flutter of hope grow wings that beat hard and fast. "Sounds as if you're working on that problem, too."

"I think so. But there's another one." Nerves swam in her eyes and he had to steel himself to stay put. To let her get all the way through whatever she'd come here to say before he gave in to the need to hold her. "The last time I saw my husband, he asked if I would have chosen him."

"Perhaps he didn't think he had enough to offer."

Her head lifted a little. Some kind of recognition or acknowledgment flared in her eyes. "He couldn't possibly think that. He's the most amazing man I've ever met. Oh, he's passably handsome and he has some charm, but that's by the by." Slowly she took a step toward him. "The thing I failed to see was how well he knew me. I kept focusing on the little things." Another step. "He didn't know what I liked to eat. I didn't know his address. He didn't know that white satin evening dresses have limited wear out west." One more step and she stopped right in front of him. Her voice dropped to a new, low resonance, in perfect harmony with Rafe's pulse. "But he knew what was important. He gave me the most precious things. My family property. A chance to have a family again. The perfect staff. And then there's the peach orchard…"

The last came more slowly, on a slightly quizzical note that dampened Rafe's stampeding hope. "You don't like the idea?"

"An orchard is a lot of work."

His eyes narrowed in alarm. "What are you saying, Catriona?"

"I'm going to need someone to share the workload," she said solemnly. "And to share the peaches."

"That sounds like a long-term project."

"Like a marriage, I was thinking. It takes a lot of nurturing and a lot of love, but then you've got something to show for your devotion and something to leave to future generations."

"Are there going to be future generations?" he asked, heart beating strong and fast again.

"I hope so." Finally she lifted a hand and touched his face. Reaching out and letting him know she was willing to give, willing to take the first step, willing to meet him halfway. "I love you, Rafe Carlisle. I want to make those future generations with you."

"You would trust me with such an important long-term project?"

"I trust you with my heart, husband."

His heart responded, believing, trusting. "Then that is all I want from you. I love you, Catriona McConnell Carlisle. Will you marry me, again? In front of family and friends?"

"Yes." Smiling her love, she moved into his arms. "I will."

* * * * *

THE RUTHLESS
GROOM

This, my tenth book, I dedicate to the wonderful editors who made it happen, Leslie Wainger and Stacy Boyd. Ladies, your blood is worth bottling!

One

I'm sorry, Alex, but I can't marry you today.

Usually it took a lot more than a single line of print to shake Alex Carlisle's carefully constructed composure, but that particular line leaped off the innocent sheet of paper and rocked him like a thunderbolt.

Jilted. Two hours before he was due to sign the marriage contract. And he hadn't glimpsed a hint of it coming.

The rest of Susannah's *I-need-some-space-and-time-to-think, I'm-sorry* explanation swam before his eyes in a swamping tide of frustration. To hell with apologies. He didn't need an explanation; he needed a wife in his bed.

Tonight, if not sooner.

"Is everything all right, sir?"

Easing his crumpling grip on the page, Alex nodded to the hotel concierge who'd handed him the message. "Thank you, Emilio. Yes."

Everything would be all right, Alex decided, setting his jaw as the first wave of reaction subsided. Once he found Susannah and got to the bottom of what the hell had changed since yesterday when they'd last spoken.

Last-minute jitters, that's all it could be. Even serene, sensible Susannah had a right to wedding-day nerves, right? Especially with the importance of what the marriage entailed to Alex and his family weighty on her shoulders.

Carefully his fingers smoothed over the note, then folded it along the existing crease lines. She'd known about his father's will from the start. He'd been honest and direct about his immediate need for a baby to satisfy that clause...or to satisfy his determination to fulfill that clause.

One baby between the three Carlisle half brothers, conceived within three months. That's "all" Charles Carlisle had asked for, and they'd made a pact, he and his brothers. One-in, all-in, to increase the odds of success.

As the eldest he considered it his duty, his responsibility, made all the more pressing by his brothers' lack of success to date. Not that that surprised him. Neither Tomas nor Rafe had tackled the problem with a strategy. Neither Tomas nor Rafe had wanted the marriage/family/baby deal.

Alex did.

He wanted his baby born within a family unit. He wanted a wife and he'd chosen Susannah, a friend and business associate, for all the right reasons. She just needed reminding of those reasons.

Discreetly the concierge cleared his throat. "The flowers were delivered to your suite half an hour ago, Mr. Carlisle. And the delivery from Cartier has been put in the hotel safe for security. I believe everything is now in order."

Everything was in order for the low-key exchange of vows they'd chosen because of the short time frame and because neither of them had wanted a media scrum. Everything was in order except for the bride.

"There is one more thing." Alex snapped his brain out of contemplation and into action. "My fiancée may be late. See if the officiant can block out a longer period of time this afternoon."

"How much longer, sir?"

"Indefinite. But I'll make any inconvenience worth her while."

"Yes, sir."

"I'll need my car out front in ten minutes." To go and fetch Susannah from wherever she'd taken those last-minute jitters. Hopefully her mother would know. Or one of her employees. "I have some phone calls to make and then I'm going out. But if the lady who delivered this note…"

"Zara."

"Susannah," he corrected, frowning.

"I believe she's a friend of your fiancée, sir. Zara Lovett. She dropped off the envelope on her way to work."

Alex's inner tension loosened a notch, then strengthened with a new sense of purpose. If this friend delivered the note, she must know Susannah's whereabouts. "Do you know where Zara Lovett works?"

"Of course, sir. She's a personal trainer with an agency we secure quite often for our guests. I have her card on file."

Susannah wasn't here.

Botheration.

Zara Lovett's leather-clad shoulders slumped a tad as she completed a second slow circuit of the cabin on her motorbike. No vehicle lurked around the back; no windows lay open to air. The single-room hut sat crouched in the center of its cleared mountain block, still sleeping off a prolonged winter hibernation. The only sign of life was the choral chortle of kookaburras in one of the mountain gums.

Laughing, no doubt, at her wasted efforts.

A two-and-a-half-hour ride out from Melbourne, ten bucks blown on a lousy roadhouse lunch, and all for nothing. She'd been so certain Susannah would be here. When her one o'clock client hadn't shown at the inner-city gym as arranged, she'd considered it a sign and a blessing.

With a whole afternoon on her hands, she could do something about the worry fretting away at the back of her brain.

Her worry wasn't over Susannah calling off today's wedding. For that she'd raised a heartfelt hallelujah. No, her concern centered on the out-of-character suddenness of Susannah's decision and the fact that she'd gone incommunicado. Susannah, who didn't go to the bathroom without at least one phone!

That's why Zara had thought of the cabin. It belonged to Susannah's grandfather and was the only place Zara could imagine her going that didn't boast communication facilities. And her early morning message—a harried-sounding voice-mail asking Zara to deliver a letter to her fiancé's hotel—had mentioned going away somewhere to think.

Zara had spent time up here herself for just that purpose. When it came to escaping, to thinking about one's life direction, this cabin was a tried and tested location.

She slowed her bike to a stop, turned off the engine and kicked down the stand. She might as well stretch her legs and fill her lungs with some clean high-country air before heading back to the city. After shucking gloves and helmet, she unzipped her jacket…then zipped it back up again when the wind snapped at her bare skin.

So much for the gorgeous spring day she'd left behind in Melbourne. Squinting up at the cloud-laced sky, she decided to limit her walk to a brisk five minutes. Then she'd be out of here if this fickle weather decided to blow up a storm.

A flash of...something...through the trees caught her attention as she prepared to dismount. Staring into the thick bushland, she waited until the gleam reappeared and took form as the highly polished panels of a car. A second later she heard the motor, heard it slow to turn in to the cabin, and she released her breath on a slow puff of relief.

"About time, Suse."

Her gaze narrowed on the dark vehicle as it crawled into view. The same prestigious European badge, the same darkly tinted glass, the same sleek lines, but a bigger, gutsier model than Susannah's.

And that definitely wasn't Susannah behind the wheel, she decided, as the car purred to a halt ten yards away. The driver's door opened and a man stepped out. Zara's heart did a half kick against her ribs.

Alex Carlisle.

Although they'd never met, she recognized him instantly. She noted that his dark suit looked as sleek and expensively European as the vehicle. Noted his broad shoulders and flat stomach as he buttoned his jacket over a crisp white shirt.

Noted how his gaze fixed on her without hesitation.

Zara had seen his picture often enough to know those eyes were the same blue-gray as a winter storm on Port Phillip Bay. She imagined they were just as cold and forbidding. Despite her leathers, goose bumps shivered over her skin as his car door snapped shut with a decisive note.

Yep, that was definitely Alex Carlisle cutting down the distance between them with long, purpose-filled strides. But what on earth was he doing out here? How did he even know about this place?

Boots planted solidly on either side of her bike, she lifted her chin and prepared to ask. Then their eyes met with a force that licked through her body like electric flame and fried her questions on the spot. By the time her synapses recovered, she'd lost the advantage. By then his gaze had narrowed a fraction, deepening the creases at the corners of his eyes. "You're Zara Lovett?"

"That's right."

He nodded, a brief, terse acknowledgment, before asking, "Where's Susannah?"

He certainly didn't waste any time getting to the point. Or any breath introducing himself. Zara supposed when your picture appeared pretty much daily somewhere in Australia's press, you assumed recognition. "I don't know," she said in answer to his question.

His gaze shifted, sliding over the cabin and its surroundings in one measuring sweep before returning to her. "She's not here?"

Zara shook her head, which he might or might not have caught since he'd started walking, past her and up onto the cabin's porch. "Don't you believe me?" she called after him, turning to watch as he peered in one window, then the second.

Hands on hips, he turned. "Your boyfriend told me you'd come out here to find her."

Her *what?* Zara opened her mouth and closed it again. He could only mean her housemate, Tim. Which meant— "You rang my home? How did you get my number?"

"Does that matter?"

"Yes. Yes, it does."

"No," he countered with the same certainty. "What matters is locating Susannah. Where is she, Zara?"

"I don't understand. Didn't you get the note I left at your hotel?"

"I don't understand why *you* left the note."

"Because Susannah asked me to."

"Don't play games with me, Zara." Something glinted in his eyes, a fierceness at odds with his even tone. "I am not in the mood to play nice."

"Are you ever?"

"When I want to—" he said, deceptively soft, deceptively smooth, as he started toward her "—I can be very nice."

"I guess I'll have to take your word for that."

When he stepped off the porch, Zara's pulse skipped. Not nerves, but the same kind of adrenaline spike that used to accompany her onto the mat before a fight. Especially one with an expert opponent.

Time, she decided, to get off her bike.

At six foot in her biker boots, Zara was used to setting men back on their heels just by standing and meeting their eyes. Alex Carlisle stood an inch or two taller and he met her gaze without a flicker of surprise. Zara looked right back and for a moment got lost in the intensity of his eyes. Not exactly blue, too vivid to be gray, and with a dark rim around the iris that sucked you into their powerful focus.

And it struck her, in that long, silent sizing-up moment, that it would take a lot to put Alex Carlisle on the ropes. That once he set his mind to something he would follow through with ruthless purpose. She didn't mind that in a person—in fact she liked purpose, she liked directness, she liked a spark of go-get-'em—but, oh, Susannah.

Now I understand your reluctance to tell him face-to-face. You wouldn't have stood a chance.

"Let's start over," he said in that same low voice. "I'm sorry I came on so strong. It's been a hell of a day."

Then he smiled and offered his hand and his name, and she realized why Susannah might have been persuaded into such a coldhearted marriage arrangement. *He's not so cold,* she realized, as the heat from his grip and the impact of that smile seeped into her blood.

"When you saw Susannah this morning—"

"No." She extracted her hand and smoothed it down her thigh. She really, really hoped the sparks she felt were only static electricity. "I didn't see her. I didn't even speak to her. She left a message on my machine, then she e-mailed the letter I left at your hotel."

Irritation pinched between his dark brows. "Why couldn't she call me? Tell me herself?"

"She said she tried to contact you this morning, before you left Sydney."

"Yet here I am."

A six-hundred-mile plane trip from his home in another state. Yet Zara didn't think the inconvenience of a wasted journey played any part in the darkened intensity of his eyes, the flare of his nostrils. For the first time, she let herself see his side of this picture. Effectively left at the altar, he had a right to some anger, some hurt and some answers.

"Suse really did try," she said on a softer note. "Her message to me sounded all flustered because she hadn't been able to contact you. When she said she was going somewhere to think, when I couldn't get her on her mobile phone, I thought she'd come up here."

"Flustered doesn't sound like Susannah."

"No, but then everything about this situation is unlike Susannah."

"Meaning?"

Zara shrugged. "Suse is careful, a bit cautious, then out

of the blue she decided to marry you. No offense, but I thought your relationship was all about business."

"We'd dated."

"Once or twice? That's hardly grounds for marriage!"

"Don't you think that's between Susannah and me?" His voice turned icy, as chill as the wind that buffeted her jacket hard against her back and whipped her hair across her face.

Impatiently she captured the long strands in one hand. "Yes, it is, but I can't ignore the way she sounded on the phone and the fact she changed her mind overnight."

His eyes narrowed. "You saw her last night?"

"We had dinner. And she sounded dead set on marrying you then."

There must have been something in her tone or her expression, because his narrow gaze sharpened on her face. "Dead set in spite of your views on what constitutes grounds for marriage?"

"I didn't force Susannah to do anything, if that's what you're implying."

"You only…what…suggested she take some more time to think about it?"

"That was my advice." Zara met his eyes without apology. They darkened with a ruthless determination that sent a frisson of alarm skittering through her bones. "Why did you come up here? Why were you looking for me?"

"To find Susannah. I have an officiant on standby."

Oh, no, he was not going to bully Susannah into this. Not if she could help it!

When he turned toward his vehicle, Zara swung around too, right into the face of the wind. It caught at her hair, her breath, and a sudden wild gust sent her bike crashing to the ground. Whipping back around, she bent to pick up the machine but Alex beat her by a second. When she attempted to take over the handlebars, their shoulders and hands grazed with a startling tingle of heat. She didn't meet his eyes as she thanked him. She didn't want to know if he'd felt that unsettling zing too.

Completely inappropriate, Zara thought, kicking at the bike stand. It broke off and clattered to the ground. If the kookaburras hadn't taken off for somewhere more sheltered they'd be laughing their heads off!

"Any other damage?" he asked.

"Only to my mood." She swung her leg over the seat and waited for him to hand over the helmet and gloves he'd retrieved from the ground. Frowning, she watched him wipe the dust from them on his very expensive trousers.

"There's no need to do that," she said, disturbed by the image. *Her* helmet, *his* thigh, way too intimate. "Give it here."

He didn't. He gestured toward the sky. "It's going to storm soon."

Zara tipped back her head. Inspected the clouds that scurried low and swift on the blustery wind. "I think we'd better get out of here while we can."

"On that bike?"

"I live in Melbourne. I'm used to weather."

"This isn't the city. That last stretch of road was tricky enough with four wheels under me." Frowning, he tapped her helmet against his thigh. "Perhaps you'd better take shelter inside until it passes."

"Oh, no." Zara shook her head. "I can't stay. I have to get home."

He stared at her a second, his expression unreadable. "In that case, you'd better ride with me."

"What about my bike? It's my only transportation. I can't leave it here."

"I'll send someone to pick it up for you."

Just like that, snap of the fingers, problem solved. Zara couldn't imagine living in a world like that. She huffed out a disbelieving breath. "I don't know if I want—"

"To be stranded here when this storm breaks?"

No, that wasn't what she'd been going to say, but he raised a good point. A point that rippled through her like quicksilver as their gazes locked. No, she did not want to be stranded here, alone, in an isolated cabin, with this man and his cold and hot eyes.

"All right," she relented. "I'll just put my bike inside, out of the weather."

"Pleased to see you can be reasonable."

"When I want to, I can be very reasonable," she countered smoothly, echoing his words and his tone from earlier. She thought about mentioning her real motivation for conceding—she wanted to be there if he found Susannah, to intercede if necessary, to ensure he didn't sway Suse's judgment—but decided to keep quiet. She didn't think Alex Carlisle would approve.

Alex didn't want her in his car, but what could he do? The wind continued to gather fury with every passing mile, gusting in uneven spurts that rocked the vehicle and dashed their path with debris. Brought up in the outback, he'd driven in worse weather, but not on roads this tortuous. He'd had to offer her a lift, and now he had to endure all that entailed.

With Zara Lovett, that was one hell of a lot.

Why hadn't someone—Susannah, Emilio, *anyone*— warned him about the legs? A million miles long and snugged in black leather, they'd catch a monk's attention. Alex was not a monk.

Eyes focused on the road, he didn't have to look sideways to picture her in the passenger seat. Her hair a spill of honeyed silk. Whiskey eyes that stretched long and exotic beneath dramatic dark brows. Face too long, nose too big, mouth too wide, she was more about impact than beauty.

Yet he'd taken one look at those long limbs and irregular features and felt a jolt of sexual energy that rocked him to the bone.

He heard her shift in the passenger seat, heard the click of studs and the long metallic whirr of a zip coming undone. Her jacket. He didn't want her taking the damn thing off. He didn't need to know what lay underneath.

Anticipation thickened the air in his lungs. Tension thickened the blood in his veins. He waited…and she settled back into her seat with a soft sigh. With her jacket still on.

What was he doing looking, noticing, responding like a horny teenager? She was Susannah's friend, for Pete's sake.

She shifted again, lifted a hand to comb back her hair, and he caught the drift of her scent, part woman, part leather, part something else he couldn't get a grip of. And he couldn't help wondering how she and Susannah came to be such close friends. They were so unalike, so unlikely.

"Is this your—"

"How did you—"

They'd both started to speak at once, both stopped at the same instant. She waved a hand and said, "You first."

"I was going to ask how you and Susannah became friends." He cut her a sideways look. "You're not what I would have expected."

Turning slightly in her seat, she looked right at him. Raised her brows. "Because I'm wearing leather? Because I ride a bike?"

Point taken. "How long have you been a biker?"

"A biker?" She laughed, a husky draft of amusement that did nothing to ease the awareness in Alex's blood. "I'm not even a wannabe. I ride a bike because it's practical and cheap. Besides, mine's too small."

"That matters?"

"You're asking if size matters?"

He heard the hint of teasing in her voice and resisted the urge to play the game. Not with this woman, not today. "You're telling me with bikes it does."

"Oh, yeah. You need to be riding something called a Dominator or a Monster to call yourself a biker."

"You look the part."

"The leathers? They're for safety, mostly. I like the idea of that layer between me and the bitumen."

"I prefer the idea of a layer of metal."

"Valid point," she conceded, and he sensed her eyes on him. Sensed a new level of interest, a new sharpness in her gaze. "Although those layers of metal don't help you get ahead in traffic jams."

"You still have to stop at the lights," he pointed out. Enjoying the banter, enjoying her eyes on him. "In my car, I can make a phone call, dictate some notes."

"I can study on my bike."

Study? This he couldn't resist. "What do you study?"

"At the lights? Something I've learned by rote. Like anatomy."

"The ankle bone's connected to the calf bone?"

He cut her a quick glance and saw that her smile was as big as the rest of her and packed the same level of impact. "Something like that."

"You're studying medicine?"

"Yup. Third year."

"Dr. Lovett," he mused.

"Okay, okay." She probably rolled her eyes—there was that in her voice—although with his attention back on the road, Alex didn't see the gesture. "I've heard it all before."

He bet she had. And the thought of a bunch of smart-mouth medical students ribbing her with "love-it" gags disturbed him on some primal level.

"You and Susannah," he began, linking their names, reminding himself who she was, why he had no business letting her disturb him in any way. Reminding her that she'd not yet answered his question about their friendship.

"We've been friends for years," she said.

"You were at school together?"

"No."

She didn't elaborate and he needed to concentrate on a tricky section of road. The car rocked hard in the wind and he eased off the gas.

"It's getting wild out there. I'm glad I'm not on my bike." As if to punctuate her words, a sizable branch flew into their path. Then, caught in the wind's bluster, it was gone. He sped up a little, accelerating out of a curve and—

"Look out!"

He saw the fallen tree that blocked the road in the same instant that she gasped the warning. Too late to avoid, but not too late to lessen the inevitable impact. Braking hard, he battled to direct the slewing car away from the thick hardwood trunk, battled to regain control when the tires lost traction and they started a slow-motion sideways slide.

Two

Half expecting air bags to deploy all around her, Zara remained braced with her eyes squeezed shut long after the car slid to a final tree-assisted halt. Apparently they hadn't hit hard enough because nothing happened. Nothing except a hissing fizz from under the hood and what sounded like the thump of a fisted hand against the steering wheel.

A second later his seat belt clicked undone.

"Are you all right?"

The tight note in his voice hinted at concern, and it brought an ache to the back of Zara's eyes that felt very much like tears. Delayed reaction, she diagnosed, since she did not do tears. Slowly she opened her eyes. "I will be."

"Are you sure?"

She managed a faint smile. "Just give me a minute."

She saw his brief hesitation before he attempted to open his door. Without success. His side of the car was jammed against the hefty branches that had halted their progress, and although he applied his shoulder to the door, the only result was an earsplitting wrench of timber against metal.

"I'll need to get out on your side," he said matter-of-factly, and Zara snapped to attention, opening her door and sliding out. The wind lashed at her hair and her unzipped jacket but she paid little heed. Her gaze had fixed on the unscathed panels on her side of the car, still gleaming despite the murky light.

Unmarked because the man currently maneuvering his body across the central console and out the passenger side hadn't panicked. He'd calmly controlled the car's slide. To protect her? That notion weaved a disquieting path through her consciousness and played games with her emotional stability.

To protect them both, she reminded herself. Nothing personal. Nothing to get unsettled and prickly throated about.

Straightening her shoulders, she followed him up front to see the real damage. The car had come to rest bumper-deep in the tree's dense foliage. One jutting branch, it seemed, had pierced the grill and the radiator still hissed its pained response.

She rested a consoling hand on the hood. "Doesn't look as if we'll be going any further. At least, not in this car."

"It could have been a lot worse," he said with a quiet intensity that brought her eyes around to meet his. "I'm rather glad you were in the car."

And not on her bike, without the protection of these sturdy metal panels.

The intensity of his look, of his unspoken message, pounded so powerfully in her chest that she had to look away. To gather her defenses with several deep breaths before she could speak. "It would have been a lot worse but for your quick reflexes."

"I didn't fancy going head-to-head with that piece of lumber." He indicated the bulk of the trunk with a brief nod, and then turned toward the towering forest that edged the road. "Or any of its mates."

She watched him walk back down the road, hands on hips, and knew he'd be reaching the same conclusion she'd just worked her way around to. This back road saw little traffic. They could wait days and not see another vehicle.

"How far to the cabin, do you think?" she asked slowly. At least the cabin had her bike, wheels they could use to get back to civilization.

"Seven miles. A decent walk."

The wind gusted up again, whipping at his suit jacket and bringing up goose bumps on Zara's bare stomach. She cast a quick glance at the sky, at the lowering ceiling of gray, and sucked in a breath thick with the scent of euca-lyptus and imminent rain.

"If we don't want to get wet," she said briskly, turning back to the car to fetch her backpack, "we might want to make that a decent run."

They started out at a walk, but with the threat of a cloud-burst hanging over their heads—literally—they picked up the pace after the first mile, despite the flinty ground that shifted underfoot and despite Alex's footwear. Zara lis-tened to those leather soles, designed for nothing more vigorous that stalking the corridors of business power, striking out a solid beat at her side.

As luck would have it, she'd pulled on her leathers over shorts and a workout top before leaving the city. Now those leathers, and his suit jacket and tie, were in her backpack. The biker boots she'd swapped for joggers but he kept up easily, his breathing measured.

Somehow she wasn't surprised. Alex Carlisle looked like a man who took everything in his long, capable stride.

She stepped up the pace again. He, naturally, kept up. From the corner of her eye she caught the easy swing of his arms, bare and tanned beneath rolled-up shirtsleeves, and her chest tightened from more than the aerobic workout.

It mystified her, the intensity and immediacy of this attraction. Sure, he was good-looking. Sure, he oozed testosterone. But she dealt with such men on a daily basis in her work. Beneath the five-thousand-dollar suits they were all just flesh-and-blood men. Not a single one affected her like this.

Why Alex Carlisle?

Because she couldn't have him? Or because she sensed a multitude of layers beneath the expensive veneer and the buff body?

In ten minutes or so they would arrive back at an empty, isolated cabin. This storm might well prevent them from leaving and they would be alone, together. That knowledge jittered through her senses, drove her to run even harder, but she couldn't outrun the man at her side or her extreme awareness of him.

Nor could she outrun the weather.

The sky broke without warning, releasing a short burst of rain that lasted only long enough to soak her to the skin. Then it turned to icy sleet. Head down for protection from the biting wind-driven slush, she might have run right by the turn into the driveway if Alex hadn't called out her name, bringing her head up and around.

At first all she saw was the man stopped by the half-secreted entrance, his dark hair whipped into disarray, his soaked shirt clinging to the hard planes of his torso. A man whose chest worked noticeably with each breath but who still managed to say in a perfectly even voice, "I don't know your plans, but this is as far as I'm going."

Zara shoved a dripping hank of hair back from her face. "I was thinking of going around the block again," she managed to gasp. "But if you've had enough, let's call it quits."

Zara had stayed at the cabin enough times to know what to expect. One room, one bed, one outside bathroom. No electricity, no hot water, no neighbors. One key hidden in the same spot behind the wood box on the porch.

Three-quarters of an hour after Alex took the key from her useless, numb fingers to open the door, Zara thought she might have stopped shivering. Finally. The fire he'd patiently built and nurtured from damp kindling into a blazing inferno helped. So had losing her wet clothes and wrapping herself snugly in one of the pair of thick sleeping bags Alex had found.

Draped over the handlebars of her bike and a chair he'd dragged fireside, her thin gym clothes would soon be dry. So would his shirt, which meant she could stop *not* watching him prowl around the cabin, all bare-chested and beautiful in the rusty firelight. She'd decided it was much safer and more relaxing to watch the flames flicker and dance over the logs in the fireplace.

Sitting cross-legged inside her downy cocoon, staring into the blaze, she could even put a positive spin to this misadventure. With Alex isolated out here, Susannah had more time to think—or to get wherever she'd gone to do that thinking—without him turning up to influence her decision. Zara might be stormbound with a man who stirred her libido in all kinds of forbidden ways, but she had willpower. She knew what she could have and what was off-limits. Take chocolate, for example…

Bad example.

With a wry grimace, she pressed a hand to her empty stomach. Thinking about food reminded her of how little she'd eaten today and how little Alex had found in his preliminary investigation of the cabin. Two pillows, two sleeping bags, two kerosene lamps, no kerosene. One box of matches.

Right now she could hear him executing a more thorough search of the kitchen cupboards.

"Any luck?" she asked hopefully, when the sounds of doors opening and shutting ceased.

"Unless there's something edible in the first-aid kit, we're dead out of luck."

She turned then to find him leaning back against what passed for a kitchen bench. And for the first time since they'd walked through the door, for the first time since he'd ordered her out of her wet clothes, since he'd busied himself with building the fire and setting their clothes out to dry, he met her eyes.

Nice that it was across the width of the cabin. Nice that the distance and the shadowy light disguised the hot lick of reaction in her eyes, in her blood, in her bare-naked skin beneath the silky lining of the sleeping bag. She wrapped it more securely around her shoulders and attempted to relax. They were stuck with each other for the duration of the storm; why not make it as easy and comfortable as possible?

"Not even an out-of-date can of beans?" she asked.

"Sadly, no."

"You know what's really sad? I stopped on my way out here for fuel and what was allegedly lunch. At the time I thought I was doing myself a favor not eating it!"

"You didn't save the leftovers?"

Zara chuckled at his hopeful tone. "No, although that's not the saddest bit. In a moment of weakness I almost bought a couple of chocolate bars, you know, for later. But I resisted."

"Damn."

"You like chocolate?"

"Like is perhaps too mild a word," he said with a slow smile. "It's my sin of choice."

Standing there in the shadows with his bare chest and flat abdomen and low-riding trousers, with that deadly little smile exaggerating the sensual bow of his top lip and deepening the grooves in his lean cheeks, he looked like a different kind of sinner. And a different kind of sin.

Temptation snaked through Zara's veins, the dark, rich, sumptuous chocolate kind. Temptation to ask how often he sinned, to suggest it had done him no harm, to ask about his second choice. To flirt and indulge herself for once while she stripped away the veneer to the man beneath.

She didn't. She couldn't. He was Susannah's.

"I resisted the siren call." Zara shrugged, a silky slide of her bare shoulders inside the sleeping bag. "It's not been one of my better days for choices."

"I don't suppose it worked out quite the way you planned when you got up this morning."

"We have that in common," she said, and regretted her candor instantly. The mood changed, grew thick and weighty with the reminder of how his day had started and what had brought them together. His wedding. Her worry.

"Why did you disapprove of me marrying Susannah?" he asked.

Zara exhaled slowly. So much for the easy banter. So much for comfortable. She felt the tension in his gaze, in her limbs, and concentrated on how to answer.

In truth, Susannah hadn't told her much about her relationship with Alex Carlisle and that was the problem. If Zara ever fell in love, she couldn't imagine clamming up on her best friend in their regular e-mail or IM or phone updates. She'd have sung it, laughed it, lived it, breathed it. Susannah hadn't. Sure, she'd mentioned meeting Alex and going out with him a couple of times, then the next thing Zara knew, she'd agreed to marry him.

"I wouldn't have disapproved," she said slowly, "if Susannah had appeared more enthusiastic about her wedding."

"She wasn't happy?"

"You're asking me?"

The line of his surprisingly full lips tightened. "We haven't spent a lot of time together, not since she moved back to Melbourne."

"You spent last weekend together," Zara pointed out. They'd flown to his family's outback station so Susannah could meet his mother and apparently there'd been a small engagement party. "Didn't you notice anything the matter?"

Heck, Zara had only seen her friend twice during the last week and *she'd* noticed her quietness, her distraction. That's why she'd prodded her at dinner last night. That's why she'd asked if Susannah was very, very sure.

Obviously her fiancé hadn't noticed. He stood in stony-faced silence for at least another minute before he asked, "Is there someone else?"

Even across the room and through the deepening twilight she could see the stormy tension in his eyes. The breath caught hard in her chest and she had to look away. Had to force her focus to that bolt-from-the-blue question. Something had definitely been going on with Susannah this last week, but another man? It seemed so unlikely that

Zara hadn't even considered the possibility. She did so now, for a long intense moment.

Perhaps she'd needed someone who gave her more time and consideration. Zara could believe that. But she couldn't believe that Susannah would cheat.

"No." She shook her head. "Not when she'd agreed to marry you."

The moment spun out, taut and silent but for the whistling howl of the wind and the intermittent crack and spit of the fire. She didn't know if he believed her, couldn't tell what he was thinking.

"What will you do now?" she asked.

"What can I do?" He pushed away from the bench. "For now we're stuck here with nothing to do but wait out the storm."

All matter-of-fact, all purpose, he crossed the room toward her and Zara jerked up straighter, eyes wide and mouth turning dry. But he skirted around to the side of the hearth, then squatted down to feed the fire with another chunk of wood. She tried to look away, some place where the revitalized leap of flames didn't limn the hard planes of his torso in golden light. Where she didn't notice how his midnight-dark hair had dried thick and wavy and ruffled, or how her fingers curled with a need to reach out and touch.

Zara swallowed and discovered that her throat was as dry as her mouth. She wriggled an arm free of her cocoon and reached for her water. She took a long swig and offered him the bottle. Then watched him drink, watched the slide of his throat as he swallowed.

Oh, gads. She had to stop doing that. Watching him. Staring.

"That's a first-rate fire," she said, turning to stare fixedly into the blaze instead. "Were you a Boy Scout?"

"Me?" He snorted softly. "No way."

"Not the Carlisle way?"

"I grew up in the outback, Zara, on a cattle station. No Boy Scouts out there."

"But plenty of fires?" She gave up and turned her curious gaze his way. Still too attractive—far too attractive, squatting there by the hearth, one hand holding a solid fire iron in a loose grip, turning it over and over in a slow, measured motion.

"The campfire was one of our first lessons, the first year we were allowed out on a muster."

"You mustered cattle?"

He huffed out a soft sound. "Is that so hard to imagine?"

So, okay, she'd known the Carlisles owned oodles of cattle country up in the north—the tabloids loved to refer to the brothers as "Princes of the Outback"—but she'd never pictured them taking an active role. If she'd pictured them at all. Now the figure of Alex the cowboy rode into her imagination, and strangely she didn't laugh. An hour or two back she would have.

Another layer peeled away, revealed, disturbing.

"How about you, Zara?" he asked, poking at the fire now. "Were you a Girl Scout?"

She smiled, despite her unsettling thoughts. "No. Obviously I wasn't."

"You like the bush, though?"

"How did you know that?"

"You said you like coming up here."

Ah, right, so she had. Earlier, out on the porch. When she'd been ferreting out the key with her frozen fingers. "Here it's like each day stretches ahead with all these hours and the freedom to do whatever I want with them. No pressure, no timetable."

"You don't mind the lack of amenities?"

"No." She smiled and shook her head. "And that's a straight-out lie. I do miss a decent shower. Steamy. Hot. Indecently long."

She finished on a husky note of yearning and looked up to find him watching her, his eyes so still and intent that she felt a hot, liquid curl in her belly. A chocolate response, she thought. Rich and sweet and tempting at the moment, but sinfully bad for her body in the long run.

"Do you come here alone?"

"Look around, Alex." She looked at the one bed and her pulse fluttered. "This is hardly the place for a group getaway."

"I wasn't talking about a group." No, she could tell he was talking about a man. About hot and steamy, one-on-one getaways. And if he weren't watching her with those deeply shadowed eyes, if she weren't sitting here naked with her sinfully chocolate thoughts, she would have laughed out loud.

She didn't.

"I come here when I want to be alone, to escape," she explained softly.

The fire crackled and hissed, the only sound for a long time. Until he asked, "What do you need to escape from, Zara? When you come up here?"

"Life. Schedules. Busy, busy, busy." She shrugged. Kept on talking when she probably should have shut up. "The last time was after my mother passed away and I was trying to escape the…" She paused, frowning as she tried to find the words to explain how she'd felt, the emptiness, the knowledge that she was all alone in the world. No family, no connections. "This might sound weird, but I was trying to escape the aloneness. Up here that's okay, but not at home. Not in the house where there'd always been us."

"Only the two of you?"

"Yes."

"I'm sorry about your mother," he said softly, after a pause. "Was this long ago?"

"Three years." Sometimes it felt longer. Other times she could picture her mum so vividly, hear her voice so clearly, Ginger might have been sitting at Zara's side, nudging her with an elbow, making her laugh at a witty observation on the world. Or on the men who ran the world.

She had been some cynic, her mum, the ex-stripper!

"You have good memories?"

"Oh, about a ton of them." She started to smile, but then her gaze snared with his and her pulse flickered and leaped like the flames in the fireplace. Like the flames reflected in his eyes.

For a long moment—too long—she couldn't look away, couldn't smile, could barely breathe. She recognized the danger in the moment. Knew her emotions, her heart, her soul were laid open and wanting by memories of her mum. And just when she thought he might say something he shouldn't, something dangerous and inadvisable, a log snapped and broke in a shower of sparks.

Alex reacted instantly, swearing roundly as he jumped to his feet. Zara couldn't contain the bubble of laughter, born partly of tension released and partly of the sight of him swatting at his trousers where the hot embers had hit.

Hunkered down, as he'd been, that was a rather delicate spot.

He shot her a filthy look. "I'm glad you find this amusing."

"Better you than me," she said, grinning. Until his expression changed and she knew he visualized her jumping about swatting at her slithery covering. Or her jumping about without the slithery covering.

"Yeah," he said softly, seeing she'd got the message. "Exactly."

And he turned back to the fire, squatting down again to poke the burning logs into submission with a fiercer than necessary hand. Despite the previous moment, she couldn't help smiling at his take-that brand of vengeance. So very un-prince-like, so very male.

"Lucky you didn't take my advice before," she said.

He paused in his energetic fire-taming to cut her a questioning look.

"When I suggested you should take your wet trousers off."

He huffed out a half laugh and muttered something that sounded like, "Self-preservation."

"You had a premonition that the fire might attack?"

He put down the tool with what looked like slow and deliberate care. Then he stood in the same measured way, and looked down at her with unflinching directness. "No. I thought one of us bare-assed was more than enough."

Zara swallowed. She hadn't expected such a forthright admission, such forthright language, or to find this new layer he'd revealed so deadly attractive. So insidiously tempting. *No, no, no.* She swallowed again and pushed that chocolate-coated temptation right to the back of her mind.

"My clothes—" Dipping her head in that direction, she tucked her legs underneath her, preparing to stand. "They should be almost dry."

Since he wasn't trussed up like a mummy, Alex got to her things first…which wouldn't have been so bad if the clothes were, say, like his shirt. Or his suit jacket or her leather jeans and jacket or even her shorts.

But, no, by the time she'd struggled to her feet, by the time she'd shuffled to his side and freed a hand, by the time she'd said, "Here, let me get them," he was holding her underwear.

Her panties to be exact. And, okay, they weren't violet lace or a scarlet G-string or anything remotely racy. They were just your practical, black, boy-leg hipsters prettied up with a pink bunny-ears appliqué. But they were in his hand and that felt incredibly intimate. The way his thumb stroked over the satin bunny ears and onto the cotton even more so.

"They appear to be dry."

"Then I'd best put them on," she managed to say, low, husky, *bad*. "Self-preservation, you know."

His nostrils flared slightly. His eyes darkened with heat and knowledge and approval, but then he shook his head as if to clear it and pushed the panties into her hand. Closed her fingers around the soft fabric with the insistent pressure of his own. And the combination of that slightly rough-textured touch and the rueful note to his final words held her rooted to the spot long after he'd walked away. Long after he'd walked out into the cold, wet twilight and closed the door behind him.

"You'd best put on everything you can find, Zara, of yours and mine. If this storm doesn't ease up soon it's going to be a hellishly long night of self-preservation."

Three

Zara dressed quickly, although not in everything she could find. Still, her brief athletic top and snug shorts seemed vastly inadequate. She fingered the sleeve of his shirt and fought the temptation to wrap herself in the fire-warmed fabric. Wrapping herself in anything that smelled of Alex Carlisle's expensive blend of man and cologne would not do her any favors.

She let go of the sleeve and reached for her jacket instead. The leather jeans, however, were too much. A minute after pulling them on, her skin felt clammy and uncomfortable. She unzipped her jacket, she moved away from the fire. Pressing her cheek against the cool glass of a window helped marginally but in the end she took the jeans off.

Self-preservation be damned. Nothing was going to happen between them, whether they were here all night or not. Nothing was going to happen because neither of them wanted it to, right?

"Right," she affirmed.

But when she pressed her face back against the window-pane, the hot-cold contrast sent a shiver of reaction through her flesh. She leaned closer to the glass and listened to the elevated thud of her heart. That, she acknowledged, had nothing at all to do with the roaring fire.

Outside, the wind drove intermittent blasts of rain hard against the log walls of the cabin and slapped wet gum branches over the corrugated iron of the outhouse roof. Alex stood in the sheltering lee of the porch and considered his options. One insistent side of his brain wanted to keep on walking, out where the icy squall might cool the heat in his skin and his blood. The other side asked what good a chill would do when the fever's source lay inside his pants.

Or inside the four sturdy walls of the cabin.

Zara Lovett with her whiskey eyes and husky laugh and steady I've-got-your-measure gaze. Zara Lovett who'd strode into his life on killer legs and lit a powder keg in his gut.

Chemistry. The kind of powerful, explosive mix Alex made a habit of avoiding. He didn't like fireworks. They reminded him of his birth father's fierce temper, of the heat he feared in his own nature, of the passion he'd worked long and hard to control.

He liked smooth and easy. He liked stability. He liked his relationship with Susannah for those very reasons.

Nothing had changed in the last six hours. He still needed to satisfy the terms of his father's will; he still wanted that within the confines of a stable relationship. A marriage to the right woman. One with the same goals and beliefs, the same background and values. One who respected the time and energy he spent on his career and who didn't demand any more than he could give.

Nothing had changed. Just because he'd crossed paths with a golden-haired beauty who made his male glands jump to attention didn't mean things would change. Once the storm cleared he would ride out of here and find Susannah and convince her all over again that they had the goods to make a marriage work.

That was his goal. That was his duty. That was what mattered. Alex set his expression to match his mindset and went back inside.

Eventually Zara gave up the pretense of ignoring him. What was the point? She'd accepted that nothing was going to happen between them and since he'd returned from outside he'd given off the same vibes.

Why not enjoy the only available form of entertainment? He was, after all, eminently watchable.

So, she'd watched him mess with the fire, watched him fetch more wood, watched him build neat symmetrical stacks beside the hearth as if rationing the supply for the hours ahead. He'd even fiddled with the broken stand on her bike, until she'd forced him to acknowledge that he couldn't fix it without a welder.

Alex Carlisle was hot, but not that hot.

For the past ten minutes she'd watched him pace, appreciating the way he moved and the muscular definition of his deltoids, his pectorals, his biceps. Obviously he worked out. Obviously he wasn't used to doing nothing.

"You're not used to having all this time on your hands, are you?"

He answered with a soft grunt of assent, essentially male, ridiculously attractive.

Zara hadn't moved far from the window, but now she leaned back against the wall and crossed her arms over her chest. "What would you be doing if we weren't stuck here?"

He stopped pacing, turned slowly and stared at her. "You mean tonight?"

His wedding night.

That significance struck her in a wave of hot-cold shock. She thought about grabbing one of her joggers—no, better make it one of her biker boots!—and shoving it in her mouth.

"How much detail do you require?" he asked with a surprisingly wry cut to his mouth. So, okay, it didn't quite make up for the dark heat in his eyes and the flare of response in her body, but she could play along with it. She could pretend she didn't notice. And if she kept on talking, maybe she could distract herself from further wedding-night imaginings.

"I meant some other night. An average night."

"I'd be working."

"Even on a Saturday?"

"Possibly." He shrugged as if the day of the week made no difference. "Depends where I am, what I'm working on. Whether there's a function I'm obligated to attend."

Obligated. What an interesting slant on social life. Not that she had a social life, but still... "No wild rave parties then?"

His lips quirked. "Not that I can recall."

"Why do you work so hard?" she asked after another moment. A moment of watching him snag his shirt from the back of the chair, of feeling the skim of sensation in her own skin as he pulled it on. Of forcing herself to say something, anything, to distract her from the thick beat of awareness in her blood.

He gave a loose-muscled shrug, one that punctuated his next words perfectly. "It's what I do."

"Work is your life then?"

"Is that a bad thing?"

"Not at all," she said quickly. "I'm pretty much the same. Dedicated—" she almost said "married," but rectified that at the last second "—to my work."

"Your dedication shows," he said slowly and she frowned, not understanding how her dedication to medical studies would show. "Your fitness," he clarified.

Ah, he was talking about the run back to the cabin. "You didn't do so badly yourself. For a desk jockey."

"Surprised I kept up?"

Zara met his eyes and smiled. "You were wearing a business suit and leather loafers. You had no business keeping up!"

"Will it make you feel any better to know I'm suffering for that now?"

For a second she became a little lost in the shadowy hint of his smile, in the delicious energy that seemed to pump between them, and then she got his meaning. Her nose wrinkled in sympathy. "Blisters?"

"A couple." His shrug was a bit tight and she figured he was uncomfortable drawing attention to anything less than a broken bone or dislocated joint. He was, after all, a man. That was something you tended to notice about Alex Carlisle.

Pivoting off her leaning post, she headed toward the cupboards. "I'll get the first-aid kit."

"It's only a couple of blisters."

Which Zara preferred to see for herself. She retrieved the kit and marched over to the chair near the fire. "Step into my consulting room and I'll take a look."

"Forget it, Zara."

"I'm training to be a doctor. I need practical experience."

"I'm sure you do," Alex said, not moving a muscle. "But you're not getting that hands-on training with me."

It took a moment, but then she got the veiled meaning in his words. He saw the little jolt of reaction, the flicker of her gaze from him to the chair and back again. He knew she'd caught a glimpse of the picture slow-burning through his brain.

Him sitting on the chair. Her kneeling at his feet, her head bent so her long hair swung loose and honey-gold in the firelight. Close enough that it brushed and snagged against the dark cloth of his trousers.

She got that he was talking about self-preservation again.

The knowledge flashed in her eyes, softened her lips, grabbed him by the throat with soft female teeth and growled in his most masculine parts. Just the image of her kneeling at his feet. He hadn't even reached the part where she placed his foot on the smooth stretch of her bare thigh.

Hell.

A couple of minutes ago they'd been talking, just talking. How did they get to this point? The point where he felt he might have to walk out into that icy slash of rain. He crossed the room, turned, paced back. They'd started out talking about what they'd normally be doing on an average night.

"You haven't told me—" he stopped and looked at her again, sitting by the fire, the first-aid kit open in her hands "—how you spend your nights."

Carefully she closed the lid and set the box aside. "Mostly I'm studying."

"You can't study all the time. What do you do to relax and take your mind off the books?"

"I visit with friends. Or listen to music. Sometimes I knit."

That tickled him. The image of this earthy, sexy, physical woman involved in such a restful, old-fashioned craft. "You knit."

Defensiveness drew her brows into a solid dark frown. "Is that a bad thing?"

"No. Just…unexpected. Did you learn from your mother? Your grandmother? Great-aunt Mable?"

She smiled. "My mother, in a roundabout way. When Mum was sick, the occupational therapist taught her and I learned as well. You kind of get addicted to the click of the needles and to watching the piece grow. Linda says—" She drew up short and expelled a breath. "You don't need to hear about this."

"No, but I'd like to."

She gave him a come-on-honestly look and he waited, patiently, until she shook her head and continued. "Linda, the therapist, says the key with knitting is that you're usually making a gift for someone else. Part of the therapeutic deal is that while you knit you're thinking about the person you're knitting for. Usually that's someone you care about so that adds to the positive vibes. Anyway, that's her theory."

"What does the doctor in training say about that theory?"

"Anything relaxing is good for a body." She looked up at him with a deprecating smile. "So, yeah, I knit. There it is—my Saturday-night confession."

"Not much of a sin."

"No." Her answer had a husky edge, and the notion of sin lingered in its aftermath and stretched the moment with dangerous tension. "Is chocolate your only obsession?"

"There's also the horses."

"As in horse racing? You gamble?"

He took that note of disbelief as a compliment and smiled. "No, that would be my brother Rafe. I race them. I study form and breeding. I can be obsessive."

"I imagine so."

Alex thought he could easily obsess about that husky register of her voice. That particular look in her eyes, part heat, part curiosity. The beauty spot below her left cheekbone that his gaze kept sliding back to, and the long, smooth length of her legs wrapped around his hips while she took him into her body.

"Do you breed your racehorses?"

It took a second to get past the hard hum of lust in his ears and really hear the question. To form an appropriate answer. "I have an interest in several stallions."

"Intriguing," she said slowly. But the change in her expression wasn't curiosity. It was a cooling, a withdrawal, and he had to know what that was about. Had to know what was ticking away in that sharp brain of hers.

"Intriguing...how?"

"I just remembered something Susannah told me. A thought I had at the time."

"Come on, Zara. You can't leave that hanging."

She eyed him speculatively for a beat. "You might prefer that I did."

"Do I look like someone who can't handle plain-speak?"

"Okay," she said, holding his gaze, accepting his challenge to speak her mind. "When Susannah told me why you needed to marry so quickly, when she told me why you'd chosen her, it put me in mind of a stud-breeding enterprise. I thought, this Alex Carlisle has studied the pedigrees. He's decided that the Horton and Carlisle genotypes would meld nicely."

Alex stared at her narrowly. Where the hell had that come from? "What," he asked slowly, "did Susannah tell you?"

"That you and your brothers won't inherit your father's estate unless one of you produces a baby. Which, I'm sorry, sounds like a disgustingly commercial reason for breeding a baby. I mean, don't you have enough of everything already? Do you really need more money?"

"How do you know it's about money? Did you ask Susannah? Did you ask me?"

She closed her mouth on whatever else she'd been about to say. He should have done the same. Her opinion of him shouldn't matter. Her words shouldn't seethe through him like a wash of acid.

"I owe Charles Carlisle for everything I have, everything I am. His last wish was a grandchild for my mother, and what we're doing—what *I'm* doing—" he tapped two fingers against his chest "—is honoring that wish. It's not about any inheritance. It's about repaying my stepfather. It's about family."

Renewed rain struck a staccato beat against the iron roof. Loud enough to mask the crackle of firewood, not loud enough to drown out the heavy thud of his heartbeat or the screaming knowledge that he'd said too much. Revealed too much of himself, of the passion at his heart, of emotions that showed vulnerability.

"I'm sorry I said what I did. That was unfair," she conceded after a long moment. But then she lifted her chin with a hint of defiance. "I was right in saying you selected Susannah though, wasn't I? You were looking for a mother for this child, and you cast around for the ideal candidate."

"You don't think she'll make a good mother?"

"She will make a splendid mother, but that's not what I asked." She huffed out an exasperated breath, then rose to her feet. "Why did you ask her to marry you? Why didn't you just offer a business deal and benefits for the child, without the marriage?"

"I believe a child deserves a stable, happy, two-parent home."

"That is so old-fashioned! Don't you think a child is better with one parent who loves and cares than in an unhappy home? Look at me." Eyes glittering with a passionate heat, she moved closer. "I'm the role model for a single-parent family. I never needed a father who didn't care about me wandering around the periphery of my life. Or in and out of it according to his whim."

Alex's gaze narrowed. "Is that what your father did?"

"Hell, no! I didn't even know who he was until just before Mum died. I tried to meet him and he didn't want to know me."

"And what if he had?" he asked, turning her argument around on her. "Would you have enjoyed joint custody arrangements? Being shunted from one house to the other?"

She hitched her chin even higher. "No, but that doesn't make a child the right reason to marry."

"What *is* the right reason to marry?"

"Love," she said without hesitation. "Falling madly for someone you want to share your whole life with. Someone who makes your heart warm just looking at him. Someone you can't bear living without."

"I didn't pick you for a romantic." Alex shook his head slowly. Then he moved a step closer, captured her gaze with the steady intensity of his as he bent closer. "So, if you were to meet someone tomorrow who made your blood hot just looking at him. If you fell madly in love and wanted to share your life with this man, you'd marry him?"

For an instant she seemed absorbed in the moment, in his eyes, in whatever the hell he thought he was trying to prove. Then some kind of resolve snapped in her eyes and she stepped away from him and the blazing intensity of that moment.

"Tomorrow?" She turned with her back to the fire and

gave a casual shrug. "No. I can't afford a relationship of any sort until I finish my studies and establish a career."

"Can't afford?"

"The time, the commitment." Laughing softly, she shook her head. "Between study and my job I don't have time to date."

"Your course is that full on?"

"Oh, yeah. And I need to maintain my grades. I'm shooting for an honors year in medical science next year." Her eyes burned with a different kind of intensity, something from within that caught at his gut in a way nothing about her had before. But then her lips curled with a curious wryness. "Plus, I promised my mother I'd get my degree."

"To make her proud?"

"Oh, I'm pretty sure she'd be proud of me with or without the degree," she said with quiet confidence. "But I deferred my studies to nurse her and she made me promise I'd go back. It would have broken her heart if I hadn't."

In the ensuing silence Alex realized that the rain had stopped, at least for now. The only sound was the crackle of firewood…that and a silence so tense that it might have crackled as well. And through that moment, he had to force himself to remain still. Not to reach out and touch her in some way. That, he knew, would be a step he couldn't take back.

"The rain's stopped." Inconsequential, but he had to say something. The silence was stretching into awkwardness, as if they both acknowledged revealing too much, too soon. The hush of darkness was falling over the cabin, too, and with it the knowledge of a decision to be made. To leave or to stay.

Her eyes met his with that same jitter of knowledge. "Are you thinking about leaving?"

"Not yet. The wind hasn't died down much. I'll give it a while."

"It might keep blowing all night."

"It might."

She seemed to give that ordinary answer an inordinate amount of consideration. She rolled her shoulders and tucked her hands into the pockets of her jacket. Moistened the full curve of her lips. "We probably should just give in to the weather and stay the night."

"Earlier you said you had to get home."

"To study."

"Is there anyone going to worry when you don't come home?"

"I have a housemate. Tim, who you spoke to. He'll wonder but he'll likely think I decided to stay up here the night. He knows I love this place."

"Staying would be sensible," he agreed, eyes still holding hers, body entertaining all manner of non-sensible ideas. "You can have the bed."

"That wouldn't be fair. I think—"

"Don't suggest we share, Zara," he interrupted. "Because *that* wouldn't be fair."

She didn't argue. They didn't have to discuss why, it hummed in the air between them. "I'm just going out," she told him, and he saw the flare of her nostrils as she drew a breath, "to the bathroom."

When she opened the door, the wind rushed in and cut an icy slice right through to his bones. That settled his uneasy mind about their decision to stay, and he set about tending the fire and setting out her sleeping bag on the bed. His on the floor as far away as possible.

And when she returned and started stripping off her jacket, pulling off her shoes, preparing for bed, he escaped to the bathroom. The cold-water shower helped for a while, but only for a while. Then she rolled over in her sleeping bag, and he knew she wasn't asleep and he couldn't control the rush of reaction that burned in his skin.

It was no surprise to find himself painfully hard. Ridiculous. He hadn't felt this out of control of his responses since his first adolescent crush.

Quietly frustrated, unable to sit still, he got up from the fireside and padded to the window. He could no more control the stir of heat in his groin than he could control the unrelenting lash of the storm outside. He felt trapped, not only within these four walls but trapped within his body. His slow exhalation fogged the cold pane of glass and he heard her stir restlessly again on the bed. A hush of movement as quiet as her breathing, and with the howl of the wind and the renewed slice of rain against the glass he shouldn't have heard.

But he did.

He didn't turn. He stood still and alert and erect.

Inconsequentially, he thought that his brothers would get a laugh out of his predicament. Especially Rafe who had a thing about fate and chance and luck. He wouldn't be standing by the window while his body ached for a woman. He'd take this meeting, the storm, the one bed, this amazing sexual fascination, and turn it into a sign.

Alex didn't hold any stock in signs but he did trust logic and gut instinct. Both had told him from the start that Zara wasn't the right woman, not for a man who wanted peace and stability and control. In half a day she'd outrun him and out-thought him, intrigued him and challenged him, made him smile and scowl and ultimately turned him into a victim of his glands.

And the night was only just beginning.

Oh, yeah. Rafe would get a real laugh out of this.

Four

Zara tried every relaxation technique she had learned and employed over the years but all to no avail. An hour or more later, she was no closer to sleep than when she'd crawled into her sleeping bag. Up here she usually slept easily, embraced by the soothing country dark and the earthy scents of pine and eucalyptus and timber. Often she was so worn out by a day spent bush walking or casting a line into one of several trout-rich streams within hiking distance that she fell into an eight-hour stretch of solid, blissful, dream-free slumber.

She probably snored a treat.

A smile touched her lips at the thought, then turned warmly reminiscent as she fixed on the day Susannah flabbergasted her with a lesson in trout fishing. It had been quite the weekend for shocks, starting with the cabin itself. When Susannah invited her away to "a little place my grandfather left me," she'd expected "little place" to be one of those classic understatements the wealthy tended to use.

She hadn't expected anything this basic, rustic, primitive.

And she sure hadn't expected her newly discovered half sister with her cool elegance and private-school accent to display such skill in casting a fishing line. They'd only known each other a couple of months—a couple of awkward, getting-to-know-each-other months because of the circumstances under which they'd met.

Zara, distressed and grief-angry at her mother's failing health, had been on a mission to meet her father. After discovering some clippings among her mother's things, she'd found him easily enough. Susannah had overheard their heated exchange, including her father's callous dismissal of Zara's paternity claim, and sought her out afterward.

She'd wanted to meet her only sibling and to plead with her to keep their relationship secret. "Mother doesn't know about his affairs. She's not well and a shock like this would about kill her."

Zara was happy to oblige. After meeting the coldhearted son of a bitch, she didn't want to acknowledge Edward Horton as her father. It had taken a few coffees, a couple of lunches, several long, bonding conversations about their respective mothers' illnesses and a defining weekend at a mountain cabin to overturn her preconceptions about Susannah.

She was no spoiled society princess, and Zara had felt mean and shamed for making that assumption. Especially when Susannah had told her why she was sharing the line-casting skill. "Pappy Horton taught me to fish. He was a wonderful man, our grandfather. He would have brought you up here and taught you himself, if he'd known about you."

Zara had stared at her with wide, stunned eyes. "Really?"

"That's why I brought you here, sis. I hate being out of

phone coverage. I hate not having a hot shower. But I wanted to share something with you, something of family. Please, use the cabin whenever you like. Pappy would have wanted that."

After that weekend, they'd become firm friends, as close as sisters, although that word had never been spoken again. As much as Zara disliked the lack of acknowledgment, she'd grown to accept it because Susannah was protecting the mother she loved.

The wrong result for the right reason...and that brought her rambling thoughts right back to Alex Carlisle.

She'd prejudged him, the same as she'd done with Susannah. She'd imagined the big man painted in the media, powerful and power hungry, self-important and self-involved. A younger, wealthier version of Edward Horton really, and if that didn't predispose her to dislike him then nothing would!

He'd asked Susannah to marry him—the wrong result— for the best of reasons. Yet she couldn't help feeling he wasn't right for Susannah. Or was she looking for excuses? Justification to stifle the guilty knowledge that she was fiercely attracted to him?

With a frustrated sigh, she flipped onto her back and kicked at the sleeping bag when it didn't turn with her. So, okay, she was attracted. She could be honest about those biochemical reactions in her body, which she couldn't do a thing to control. The isolation didn't help. Being alone with an enormously attractive man, especially after the adrenaline-producing crash and the run back to the cabin, was suggestive.

But nothing was going to happen. Not even if Susannah appeared at the door right now and said, "Go ahead, be my guest, he's all yours!"

She didn't have time for a relationship, not even a brief fling, not with Alex Carlisle. It would be too intense, fierce, hot, consuming. She knew this without question, as surely as she knew where he stood right now, still and silent and watchful.

Watching her.

Physical awareness washed through her body, more potent than anything she'd ever felt. The wind had died down but the rain had started up again, a steady drumming beat on the iron roof that echoed in her body. The heightened beat of her pulse. The restless throb of desire in her veins.

Lying on her back staring up at the faint play of shadow over the darkened ceiling, she should not have known where he stood…or that he stood. She should not have heard him move, either, above the noise of the rain, but she did.

She sat up, found him by the sink, a dark, solid silhouette beyond the low glow cast by the banked fire.

"I was just getting a drink," he said. "Did I wake you?"

Zara shook her head. "No. I've been awake a while. I couldn't sleep."

"Are you cold?"

The husky edge of concern in his voice rolled through her, a shiver that had nothing to do with the cold. "No. Not cold."

Hot, much too hot. And dry, she realized, as she watched the shadow of movement as he lifted an arm to drink the water he'd poured. As she attempted to moisten her mouth.

"I'd love some water, actually." She started to unzip her bag, to swing her legs free.

"Stay there. I'll bring it."

The faucet hissed again as he refilled her bottle from the rainwater tank, then he started toward her and there was an almost expectant hush in her body, a still anticipation as she waited for him to walk from the deep shadows into clearer sight. He wore his trousers and shirt, unbuttoned and hanging loose. A tousled, disreputable version of the polished man who'd climbed from that car six or so hours ago.

He paused beside the bed long enough for Zara to notice, right there at eye height, that several sparks from the fire had burned right through the fine cloth of his trousers. Long enough to see that he wore white underwear. And that both underwear and damaged trousers were distended by the jut of his arousal.

That all swam dizzily before her eyes another second before he sat on the side of the bed. A frown colored his voice as he asked, "Are you all right?" and she opened her eyes and discovered how close he sat.

Her heart thudded. Close, hot, aroused. "Just overheated. And thirsty."

He handed her the bottle. She thanked him politely and lifted it to her lips. Then, as she drank, she made the mistake of meeting his eyes and the burn of heat in their deeply shadowed depths sucked at her breath. And her mouthful of water went down the wrong way, leaving her choking and coughing and disconcerted.

She couldn't meet his eyes. And because she looked away, she had no notice of what he was doing, no warning that he was going to touch her. The pad of his thumb stroked across her chest, spreading dampness against her hot skin.

Air hissed between her teeth, and for a moment she thought that was the sizzle of his touch on her skin. Her eyes shot to his, connected with that same scorch. "What are you doing?"

He took his hand away and disappointment tightened hard and low in her belly.

"Spillage." His gaze slipped down to where he'd touched, then lower. "Best I leave the rest to you."

She looked down too, saw what she hadn't even felt. The damp circle over one half of her breast. The clear outline of her nipple. She swallowed. "The water went down the wrong way."

"I noticed."

Their eyes connected again, with a glint of knowledge at what they'd both noticed. In her, in him.

And before she did something or said something regrettable, she searched around for a safer topic. The first thing her eyes lit upon was his sleeping bag spread on the far side of the fire, on the perimeter of its red-tinged glow. Smooth and untouched. "I know I'm having trouble sleeping," she said, "but it looks like you haven't even tried."

He turned a little, followed her line of gaze. "The floor wasn't so inviting."

"Your choice," she reminded him. "We could be sharing the bed."

Slowly his gaze slid back to hers. Something that looked like *are-you-kidding-me?* crossed his expression and she felt the heat, the color, the knowledge flare below her skin in her throat and her cheeks. But she lifted her chin and met that incredulous look.

"We both have sleeping bags. It's not as if I'm inviting you to slide between the sheets with me." She lifted her shoulders in an attempt at a casual shrug. "We can top and tail if that helps."

"I doubt that would help, Zara."

She inhaled sharply, swamped by the vivid imagery he painted with that one line. With the wry intonation and the burn of heat in eyes she had once thought cold as the winter ocean.

That seemed so very long ago.

"If I trust you," she said, straightening her shoulders and meeting those eyes steadily, "can you agree to trust me?"

"Why would you trust me?" he asked warily.

"Because you're my best friend's fiancé and a gentleman." She paused a beat. "Because we're both adults and neither one of us wants anything to happen between us."

He continued to eye her with a curious mix of circumspection and concentration, as if he were searching back through her words looking for hidden traps. She scooted to the other side of the bed, which, being a double, wasn't a terribly long way.

But it was a stance and a demonstration of intent. *Me on my side, you on yours.* When he still didn't move, she patted the mattress she'd cleared. "Don't be a chicken, Alex. Get your pillow and sleeping bag and give it a try. "

The coward taunt worked. When he got up to fetch his things, Zara silently congratulated herself. She also took the opportunity to drink without choking, and it was only after he'd returned and stretched his long body out on top of his carefully positioned sleeping bag that she questioned what she'd just done.

Nothing, she answered herself. *Nothing is going to happen.*

That's what her brain said while her breathing grew shallow and her heart rate blew up and her glands pumped a steady stream of I-want-stuff-to-happen hormones into her blood.

From the corner of her eye she could just make out his figure in the low light. On his back, hands resting on his abdomen, bare feet crossed at the ankle. A couple of feet separated them, yet she could feel his proximity in every cell of her body.

She could not just lie there, saying nothing, doing

nothing. She wanted to talk about something light and easy and safe. Her gaze fastened on the ghostly silhouette of her bike. Their only means of transport in the morning.

"I bet I know why you can't sleep," she said.

He didn't answer.

"I can hear you thinking."

"That's my stomach rumbling," he said.

Zara smiled. "No, it's definitely your brain. You're worried about tomorrow."

That got his attention. She felt the shift of interest, heard the subtle friction as his head turned on his pillow. "What am I worried about, exactly?" he asked slowly.

"About putting yourself in my hands. When you get on the back of my bike."

She'd expected him to scoff at that. Or to suggest that he'd be in charge and she would ride pillion. She didn't imagine Alex Carlisle rode in life's passenger seat too often.

She sure didn't expect the long, still stretch of a pause or his quietly spoken answer. "I'm not worried about putting myself in your hands, Zara."

That answer seemed laced with everything she felt. Every wired strain in her body, every thud of her heartbeat, every shiver of heat in her blood. Man, but she ached to turn on her side, to look into his eyes, to see if they reflected the sensual ache low in her body.

But she didn't, she couldn't, in case she did something silly like inviting him into her hands. He wasn't hers to touch, he wasn't hers to hold.

"What's the first thing you're going to do?" she asked instead. "When we get back to town? I'm thinking about a long, hot shower."

"I'm thinking about eating."

She smiled at that, at the tone, at the certainty, at the dryness. At the fact that she'd inadvertently hit upon the one thing that would take her mind off her other hunger. "Well, yes, but I figure we'll do that at the first roadhouse or café we come across. I'm thinking about one of those big truckie's breakfasts. Bacon and eggs and sausages."

"With mushrooms?"

Her tummy growled and she did too, in sympathy. "Oh, yeah."

"Tomatoes?"

"Grilled and drizzled with cheese."

"Coffee," he said, low and sybaritic. "I don't even care if it's instant."

She made a low *mmm* of assent as she pondered her cup of hot tea. "Afterwards," she continued dreamily a few seconds later, "I'm going to have one of those chocolate bars I foolishly denied myself yesterday."

"For breakfast?"

Frowning, she turned to look at him. "I thought you loved chocolate."

"Never before noon."

"Are you always so disciplined?"

For a moment he continued to stare up at the ceiling, then slowly he rolled his head on the pillow and she felt the burn of his gaze as it fixed on hers. "We'll see."

The breath caught in her throat, a hitch of sound they both heard and understood. A hitch of the knowledge that, despite her earlier avowal of trust, only her sleeping bag and his discipline separated them on this bed.

We'll see.

Those words beat through her with the same constant driving rhythm as the rain on the roof, with the same beat as forbidden desire, strong and thick and unrelenting. "I guess you'll be going back to Sydney," she said. "Once we get out of here."

"If I can't find Susannah. Yes."

"You'll go looking for her? Do you still think you can change her mind?" she asked on a rising note, alarmed at the prospect that nothing had changed.

"Yes, I'll look for her. We need to talk. But I can't make her marry me, Zara."

No, but if he looked at her with that intensity, if he spoke to her in that low, smoky voice… "I'm sure you can be very persuasive."

"When I want to be," he said, and that confidence shivered through Zara in a contradiction of desire and disquiet.

Yet she couldn't leave it alone. Despite the moody heat that licked between them, she was enjoying this soft-voiced exchange in the near dark. "Do you want to be married?" she asked after a second. "I mean you, yourself, not because of the will or your family."

"Yes. I want a family, a wife, a marriage."

"You're…how old?"

"Thirty-five."

"And you waited this long to decide you want to marry? Forgive my bluntness, but I imagine you've not been starved of opportunity."

This time he didn't answer straight away, and she sensed a different tension in his hesitation. "I almost married once before."

Zara felt an odd pressure in her chest, a tightness, a lack of breath. "What happened?"

"She married someone else."

Oh, Alex. What could she say? She recalled his closed, hard expression when he'd asked if Susannah had met someone else. The second woman to have changed her mind. How could Suse have done that to him? The day of the wedding, no less.

Yet she knew he wouldn't want her sympathy. Knew that reaching out to touch him would be a bad, dangerous move. Instead she shrugged, as best one can when lying down, and said, "Her loss."

"Yeah," he agreed, and Zara sensed an ease in his tension. Her heart skipped with a kind of gladness because she had picked the right tone, because she had lifted the mood out of murky waters. "I couldn't marry a woman who didn't want me."

She wasn't sure he meant Susannah and she didn't ask. Suddenly she felt less sympathetic toward her friend and much too sympathetic toward this man she'd grossly misread. So many layers, every one more intriguing, every one adding to her fascination.

"I believe I owe you an apology," she said softly. "I misjudged you."

And Lord help her, this time she couldn't help turning and touching. Just her hand on his. A brief touch, a quick kiss of heat in the dark.

He didn't thank her. He didn't say anything for a moment and then he shook his head and she heard the heavy expulsion of his breath. "I want to get an early start in the morning. How about we try to get some sleep."

"I'll try," she said dubiously and closed her eyes.

Amazingly she slept.

Hours later Zara woke and for a long moment lay perfectly still while she made sense of her surroundings. The storm had passed, leaving behind a quiet broken only by the creak of wet timber expanding and the faint drip, drip, drip of water somewhere outside. The darkness was more complete, and she realized the fire had gone out. Not even an ember sparked to break the solid wall of black. Yet she wasn't cold.

Oh, no, she was very, very warm, snuggled as she was against the intense body heat of the man in her bed.

Surreptitiously she stretched a hand toward the edge of the mattress. The distance she needed to stretch confirmed her suspicion. She had backed into the center of the bed. She had spooned into his hips and curved her legs to trace the line of his.

His arm was thrown over hers, trapping her there. So close she swore she could feel the hard line of him against her backside. Despite at least one sleeping bag in between.

Heart thudding hard in her chest, she fought an almighty surge of temptation to press back against him. To unzip the cursed bag. To turn and touch.

No, no, no, she whispered silently in time with the dripping rainwater. *Move your backside forward. Away. A little wriggle forward, one hip and then the other—*

"Zara." The hush of her name washed over her, quiet as the night. Dark as temptation. She stopped wriggling but the impact of his voice—the notion that he too lay awake, hard and hot at her back—rolled through her like molten chocolate. Sweet and thick in her veins and her senses.

"Yes?" she managed to breathe.

"Best you don't do that."

Oh, man, did he think she was shimmying up against him on purpose? That was altogether possible seeing as he still lay on his side of the bed.

Mortified at being caught out, at unconsciously seeking his heat and shelter while she slept, at thinking of doing exactly what he suspected, she resumed her effort to twist away. He made a sound low in his throat that might have been a groan of discomfort. Or disapproval. Then the arm impeding her escape tightened, pulling her back against him.

Zara swallowed. Yup, he was definitely aroused. Very much so.

"I thought you didn't want me to know about that," she said.

The hand at her waist twitched, but when he spoke, his voice was coated with dry amusement. "I think you pretty much know every inch by now."

What could she say to that? Certainly not the wicked response that leaped into her mind and pooled low in her body. Nope, she better not make any crack about how she could get more intimately acquainted with those inches.

"What did you mean by 'best you don't do that'?" she asked.

"You were squirming."

"I was trying to move away without waking you. Why did you pull me back?"

"I like the feel of you against me," he said frankly. "If you just lay still like you've been doing for the last couple of hours, we'll do fine."

Zara exhaled slowly. Felt the spread of his fingers on her abdomen, the tiniest shift in pressure. He expected her to lie still? Now she knew that he touched her, now she knew that he wanted her?

"You've been—" she moistened her lips "—lying there...awake...for hours?"

"Yeah. Awake."

Again that lick of dry amusement. Oh, yeah, he recognized her slight pause for what it was. He knew she'd been thinking of him lying awake and hard for hours.

"Go to sleep, Zara," he said quietly.

Go to sleep? Was he for real? Or had she missed something in the translation?

Using her shoulder and elbow for leverage, she managed to push free of his hold and roll onto her back. Then onto her side to face him. "You expect me to just go back to sleep? As if I don't know that you're aroused?"

"That bothers you?"

She blinked, unsure how to respond. Wishing the night weren't so dark so she could see more than an impression of his strong, dark face. "Shouldn't it?"

"I'm not going to use it for anything. No matter how nicely you ask."

To her credit, Zara's mouth didn't fall open. Much. She drew an audible breath and let it go. Replayed that shockingly candid admission in her mind and let its impact settle. She believed him. Even if she made the moves, if she reached out and put her hand on that hot, hard body, he would resist.

Reflexively she curled her fingers tight into the palm that tingled with the suggestion of touch. Deep inside she felt a rush of sensation, not wild and hot like so many times during this long night, but steady and strong.

A knowledge that this was a man she could trust.

"Because of Susannah?"

"Until I talk to her, until I hear it from her lips, we're still engaged."

And then? The words jumped from her mind to her mouth but she bit them off. And then he would be in another city, another state, another lifestyle far removed from hers. Then, no matter how nicely he asked, there would be nothing.

Susannah might keep them apart now, but in the end there was nothing to keep them together. Nothing but a cabin-fever attraction he had the willpower to resist.

She would do well to take a lesson.

Five

Alex went to sleep hard and woke the same way. No surprise there, since he lay wrapped around a woman who'd stirred his juices from the instant he'd clapped eyes on her.

He wasn't sure why he'd insisted on dragging her back into his embrace when she'd woken in the night, except that he did enjoy the feel of her long, strong body matched to his. In his sleep he'd enjoyed the fantasy of unzipping her sleeping bag and running his hands over that amazing body.

The fantasy of starting the day with long, slow morning sex.

With a low groan, he edged away from that fantasy and the torturous pleasure of her derriere nestled against him. He must be turning into a masochist. And a supreme optimist if he imagined himself capable of long and slow anything right now.

Rising on one elbow, he stroked a fall of hair back from

her face, then held his breath when she stirred. She slept on but with a frown puckering the skin between her eyebrows. Tension ticked one of the fingers curled around the top of her sleeping bag and her legs shifted restlessly inside its bulky warmth.

She'd moved in her sleep too, not only snuggling closer to his body heat but shifting uneasily as if her mind never rested. Perhaps it was his presence or the aftermath of what must have been a harrowing day. Or perhaps she was simply reciting her anatomy lessons, like she'd told him she did at the traffic lights.

Smiling at that, he slowly traced the length of her exposed arm with the back of his hand. *Scapula. Humerus. Radius and ulna.* He stopped at her wrist, frowning in concentration as he struggled to remember the name of the next bone. She shifted again, rolling her shoulders slightly as if responding to the light pressure of his touch.

He gave up on the bone thing to watch her face, unobserved, in the thin dawn light. To torture himself with not touching more of her smooth skin, with not kissing the sleep-soft fullness of her lips, with not flicking his tongue against that beauty spot on her cheek.

He wanted all that, and sometime during the night he'd accepted that he could want more. He'd entertained the notion that his first gut instinct may have been wrong. That she might be the right woman, but at the wrong time. But until he'd talked to Susannah, he could not tempt himself with possibilities.

I'm sorry, Alex, but I can't marry you today.

In his head he heard Susannah's voice, heard her emphasis on that last word. Until he found her, until he heard her voice finish that statement with *any day,* he was bound to her and to his marriage proposal.

He rolled from the bed, stood and stretched a dozen tight muscles, and watched Zara come awake. It didn't bother him that she caught him standing there beside the bed, sporting only underpants and a massive morning erection. Apparently it didn't bother her either because she took her time looking.

Alex finished rolling his head and shoulders and smiled down at her. "Good morning."

He liked the hazy distraction in her eyes when they rose to meet his. The husky morning edge to her voice when she returned his greeting. "What time do you want to get going?"

He reached for his trousers and started to pull them on. "What time do you suppose that roadhouse will be open for breakfast?"

Unable to get around the obstruction of the tree and his incapacitated rental car, they detoured via a longer alternate route. Several miles before connecting up with the highway, they came upon a tiny settlement with a café-slash-petrol-station-slash-general-store and a handmade sign advertising Home Cooked Meals. Carmel, the cook-slash-waitress-slash-store-owner, told them she did a good trade in lumber trucks.

She told them quite a bit, actually, in intermittent slices of monologue each time she returned to plunk something else on their table. In return they told her how they'd missed dinner and she promised to fill them right back up again.

She'd been working on that ever since.

Between feeding their hunger and Carmel's voluble presence, they'd barely spoken to each other since sitting down at the worn Formica table. But with the edge now off, Alex watched Zara spoon the last of a generous serving of scrambled eggs onto her plate.

She ate with a refreshing lack of self-consciousness, only pausing, her fork midway between plate and mouth, when she caught him watching her. "Please tell me you're not staring at a big smudge of sauce on my chin."

"No. I'm enjoying your appetite." Alex reached across the table and tapped her wrist. "What are these bones called?"

She stared at him, obviously perplexed.

"I was trying to think of the name this morning. Scapula. Humerus. Radius and ulna. I couldn't remember the wrist bones."

"Carpals," she said, frowning.

Carmel returned to gather and stack the finished plates, to ask if they enjoyed it all, to see if she could get them anything else. Alex leaned back in his chair, enjoying the look of confusion on Zara's face as she tried to work out what the bones thing was about. He decided to let her wonder. He liked the way concentration drew her heavy brows together, giving her an almost fierce look. Like an Amazon warrior queen.

"I wasn't going to ask." Carmel paused, her hands filled with plates, her gaze narrowed on his face. "All the while I cooked your breakfast I've been trying to work out why you look familiar, and I just can't work it out."

Alex gave a casual shrug. "I get that a lot."

"You're not on the television then?"

"Not that I know."

"Huh." She shook her head. "You must look like somebody famous."

"I guess that's it." He eyed his empty cup. "Could I trouble you for another coffee, Carmel?"

"That won't be any trouble at all. How about you, love? More tea?"

"Lovely. Thank you," Zara replied but she continued to study him intently, her frown now about curiosity more than confusion. "Do you get recognized often?"

He tracked Carmel's exit to the kitchen. "She only thought I looked familiar."

"Hardly surprising. Your picture's always in the papers for some reason or other. I recognized you as soon as you stepped out of that car yesterday!"

"You had reason to."

She dismissed that with a wave of one hand, then sat in silence while Carmel filled his coffee and muttered something about his TV face.

"Why didn't you tell her who you were?" she asked when they were alone again. "That would have made her day."

"I suspect my generous tip will do that," he said dryly.

"Well, yes, but a celebrity sighting would have been the cherry on top."

"She wanted a TV star."

"Oh, I think royalty would have done just as nicely."

Royalty? Alex made a disparaging sound and shook his head, but her eyes continued to shine with unfulfilled curiosity.

"Does it bother you, the way the magazines love to label you and your brothers with those Aussie royalty tags?"

"No."

Her *huh* sound could have been acceptance. Or disbelief. "You don't mind being referred to as one of the 'Princes of the Outback'?"

"I don't read that garbage." He reached for the sugar bowl. "That's not what bothers me about media interest."

"What *does* bother you?"

"When someone gets hurt."

For a second he concentrated on stirring sweetness into

his coffee, ignoring the bitter taste of experience that rose to coat his senses. But he could feel her sharpened gaze on his face, could feel her curiosity change from teasing interest to serious attention. "Anyone in particular?" she asked.

"My mother." Across the table he met her eyes, sincere and unwavering, and he realized that for once he didn't mind talking about this. He wanted her to know the truth instead of the half-truths and outright lies that had been printed by the gutter press. "They gave her hell when she lived in Sydney, after our sister died of SIDS. Not a great time to have a dozen lenses trained on your face everywhere you went, but they loved capturing Maura Carlisle looking less than glamorous."

"I'm sure they loved the whole story," she said softly. "A beautiful model married to one of Australia's richest men, suffering the same as any grief-stricken mother."

"Couldn't get enough of it," he confirmed. "In the end Chas moved us all to the outback station where he grew up. Mau's rarely left there since."

"Is that why your father wanted this grandchild?" she asked after a thoughtful length of pause. "Because of what losing her baby girl cost your mother?"

"Cost?" Alex frowned at that choice of word.

"She lost a child, a part of her, a piece of her heart. And she also lost her freedom to live where she chose." Her eyes, astute and serious, held his across the table. "I can't help wondering if your father maybe felt some guilt over that. I mean, if he weren't so high profile, the press wouldn't have cared and your family wouldn't have been uprooted."

"She was famous in her own right."

"Ah, but never so much as when she married 'King' Carlisle," she said with an edge of wryness. "Then she became the next best thing to royalty."

It bothered him, that sarcastic bite in her voice. Bothered him because this was his family. His parents. "Sounds like you read too many tabloids."

"I try to avoid them, actually. I know how bloody they can be."

"Are you speaking from personal experience?"

She gave the merest shrug, not offhand, not casual. Then she lifted her gaze and the expression in her eyes, fierce and dark as if she were fighting to keep emotion at bay, drove the air from his lungs. "Would you believe my mother suffered at their hands once, too, a long time ago?"

"She was famous?"

"She had her fifteen minutes." A smile drifted across her lips, a lopsided smile tinged with irony and with a sadness that squeezed tight in his chest. "Nothing in the Carlisle mold, of course."

He didn't smile back. "Was she an actor or—"

He broke off when Carmel returned for their cups, tidying and wiping and asking if they needed anything else. "Just the bill," Alex told her, his eyes not leaving Zara's face. And when Carmel finally left he leaned forward, intent on finding out what had happened in that fifteen minutes. "Tell me about your mother."

"Oh, that's a long story," she said with another smile.

"It's one I want to hear."

Something shifted in her expression, opened and softened for a singular second. Then she gathered herself and shook her head. "Don't you think we should be going?"

"I'm not in that big a hurry."

"You're not afraid Carmel will suddenly look up in the middle of washing dishes and go, 'I remember now. It's Alex Carlisle. One of those filthy-rich princes!'"

"All right," he said agreeably after a short pause. He saw

her surprise in the slight widening of her eyes and smiled as he got to his feet and walked around to pull out her chair. Then, when she was on her feet, he looked right into those eyes and said, "You can tell me the whole long story another time. When we're alone and won't be interrupted."

Zara told herself it was a throwaway line. He didn't mean that he intended seeing her again, but that didn't prevent the swift grab of longing that shadowed hard on the heels of his words. Not that it mattered. There would be no "another time." No more sharing of confidences or beds.

No more desiring what she could not have.

The ride back to the city, unfortunately, only served to intensify the potent physicality of that desire. Mile after mile, she became more aware of his solid presence at her back, his hands spread over her rib cage, the vibration of the bike between her legs.

Oh, God.

Heat shuddered through her. Heat and memories and the knowledge that only inches separated their bodies. No. She huffed out a quick breath. She did not need to think about the intimacy of his body hard against hers. Or the edge of vulnerability she detected deep in his storm-gray eyes when he talked about his mother's loss.

She needed to picture him looking ridiculously out of place riding pillion in a business suit. She needed to picture him looking out of place on her bike and in her life. In the living room of her tiny Brunswick terrace, for example, among the eclectic mix of furniture slung together from estate sales and secondhand shops.

She needed to picture him sitting on her red leatherette sofa surrounded by her mother's collection of cushions, a rainbow palette of silky fabrics and girlie adornments, while she told him the story of Ginger Love, the stripper. Except she wouldn't because after she dropped him at his hotel, she would never see him again.

Providing Susannah doesn't change her mind.

The possibility fluttered through her consciousness, then lodged tight in her brain and her throat. If Susannah changed her mind and married this man, how could she face them? Her best friend—*her only known family*—and the man she'd fallen in lust with.

Last night he'd told her he couldn't marry someone who didn't want him, but what if Susannah returned ready to wed him and have this baby that mattered so much to his family? How could he refuse?

Sucking in a hard breath, she forced herself to grab hold of the wild black churn of resistance before it spun out of control. She had no business craving Alex Carlisle, even if Susannah didn't want him back.

His home was in Sydney, hers in Melbourne. Their life-styles were diametrically opposed, their goals in conflict. He needed an immediate family, she needed her degree. She barely kept up with study and the work necessary to pay her bills without thinking about a relationship.

She told herself all this, silently reciting the logic point by point as the miles whizzed by, as the landscape changed from bushland to paddocks to suburbia. Less than twenty-four hours since they'd met, so why did she feel as if she'd known him so much longer? Why did she feel a gathering anxiety as the suburbs turned to cityscape, as they drew closer and closer to their destination?

To the moment when she would say goodbye.

That restless stir of nerves and blood and mind made her drive a little too fast, zipping in and out of traffic and tak-ing side streets to avoid the lights. But no matter how many turns she made, she could not escape the pervasive sense that this last twenty-four hours had changed something key to her happiness.

Oh, the scientist in her scoffed. The cynic sneered and the realist just shook her head and suggested she couldn't afford a speeding ticket.

And when she pulled up outside the elegant facade of the Carlisle Grande Hotel, on the terra-cotta pavement under the gleaming stretch of awning, she still hadn't shaken that unsettling anxiety from her body. It bugged her, the unaccustomed sense of nervous uncertainty, enough that she gave the throttle a half turn, amplifying the high-pitched roar for a few revs, before she turned off the engine.

A liveried doorman started toward them, his face a stern mask of disapproval, but then she saw him double-take. Alex had stepped from the bike and removed the helmet and jacket he'd borrowed from Carmel. The doorman dipped his hat and asked if everything was all right, sir, and various other staff lurked nearby, obviously awaiting instructions.

Alex lurked, too, obviously waiting for her to…what? Because of the broken stand, she couldn't get off the bike but after a couple of seconds she did take off her helmet and shake out her hair. Hard to say goodbye through a Plexiglas visor.

Hard, too, to meet his eyes with her usual directness and to find the words to broach the awkward silence.

"It's been—" *Was there an adjective to describe this last day?* "—interesting. You are not what I imagined, Alex Carlisle."

His gaze slid over her, her bike, the helmet resting on the tank. Back to her eyes. "Likewise, Zara Lovett."

Zara moistened her lips. Her fingers played over her helmet, lifting and releasing the hinged visor, as she struggled over what to say. Goodbye seemed vastly inadequate, yet what else was there?

"I thought you would be ruthless and arrogant and full of yourself."

"What makes you think I'm not?"

For a second she stared back at him, knocked off balance by the impact of that question. Low, quiet, dangerous. "Last night," she told him, recovering. Lifting her chin. "You know you could have had me."

Heat flashed in his eyes. "I know."

Behind them a car pulled up, a distraction, a reminder of where they were and a focus for her thoughts. There wasn't any point extending this. There wasn't anything to say. "Well, you have a fiancée to find and I have study to catch up on. I'd best get moving."

But when she reached for her helmet, he put a hand on her shoulder. She felt the charge right through her leather. "I want to see you again. Is night the best time to call?"

"Don't call," she said quickly. "It's pointless. You're in Sydney and I'm in Melbourne. You want a wife and family. I don't even have time to date. I'm not the woman you want, Alex."

"I'm not asking you to marry me, Zara."

And while she was still dealing with all the conflicting implications of that statement, his hand slid from her shoulder to cup her neck. Then he leaned down and kissed her.

Oh, man. He kissed her, and after the first shocked second of pressure from those unexpectedly cool, amazingly supple lips, she kissed him back.

The response was instant. Her brain shut down. Her complete sensory system quivered with pleasure.

Against the sensitive skin of her nape, his fingers moved

infinitesimally, their touch as soft as the finest silk, the effect a lightning streak of fire in her skin and her veins. Her nostrils flared, drawing in his scent. Not yesterday's cologne but just the musky impression of man.

Not the filthy-rich tycoon, not the ruthless groom, just the man.

Dimly, that registered as significant. Dangerous. And then his tongue stroked her bottom lip and her whole body embraced the glorious idea of danger, heat, *him.* Starbursts of pleasure peppered her senses as she opened her mouth to deepen the kiss, as she silently acknowledged the overpowering sense of rightness that tightened in her chest, then unraveled in a swift silken flow of delight.

Then it was over, gone, a shift of air against her heated face and the blare of a horn from the street. She'd been completely lost in that kiss, and yet she wasn't surprised. Some part of her had known they would be like this together.

His hand slid from her nape to cup her cheek for a moment, and he looked right into her eyes.

"I do want you, Zara. Make no mistake about that."

"We can't always have what we want," she said softly and a muscle ticked in his cheek.

"I know that." He straightened, and as his hand slipped from her face, she felt an intense sense of loss. It wasn't only the breaking of that physical bond, but the sudden grimness she saw in his eyes.

Then he turned and was striding away before she could say the one word she'd been so intent on saying.

Goodbye.

Six

Not having his hands on something he wanted didn't usually perturb Alex. If he wanted that something badly enough, he devised a plan and went after it. In the case of wanting Zara Lovett, however, his hands were tied.

By lunchtime Monday he'd determined that no one knew Susannah's whereabouts and short of implementing a search—he put an investigator on standby, in case she didn't turn up soon—he could do nothing but wait.

And that inactivity, that lack of action, perturbed the hell out of him.

So did the tick of the clock counting down on the deadline for conceiving a baby.

During the long, dark stretch of Monday night, while he stared at the shadows on his bedroom ceiling with the taste and texture and heat of Zara's mouth alive in his senses, he could hear the time passing in endless pulsing beats of his blood. The frustration of knowing he might fail kept him awake. The conflict over what he wanted—Zara—and what he needed—a wife—brought him close to howling.

If Susannah returned wanting to be that wife, what then?

He could go ahead, marry her, and still not make a baby within the tight time frame. And if he did succeed on that front, would it really count as success if no one was happy?

His mother had made her feelings clear when he'd called with the news of his non-wedding. "I watched you together, darling, the night you brought Susannah to Kameruka. I'm so glad she was sensible enough to see what you're too stubborn to admit."

Not stubborn, Alex contended. Just focused on what had to be done. His duty, his responsibility, his contribution to the family that meant everything to him.

Even if that makes no one happy?

Tuesday morning dawned without any answers, and Alex took his simmering frustration to the racetrack to watch his favorite horse gallop. When he saw his brother strolling toward him in the pale, early morning light, he swore softly. He'd learned to deal with Rafe's smart-aleck observations over the years. He no longer let them get under his skin and wind his temper as they'd done in his youth.

Not after his mother had sat Alex down and told him about his biological father, about the tearaway temper that had destroyed his career, his reputation, his every relationship. Alex didn't want any part of the man who'd abandoned his mother. He couldn't do a damn thing about his coloring or the set of his eyes or the distinctive mouth he'd inherited, but he could control his wildness.

And, with Charles Carlisle's steady influence, he had controlled it and mastered it. Most days now Alex didn't even have to try. Today, if Rafe was true to form, it might take some effort.

"Morning, bro." Rafe thumped him on the back in greeting. "Has Irish galloped yet?"

"About to go. Your timing's inspired."

"It is, isn't it?" Rafe often made it to early morning track work, but grumbling and yawning and complaining about the godforsaken hour. This morning he practically hummed with bonhomie.

"Why are you in such a good mood?" Alex asked, lifting his binoculars toward the far side of the track and remembering his brother's distraction the previous week over his brand new wife. "I thought you were having marital problems."

"We were." Rafe sounded happy *and* smug. "But we spent the weekend making up."

"Congratulations."

"You too. Although I gotta say I didn't expect to see you this morning. Shouldn't you be honeymooning?"

Although he gripped his binoculars tighter, Alex managed to keep his voice even, his tone conversational. "It appears you haven't heard my news. The wedding didn't go ahead."

"No shit."

"None," Alex confirmed dryly, binoculars trained on the group of horses milling on the far side of the racetrack and the trainer giving instructions to the jockeys. "She's about to send them off."

Side by side they watched a trio of thoroughbreds set off on their training run, tracking their progress through the whispery threads of mist that curled up from the thick, damp turf.

"Glad to hear you came to your senses," Rafe said after several seconds.

"I didn't. Susannah did."

He felt Rafe's focus shift from the horses to his face. Steeled himself for a smart-aleck observation that didn't come. Instead, when he spoke, his brother sounded serious, if slightly suspicious. "You want to tell me how that happened?"

Alex told him, in a bare-bones fashion that skimmed over the night in the cabin and ended with his current situation in limbo-land. And despite his best intentions, frustration coated every word. "Until I hear from her, I don't know where I'm at."

"I think her not turning up on Saturday is a clear enough message of where you're at, bro."

Irritation crackled in Alex's blood. "'I can't marry you *today*' is not definitive."

"Are you saying you'll marry her if she turns up tomorrow?" Rafe's voice rose, incredulous. "After she left you cold at the altar?"

The horses thundered past their vantage point at a full-stretch gallop. Exasperation and a sense of hopeless futility pounded through Alex with the same thick drumbeat. The binoculars came down. Slowly he turned his head to stare at his brother. "Maybe I don't have any choice."

"Because you like being a martyr? Or because you won't allow Tomas or me our part in this?"

A muscle ticked hard in Alex's jaw. He felt it and took it as a warning to cool down, to take a second before answering. "I gather you're doing your bit."

"As was Tomas, before Angie walked. She could be pregnant now. Catriona, too." Rafe's voice softened on his wife's name. His expression, too, as if that possibility enthralled him. As if his new wife enthralled him.

"You love her, don't you?"

"Like crazy."

Alex shook his head slowly as he watched another bunch of racehorses flash by. Rafe Carlisle, confirmed playboy, struck by Cupid's arrow. Amazing. "I never thought I'd see the day."

"The rest were for fun. I knew Catriona was serious stuff the second I clapped eyes on her."

"Weren't you concussed?"

Rafe shrugged negligently but his gaze remained steady. "Unconscious I'd have still known she was the right woman."

The space following his pronouncement echoed with the retreating beat of galloping hooves for a good thirty seconds. Alex's head echoed with the beat of his brother's words. "What if this right woman—your Catriona—hadn't wanted to marry you? What if she wasn't ready for having babies?"

The creases around Rafe's eyes deepened, his gaze narrowed astutely. "If she's the right woman," he said slowly, "then the baby part isn't going to matter…especially if, for example, my brothers had that covered already. In that case, I'd say 'thank you, bro,' and I'd set about convincing her that I was the right man."

Alex didn't thank his brother for that advice before he left the track. He didn't thank him later that night, either, when Rafe called to let him know that Tomas and Angie were back together and setting a wedding date. Rafe used the occasion to casually ask, "Who is she?" to which Alex deadpanned, "I have no idea who you're talking about."

He had no intention of saying anything or doing anything until after he'd talked to Susannah. He didn't know if he could take Rafe's advice, if he could dispense with his familial responsibility, if it turned out he had a choice.

On Thursday, Susannah called.

She told him she couldn't marry him and relief flooded through Alex like a dam gate had opened. Later, he knew, that sense of reprieve would get spliced with guilt and the sense that he was letting down the man who had given him so much, who had made him everything that he was and everything that he wasn't. But for now, he could think no further than the moment, could feel no more than delight and satisfaction because now nothing stood between him and Zara.

That night he picked up the phone and then put it down again. He didn't call her on Friday either because he knew a phone call wouldn't be enough. He flew down to Melbourne instead.

Before his jet landed in the southern capital late on Friday afternoon, Alex knew exactly where to find Zara. Inside *this* fitness club. Satisfaction and anticipation jostled for supremacy in his gut as he flashed a smile at the receptionist.

The smile—and the fact that her eyes widened in recognition—helped when he asked if he could take a look at the facilities. Of course, then he had to stave off her enthusiastic offer to act as tour guide.

"Not necessary," he told her briskly. "I'm only interested in seeing your weights room."

"To your left and you'll see the sign, but it's no bother, Mr. Carlisle, really…."

Alex was already moving, and with every long stride his expectancy sharpened. For the last twenty-four hours he'd kept that keenness under tight restraint, but as he pushed through the door the rhythmic clank of weights swelled in the air and through his senses. So did his anticipation. His eagerness to meet Zara on equal terms, man and woman, without the will or Susannah strong-arming them apart.

He sensed she would have used this week to shore her I-don't-have-time-for-dating defenses. That's why he hadn't rung, why he'd chosen to surprise her and put her off balance again.

His eyes zeroed in on her instantly…or on her reflected image in the long mirrored wall. For a moment he stood riveted to the spot, drinking in the sight of that killer body at work.

She wore a similar outfit to last weekend. One of those racing-back athletic tops that bared shoulders and arms and the flat stretch of her midriff. Matching shorts—today's color was sunshine yellow—with a pair of stripes tracing the flow of her hips and outer thighs.

He watched the stripes bend and flex as she demonstrated a deep squat, then uncurl in a long, easy flow of limbs. The need to touch, to trace that path with the slow glide of his palms, crackled hot in his blood. When she switched modes, from demonstrator to hands-on instructor, Alex noticed she wasn't alone.

He'd known, of course. That's why she was here. It's what she did as a personal trainer.

He knew all this, yet when she put her hands on the man—when Alex saw the sandwiching touch, one hand on his abs, the other his lower back—an acid burn of jealousy seared his gut. Perhaps she actually heard the steam of that reaction, because suddenly she stilled. Her spine stiffened, her shoulder blades snapped back, and their gazes collided in the mirror. Her eyes widened, sparking with shock and something else.

Oh, yeah. It was still there. The same bolt of attraction. The same smoldering charge of awareness.

She said something to her client, bent to pick up a towel, then started to cross the room toward him. Her eyes flicked over his suit, rested a tick on his mouth. Remembering the heat of their kiss? Recalling his taste in her blood?

Heat burned in Alex's veins. He wondered what the half dozen or so members working on the resistance machines would think if he greeted her like he ached to. If he put his hands on her shoulders and rolled her around against the wall and kissed her until neither of them could remember where they were or why they hadn't kept on kissing last Sunday.

She stopped in front of him. Alex managed to keep his hands at his sides but he couldn't manage another smile. "Hello, Zara."

"Alex." With her usual steady confidence, she met his eyes but a note of wariness crept into her voice. "Why are you here?"

"To see you," he said simply.

Expression guarded, she stared back at him. "Why didn't you call first?"

"Would you have agreed to see me?"

Her lips tightened and her gaze rolled away. Perhaps he should have skipped the awkward introduction and explanation and gone with the kiss.

"So, you found out where I was working? How did you do that?"

"I called Personal Best. Jen was very helpful."

Her brows pulled together in vexation. "She shouldn't have told you I was here. That's not—"

"Don't blame Jen. I told her you would want to see me. I said we were…friends."

The way he lingered over that last word, investing it with an extra layer of meaning, brought her gaze rocketing back to his. "And she believed you? She actually believed I was 'friends' with Alex Carlisle?"

"Apparently," he said mildly. "Or she wouldn't have told me where to find you. Would she?"

No. The answer sparked in her eyes a second before she exhaled an audible breath. Before she lifted her towel to wipe the sheen of perspiration from her face. "Well, I can't talk now. Even to 'friends.' I'm working. I have a client."

"I noticed," he said evenly, taking the towel from her hands. Dabbing at her throat. "You missed a bit."

Under his hand, he felt her reflexive swallow and paused with the towel against her skin. His eyes lifted to hers in time to see the spark of response. It caught alight in his body.

"Are you always so hands-on?" he asked, slowly wiping across her collarbone, dipping into the hollow above. "With your clients?"

"Robert wasn't using his core muscles. I was instructing. Doing my job."

Of course she was. He had no right to this primitive possessive burn. None.

He slung the towel over her shoulder and met her eyes again. "Have dinner with me."

"I can't. I—"

"Don't make excuses. Jen told me this was your last client. You have to eat, I have to eat. I would enjoy your company."

She started to shake her head.

"Come on," he coaxed. "You know you want to."

For some reason that made her take a step back. Not physically, but mentally. He saw the grab of focus in her eyes and could feel the rejection coming off her in waves.

He'd expected this response, had planned for it, but that didn't make it any easier to take.

"It's just a meal, Zara. And while we eat I can tell you about Susannah."

Her eyes widened. "She's back? You've seen her? When? Where was she? Why hasn't she called me?"

"She isn't back. She's on her way to America. Come to dinner and I'll tell you the whole story."

Zara agreed to meet him at the restaurant because, a) she had to know what was going on with Susannah, and, b) if she wanted to keep this "just a meal" then she wasn't inviting him anywhere near her home, and, c) same with his hotel, only more so.

But when she stepped off the tram and saw him on the opposite side of the road, waiting outside Caruso's and scanning the street with the kind of restless impatience she recognized in her own blood, she knew she'd been fooling herself about why she'd agreed to meet him.

She'd been fooling herself, too, in thinking her choice of restaurant—a friendly, boisterous, Italian place—might make him feel uncomfortable and out of place. Ha. He'd dispensed with the corporate suit but still looked like a million dollars in dark trousers and a blue-gray shirt.

The same as in the gym two hours earlier, she couldn't stop staring at the hard, chiseled beauty of his face. Couldn't stop the memories of his kiss from unraveling in silky ribbons of response, a long yearning streamer of desire for *this* man, no matter how wrong, no matter how inopportune, no matter how destructive.

You shouldn't have agreed to see him, Zara. You know that. Turn and walk—no, run!—away before it's too late.

Except her feet remained rooted to the spot, not going

forward but not doing the smart thing and running away. And he saw her then, his restless gaze finding her face through the traffic and not veering for several long, breathless moments. *Run now,* her brain screamed, as he started toward her, his progress stalled by the rattling passage of two trams, one after another.

By the time he'd dodged both trams and several cars to reach her side of the road, by the time he'd paused to take in her batik skirt and vintage silk shirt and loose flow of hair, it was much too late to run. Then he smiled and took her hands and drew her so close she could feel the heat emanating from his body and her knees went weak with longing.

She swore he sniffed at her throat, just below her ear, before he kissed her cheek and drew back, still holding both her hands.

"What?" she asked, mesmerized by the hot pall of appreciation in his eyes and the kick of his smile.

"Just seeing if you smell as good as you look."

Oh, yeah, it was much too late.

She was an absolute goner.

Seven

After they ordered, Zara asked about Susannah and Alex told her about the phone call.

"Apparently there's another man," he said in an even voice.

Zara's heart turned over. *Oh, Alex. Why would she want another man when she had you?* "Who is he? When did she meet him? How?"

"Someone from her past, apparently, who turned up again out of the blue. An American, obviously."

Bowled over by this turn of events, by not knowing about any major man in Susannah's past, Zara slumped back in her chair. She mulled over the signs from last week, when Suse had seemed distant and distracted. Then she considered the even, impassive way in which Alex had imparted the news. "Are you okay with this?"

"It would be hypocritical of me not to be," he said wryly. "Given last weekend."

Given meeting her. Given that kiss. Given the way he was looking at her now.

"Nothing has changed since last weekend," she told him, wishing she could make her body believe the words. "I don't want you to read anything into me being here."

"This is just a meal." He lifted one shoulder and both corners of his mouth, ever so attractively. "That's all."

Except dinner with Alex Carlisle was so much more than "just a meal." One moment she talked and laughed in complete relaxation, the next she was struck dumb by the rush of heat when their legs brushed under the table and their eyes caught and captured the flame.

But there was more than the sexual thrall, more than the mesmerizing swirl of storm-blue eyes and her fascination with the lines that bracketed his face when he smiled, in the dusting of dark hair on the back of his hands and forearms. There was the sultry beat of desire when she thought about those hands on her body, and the ache of restraint because hers weren't on him.

But mostly there was captivation, in his company and his conversation, in the connection she felt as they shared slivers of their lives, and in his attentiveness. Having a man like Alex Carlisle hanging on her every word was a heady, rich, empowering sensation that transcended anything she'd ever felt.

If she weren't so enthralled and, yeah, turned on, she knew that would bother her on numerous levels. She shouldn't need a man's approval and attention to feel *this* good, *this* alive, *this* female. But she did feel all those things and for once she shoved all the be-responsible, think-about-tomorrow, look-after-your-own-happiness stuff aside, and immersed herself in the moment.

When he finally asked about her mother—as he'd promised after breakfast five days before—she only smiled and met his eyes over the rim of her coffee cup. "I wondered when you'd get to that."

"I wondered if you'd volunteer the information."

"What do you want to know?"

"Everything."

And despite the casual exchange of lines, despite the smile on her lips and her relaxed posture, Zara felt a shiver of trepidation deep inside. This represented a new level of dinner conversation. This was the most important part of her life. This was everything that had shaped her world.

One part of her wanted to share, but another part warned her about the promise she'd made to Susannah and how easily that could be exposed if she didn't tread warily. "You want to know why Mum was in the papers?" she asked, knowing she couldn't avoid sharing this part. Hating what this would expose, nonetheless.

"That's a start."

Zara nodded. Drew a breath. And decided she might as well tell it like it was. In straight, bald terms. "One of the tabloids found out she was mistress to a powerful man. He was a big name in business and society and he'd set her up a flash house, bought her all the pretty things."

"Doesn't sound like much of a story," he said mildly, meeting her eyes across the table.

"Possibly not. Except Mum was pregnant. At the same time as his wife, as it happens. Big story, big scandal, big scarlet woman."

"She didn't know he was married?"

"She didn't know Mi—" She caught herself before the name slipped out. "His wife was pregnant, that's for sure. She didn't talk about him much, but I rather think he'd spun her the usual lines. His marriage was over but he couldn't end it for business reasons. To protect his fortune and his status, I imagine. Then, when this story broke, she found out he'd been less than truthful."

He didn't say anything for a long moment and Zara resisted a fierce urge to fill the silence by defending her mother for the unforgivable. To justify something Zara had only started to comprehend in the last week, since she'd met this man. Because, even knowing Alex Carlisle belonged to another woman, she had been tempted.

You know you could have had me.

I know.

"This was your father?" he asked, breaking into her thoughts.

"Yes, but please don't ask about him. Nothing personal. I don't talk about him to anyone." She attempted a smile and felt the tug of its tight, bitter edges. "It's not good for my sanity."

"What about your mother's?"

"Oh, she got over him. She had her pride and she was always practical. She had a baby to raise."

"Appears she did a fine job."

"Yes. She did," Zara said with no false modesty. "No one had a better mother than I did."

Something flitted across his expression as he watched her, an element she'd not seen before. Intense but with softer edges, it stole her breath and sounded alarm bells in her head. A warning that this man could steal so much more than her breath, that he could make her want too much and leave her wanting more.

Then his eyes narrowed a smidgen, deepening the creases at their edges.

"What's that look about?" she asked suspiciously.

"I'm just picturing you as a little girl." His lips lifted into a smile and as quickly as that he turned the mood around. "Did you play at being a doctor?"

"Yes." Relief washed through her as she smiled back at him. Relief that he'd not wanted to pursue that serious moment, or press her about the father she didn't want to know. That instead he'd chosen to lighten the tone. "I loved my red plastic stethoscope and the medical encyclopedia best."

"Interesting choice of reading."

"Oh, my mum read me traditional stories, too."

His lips quirked again. "Fairy tales?"

"You betcha. She wanted me to know that Little Red Riding Hood and her girlfriends made some singularly bad decisions regarding big, bad wolves and kissing frogs and the like. She brought me up to believe I could rescue myself rather than waiting around for a stray prince or woodcutter."

"Cynical," he said, eyes narrowed, thoughtful, "but interesting."

"Realistic," she corrected, "but why interesting?"

"At the cabin last weekend you said you would only marry for love."

"Yes, and one day I will. In the meantime I'm not hanging around waiting for my prince."

Unfortunate wording, she realized, when his eyes darkened with the impact of her word choice, but she refused to acknowledge that link to him. He wasn't her prince. He wasn't a prince at all, to anyone but the trash media she despised.

Lifting her chin a fraction, she met his eyes. "In the meantime I'm doing what I've always wanted to do."

"You've always wanted to study medicine?"

"Pretty much. I danced when I was little, and then I got into sports. Along the way I developed a fascination for the human body and how it works, so that was always my first choice for university. I'd only done one year when Mum got sick."

"You deferred your course to look after her?"

"Yes." She shifted in her seat, uneasy talking about that soul-destroying time as her mother's damaged nervous system gave out and her muscles wasted away. "Afterwards it took a while to get myself together. When I did resume my course work I was even more determined to get my degree."

"Because you promised her."

"There is that, but also…I wanted to do something that would make a difference. It's hard to explain but it's like…it's like I didn't want her suffering to have been in vain." She finished up in a rush and then rolled her eyes self-consciously. "I know that sounds ridiculous."

"No. It doesn't."

The quiet certainty of his voice, in his expression, made her heart trip in her chest. She drew a deep breath, cautioned herself again about feeling too much, responding too much. Falling too hard.

"What about your father?" he asked after a moment. "Would he be proud of you too?"

The automatic response, the I-don't-give-a-damn-what-the-bastard-thinks, froze under his serious regard. For some reason she felt a connection, an emotional accord, and another answer altogether slid easily from her tongue. "I always thought I didn't care, but before he died you know what I discovered? There was this rogue part of me that wanted to make a mark. To be a somebody, a success, so that one day he might come looking for me. That he might want to know me."

"You went looking for him?" he asked slowly. Astutely.

"When I couldn't look after Mum anymore, when she

moved into care, I had to sell the house. Anyway, I found those paper clippings. She'd kept them all, I don't know why, so he wasn't difficult to find."

"And you wished you hadn't bothered?"

"No. Actually, I'm glad I found him." Frowning, she searched for the words to explain what sounded like a paradox. "I guess I'd always wondered if things had been different—if he hadn't been married or if he'd divorced his wife—what might have been. Meeting him cemented that we were better off on our own."

"You didn't hit it off, huh?"

"Nicely put." And for once she realized that talking about Edward Horton hadn't twisted her insides into knots. No aftertaste soured her mouth. An ironic smile curved her lips as she considered another aspect of those dark months. "On the positive side, I was into kickboxing at the time and meeting him had a big impact on my aggression."

Smiling at that, he reached across the table and trapped her hand in his. And when she looked into his eyes Zara actually felt something inside her give. "We had that in common," he admitted softly.

"You kickbox?"

A joke, sort of, but he didn't laugh. "The aggressive streak because of a father who didn't want to know me. Except I got lucky when my mother married Chas. I didn't need to go looking. There was nothing I wanted from my biological father, I had nothing to say to him."

"Is that why honoring your stepfather's will matters so much?"

"It seemed the least I could do."

"And now?" she asked.

"My brothers tell me there's still hope. Tomas and Angie

are back together. Rafe and his wife have worked out their problems, apparently."

"That must be a relief."

"Of sorts." His shrug looked tight, not quite casual. "I don't like that I can't uphold my end of the pact."

No, he wouldn't. Zara could see that in the stormy swirl of his eyes and the tight set of his mouth. He would view it as failure. "Worse," she said solemnly, "to have married for the sake of the pact and then regretted it afterward."

"Do you regret coming here tonight?" he asked after a moment.

"No."

Heat sparked in his eyes as he turned her hand over and linked their fingers. Heat and everything else that had passed between them during what had never been "just a meal." And in that instant she was back on the street, her gaze trapped by the smoky intensity of his, thinking *I am a goner.*

"What are we going to do," he said, low and gruff, "about this?"

The background noise faded to a dull blur as all Zara's focus centered on him. The unsmiling intensity of his expression, the silent appeal in his eyes, the heated charge of his touch. "I don't know."

"Would you like to come back to my hotel room?"

Her simple "yes" almost brought Alex to his knees. So unexpected, so honest, so exactly how this night had to end. He didn't question her motivation. He paid the bill; he ushered her outside; he made small talk about the food and the balmy spring night while they waited to hail a taxi in busy Sydney Road.

On the surface he maintained his cool. Inside anticipation

honed his focus to a keen knife's edge. He had to get this woman—this woman he wanted more than his next breath—back to his hotel and into his bed before she reconsidered.

A cab pulled up on the opposite side of the street and he took her hand, towing her through the traffic until he could steer her into the back seat. He didn't see any reason to let go of her hand. He liked the strength of her grip, the intimacy of their linked fingers, the charge of heat when he rested their joined hands on his thigh.

The grip of tension when her fingertips brushed the fabric of his trousers.

That touch, innocent but incendiary, blew whatever he'd been discussing with the cabbie clean out of his brain. Finals football? The pre-election polls? The upcoming spring racing carnival? Frowning, he struggled out of the lust fugue and forced himself to focus on the driver's laconic commentary because, hell, if he started thinking about those fingertips on his skin, if he gave in to the urge and lifted her hand to his lips, if he tasted a hint of her sweet scent then he would be lost.

"Got a runner in the Cup this year?" the cabbie asked.

Alex knew he'd been identified before this giveaway question. The driver's eyes kept darting to his mirror, watching, not missing a thing. Hence his caution with Zara. He'd kicked himself to kingdom come and back again after last week's recklessly public kiss outside the hotel. It's a wonder *that* hadn't appeared front page in the tabloids!

Tonight he was being more circumspect. Hand-holding was fine. Anything involving tongues was definitely behind closed doors.

"Irish Kisses is entered," he supplied in answer to the cabbie's question about the Melbourne Cup. "We'll see how her form holds up in the meantime."

"Guess a lot can happen in…how long till the big one?"

Alex did the calculation. "Five weeks next Tuesday."

And, yes, a lot could happen in that length of time. His horse could go lame, get sick, train off—any one of a dozen variables could rob him of a starter in Australia's richest horse race.

Yet tonight all he could think about was whether or not, in five weeks' time, he'd still be holding Zara Lovett's hand. If she would be at his side in the stands cheering Irish home. If she would celebrate with him, or console him afterward with her silky sweet-tasting kisses.

Reflexively his grip on her hand tightened. Her fingers curled hard against his thigh and that touch arrowed straight to his groin. Heat washed through his skin, so intense he felt perspiration break out down his spine.

"I'm not going anywhere," she said softly, squeezing his hand. Subtly reminding him to ease off the pressure. He did, stroking his thumb across her knuckles, rolling the tension from his shoulders, breathing a silent sigh of relief when the taxi pulled in to the hotel driveway.

Finally—and only because he had to—he released her hand so he could pay the fare.

And when he closed the door and straightened, he realized they were standing in the exact spot where he'd first tasted the lush temptation of her mouth on Sunday. Their gazes met and everything he'd felt in that moment, everything that clamored through him now, was reflected in her whiskey eyes. All he could think about was kissing her again, same place, same way, except this time they would walk away together. All the way to his bed.

Circumspection be damned, he closed the car's-width space between them, cupped her face in one hand and gave in to his fierce need.

One kiss, tempered with a world of restraint, while the stroke of his thumb along her jaw and the burn of passion in his eyes told her that this was only the start. Never dropping his gaze, she stretched closer so her body brushed his in a dozen fleeting places and the subtle flick of her tongue drove a groan from his lust-tight throat.

"Inside," he growled at her ear. "Before we draw a crowd."

She laughed, low and husky and erotic.

Oh, yeah. He would definitely have to find a way to make her laugh once they got naked. Her laughter, her hands, her legs, the silky shimmer of her shirt as she turned into the glare of the lobby light—she blew him away on so many levels, had done so too many times to count these past hours.

This woman, his gut told him as he took her hand and led her through the lobby, *is the one you've been waiting for.*

The clarity of that knowledge didn't shake him. Last weekend he'd known, at the same instinctive level, that more than physical attraction forged this connection. But he'd walked away because of the will and what he took as his duty.

"Hey." Tugging on his hand, she drew him out of his reverie. "Whatever you're thinking about—stop!"

"What if I'm thinking about you?"

"I hope you weren't, actually."

Alex pulled up short and turned her toward him. "You don't want me thinking about you?"

"Not if it makes you look so…intense."

"Ah, but you do make me feel intense," he said, tightening his grip on her fingers. "Whenever I think you might change your mind about stepping into this elevator."

Their gazes tangled and the moment hung with renewed tension, with the hint of wariness that stole across her face.

Alex's heart kicked with sudden fear but he kept his gaze direct. Unflinching. A part of him warned against pushing too hard and scaring her off, but at this moment he simply could not do light and easy. Until he had her upstairs, a smile was impossible. "Make up your mind, Zara. Here and now."

"My mind is made up," she said after the briefest pause. "If I don't do this, I will only spend another week wondering."

"Wondering?"

One corner of her mouth lifted in the smallest hint of a smile. "About whether this will be as good as I've imagined."

Relief poured through Alex as he pulled her closer, relief and a parallel stream of desire because she'd been imagining this—imagining him in her bed—all week. He threaded her hair behind her ear, stroked his fingers down its silken length and saw the spark of response in her eyes.

"Don't worry, sweetheart." He pressed a brief, hard kiss to her lips, then turned them both back toward the elevator. "It'll be better."

Eight

Alone in the elevator, Alex gave in and kissed her like he'd wanted to in the lobby, under the portico, in the taxi. In the street outside the restaurant. In the gym earlier that afternoon. He wound his fingers in her hair and pulled her hard against his body and simply immersed himself in the mind-numbing sweetness of her mouth.

That taste, he knew, was already under his skin, in his blood, hot-wired into his hormones. One sip and they raged into life, screaming for more. He kissed her until the doors opened on the hotel's top floor, and once he had her inside his suite he backed her against the door and kept on kissing her until they were both breathing harder than after their run through the sleet.

Winded, knocked off center by the power of his need, by the fevered roar of blood in his ears, Alex leaned his forehead against hers, flattened his hands against the door and struggled for control. He had, at least, to get her into his bedroom before he tore her clothes off and gave himself up to this raging need.

The hell of it was he didn't want to tear her clothes off. He wanted to undress her slowly so he could savor her amazing body, inch by silky inch. He wanted to seduce her, for Pete's sake, into giving him much more than her body.

"I had hoped to offer you a drink." His voice was a deep mixture of arousal and wryness. "To put on some music. To show you my smooth side."

After a second her hands slid from his neck, down his chest to his sides. "Which *is* your smooth side, Alex? Left or right?"

That surprised a laugh from him, a laugh that snagged in the middle when she stroked a hand up and down one side and then the other. A simple touch made intricate by the extravagance of his body's response. Or perhaps by the way she tipped her head back against the door and studied him through half-lidded eyes, her hair mussed by his hands and her lips full and sultry from his kisses.

"Maybe you need to work that out for yourself," he said, levering himself slowly off the door. Spreading his arms wide, he dared her with both body language and his steady gaze to find her own answer.

Heat flared golden in the depths of her eyes and resounded low in Alex's body. A challenge given. A challenge accepted.

She rolled off the door and Alex smiled at his own unconscious description. Yeah, she rolled...or maybe flowed. Whatever, it was a long, sinuous unraveling that he wanted to freeze-frame in his memory.

Hell, who was he kidding? He loved everything about the way she moved. Sometimes full of energy and purpose.

Sometimes loose and athletic. Sometimes with smooth leonine grace.

Like now, he thought, as she circled him, not touching, just studying him like a hunter on the prowl. A lithe, agile hunting cat, hungry for his body. His every muscle bunched with anticipation, tightened with heated arousal at the thought of her stalking him, taking him down, her mouth on his body.

She disappeared behind him, the flutter of her exotic patterned skirt a whisper of sound and motion, her scent in the air and in his nostrils as he waited. Waited for her touch until he thought he might snap. And then he sensed her closeness, felt the warmth of her breath between his shoulder blades an instant before her hands skimmed down his arms, then repeated the flat-palmed glide up his sides and down his back.

Frustration twitched in his flesh. He wanted more. He wanted those hands beneath his shirt, that breath on his skin. That mouth on his body.

She circled back to the front and their gazes collided. "Hard to tell which is your smooth side." Her voice reflected her eyes. Hot. Aware. Turned on. "You're hard as a rock."

And she hadn't touched him anywhere below the waist.

"You need a closer inspection." He lifted a hand, brushed his thumb across her lips. "Why don't you undress me?"

Her lips quivered under his touch. "Here?"

She had a point. They stood a scant two feet inside the door. A whole spacious suite beckoned. A king-size bed, with the best linen Carlisle money could buy, lay turned down and waiting.

But still…

His thumb ghosted across her cheek, lingered on the

beauty spot. "I'm not fussy about where. You walk into a room and you're all I see. You touch me and everything else fades to black."

Her breath hitched, a sound of wonder, of wanting, and she turned in to his body, so close her skirt skimmed against his thighs and their knees brushed. Warm breath shuddered against his chin, his throat. "I think I just discovered your smooth side."

"It's not a line, Zara. It's the truth."

For a second she went still, and he sensed her weighing that, analyzing it in her sharp brain, and then her fingers lifted to touch his abdomen and chest in a half-dozen places. The merest drift of a caress. The hottest lick of flame.

Alex sucked in air. Her scent, sweet, warm, female, went straight to his head. He trapped her hands against his chest, held them against the thickened drumbeat of his heart, before drawing them to his top button. "Take off my shirt. Please, Zara. I want to feel these hands on my skin."

He felt the flutter of response in her hands, or perhaps it was his flesh that shuddered because when he dropped his hands away she started unthreading buttons with surprising sureness, her fingers quick and steady until they neared his waist. Then she fumbled with delicious effect. Warm breath huffed against bared skin and her knuckles dragged over his tensed abs while she battled with that last button.

Finally, she grabbed two handfuls of shirt and pulled it free of his trousers and the last button gave. Then her hands were on his chest. Her hands and her mouth and the hot murmur of her breath as she said, "I've thought about touching you like this. All night."

"I've been dreaming about it." His hands combed through her hair, let the cool tresses play against his hot skin. "All week."

"Really?"

Oh, yeah. And not just like this. He'd dreamed of those long, elegant fingers, that lush siren's mouth, on him everywhere. "You have no idea."

"Maybe I do."

"Really?" he asked, echoing her question, her tone.

He felt her smile against his skin, felt it seep into his flesh and saturate his blood. "Did you only dream about *me* touching *you?*"

"Is that a hint?"

Her thumb grazed his nipple. "Was I too subtle?"

Alex laughed, low and lazy. He let his hands slide to her shoulders and down her back. Less than a minute ago he'd been too edgy to contemplate lazy or any laughter that wasn't wound as tight as his impatience. But she'd surprised him again with her humor.

Surprised him with how easy she was to be with.

Dipping his thumbs under the hem of her shirt, he stroked the warm skin beneath. His fingers spanned her waist—beneath the silky drape of her shirt—and he started to walk her slowly backward, into the sitting room. "When I was waiting outside the restaurant, wondering if you'd show up—"

"I wouldn't have sent you out there," she cut him off, sharp and affronted, "and then stood you up!"

"Good to know."

"I would have called."

He stopped walking. Ducked down to look into her face. "You thought about doing that, didn't you?"

"At least a dozen times," she admitted. "Every time I tried to call Susannah. Every time I changed my clothes."

"I'm glad you didn't."

"So am I."

The honesty in her words and her steady gaze settled rich and warm in his chest. He had to kiss her again, not with the unrestrained hunger of before but slow and deep and giving. He kissed her mouth and the strong line of her jaw and the little spot on her cheek. "I approve your final choice," he said when he moved on to her ear. "In case you were wondering."

"My final choice?"

Gathering the soft fabric of her shirt in his hands, he slowly pulled it up and off. "Of clothes. You said you changed a dozen times."

"Well, it wasn't quite that many, but close. I'm not used to thinking about what I'm wearing."

"That's okay." Alex fingered the strap of her bra, let it slide down her arm then followed it with his mouth. His hands glided down her back and over her hips. "I'll think about it for you."

"You're offering to act as my wardrobe consultant?" Her amused question ended on a breathy hitch when he gently bit the skin of her shoulder then laved it with his tongue.

"Sure." Slowly, inexorably he bunched up the material of her skirt. "I'll choose your clothes for you as long as I get to take them off."

A smooth line, Alex thought, liking that he had his edginess, the wildness he loathed, back under control. Rewarding himself by drawing up her bunched skirt and letting his knuckles graze the backs of her thighs and the tight curve of her backside...the tight *naked* curve of her backside.

For a fleeting second his fingers fisted in the soft fabric of her skirt. He sucked in a quick breath through his teeth. Then he let that air—plus all the gathered folds of her skirt—go so he could cup those tight naked curves with his palms.

"A G-string," he breathed.

"Is that the underwear you would have chosen, as my wardrobe consultant?"

In answer he drew her hard against his body. Stroked his hands over her warm, smooth skin and absorbed her shudder of response with a long, wet kiss. And when the lust dimmed to a dull roar and his brain cleared enough to distinguish his surroundings again, he resumed walking her toward the bedroom.

Before they made it to the bed, he managed to prize his hands from her body long enough to undo the waistband of her skirt. He took a half step back to watch it slither past her hips, to study those long, toned, runner's legs, to imagine them locked around his hips, holding him deep inside her body. The pulse of sex started to beat through his blood, a hard hum of insistence that filled his senses, and then her hands were on his trousers, an exquisite torture of unbuttoning and unzipping, of touching but not touching nearly enough.

Their eyes met and shared a wordless message of heat and urgency and need. With swift hands and quick catches of breath, they shed the rest of their clothes and sank together to the turned-back bed, rolling in a heated slide of skin against skin, of passion-warmed bodies against the cool expanse of sheets. Again their eyes met and of an accord they slowed, steadied, stilled...until Alex turned them one more rotation and settled on his back.

For the moment he had Zara exactly where he wanted her. Stretched on top of him, her breasts grazed his chest with every breath, her legs tangled with his. She was all sleek curves and finely toned muscles, long and strong and perfect. Slowly he slid his hands over her back, adjusting the weight of her hips until she cradled his arousal between her thighs.

But what froze him in that instant wasn't the fit of their bodies or the teasing lure of her moist heat. It was the intensity of her expression as she looked down at him.

The rush of empowerment, the sense that he'd waited forever to look into this woman's eyes while she took him into her body, stalled the breath in Alex's lungs and squeezed viselike in his chest.

For a second it was too much, a blinding flash of fear that he might give more than he wanted, and then she leaned down and kissed him and drove the beast away with the honeyed taste of her passion. He twisted his hands in her hair and held her there, bound to his mouth and slowly melting over his body, yielding to the thick, insistent heat between his legs.

Longing coiled strong and low in his gut. The desire to spread her wider and push inside. To claim her in the most primitive way, naked and unprotected. His hand traced the length of her spine, and she arched and stretched against the pressure, humming with pleasure into their kiss, against his lips, into his mouth.

Alex's need flexed, stretched, pulsed. He palmed her hips and held her there, hot and wet against him, the worst and the best of tortures. Then with a low growl he rolled her onto her back. "You have no idea how much I want this." All the primitive fire of his need blazed in his eyes and grazed the edges of his voice as he rocked slowly against her. "To forget myself. To forget to ask about protection."

His words seemed to take a second to sink in, but then her eyes widened with understanding, alarm, dismay. Alex felt a jolt of remorse. He shouldn't have admitted to that primitive temptation. Not after last weekend and all they'd talked about. Quickly he rolled away, over to the bedside table and the condoms he'd bought after leaving the gym. *Just a meal* he'd said, while he prepared for much more.

"I can't believe I would forget."

Frowning at the appalled note in her voice, Alex looked back over his shoulder. Her stricken expression caught hard in his chest. "Hey, it's okay."

"No, it's not okay. My mother taught me better. I always carry protection. Always."

He came back to her, pressed a kiss to her mouth, another to the pucker of worry between her brows. "I didn't forget. I'm sorry I sowed that doubt. It was unforgivable. I'll always protect you, sweetheart."

Something flickered in her eyes. Doubt? Skepticism? Whatever, he didn't like it.

"Don't you trust me? If that's—"

"It's not you," she said quickly. Her gaze rested, dark and serious, on his. "Or maybe it is you. You make me forget my common sense." She touched a hand to his mouth and her voice grew husky. "You make me forget…everything."

Her fingers skimmed his lips with silken heat, the sincerity of her words stirred much deeper, richer, hotter. Alex closed his eyes for a second, two, and then he trapped her fingers against his mouth. Opened both eyes and lips as he murmured, "Fade to black."

"You're dangerous," she breathed as he licked across her fingertips. As her quiver of reaction echoed through his body.

"You must have me mixed up with someone else." Eyes never leaving hers, he took her hand from his mouth. "I'm safe." Drew it down his body to touch the part of him he'd made safe. "Steady. Dependable. Reliable."

"Is that how you see yourself?"

"Yes."

For a second she gazed at him speculatively, then her

fingers slid down his shaft and her look turned hot, wicked, erotic. "I'll give you safe." Those teasing fingers wrapped around him and he jerked in response. "But not so steady."

With her hand still on him, Alex's snort of laughter sounded tight and broken. Not steady at all.

"I do believe you're dependable and trustworthy." Her eyes glazed with more than heat, she leaned into him and traced the grooves in his cheeks. With her fingers and then her tongue. "You're hard. And dangerous. And beautiful."

Completely undone by her words, by the sensual whisper of her mouth, Alex struggled to breathe. "That would be you," he managed to say finally. "Beautiful."

"Oh, I'm not beautiful. My sister's beautiful."

"You have a sister?"

"Half." And there was a new tension in her eyes, a dark flash of self-castigation. "Can we not talk about my family?" She cradled him fully in her palm, squeezed gently, insistently. "Can we not talk, at all?"

At the moment Alex couldn't imagine saying anything that wasn't a groan or a plea for mercy. Later, he thought, as he kissed her and palmed her breasts and struggled to contain the swamping wave of desire. Later he would ask questions and inveigle the answers from her sweet mouth. Everything he wanted to know, everything that went on inside her mind, everything that made her strong and vulnerable and completely captivating.

Everything that made her so damn beautiful he ached.

For now he contented himself with learning her body. Everything that made her arch her back and stretch her legs in restless need. Everything that made her hum low in her throat and clutch his head between urgent fingers, holding him to her, enticing him to use tongue and lips more boldly until he lapped up the strong shuddering wave of her first climax.

And when he rose above her, hard and aching with the need to be inside, she met his eyes and slowly drew him into her wet velvet heat. As if she'd divined his need for slow, his craving for self-control, his fervent desire to keep a grasp on the sweat-slippery reins of restraint.

He curbed the incessant need to close his eyes and give himself up to the wild primal instincts of his blood. He needed to be that steady, solid, reliable man he'd created.

"Beautiful," he breathed as she took him to the hilt, and then she squeezed some internal muscles and drove the air hissing from his lungs. Dizzy with lust, with need, with *her,* he struggled to hold himself still, to withdraw inch by inch, to not drive himself all the way in, again and again.

Slowly he pulled back, and she wrapped those amazing legs around him and held him there while she stroked his face and then licked at his mouth. Her taste was on his tongue, in his blood, wrapping him in a thick, sweet cloak. He kissed her throat, nuzzled his face in her shoulder and bit her earlobe as he moved with a slow rocking cadence while the pressure built in the back of his brain and in the tightly bound tension of his muscles.

Her hands slipped through his hair, caressed the long muscles of his back and then gripped his biceps as she arched up to meet a stronger thrust, changing the angle, driving him even deeper and crying out with her pleasure. That was it, that guttural cry of pleasure, that sound of complete abandon, the buck of her hips and the drag of her flesh against his.

"Let yourself go," she murmured, her voice as thick and tight and hot as his body. "Now, Alex, please."

Heat engulfed him. A blazing sensual storm he could no longer fight. He drove faster, harder, deeper until his breath exploded, fast and furious, as his climax came in a blinding explosion of pleasure that swallowed him whole. For a long while he remembered nothing, nothing but the frantic beat of hearts and the cooling sweat of bodies, and running beneath the harsh physical reality like a vein of pure gold lay the innate knowledge that he knew this woman.

That every broken relationship, every woman who hadn't worked out was because he hadn't met this one.

He knew he had to rouse himself, to dispose of the condom. Even through his languor he felt a fierce need to protect her as promised, to protect her during the dangerous afterward. But before he forced his utterly spent muscles into action, he buried his nose in her throat for a second and it came to him, clear and unbidden.

The unnamed element in her scent.

"Almonds."

Zara recalled that one perplexing word muttered against her throat as she stood blinking at herself in his bathroom mirror the next morning. "Almonds," she mouthed silently, shaking her head in bewilderment. What was that all about?

It was an easy something to focus on. One distinct, unthreatening word she'd picked from a thousand that fluttered through her early-morning brain. Not that she was trying to forget or to discount the hours spent in Alex Carlisle's bed. As if she could do either. As if she would ever forget the way he'd loved her, so many times, so many ways.

The hand she lifted to touch a mark on her throat, another on her breast, trembled.

While her pragmatic self came awake knowing what she must do—get dressed, leave while he slept, acknowledge this as a one-night stand—an inner voice murmured that walking away would not be that easy.

Alex Carlisle made love as he did everything—slow,

thorough, intense, with an underlying thread of ruthlessness. As if he couldn't stop until he had bound her to him, body and soul. Her hand dropped from her breast and a shiver of reaction rippled through her over-sensitized skin.

Dangerous. Oh, yes. He was one very dangerous man, making her feel this sated, this different, this beautiful.

Shaking her head at that piece of silliness, she turned away from the mirror. *For heaven's sake, Zara, your nose is still big, your shoulders too wide, your face too long. The mole on your cheek is still a mole no matter how many times he calls it a beauty spot. A masterful mouth and a clever tongue and half a dozen orgasms do not change facts!*

A wry smile curved her lips as she sorted through the items of clothing she'd scooped up from the floor in the near-darkness. Her favorite shirt, her best skirt, her only bra that wasn't a racing-back sports model. And a pair of men's boxer briefs with a designer monogram on the elastic waistband.

Damn.

Quickly she pulled on the rest of the clothing. If she found her underwear on her way out, well and good, but she couldn't spend time searching. She didn't want to wake him. She didn't want to explain. She wanted to get home where she could indulge herself with a long shower, and then she would get dressed in her usual practical, comfortable clothes—with underwear—to face a big day of study.

Right. She inhaled a deep breath, opened the bathroom door, and let out a startled squeak. He stood just outside the door, waiting.

The dark shadow of morning beard, the bed-tousled hair, the broad naked chest made him look not quite civilized. Made her heart thump hard in her chest. So did the look in his eyes as they slowly trailed over her, head to foot.

And the raspy edge to his morning voice as he said, "Good morning. Did you sleep well?"

"Sort of."

He studied her for another second, something dark and primal in his eyes, then he closed the space between them, held her still with a hand cupping her neck and kissed her. Not briefly, not as long as last night's marathon, but very thoroughly. By the time he finished, her heart was racing and the bottom had dropped out of her stomach.

"You're dressed." He rubbed her nape and she curled into that caress like a cat.

Her response resembled a purr.

"Why?"

Frowning, Zara forced herself to straighten and pay attention. "Why…what?"

He curled a finger into the neckline of her shirt and tugged gently. "Why are you dressed?"

"I have to get to work."

"Damn."

And suddenly it was all right, this morning-after intimacy thing. The overwhelming urge to forget work and climb back into his bed was all right, too, since it was an urge he obviously shared. Since it was an urge she couldn't give in to.

She sighed heavily. "Yeah."

"Will you come back?" he asked. "After you finish work?"

How easy it would be to say yes. His hand dipped lower inside her neckline, tracing the slope of her breast, enticing her to accept that easy answer. Her nipples tightened, her heart skittered, but she lifted her eyes and met his gaze steadily. "I have a lot of studying to do. I intend spending the day at the library."

"And after that?"

She moistened her lips. "Alex, I don't think—"

"This wasn't a one-night stand, Zara."

"It was supposed to be just a meal," she countered, not stepping down from the steely resolve in his eyes.

"Let's just see what happens," he said evenly. "I know study is your priority. I know you have your job and not much time."

"No time for a relationship."

Something flickered in his eyes, but before she had a chance to acknowledge the danger, he'd moved closer, cupping her face in his hands, easing her back into the bathroom until she'd backed up against the vanity.

"I'm not going to rush you. I'm not going to impinge on your time." Very, very slowly, he trailed his mouth over her cheek, nuzzling her ear, turning her knees to jelly. He was not playing fair. "Let's just see where this goes? No promises. No commitment. No tomorrow. Just now."

Nine

When Zara exited the library at four o'clock and found
him waiting outside, she pulled up so suddenly that a couple of students following behind plowed right into her. She
murmured an apology but her eyes didn't shift from his and
her feet seemed incapable of resuming motion.

He'd seen her, of course, and as she forced herself to
get moving again, as she casually descended the flight of
steps to the roadside, he smiled and all those tightly wadded emotions softened to mush. She smiled right back
and thought life could only get better if he met her halfway across the wide, pebbled concrete footpath and
kissed her.

He didn't. He stood still and straight beside a dark vehicle, and something primitive flitted across his expression.
It resounded through her body, heavy in her breasts and
tight in her chest and rich in her belly. And beneath the hard

hum of that instinctual response, she heard the dull clang of a warning bell.

Caution, Zara. Remember this morning? You only agreed to see him again because he'd promised to take it slow, to make it easy.

Smile tamped by caution, she stopped in front of him. "What are you doing here?"

"Waiting for you."

She gave him a *well, duh* look. "How did you know where to find me?"

"From your housemate."

"Not my boyfriend?" she countered, recalling the first time he'd called her home to finagle information from Tim.

"Not your boyfriend." And there, in his eyes, that same territorial darkness as before.

Zara stiffened her spine, determined to control her female flutter of response. Determined to muster some kind of affront. "You called my home and you asked my housemate about my plans for today?"

"I needed to know what time you'd be finished," he said evenly. "Since you left this morning without saying."

"What if I'd changed my plans? What if I'd told Tim I would be at the library and then I'd left early?"

"Then I'd have missed you and you wouldn't have had the pleasure of my company."

As if that answer weren't enough, he railroaded her with a slow smile and before she could recover, turned and opened the door of his vehicle. A charcoal dark four-wheel drive, probably some luxury model and so up to the minute she could smell the new-car aroma.

He took her backpack, heavy with books, from her arms but Zara stood her ground. "I can't go with you, Alex."

Half-turned toward the vehicle, he paused. His eyes narrowed a fraction. "You said you would see me tonight."

After he'd lifted her onto the cool, wet vanity in the hotel bathroom. After he'd discovered, with devastating effect, that she hadn't found her panties.

That knowledge, that memory burned dark in his narrowed eyes and sparked all kinds of embers in Zara. "You didn't play fair," she said.

"All's fair, sweetheart." As if to prove that point, he hooked a hand around her neck and drew her into his kiss. Brief, bone-melting, breathtaking. Then he opened the back door and slung her bag inside.

"I have my bike."

"Tim took it home."

"Come again?" she said, stiffening. Incipient outrage chased away the shimmery warmth of his kiss. "Are you saying you *arranged* for my bike to be gone?"

He didn't deny it. In fact—smart man—he didn't say anything. He studied her quietly and then he touched a hand to her hair, threading a loose strand back behind her ear. "I'm sorry.

"Tim said whenever you needed to borrow his car he would take your bike." His thumb caressed the curve of her ear, and he shifted his weight, moving close enough that his breath warmed her forehead. "I wouldn't have made arrangements if I'd thought you would mind."

He sounded sincerely apologetic. Between his scent and his touch and the deep, earnest quality to his voice, Zara felt her irritation give and bow. She leaned into his touch and, maybe it was her imagination, but she swore she felt satisfaction in the smile he pressed to her forehead.

Damn him, he'd gotten his own way again. She was seeing a pattern here.

Eyes narrowed, she climbed into the car, pulled on her seat belt and waited. Once he'd joined her and angled the big vehicle onto the road, she turned to study him. "You're very used to arranging things to suit yourself, aren't you?"

One brow raised, he cut her a slow look. "You make that sound like a bad thing. What I'm doing is making things easier all around."

"For you."

"And for you."

That was what disturbed her about a relationship with Alex Carlisle. He tempted her to let him take charge. He weakened her resolve with a look, with a kiss, with a smile. He changed her mind as swiftly as a heartbeat, and made her lose control of her logic and her senses.

Last night she'd gone to dinner firmly resolved not to sleep with him. Then she'd convinced herself she deserved one night in his bed, one night of taking the pleasure and letting it fill the ache of loneliness that had felt more acute in the week since they'd met.

And then, in the bathroom this morning, he'd had his way again. She'd let him change her mind. She'd let him talk her into another night.

That weakness of willpower was all kinds of wrong.

Lost in her unsettling thoughts, she only realized he'd taken a left out of the car park a couple of blocks after the event. "Aren't we going back to your hotel?"

"No." His sideways glance was narrow, assessing. "We're going out of town."

That made her sit up straight, riled again by his high-handedness. "What if I have work tomorrow?"

"Do you?"

"I have to study."

"You have your books with you." He tipped his head to indicate her backpack. "Do you need others?"

"I…" Frowning, she let her breath go with a hiss of exasperation.

"Remember this morning when I asked you to spend the night with me?"

How could she not remember? Stunned after another shattering orgasm, from the tenderness in his face as he carried her into the shower, by the deep gravity of his voice when he asked.

"I remember," she said, her voice laced with those memories.

"You said you weren't that comfortable with five-star hotel suites. I decided we should spend tonight somewhere you would be comfortable." He kept his focus on the road and the city traffic as he switched lanes. "Do you want to go home to change? To get some more things?"

"Where are you taking me?"

A suppressed smile twitched at his mouth. "That's a surprise."

"You can't just pick me up and cart me off to God-knows-where," she said, trying for offended but sounding more intrigued than anything. Her heartbeat thickened. Where did he think she would be comfortable? How well did he think he knew her?

"I'm not abducting you."

"No?"

"Although I did think about it." His tone was conversational. The look he cast her wasn't. "Blindfolding you, taking a few wrong turns to throw your sense of direction off."

"No handcuffs? No tying me up?"

"We can still manage that…if you ask nicely."

Whew. His voice turned silky and the picture he painted

rippled through her, dark with erotic promise. Zara's nipples tightened sharply, and when she shifted in her seat, trying to ease the restless prowl of arousal, her camisole rasped against those hard points. She rolled her shoulders forward to ease the pressure. Saw him looking. Knew he knew he'd turned her on.

"No need to look so smug."

He laughed, a soft, dark sound that wasn't smug at all. "Don't worry, sweetheart. I turned myself on, too."

Okay, so that comment was just begging for her attention. Giving up on hiding her own reaction, she turned in her seat. Enough for her gaze to slide over him, touching the freshly shaven contours of his face and neck. The smoky-blue polo shirt, designer issue, natch. The hand he dropped from the wheel to rest lightly on his thigh, blocking her view of his lap.

Except then she got completely caught up in the slight tension in that hand, in the smattering of dark hair and the curve of muscle in his forearm. In the spread of his thighs against the car seat and the memory of them naked, thick and achingly male as they slid between hers, urging them apart, opening her to his first powerful thrust.

Omigod. She had to stop thinking about sex. She had to stop herself before she demanded he pull over, before she gave in to the wanton urge to reach out and touch the hard line she imagined inside those soft denim pants.

Before she caused a damn traffic accident.

Staring sightlessly through the windscreen, she breathed deeply until she'd centered herself. Her fingers, she noticed now, were curled tightly into the heels of her hands. Lucky she didn't have nails worth a razoo or she might have done herself an injury!

An awkwardness stretched in the silence, or maybe just

through her still-jangling hormones, and she felt she had to say something. The first thing that came to mind was naturally, situated below his waist. "You're wearing jeans."

"Is this a problem?"

"No...just unexpected."

"I grew up wearing jeans."

In the outback. She kept forgetting that, blinded by the man in the suit or the exclusive designer casuals of last night. Even naked—and that's how she'd been picturing him a lot today—his first-class body was framed in sheets so soft, so fine, so exquisite, she'd been afraid they would melt under the heat of their joined bodies.

She'd forgotten last weekend and all the layers uncovered at the cabin.

Clarity snapped in her brain. That was it. How slow could she be in putting the clues together? His jeans. The four-wheel drive. A place he knew she enjoyed.

She whipped around, leaning into the center console. "You're taking me back to the cabin, aren't you?"

"Is that okay?" Their gazes met for a brief moment before his returned to the road. "You said it was your favorite place."

Wow. Yes. She probably had. But what stole her breath, tightening her chest and creeping beneath her defenses, was that he'd remembered. That he could have taken her anywhere—could have put her on his private jet and flown her anywhere in the world, most likely—but he'd chosen the simple. Her perfect place. That disturbed and delighted her in equal measures.

"I'm gobsmacked."

"Is that good?" he asked, and she might have imagined the hesitancy. The hint of uncertainty in his smoky gaze before it switched back to the front. "I thought you'd appreciate the quiet to study."

"What about you?"

"I can fish."

She probably gaped at him like an aquarium guppy. Luckily he was watching the road and didn't see. Quite simply, she couldn't picture him doing anything so restful. Despite the hidden layers. She remembered his pacing, prowling, unable to sit still for more than a few minutes that night at the cabin. "You fish?"

"Not in a long while," he admitted.

"I bet you haven't had a weekend off in a long while."

When he didn't answer, Zara knew she was right.

"Did you bring work with you?" she teased, turning to peer into the back. Her attention snagged, not on a computer case or a briefcase, but on several boxes of camping supplies. Bedding. What looked like a stereo.

"Wow. You've come prepared."

"Impressed?"

No, she refused to be impressed by what he'd probably asked the hotel concierge to organize. "Are you trying to impress me?"

"Isn't that what first dates are all about?"

Is that what this was? A first date? Zara narrowed her eyes at him. "What was last night, then?"

He smiled, and the sideways look he cast smoked with meaning. Yet, somehow, despite that look of pure sex, he managed to keep his voice completely even, completely innocent, when he said, "That was just a meal. Remember?"

"In which case, I'm really looking forward to what you can do with a real date."

His laughter, rich with amusement, hot with promise, rolled over her and for a long minute she let herself tumble with it. Completely turned on. Completely unrepentant about wanting him and wanting to spend the rest of this weekend with him.

Later she could regret it. Later when, again, she would have to find the words to say goodbye.

Something in his expression shifted, stilling the laughter and thickening its warm resonance in her body. "What?" she asked, needing to know what that look was about.

"I was just thinking how beautiful you are."

And, yes, when he looked at her like that, she could almost believe him. Yet, instinct cautioned her to shake her head dismissively. He caught the gesture and didn't let it go.

"You have a beauty spot on your cheek." His gaze touched her there. "Another on your neck." And shifted to that spot, exposed by her open-necked shirt and her hair pulled back in a ponytail. "And then there's the third…"

On her breast. She felt his gaze lower, the stroke of heat, the sweet yearning for his hand, his mouth. The magic way he had with his tongue.

"Three proves it."

She shook her head, to clear the sexual heat. To counter with her own show of three. "My nose is too big. My face is too long. My teeth are too big."

"You have big teeth? Show me?" She bared them in a fake snarl and he laughed. "Sweetheart, you can bite me anytime."

"We can manage that…if you ask nicely."

Their eyes met again, a glancing slide of promise and anticipation that made Zara wish for the hotel suite. Any hotel suite. And then to decide that, no, she liked this teasing foreplay. The verbal sparring. The knowledge that she'd found a man—*a lover!*—with a clever mind and a clear focus.

A man she couldn't intimidate.

A man who'd vowed to protect her. Always.

"You need the left lane here," she said quickly, pointing out the sign off the freeway, and for several minutes he concentrated on crossing traffic and finding the road that wound into the Dandenongs. Young gums, as tall and straight and slender as supermodels, edged the road and Zara relaxed a little, imagining their calming eucalyptus scent in her nostrils.

Oh, yes, he had chosen well. She would enjoy tonight and tomorrow. She closed her eyes and—

"Tell me about your sister."

Damn. A dormant memory awakened suddenly to grab her by the throat. Last night, in bed, she'd murmured something about her sister and then she'd distracted him and distracted herself.

How could she have forgotten that slip? How could she have imagined that he-of-the-clever-mind would forget?

"She's my half sister, actually," she said. "Four months older than me, although she swears I act like the big sister."

"His legitimate daughter?"

"Yes." And without mentioning names, she told him how she'd met Susannah and how they'd become friends. How Susannah acknowledged their blood relationship when none of her family wanted to know, and how she'd promised to keep that relationship secret for the sake of her mother. "She's quite fierce about protecting her mother."

"I think I'd like your sister," he said, and Zara's heart thumped hard in her chest.

"I'm sure you would."

Hard as she tried, that statement did not come out level and free of irony. Breath held, Zara waited for him to comment, to stop looking at her in that puzzling way. In the end she couldn't stand the weight of the tension. "Why are you looking at me like that?"

"Trying to imagine how she could be more beautiful."

"Look, I'm not being precious about this beauty thing. I know I stand out in a crowd, but that comes with being an Amazon. People can't help but notice me." Frowning, she struggled to explain without even knowing why she needed to explain, why she couldn't just accept that this man found her beautiful and run with the lovely feelings that invoked. "I matured early. I can't remember a time when I wasn't the tallest in my class, but I wasn't always this lean, this fit."

"You worked hard at that?"

"I drove myself," she admitted, "after Mum got sick. I started running as a way of getting out in the open air for a while. Then I started to run to escape. Then I ran until it hurt."

"And when that didn't hurt enough, you took up kick-boxing."

She smiled tightly, acknowledging his astuteness. "I shouldn't have. It wasn't for the right reason."

"An aggressive release because your mother was hurting? Because you were hurting? What's wrong with those reasons? Better than having a breakdown from holding it all inside."

He would know, she realized, thinking about his mother. How she'd broken down from grief and the pressure of media hounding. They lapsed into silence for several minutes, several miles, and despite the aching sadness she always felt when remembering her mother's pain, Zara also felt a measure of comfort in knowing she could share this part of her life, so long held closely guarded, with another person.

How easy it was to share with him; how unexpected he was.

"She shouldn't have suffered so cruelly," she said softly,

the ache of remembered sadness thick in her voice. "No matter how hard I ran or how hard I punched and kicked, that never got any easier to take."

Zara woke with a start, surprised she'd relaxed enough to nod off in the passenger seat. Sitting up straight, she stretched the kink in her neck and the arm scrunched against the door handle and looked around.

They'd stopped. Her heart skipped a beat as she noticed where they had stopped. Her gaze zeroed in on the familiar outpost store and the couple she could see through the large front window. Alex, of course, looking tall and broad and heart-kickingly gorgeous in those jeans. He leaned against the counter watching Carmel, her mouth in nonstop motion, stack supplies into a large box.

A strong strand of emotion wound through Zara's chest. Instead of buying their food from an upmarket city deli, he'd taken a detour to give his business to someone who needed it more. To someone who'd done them a good turn.

In assuming he'd palmed off the details of this trip to a hotel concierge, she'd done Alex another disservice. He was so much more than she'd anticipated and for the first time this acknowledgment didn't ring cautionary alarms or cause stomach flips of anxiety.

For the first time she accepted that he could be more than her weekend lover. More than the man who'd awoken her dormant sensuality. This was a man she liked. A man to share her cares and concerns, her laughter and her tears.

She pressed a hand to her mouth, to still her burgeoning smile, but she couldn't suppress the knowledge that unfurled like a flower's petals in the morning sun.

This was a man she could love.

* * *

Unlike a week earlier, the evening was mild—warm enough inside the cabin that they could have done without a fire. Alex built one anyway. "So I can undress you in the firelight," he told her, and anticipation flared through Zara like a match to tinder.

He'd brought candles, too, and linen and crockery and fine crystal glasses.

"Your smooth side?" she asked, watching him pour wine. Watching the dance of candlelight and shadows over the raw angles of his face and thinking she would never describe him as smooth. He was too intense, too strong-minded, too male.

Naturally, he made a mockery of her judgment by producing the battery-operated stereo with all the flourish of a conjurer unveiling his best trick. He'd said a first date was all about making an impression. This, she knew, would be an impression that lasted a long, long time.

"You told me you liked to relax to music." The voice of a silver-tongued crooner drifted through the cabin as he held out her chair, inviting her to sit. "I wasn't sure what style."

"Bublé is a pretty nice choice. Very smooth. And considerably more romantic than knitting." She met his eyes across the table, letting him know she remembered that conversation. And that she appreciated him remembering.

"What has Carmel cooked up for us?"

A trout pâté, chicken, salad side dishes and freshly baked bread. Simple stuff, all beautifully prepared, all delicious. But how could she find room for food, when her appetite was all for the man sitting opposite her? The man who hadn't touched her since they'd left Melbourne. The man who watched her over the rim of his wineglass, his eyes lambent with the same desire that prowled through her blood.

The same restless energy that crackled in the air.

"Dessert?" he asked.

Zara shook her head.

"It's chocolate mousse."

"I know."

His nostrils flared. His eyes blazed with speculation as they drifted over her. "Take off your shirt."

Zara didn't bother with buttons. She simply lifted from the hem and peeled the shirt off. Underneath she wore a camisole, but it wouldn't have mattered if she'd worn nothing at all. She would still have stripped the shirt off.

"Only the shirt?" she asked.

"For starters." His voice was thick, low, aroused. She watched him sip from his wine and swallow. Felt the swell of response in her body, the tightness in her nipples, the ache of emptiness between her legs.

"Come over here."

She went without hesitation, her pulse a loud drumming of want in her ears. The blaze of heat in his eyes all the confidence she needed. Eyes locked on his, she took the glass from his hand and placed it on the table.

Then she straddled his lap and kissed him with all the pent-up hunger of a day without. He tasted of wine, rich and intoxicating. He turned her dizzy on the first sip, freed her ponytail on the second, stroked the length of her hair over her shoulders and breasts on the third.

Man, but he was some kisser.

"This is unexpected," he said when they came up for air. *This* was the silk camisole, one of the few pieces of sexy frippery she owned. He fingered the thin strap, the edge of lace across her breasts.

"Take it off," she whispered and he did.

But he didn't toss it aside. Instead he held it bunched in

his hand a second while his gaze glinted with wicked intent. Then he feathered it over her skin, tracing the slope of each breast, teasing her nipples into aching points.

Eyes closed, she arched her back into that gossamer touch. "I didn't take you for a tease."

He dragged the silky fabric over her again. "Doesn't that feel good?"

"Not as good as your hand." She stretched up straight and met his eyes. "Or your mouth."

His response, rough and hungry, growled in his throat.

Zara would have smiled with satisfaction but then his hand stretched wide on her back, pulling her to the strong, wet suction of his mouth, to all the magic he could do with her body, there in a straight-backed chair and on a linen-spread table amid the remains of their meal.

They didn't ever get to the mousse because he said he preferred the taste of her and he showed her how much, satisfying her cravings again and again, and it struck her in one dark molten aftermath that with Alex Carlisle in her life she might never need chocolate again.

They made love by the fireside, and in the midnight dark when she woke surrounded by his heat, and Zara wondered how many times she could come apart, how many times he could shatter her into tiny shards and then put her back together with the stroke of his hands and the blaze of those storm-blue eyes.

At some point she remembered asking him about almonds and he licked her throat and said, "That's what you taste of, sweetheart. Amber and honey and almonds," and she slept, too exhausted to tell him that was her perfume, a gift from her sister, as was the silk camisole.

A gift from Susannah, she thought as she drifted into sleep. Just like you.

Ten

She didn't study much, unless she counted studying Alex's very fine anatomy as they lazed in bed together Sunday morning. Alex didn't fish much, either, although they did take all the gear and trek down to Bad Barry Creek, mostly because he wanted to see her execute the specialist cast she'd bragged about over breakfast.

Relaxed and cocky, she almost slipped up telling him how she'd learned the skill.

"Pappy said it's all about feel and timing," she said as she commenced her forward cast, and he looked at her funny.

"I thought you said Susannah taught you."

Damn. She'd been quoting Susannah, but somehow in her memory she "heard" the instructions in the voice of her unknown grandfather. Ridiculous, but there it was. "Susannah's grandfather taught her," she covered smoothly. "I got used to her saying, 'Pappy said this, Pappy said that.'"

Which was the truth, after all.

She continued her demonstration but refining Alex's technique was another matter. She pointed out that his grip on the rod was too firm to make a smooth cast. He suggested she demonstrate on his rod—seeing as she'd mentioned the importance of choosing the right rod—and, well, things just deteriorated from there.

Later, they stretched out on the soft spring grass beside the stream, and Zara couldn't remember the last time she'd felt this relaxed, this carefree, this happy. She astounded herself by saying the words out loud.

"You want to stay relaxed and happy a bit longer?" Alex asked.

Nestled in the crook of his arm, Zara had to twist around to see his face. She could feel her heart fluttering just from looking into his sleepy eyes. Just from imagining what he might mean. "A bit?"

"Yeah." He grinned and tickled her bare belly with a blade of grass. "We could stay another night."

"What about work tomorrow?"

"We could play hooky."

She laughed softly and shook her head. "I can't imagine you playing hooky."

"You couldn't imagine me wearing jeans."

Point taken. Her gaze drifted down his body, relaxed, sated, not wearing jeans anymore. As always, her pulse picked up just by looking. "When did you last take a weekday off?" she asked.

"My father's funeral."

"For pleasure." But she pressed a kiss to his chest, not for pleasure but for comfort. Her unspoken message to say *I'm sorry you had to take a day off for that purpose.*

"I guess that would have been last November. Melbourne Cup day."

Zara snorted. "Half Australia takes Melbourne Cup day off. That does not count!"

"Have you ever been to the Cup?" he asked, conveniently changing the subject.

"No."

"I'll take you this year."

In five weeks' time? Her stomach tightened with longing but she didn't know how to respond, whether he was teasing, whether he was serious. His expression gave nothing away.

Wrinkling her nose, she chose the safe option. Light, teasing, dismissive. "I don't have a hat."

"So?"

"So, ladies have to wear a hat to the Cup. It's a rule!"

His brows dipped a fraction and she thought he was about to take issue with that rule. Then he reached over his head and retrieved the trucker's cap she'd been wearing earlier. Before he'd hauled it—and all her clothes—off her.

"There you go." He pulled it on her head, back to front. "A hat."

Amused by the mental image of an almost six-foot-tall woman strolling through the toffy Flemington members' enclosure wearing a pretty floral spring dress and a trucker's cap—especially on the arm of Alex Carlisle in one of his stylish Italian suits—she laughed long and hard. But then she caught a flash of emotion in his eyes, something that grabbed at her chest and squeezed all the air from her lungs and the laughter from her lips.

And there, lying beside an isolated mountain stream, naked but for a backward trucker's cap, she knew she'd gone and fallen in love.

Damn.

* * *

In the end, they didn't play hooky because Zara had a full day of lectures on Monday. *That's what really matters,* she reminded herself. *Your degree. The honors-year program. All-important exams in a month's time.* But when they arrived back in Melbourne Sunday evening and he asked, "Where to?" she couldn't bring herself to say *home.*

She spent another night in his hotel room, in his bed, and by the time she kissed him goodbye in the morning she'd convinced herself she could handle this affair. Driving back to the city, he'd repeated all the right things about not wanting promises or commitment. He wasn't going to be demanding. He lived in Sydney. He had the means to come and see her some weekends.

Others he would be too busy with work or travel.

Carlisle's international dealings took him away often, sometimes for a day or two, sometimes a week or more. Later this week he was flying to London to meet with U.K. executives, so she wouldn't see him for at least two weeks and that was okay. She would not let this euphoria of infatuation overwhelm her.

Surely, one day soon, she wouldn't grin like a loony every night when he called. Every time she heard "hello, Zara" in a voice as deep and dark as the late-night hour, she would not turn weak with longing.

She would not tell him she missed him. Absolutely not.

Over the next few days, she managed to keep her feet on the ground during the busy daylight hours. Whenever she found herself daydreaming about, say, spending the summer break in his Sydney harborside home or visiting his family's outback station, she gave herself a good mental shaking.

No promises, no commitment, remember?

She forced herself to remember that first weekend at the

cabin and their conversation about why he'd asked Susannah to marry him. He wanted a family; he was at that stage of his life.

Zara, most definitely, was not.

And thinking about that first weekend, about how they'd met, about Susannah, never failed to produce a twinge of guilt.

For a start, there was the whole sister-secret thing crouched like a dark phantom in the shadows, waiting to catch her out. She wanted to tell him—she *would* tell him—once she had Susannah's permission. Once she heard from Susannah who, apparently, was still in America.

During one of their long, late-night phone conversations, she asked Alex if he'd heard from her again. He hadn't.

"If she calls again, please get her number or ask her to ring me," Zara said. "I need to talk to her."

"Okay, but I doubt she'll call me."

"Why ever not?" And some inner demon reminded her that this was the woman he'd chosen as his wife. "What if she changes her mind about marrying you again?"

"She won't."

The certainty in his voice stilled her for a second. "Because of this other man? Does she love him?"

"I don't know. She said she'd never forgotten him; that she couldn't stop thinking about him. I said I understood."

Zara's heart started to thump so hard she barely heard the question she asked. "Do you?"

"Yes. That's exactly how I felt. About you."

Infatuation, not love, Zara cautioned herself afterward, but her heart didn't want to hear. It took off soaring and didn't touch down until later that week when a weekly gossip magazine hit the newsstands.

When she became front-page news as Alex Carlisle's "Mystery Melbourne Blonde."

* * *

She didn't even know until Tim brought the magazine home and tossed it on the kitchen table. "I talked to this dude on the phone, Zee. Twice." He picked up the magazine and studied it again, shaking his head accusingly. "You didn't say you were sleeping with a freakin' prince!"

He didn't notice Zara's face pale as she stared at the front page.

She hadn't seen a photographer. The series of pictures were obviously taken outside the Carlisle Grande last Friday night, after he'd taken her to dinner. Their clothes gave that away. So did their absorption in each other. The moment before the kiss. The kiss. Walking hand in hand into the hotel.

No need for any caption to say what was going on, she thought bitterly. It was all there on the front page.

How could she have been so stupid, so shortsighted, so oblivious? They'd talked about the media interest in his life, for Pete's sake. Why hadn't she paid attention? Why hadn't she realized?

A sick feeling clutched at her throat as she grabbed the magazine from Tim's hands and scanned the copy with swift eyes. *Mystery blonde...unknown beauty...latest lover.* No mention of her name, thank God.

She could feel the sheen of cold sweat on her skin as she slumped into a chair, weak and dizzy with relief.

"You all right, Zee?" Tim shifted uncomfortably, finally clued in to her distress. "You look like you've seen a ghost."

"Shock." She shook her head. Put down the magazine. Sucked in a deep breath. "I didn't know anything about this."

"You didn't know he was this 'Prince of the Outback' dude?"

"I knew that. I didn't think anything like this—" she waved a hand at the offending article "—might happen!"

"It's not that bad, is it? He's not married or anything."

Zara shook her head.

"And it's not like they're poxy photos. He caught your good side. Hey, you're even wearing a dress."

"Well, thank you, I think."

One of the things Zara liked about Tim was his sense of humor, and within five minutes he had her laughing at his Zara-as-Princess tomfoolery. By the time she traipsed upstairs to hit the books, she'd convinced herself that she'd overreacted.

She was only the mystery blonde. A five-minute fancy that wouldn't create any lasting interest because she wasn't a celebrity. They didn't know her background. They didn't know about her mother, right, so why should she worry?

Because one day they might find out, an inner voice whispered, *and then what?*

Alex didn't call that night and in a way she was glad. She needed perspective on the magazine piece, time to work out her true feelings, although none of that stopped her from sitting up past midnight in case the phone rang. Hours later she woke with a start, jackknifing upright in her study chair and spilling the remnants of her midnight milk all over her cytology notes.

Dumbly she stared at the mess, her heart racing from coming awake too quickly. From the horror of her dream. She grabbed a sweatshirt to sop up the milky puddle. In the bathroom she rinsed it clean and splashed water on her face, then rubbed at her eyes.

Nothing obliterated the nightmare front page stamped in her brain.

Mystery Blonde Exposed the headline screamed. The picture underneath was a sleazy pole dancer with her mother's face. The copy exposed Zara as the daughter of Ginger Love, former stripper and infamous mistress of transport tycoon Edward Horton. Illegitimate, unacknowledged, half sister of Alex Carlisle's former fiancée, Susannah Horton.

Weren't dreams supposed to be less overt? More open to interpretation?

Zara's sat cold and heavy in her mind and her stomach. A journalist would not have to dig too hard to come up with that front page. She'd never hidden her identity; she'd never felt any need to. She was simply a mature-age medical student, intent on making something of her life.

Linked with Alex Carlisle, she was all kinds of scandalous headlines, things he would not see coming.

Bracing herself on her forearms, she stared at her reflection in the bathroom mirror. Saw the churning ache of what she must do to reclaim her independence, her anonymity, her own identity.

She had to say goodbye.

Alex resisted the urge to push hard through his London meetings so he could fly home a day earlier. What difference would that make? He'd still be two days away from the weekend. Better he remain a full day's flying away from temptation, from this restless urge to see her sooner, to consign his take-it-slow declaration to hell.

Except, he had vowed to play it cool. To Zara and to himself.

He didn't want her ambushing his thoughts, night and day. He didn't like the ache of anticipation, waiting for the hours he knew he could call her at home. And he loathed the savage plummet of disappointment when all he got to hear was her short, perfunctory voice-mail message.

Zara here. Leave a message.

In the end he did leave a message. His contact number, instructions to reverse the charges, a couple of suitable times. And, because he couldn't help himself, a simple, sincere message.

"Call me, Zara. I miss talking to you."

But she didn't call him back and he hated the ensuing frustration more than everything else put together. He hated not knowing if she'd received his message. He hated the biting, gut-deep worry that something might be wrong. And he hated the sense that he no longer controlled their relationship, that he might no longer control himself.

On Wednesday morning he arrived back in Sydney and headed straight to his office. And there, on his desk, on top of a stack of personal correspondence his PA had left for his perusal, he found her note. An innocent sheet of white notepaper, six neatly handwritten lines that turned his simmering frustration cold.

Alex read it again, searching for hidden meaning, feeling the cold turn to ice and the stab of each shard, word by word. Her message was clear: She'd reconsidered; she couldn't do a relationship; she was sorry.

Yes, she'd dressed it up in pretty words, words he'd heard before about not being the right woman for him, about not being able to handle the media attention he attracted, about how great that weekend had been but she believed they were better off to end it now.

Alex crumpled the note in his fisted hand and aimed it at the bin. He wasted half an hour pretending he could concentrate on work, pretending to listen to his PA's update, pretending he could deal with being cast aside as if that last weekend hadn't meant a thing.

As if she hadn't looked into his eyes and told him she'd

never been this happy, this satisfied, this contented. As if she hadn't told him on the phone, forty-eight hours later, her voice low and raspy with emotion, that she missed him already and wished he were there in her bed.

In her body.

He stood up abruptly, slapping the report file shut in the same single motion. "I'm going to Melbourne."

"Now?" To her credit Kerri's voice only rose slightly, although her eyes were wide with astonishment. Alex felt a sharp satisfaction. He wanted to shake things up. He needed to take control again. "When will you be back?"

"I have no idea," he said with grim determination. "But I sincerely hope it's not too soon."

Eleven

If Alex had stopped and thought this through, he'd have realized that finding Zara on a Wednesday might not be easy. If he'd employed a cool, calm, logical approach, he might have saved himself half a day of chasing his tail around Melbourne.

Not that he was chasing after Zara, exactly. His pride would not admit to that. He was chasing answers and some face-to-face honesty.

Except she wasn't at home. She wasn't answering her phone. She didn't have a client appointment until mid-afternoon. And finding her on campus proved an exercise in frustrating futility. As did sitting outside her empty Brunswick terrace on the off chance she arrived home.

By mid-afternoon when her personal training job was underway, Alex's temper crackled with impatience. It itched to surge through the door of the hotel gym, to interrupt her session five minutes in, to demand her time and her attention and her explanation.

Only the heat of that impulsive urge held him back. He'd spent too many years learning to control himself, to countermand that heat with cool control, not to recognize the danger signs. So he waited out the whole hour, waited until her client, red-faced from exertion, came out the door and headed for the elevators.

Then he slowly got to his feet and walked into the small gym.

She was alone. That's all he noticed in the first twenty seconds. That and the wide flare of her eyes when she turned and saw him standing just inside the doorway. Her mouth formed a silent word of surprise—possibly his name—and then she drew herself taller and attempted a smile.

"I didn't know you were back," she said around that fake smile, "let alone in town."

"Why would you? You didn't return my call."

"Your…call?"

Her breath caught in the middle of her question as he started toward her. Six slow, deliberate steps that brought him close enough to see the guarded expression in her eyes. To see the beat of elevated pulse in her throat. "Didn't you get my message? From London?"

"Yes, but with the time difference…"

"You couldn't find five minutes that might have worked for both of us?" Alex forced himself to speak evenly, coolly, conversationally. "So you decided a note would be enough. Is that a trick you learned from Susannah?"

Her gaze snapped back to his. Shock radiated from their depths. "No. I'm sorry, Alex. I did try to call and then—"

"Forget it," he cut in, hating that he'd exposed himself to her sympathy with the reminder of Susannah's note.

"The thing about notes," he continued even more dispassionately, "is what's left out. What's open to interpretation."

"You didn't think my note was clear enough?"

"Oh, your message was clear enough. It was nice while it lasted. Goodbye."

She pressed her lips together and looked away, and Alex set his jaw against the simmer of his temper.

"Did you consider who might read that note? Did you think that my PA might open all my mail?"

That brought her gaze whipping back to his. "Your PA read my note? When I marked the envelope as personal?"

The sharp rise of her voice, the irritation in her eyes, snarled mean knots in his mood and all he could think was *Good.* He wanted her mad. He wanted an argument.

"Yes, she read it," he said tightly. "Yes, she knows I'm the best sex you ever had."

Color flared along her cheekbones. "I did not say that!"

"You inferred it." And it gave him no satisfaction at all, he discovered as she turned away to pick up her gym bag from the floor. None at all. "Don't worry. I pay Kerri enough money. She's not about to tell the world."

Bag in hand, she straightened. "The world already knows."

Alex stiffened, his attention snared by her comment and the odd note of resignation in her voice. By the sudden bolt of understanding that tightened the muscles in his shoulders and back and jaw. "Was there something in the papers while I've been away?"

She nodded. "Last week. Front page of *Goss.*"

Damn. "Photos?"

"Outside the hotel. And going into the hotel." Her mouth twisted into a smile that didn't take. "I was your mystery blonde for two days and then a couple of the weekend papers ran my name in their society gossip column."

"And this is when you decided we were over?" he asked slowly. His heart beat harder, lacing his blood with a new optimism. *This* was an answer. *This* he could understand. "Because of a magazine that isn't worth the paper it's printed on?"

"I don't want someone taking my photo when I know nothing about it. I don't want to be on any front pages. I don't care which magazine or which paper." There was a fierceness in her voice he'd heard before, over breakfast at Carmel's café when she'd told him about her mother's exposure to the media.

When he'd sensed a strong connection because they'd understood each other.

"Not even a medical journal?" he asked, letting her know he remembered that conversation.

"I'm talking about being on the front page for no reason other than being your lover."

Hurt and regret and something else shimmered in her eyes and Alex couldn't stop himself from reaching for her, to hold her, to reassure her. But she hugged her gym bag to her chest like a barricade. A clear sign that she didn't want him any closer.

"If it was only me on the magazine cover I wouldn't care quite so much," she continued. "But last week it was an anonymous blonde and then it was Zara Lovett and next time it will be Stripper's Daughter and they'll find photos of Mum and run them next to yours."

"And you think…what? That I'll be shocked to find out your mother was a stripper?"

She frowned. Hugged her bag even closer. "You knew?"

"No, and I don't care." He started to reach for her again, but she flinched before he got within six inches. "I don't care what the papers say, Zara. I told you that."

"You told me you care when it hurts other people."

This time he didn't let her pull away. He took her by the shoulders and held her still and forced her to meet his eyes. "What did the magazine say, Zara? How did it hurt you?"

"Not me, my mother. I don't want her name and her memory dragged through the muck."

"You would rather walk away? From this? From us?"

"I would rather walk away now," she said softly, but her gaze was strong and sincere. "Before we get any more involved. Before they start digging for dirt."

"I don't care—"

"You *do* care, Alex, and that's the thing. This isn't only about me or you or us, and it's not even just my mum. You said your mother hates the media muckraking. Don't you see?" She let go of the bag, let it drop to the floor beside her with a thick thud, and then her hands were on his, giving them a little shake as if that might jostle his obdurate stance. "They'll drag up Mum's old story from the archives and then they'll jump onto your mother's, too. They'll have a field day rehashing those old scandals, all juicy details, all the lies. The heartache. I couldn't stand that and I know your family couldn't either.

"I'm sorry, but I just…I just can't!"

The husky ache in her voice gripped Alex by the throat, turned his voice sharp and harsh. "So, you're taking the coward's way out and giving up? Would that make your mother proud?"

Her head reeled back as if he'd struck her. "Yes," she said distinctly after a second. "Yes, she would be proud that I'm unselfish. That I'm thinking about the other people this would hurt."

"I'll look after my mother's concerns."

"And what about my father's family? What about his widow? She won't want to see her husband's cheating affair rehashed again and for what? So we can have a good time between the sheets whenever we can find time!"

"Is that how you see our relationship?"

"What else is it, Alex?"

He stared into her face, into the resolute darkness of her eyes, and felt all the frustration of the long day return tenfold. *Damned if he told her all he wanted to; damned if he didn't.*

But he had to keep trying. He wasn't nearly ready to let her go. "It's nothing if you give in to the guttersnipes. If you let them run your life and rule your decisions. We're nothing if you toss what we have aside without giving it a chance."

"I have to. I'm sorry."

"Are you? Or is this a convenient out?"

A spark of heat lit her eyes and for a second he thought he might yet get a chance to argue hot and strong. But with a slow expulsion of breath she banked the fire.

"It doesn't matter why, does it? Just…let me go. I have to shower and change. I've got a study date."

Zara knew she'd made a mistake using the *date* word. She saw his eyes narrow, saw the twitch of a muscle in his jaw just before she ducked down to scoop up her bag.

But she hadn't expected him to follow her into the ladies' locker room.

Intent on keeping her legs moving forward, on not buckling to the urge to turn around, to go back for one last kiss, she hadn't even heard him follow. Not until the door shut behind her with a firm snap. As if propelled by a hand.

She swung around. Her gasp sounded way too loud in the tiny room, as if it bounced off the white tile walls and came back at her from all directions, amplified a hundred times. "What are you—" Her throat was tight, her voice so faint that she licked her lips and tried again. "What are you doing?"

His gaze rolled from her lips to her eyes. His, she noted with a spike in her pulse, were no longer cool. No longer contained. "A study date?"

"In half an hour." Pleased her voice had regained strength, she flung her bag on the bench and folded her arms across her chest. "So I'd appreciate if you left me to get ready."

"This won't take long."

"To walk back out that door? No, that won't take long."

She crossed to the single shower enclosure and turned on the taps as far as they would go. Hot water gushed, a stream of liquid sound, a statement of her intent. *Conversation closed, Alex Carlisle. Now leave.*

But as she returned to her bag, she heard the snick of the lock catching and her gaze jolted back up. "You locked the door? What are you doing?"

"Ensuring we're not disturbed."

Zara was gripped by an insane urge to laugh. The sound of that door locking disturbed her. *He* disturbed her with the way he watched her through the gathering cloud of steam.

Predatory intent, narrow, sharp, purposeful, flitted across his expression and Zara felt a frisson of alarm in her skin. And deeper, in her flesh and the female core of her body, a much stronger bolt of anticipation and heat and all the things she should not be feeling.

Damn him. Why couldn't he make this easy? Why couldn't he accept that she couldn't have a relationship with him?

Because then he wouldn't be the man he is, her inner voice of honesty retorted. *You wouldn't have fallen for him. You wouldn't be locked in this room with him, dreading his next move and craving it in the same breath.*

She had to stay firm. She had to keep him at arm's length. She had to convince him that she meant no.

"Alex, there's nothing else to say. Please, will you just accept that?"

"I wish I could. It would make my life a hell of a lot easier."

"Then try harder," she countered.

But he'd started toward her, his eyes as fiercely insistent as his voice. "I can't, Zara."

Zara had nowhere to go, no escape from the man or from the awareness that engulfed her more hotly, more surely, a thousand times thicker than the steam swirling from the shower.

She didn't know she'd been backing up until she hit the wall, until he stopped right in front of her, his hands flattened on the tiles on either side of her head.

"Don't," she breathed.

"Don't?"

"Don't touch me."

His eyes narrowed. "I'm not."

Technically, he was right. But he stood so close she could feel the heat rolling off his body in stark counterpoint to the cold tiles at her back. When their eyes clashed she felt the jolt of electricity course through her veins. Felt the tingle in her breasts.

Oh, the danger. This much electricity in a wet room spelled doom.

Zara tried to shrink back farther, away from the sparks, away from the temptation. She saw the corners of his mouth tighten and knew she had about a second to regain the ascendancy.

"You're not touching me. Fine. Then what do you want?" she asked on a note of desperation. "What is your point?"

He stared at her a moment and she had the distinct impression he didn't know. That he'd acted on impulse, instinct, perhaps on thwarted pride. Because the way she'd done it—the note and the media exposé reason—punched his hot buttons and because he'd had enough of women leaving him.

"Is it because I wrote you a note?" she asked, against her better judgment. "Is that why you won't accept that I meant every word of it?"

"Perhaps I need to hear it again." His voice as soft as the billowing steam, he leaned infinitesimally closer. So close that each word stroked her skin with the sweet warmth of his breath. "Tell me you don't want me, Zara. Tell me you don't ache for me, that what I'm seeing in your eyes isn't the burn you're feeling in your blood."

"Don't do this, Alex," she whispered. "Don't use sex to try and manipulate me."

He stilled. She felt his tension like a renewed blast of heat. "Is that what you think I'm doing?"

"Yes!" *Damn him.* And a sudden burst of anger came to her aid. Straightening, she met his gaze full on. "You came in here and locked the door. You stalked over here and trapped me against this wall after I asked you to leave. You knew you only had to get close to manipulate this chemistry we have—"

He slapped his hand down on the tile beside her head so hard she recoiled. For a second he just stared into her eyes and what she saw there, the seething, burning heat, shocked her into action. With both hands, she pushed at his chest until he ceded several inches.

"Do you really think that's all this is? Chemistry?"

"Yes," she said with quiet intensity. "And I can't deal with that kind of stuff. It's too much."

"Do you think I like it? Do you think I want to feel like I'm—" He stopped abruptly, eyes blazing in his tightly drawn face. "Hell, Zara. In your note you said it was great. Your best time ever."

Her heart wailed a protest, but she lifted her chin and refused to listen. It didn't matter what she felt because she couldn't have him. He was the pain and the dread of front-page revelations. He was a man used to getting his way, a man not used to compromise. Ridiculous that she'd thought they could work out some basis for a long-distance relationship.

Ridiculous that she'd considered he could be her man, her soul mate, her love.

Abruptly he swung away, slamming a hand through his hair in a gesture of abject frustration. But he turned back just as quickly, fire still blazing in those razor-sharp eyes. "What do I have to do to change your mind, Zara? Do I have to ask you to marry me? Will that make you reconsider how much I want you?"

"Marry you?" she repeated, her eyes wide with disbelief.

And then she started to laugh, an edgy stop-start sound that did nothing to soothe the roar in Alex's ears and in his blood. The temper he so badly needed to control.

He turned away, focused on an irritant he could control. The damn shower still spraying at full blast. Quickly he strode over, reached into the enclosure and shut it down.

"You find that funny?" he asked, turning back around.

As quickly as it had started, her laughter shut down too. "That wasn't amusement. That was astonishment."

Which she hardly needed to state. Alex saw it in her eyes, in the soft set of her mouth. Stunned, yes, but also taken aback by his uncharacteristic outburst.

"Nothing will change my mind or anything else about this situation. Including any other temper tantrum you might be thinking of throwing."

Her calm words hit him with the cold dose of realization he needed. He'd almost lost it. Like some spoiled rich kid denied his candy.

You can't always have what you want.

Hell.

He'd almost let passion and frustration override his usual cool counsel and that shamed him and horrified him and scared him in equal measures.

"You're right, of course," he said stiffly. "It seems you bring out the best in me and the worst in me."

"I'm sorry, Alex."

He met her eyes and knew she'd slipped away as surely as the rapidly dissipating steam. Knew there was nothing he could do to keep her. "Not half as much as I am."

Zara didn't have anything else to say because there was nothing left to say. Her expression as rigid as her posture, as tight as the cloying atmosphere in the tiny room, she watched him turn and walk out the door without any word of goodbye. And that was okay. Her emotions did not need any further battering.

And when he was gone, she expelled one long, broken breath and got on with what had to be done.

She showered, she dressed, she got herself to her study session and forced her mind to participate at some remote automated level. She kept it all together until later that night when Tim wandered into her room and flung himself on her bed, as he was wont to do when he needed a break from study.

He took one look at her face and asked who'd died.

A tightness grabbed the back of Zara's throat and, dammit, she felt the raw burn of tears. "PMS," she muttered.

"Ah, The Hormones," Tim intoned with suitable gravity. Then, bless his heart, he fetched her two Tim Tams from his secret stash and the chocolate cured her ridiculous urge to cry.

For the moment.

Over the next few days, she resorted to the chocolate fix frequently and unrepentantly. This breakup—and, okay, she'd only met Alex three weeks ago but their connection had been so intense, it felt like much longer—could not have happened at a worse time.

Her hormones were doing a crazy dance with her emotions. She wasn't sleeping well and the pressure of approaching exams and of watching the papers every day with a sick feeling they may yet pounce on her mother's story or her relationship with the late, esteemed Edward Horton, had delayed her period.

That had happened before. She wasn't worried; she was just…stressed. They'd had sex—a lot of sex—that weekend but they'd always used condoms.

And thinking about that, about the powerful pleasure of making love with Alex, did not help her insomnia.

Hands fisted in her pillow, Zara squeezed her eyes shut tighter against the memories and the tide of longing that rose swift and strong. This was the part she hated most. The doubts that swelled in the dark of night, in the hours when she felt her loneliness most, when her heart asked why she hadn't admitted her feelings when he'd given her the chance.

In the light of day, the answer came all too easily.

Why admit she loved him when they had no future? One day she did want love, commitment, marriage, but with a man she could spend the rest of her life alongside. One she could be honest with about every aspect of her past. One she would have gladly taken home to meet her mother, Ginger Love, stripper and scarlet woman.

She could not see Alex Carlisle in that role.

Besides, the marriage thing had been an expulsion of his frustration. A taunt rather than a proposal. Imagining they could make a marriage work because they had great sex was ludicrous. Her life plan was based around finishing her interrupted degree. That's what mattered to her.

She'd worked her butt off to keep up the distinction average needed for a shot at next year's honors program. She couldn't blow it now. She couldn't allow the distraction of Alex Carlisle to encroach upon her study time.

He was gone, done, over.

During the next week, she trained herself not to jump whenever the phone rang. Forced herself to stop checking the door of the gym every session in case he suddenly appeared. And because this was driving her nuts, she told the Personal Best receptionists not to give out her schedule or whereabouts to anyone—*anyone!*—without her approval.

But he didn't call or try to contact her.

This is good, Zara told herself, as she paid for her purchase and strode out of the campus pharmacy. Her stomach churned with anxiety and she gripped the paper package more tightly. Outside she paused—she had to pause because she suddenly felt a bit dizzy. Light-headed.

"Are you all right?"

"Yes. Thank you," Zara said, recovering. And when she looked around at the woman who'd expressed concern, her eyes widened in recognition.

So did Professor Mark's. "Zara! I haven't seen you in months and now today of all things peculiar!"

"Why is today peculiar?" Zara asked before she could stop herself.

Her favorite professor, her mentor through the tough first semester when she'd resumed study, smiled. "Oh, I've just come from a meeting where we were discussing some of the honors candidates for next year." She pursed her lips. "No guarantees, you understand, with this year's finals still to come. But there is a short list."

Zara's heart lurched and raced, but she didn't whoop and yell. She did smile very broadly. "I understand. Of course."

They talked a little more about how she was managing her course load before going their separate ways. Zara's stride bounced with elation. No guarantees, but she was short-listed.

All she'd aimed for, all she'd strived toward, was within her grasp. All she had to do was keep up her study schedule so she performed in her exams next month.

Smiling like a fiend, she punched the air with her fist…and came back to earth with a dizzying thud. Her fingers tightened on the little bag in her hand and her stomach lurched sickly.

Okay, she told herself, sucking in a deep breath. No need for alarm. This test is just in case. To eliminate the likelihood. To stop the clutches of night panic.

All the way home she dealt with her gathering nerves by refusing to accept the possibility. She could not be pregnant. Fate could not be so cruel.

Half an hour later, she sat on the edge of the bathtub and the bottom fell out of her world.

She stared at the distinct second line on the stick, compared it again with the control band and with the instructions, and accepted the inevitable.

Fate could be that cruel.

She was pregnant.

Twelve

She had to tell Alex, but after the disastrous episode with the note, Zara was leery about how. In her heart she knew this deserved face-to-face—in her heart, she *wanted* to tell him face-to-face—but the logistics defeated her. She couldn't jump on a plane and go to Sydney. Not when she was having trouble jumping out of bed each morning.

And therein lay the biggest logistical problem.

As if triggered by the appearance of that second pink line, morning sickness had struck instantly. She wasn't completely debilitated, just severely limited. And tired. And anxious about how long this would last and how many lectures she would miss and how this might affect her ability to concentrate for her upcoming exams.

Yup, a trip to Sydney was out of the question, which meant she would have to ask Alex to come and see her. That provided her next challenge. A dozen times she'd composed her side of the conversation. Two or three times she got as far as picking up the phone.

But the thought of asking him to come and see her without telling him why, imagining him jumping to several different conclusions and insisting on the full story over the phone, never failed to churn her stomach into a new bout of nausea.

If only she could pick the perfect time to leave a message on his voice mail. That seemed like the perfect, simple solution. She'd started working on the message.

Hello, Alex. This is Zara. I need to see you. It's rather important. When you're next in Melbourne could you give me a call?

At which point, she would see the flaw in her perfect, simple plan.

He would have to call her back to arrange the meeting. He would want to know why, and she didn't want to blurt out, "I'm pregnant," in a tense, overheated telephone conversation.

She wanted…oh, gads, she didn't know what she wanted.

When she wasn't being sick or recovering from being sick or worrying over her life falling apart, she teetered between fear and burgeoning wonder. A baby. Would she be able to manage all the change and the challenges that entailed? Would she make a good mother, the kind a child could laugh with and learn from and love with all their heart?

Oh, she hoped so. She'd had the best example. And then she would think of Alex and his part in her baby's life and worry would pitch her stomach again.

She recalled his strong opinion on two-parent families, their heated debate the night of the storm, his reasons for wanting to marry Susannah.

And she could not bring herself to pick up the phone.

Next week, her newly discovered inner coward whispered. *Next week you might be handling the morning sickness better and next week he might be in Melbourne for the races and you can leave a message saying you'll meet him at his hotel at a specific time.*

A decent plan. Better than decent, really, because she wasn't asking him to fly down here specially. Except then she remembered him joking about taking her to the races in her trucker's cap, which made her remember him undressing her beside the mountain stream and tossing the cap aside.

She remembered how he'd looked at her when he pulled the band from her ponytail and let her hair fall around her face. How he whispered the word *beautiful* over and over when she came apart beneath his body.

And tears clogged her throat because she knew they could never regain the magic of that weekend. Not with the complications of an unplanned pregnancy and all kinds of compromises and decisions to be made.

Then, the day before the Melbourne Cup, her plan backfired.

Tim was studying the form guide, pretending that might help him pick the winner. Since this was the only horse race and only form guide he ever looked at, year to year, Zara sincerely doubted it. She was studying histology and paying no attention to his occasional muttered comment.

Until she heard the magic word.

She swung around, staring over the top of her reading glasses. "Did you say Carlisle?"

"His horse is scratched. Tough break," he added, with no sympathy whatsoever. Although he continued to read out the newspaper piece about Irish Kisses, Zara barely listened.

All she could think was: his horse isn't running; there goes my plan.

"When are you going to tell him?"

Tim's quiet question twined through her thoughts and she sighed heavily. "I thought he'd be in town for the races. I was planning on seeing him tomorrow."

"There's always the phone," he said after a pause. "In case you hadn't thought of that."

"I'm still working on what to say."

Tim snorted. "Call him now, Zee. Don't think about it. Just pick up the phone and do it."

"Tomorrow," she decided, turning back to her books, and her inner coward breathed a sigh of relief at the reprieve. "I'll call him tomorrow."

Alex didn't want to be in Melbourne. It might be a big city, one he loved for its racing and its restaurants and its people, but now his mind only conjured up one of those people. Zara. As soon as his jet landed, he felt a new tension in his muscles and an edginess in his veins.

He wasn't going to see her. She'd made her feelings perfectly clear on his last visit and he sure as hell didn't need to haul his pride through those hot coals again.

That same bruised pride wouldn't allow him to call off his Melbourne Cup trip, either. Despite the disappointment of Irish's injury, he wanted to be at the track on Australia's biggest race day. It was a tradition and he supposed at some level a test.

Go to Melbourne, Alex. Prove to yourself you can spend two nights and a day in the city without tracking her down.

Well, here he was. One night down and this morning he hadn't given in to the temptation of calling Personal Best and booking her for a training session. And, yeah, he was man enough to admit that he had been tempted.

"Masochist," he muttered, shaking his head.

Instead of facing memories he'd as soon forget in a hotel gym, this morning he'd swum. Exercise for his body and to clear his head from a late night at the Cup Eve Ball. He showered, he dressed, and while he had coffee he checked for messages with the hotel and then on the phone he'd not taken with him last night.

When he got to the last of the voice-mail messages, everything inside him stilled.

"Um. This is Tim Williams. In Melbourne. Zara's housemate. I, uh…can you call me…if you get this message tonight?"

The voice paused, then came back with a phone number. Alex didn't bother writing it down. He knew it by heart. And all he could think was that something must be wrong.

Why else would her housemate call?

He started punching in the number. Then stopped and closed his phone. Tim had asked him to call last night. On a Tuesday morning he would probably have already left for classes.

And if he was home?

Alex reached for his suit jacket and started for the door. If he was home, then Alex would soon know why he'd called.

If she started the day slowly, if she ate some dry cereal in bed before moving at all, if she concentrated on relaxation and not on that wasted first hour, Zara's morning sickness was bearable and she could function for the rest of the day. Skip any of those steps and the first wasted hour could stretch to two, three, or right through the rest of the day.

Today she'd woken too early and after too little sleep,

already anxious over the phone call she'd vowed to make and with no bedside snack. Three strikes and with no one to blame but herself. Shivering from however long she'd spent on the cold bathroom floor, she crawled back into bed and closed her eyes.

Half an hour, she thought weakly. I just need thirty minutes to gather the strength to go downstairs and eat. To dress and get to the university.

She must have slept. She didn't remember nodding off but she woke with a foggy head and a dry mouth and a surprisingly steady stomach. When she turned her head and saw the mug and bowl on her bedside table, she managed a feeble smile.

"Tim, you are a sweetie."

Moving slowly to guard her precious equilibrium, she sat up and started the breakfast he'd left. Dry cereal and raisins. Tea gone cold. And suddenly it wasn't her physical or gastric stability at risk, but her emotional calm. Tears thickened her throat until she couldn't swallow and she had to cradle her mug in both hands to stop it shaking.

Damn, damn, damn.

She hated these debilitating, emotional jags that waylaid her at the least provocation. This one because of Tim's thoughtful gesture. And because he'd remembered what she'd forgotten and because her prized self-sufficiency was as shaky as her hands and because she didn't know how much longer this would go on and because she hated feeling incapacitated, weak, reliant.

And because, she realized as the tears brimmed and started to roll down her cheeks, she would likely lose Tim as a housemate and surrogate brother. How could he stay and study with a baby crying through the night? How could she keep this house with its steep stairs and temperamental heating? Where would she be in twelve months and how would she be managing?

Gripping her mug a little tighter, she controlled the fretful tears by thinking about what she needed to do. She had to start making decisions, thinking about her future and all the changes this would bring.

Today she would call Alex. Today it would start.

With renewed resolve, she finished her breakfast. She wouldn't rush to try and make her nine o'clock lecture. She needed to let the food settle. Then she would shower and dress. She could be out the door by—

Above the muted music downstairs she heard the leaden rap of their front-door knocker. Her pulse lurched, for no good reason, and she rolled her eyes at herself.

It isn't him. It can't be him.

Still that didn't halt the prescient quiver that snaked up her spine.

The knocker sounded again and she put down her mug. Carefully, since her hand was shaking again. Perhaps Tim had already left. Often he did that, waltzing out the door without turning off the radio or the lights or his computer.

She started to swing her legs out of bed and then stilled—everything stilled—when she heard the distinctive creak of the front door opening. And voices. Tim's droll drawl and a deeper, stronger pitch that sent her recently subdued emotions into another fever pitch of turmoil.

Alex was here. Downstairs. In her home.

And she was about to lose her breakfast.

Another minute. Alex eyed the door of the front room where Tim had left him waiting, pacing, putting his patience through the wringer. He eyed the door but he pictured the stairs in the narrow hallway beyond, the stairs he'd heard the housemate bound up at least five minutes ago.

Another minute and then he'd…what? Go and find her for himself? Force her to see him, when the message delivered by her nonappearance was as clear as the scowl on his face? As loud as the female rocker screeching on the radio in the room next door?

Alex paced another round of a room not designed for pacing. He'd tried sitting, on the bright red sofa that dominated the tiny room, but he'd sunk so deep that the cushions heaped all over the thing had spilled into his lap. And then he'd heard the sound of running water upstairs and he'd sprung to his feet in an instant.

She hadn't appeared then. She hadn't appeared since.

What the hell was he doing here anyway?

Yes, Tim had called. But when he answered the door this morning, he'd looked sheepish and ill at ease. "Look, man, I might have overstepped, y'know."

"You did call about Zara?"

Tim had scratched at his chin and winced. "Sort of. I didn't expect you'd call in person."

"Is she home?"

"Yeah, but she's still in bed."

"Is she sick?" he'd bit out instantly, remembering the morning at the cabin. Remembering her languid stretch and her guilty grin when she admitted she never slept in. "Is that why you called?"

"She's, um, a bit off color. Look, why don't you come in and I'll see if she's up yet."

Running water and every screaming instinct told Alex she was up, but avoiding him. His pride suggested he take the hint and leave. But then he heard footsteps in the hall outside and he whipped around just as the door opened.

He saw her and didn't see her; felt too much, too swiftly, to take in anything except the fact that she was here, and he still wanted her more than his next breath.

Then she flipped back her hair, loose, no ponytail, and that simple action steadied his first rush of response, focused his gaze on the woman who stood in the doorway looking gaunt and pale and still.

Realization hit him like a tidal wave, knocking the breath from his lungs, sucking the sand from under his feet. Slowly his gaze dipped to her waist and he heard the intake of her breath and saw the flutter of nerves in her hand the second before she pressed it to her flat stomach.

Reflexive, protective, and more revealing than any words.

"When were you going to tell me?" His gaze rolled back to her face. "Or weren't you going to bother?"

Her eyes widened slightly, hurt, shocked. "Of course I was—"

"When?"

"Today. I was going to call you today."

Right. "And that's why your housemate felt he should intercede?"

Her lips tightened visibly. "Tim thought he was doing me a favor."

"Yes. He was."

For a second he just stared at her, battling a barrage of conflicting emotions. At the moment anger was ahead on points and she must have read that on his face and in his body language because she sucked in a breath and lifted her chin a little. "Please, Alex, can we not do this now? I can't—"

"You want me to come back later? You want me to walk away and go about my business after finding out you're pregnant?"

"No," she said in cool, clear contrast to the rising heat in his voice. "I want you to understand that I'm not up for a fight. Sorry, but if that's what you want then you will have to come back another time."

Their eyes met, clashed and he felt a gut-punch of remorse. "You look like hell."

"You noticed?"

And that one wry question wiped away his anger, wiped away everything but a powerful wave of protective concern. "How long have you been sick? Have you seen a doctor? Isn't there something they can give—"

"Slow down. Just…sit down." She waved a hand toward the sofa. "I'll make some tea."

Alex set his jaw. "I don't want tea. I want answers."

"Well, I do want tea, as it happens." She pressed a hand to her stomach again and he was struck again by how thin she was. "And another breakfast."

"You've lost weight."

"I dare say."

How could she be so blasé? This was her health, the baby's health! *His* baby's health! "Dammit, Zara, sit down. I'll make you tea and…what can you eat?"

Too wrung out to object, Zara let him feed her. Sitting at the kitchen table, she gave him directions on what to make, where to find things, and tried to focus on how small and shabby he made her kitchen look, with his elegant navy suit and red silk tie and perfect grooming. Focusing on the superficial and reassuring him about her health—several times—helped keep her trepidation down to a dull roar.

But then, while she ate, he leaned against the counter and watched. He was so quiet, so cool, that for a second she wished back the dark slice of anger he'd displayed earlier. At least that was an emotion she understood.

This Alex was infinitely more dangerous because she didn't know how he'd strike and therefore she couldn't prepare to defend. And if he kept watching her like that, if her stomach kept churning with her rising anxiety, then she wouldn't have to worry about anything except making the bathroom in time.

"How did this happen?"

Zara looked up from spreading a second slice of toast. She didn't know that she wanted to eat a second slice, but she liked having something to do. She liked the cool and solid strength of the knife in her hand, too. Not so much a defense as a prop.

"The pregnancy?" she asked, meeting his eyes. Resisting the smart-mouth answer that sprang to mind. "Well, you were there."

"We used protection. Every time."

Oh, yes. So many times, so many ways. All of them completely mind-blowing.

Zara looked back at her toast, away from the heat of that thought reflected in his darkening eyes. Away from the flare of color along his cheekbones. The look she'd seen so many times when he came to her after donning protection. Or while she'd rolled it on, slowly, carefully, tormenting and teasing.

The knife clattered from her hand, breaking that dangerous thread of thought.

"Condoms don't offer one hundred percent protection." She adopted a practical, professional tone. "For various reasons, but mostly user error."

He didn't say anything for a long moment but she felt his tension, felt it stretching between them like a physical entity. "Did you know the last time I was in Melbourne?"

Zara shook her head. "I would have told you if I'd known. I know how important this is to you."

"You're going to have the baby?"

"Of course I am! What did you think?"

"I don't know. You haven't given me the chance to think."

Oh, but that hurt. The words and the insinuation, the cool tone and the spark of accusation in his eyes. "You know, it came as something of a shock to me, too. I've had a lot to think about and to deal with—"

"Dammit, Zara, I could have shared all that!" He rocked forward off the counter, as if he couldn't maintain that fake-casual stance any longer. "I could have been looking after you, getting you medical care, making sure you were eating properly."

"I hope you're not implying I've been neglectful."

"How can you look after yourself here?" He waved a hand around. "Alone? With your study and your work. You look like—"

"Hell. I know. You have pointed that out."

And somehow they were back at glaring odds, except this time the anger simmered just as strongly in Zara. How dare he imply that her home—bought with her mother's estate, her only asset, and perfectly adequate for her needs—wasn't good enough?

How dare he imply that she couldn't look after herself and her baby?

Instinctively, her hand dropped to her lap. "I have been looking after myself," she said coolly, "since before I turned twenty. For four of those years I also nursed my mother through a debilitating illness. I'm a medical student and I know how to protect my health."

His look suggested otherwise but he didn't say so. He

didn't say anything for a long, tense moment. Then he blew her right away. "I want to marry you, Zara. As soon as we can make arrangements."

Zara sucked in a breath but it wasn't enough to stop the giddy whirl in her brain. "You want to marry me? Because I'm pregnant?"

"Because we're going to have a baby together. Yes."

"I…" Her voice trailed off. She licked her lips and tried again. "I don't see how that would work."

"Why not?"

"Well, because you live in Sydney for a start. Your work is in Sydney and I have my degree to finish."

"You can transfer to Sydney," he countered, cool and logical. "I know people. I can pull some strings—"

"No." Both her hands came down on the table hard enough to rattle her plate. "You absolutely cannot pull strings. I got where I am on my own and I will continue to do so."

"Because you're too independent to accept help?"

"Because I value what comes from effort. Everything I have and everything I am comes from hard work."

His eyes narrowed slightly. "Unlike me?"

She met his eyes and knew, in her heart, she was doing him another injustice. But then she also recalled where this argument had started and how every argument ended with this kind of vehemence. "How can I marry you," she asked, "when every debate ends in this kind of frustration?"

"If we were married, perhaps we wouldn't be frustrated. At the cabin we got along just fine. Remember?"

"How can I forget?" she asked with a twisted smile. She remembered all the getting along just fine. "I also remember the first weekend at the cabin and our discussion about marrying for the right reason. Do you remember that?"

"I remember."

"Then you know that I don't believe two parents are necessarily better than one."

He stiffened so perceptively Zara swore she heard a snap. "Are you saying you want to raise this baby—*our baby*—alone?"

"I'd prefer if he or she—" she paused, overcome for an instant by the concept of this baby as a boy or a girl, as a real, living, breathing baby "—if our baby has two involved parents. But I don't believe they need to be married."

"You'd rather live together?"

"I'd rather we reach some agreement for shared custody—"

"No. That's not the best thing for a child, being tossed between two homes."

Zara lifted her hands, palms up, in a helpless gesture. "See? We can't agree on anything. I told you the last time we talked why I couldn't handle a relationship with you. None of that has changed just because I'm pregnant."

He looked away, and she could see the flick of a tensed muscle at the corner of his jaw for the second before he turned back. "Think about it, Zara. Think about how much easier it would be for everyone if we married. As my wife you won't have to worry about what the papers say about you. Have you thought about that? About what happens if they latch on to the fact that you're pregnant and I'm the father?"

No, she hadn't. Zara's stomach churned. How could she have not realized that?

"Marry me, Zara, and I'll protect you from all that. You'll have the best medical care and afterward we can hire a nanny. You can study, you can work, you can have whatever you want."

And that last phrase lodged in Zara's chest, thick and unshakable. Yes, he could give her opportunities and care and everything money could buy. Yes, his name and his position might protect her on some level, once the tabloids had their initial fun dragging her through the mire.

But sitting there at her little kitchen table listening to his deep voice and his fervent promises only made her realize the one thing he hadn't mentioned. The only thing that mattered and the only thing that could make a marriage work.

He hadn't mentioned love.

"I'm sorry, Alex, but I can't marry you," she said quietly. "I don't believe you can give me what I want."

Thirteen

Alex had thought he couldn't marry a woman who didn't want him. He recalled telling Zara those exact words the weekend he'd met her. Yet in the days after she turned him down—after she turned his world upside down—he discovered that he'd lied.

He wanted to marry Zara Lovett, despite her rejection. He wanted to marry her even after she'd looked him in the eye and coolly told him he couldn't give her what she wanted. He didn't have to ask her to elucidate.

He remembered her exact words when they'd first discussed marriage, that same night at the cabin. She'd told him she would only marry a man she wanted to share her whole life with. Someone she couldn't bear living without.

Obviously he wasn't that man and she was not prepared to take anything less.

And, dammit, he wasn't going to beg. Nor was he laying his pride out for her to stomp all over again.

But that didn't mean he was about to give up. He wanted her as his wife; he wanted his child's parents together, preferably married, before the birth. He just had to work out a plan to make it so.

For now he'd agreed to give her the time and space she'd requested to get through her end-of-year exams. After much pressing, she'd finally thrown her hands in the air and agreed to accept his financial help immediately, since she'd had to resign her job at Personal Best. But she refused his proposal to send his housekeeper/cook to look after her and his offer to buy her a car.

The second was nonnegotiable. He would buy her a car. She just didn't know it yet.

She had, however, relented on a couple of key issues.

At first she'd not wanted anyone else to know until she was further along in the pregnancy, since things could go wrong, but then she'd conceded that his mother and brothers should know because of the will.

Secondly, she'd agreed to him accompanying her on her first prenatal visit, after she'd finished her exams. That had surprised him. Perhaps she'd seen the obdurate set of his jaw or perhaps he'd swayed her with his reminder that this was *their* baby.

"I will let you know once I've made an appointment," she'd told him, and Alex had dipped his head in acknowledgment. "I appreciate that. Thank you, Zara."

He knew that was the only way to make any ground with her. With polite, controlled, nonconfrontational exchanges. He knew and yet he'd struggled—each time he'd called her since—to keep the heat of frustration from his voice.

He'd struggled, too, against the impulse to ask all kinds of incendiary questions. When he asked how she was feeling, he wanted to then ask if her body was changing. If she felt any different. Did she ever lie awake at night thinking that this was *his* baby inside her, a part of him that would forever bond them together, whether she wished it or not?

He wanted to remind her of the other nights they'd talked on the phone, when they'd laughed and shared details of their days, when she'd sighed and told him she missed him in her bed.

But these conversations were short and awkward, punctuated with fraught silences and always ending with her saying she needed to get back to work.

Tonight Alex had called with a purpose beyond asking after her health. He'd invited her to Kameruka Downs to meet his family the weekend after her exams finished and, dammit, he'd felt as tongue-tied as a teenager asking a girl out for the first time.

The silence after he finally got his tongue around the invitation felt damningly thick.

"I want you to meet Mau," he said stiffly. "My mother. And she will want to meet you."

"Have you told her yet?" she asked. "About the baby."

"This weekend. I'll tell her then."

"Will the rest of your family be there?"

"Yes. Tomas's wife is throwing a small party for Cat. Rafe's wife. This will be her first visit, too. I thought that might help. You won't be the only new—" God, he almost said *wife* but stopped himself in time and pinched the bridge of his nose "—newcomer."

"I don't think so," she said after a brief pause. "This is your sister-in-law's party."

Alex gripped his phone tighter. For some reason, without even knowing it, he'd been banking on her accepting. Banking on getting her out into the country where they might recapture a glimpse of what they'd shared at the cabin. A place where she would be comfortable and re-laxed, where he could show her how it could be between them. "It's not like that," he told her, pacing the room, try-ing to control his gathering frustration. "Angie throws a party at the drop of a hat. It's no big deal. Just an excuse to dress up and invite a few neighbors over."

"I thought those outback neighbors were hundreds of miles away."

"They fly in."

He heard a sound that could have been laughter, but it was too short and sharp to tell. "Alex, I appreciate the in-vitation. And I do want to meet your family one day. But by this weekend I'm going to be exhausted. I'll only want to sleep."

"We have beds at Kameruka Downs."

She sighed and he could actually picture her tired face, her worn-out eyes from that day in her kitchen, and he felt a pressure in his chest. A pain born of helplessness because he could do nothing for her. She wouldn't let him. "Look, I have to go. I have studying—"

"To do," he finished over the top of her. "I know, Zara. I've heard it before."

And this time he didn't even bother telling her not to work too hard, to look after herself, to get some sleep. He knew that was a waste of breath. And after they'd said their stilted goodbyes, after she'd reminded him of the time of her doctor's appointment next week, he allowed himself to consider if he was also wasting his time and his hopes.

She didn't love him. She wouldn't marry him. How the hell did he think he could change that?

Alex didn't tell anyone about the baby straight off. At the back of his mind he'd been wondering about his sisters-in-law. Waiting for some announcement, he supposed, but so far there'd been nothing. If either Angie or Cat was pregnant, they sure weren't showing the same signs as Zara.

He heard Angie's distinctive laughter and turned to see her, the life of the party, surrounded by a group of neighbors. Mostly male. He smiled, but as always lately, the gesture felt tight and the smile didn't stick. He did feel a degree of satisfaction, however, when he noticed that Tomas was one of the group. And that he—his formerly morose little brother—had a grin as wide as the north all over his face.

Angie was good for him. But she looked the same as the last time he'd seen her, strong and healthy and vibrant. If she was pregnant, she sure as hell wasn't suffering.

Turning a slow half circle, he scanned the small assembly in the central courtyard of the sprawling homestead that was now Tomas and Angie's home, until he located his other sister-in-law. Catriona. He found her sitting in a quiet corner, head bent toward Mau, listening intently.

Rafe had told him how she'd resisted making this trip for the two months since they'd married, how shy she'd been of meeting all the Carlisles, but finally he'd talked her into this weekend. Alex had wondered if that was significant. But then he couldn't imagine Rafe keeping quiet about anything, let alone impending fatherhood.

Right on cue, he felt a familiar thump between the shoulder blades.

"That's my wife you're ogling," Rafe said. "Do I need to punch your lights out?"

Alex snorted. "You could try."

They both watched Rafe's wife a second longer.

"She seems to be getting along fine with Mau."

"Are you thinking Dad knew what he was doing?"

Alex swirled the contents of the glass he'd forgotten he was holding. Whiskey. The color of Zara's eyes. The knowledge tightened his chest as he considered Rafe's question. "We assumed he wanted to see Mau happy again." He dipped his glass in that direction. "She's smiling now."

"My wife has that effect."

The tightness in Alex's chest constricted further at those words. *My wife.* As he noted the proprietary look on Rafe's face.

"The deadline's past," he noted. The three months they'd been granted to conceive, according to Chas's will.

"Don't take it too hard." Rafe cut him a look. "Tomas and I both consider we've won even though we've missed out on the inheritance."

"Neither of you?"

"Nope."

"Are you sure?"

"Pretty much."

Alex considered the depths of his whiskey another second. Cleared his throat. "I have some news."

Alex felt his brother's gaze shift and fix on his face. "Jeez, Alex, don't tell us you've been jilted again."

As far as jabs went, that one was pretty effective. And Rafe didn't even have a clue. Alex huffed out a breath and then looked up to meet his brother's eyes. "It seems I've made the deadline."

Rafe stared. The realization came slowly, in degrees, sharpening his gaze and curving his lips into a smile. "You sly dog." He slapped Alex on the back and then turned and called out across the courtyard. "Hey, little bro. Get over here."

Everyone turned and looked. Rafe grinned and shook his head. "I did not see that one coming."

* * *

Alex ushered his brothers inside, before Rafe decided to yell the news to all and sundry. In the office where this had all started the afternoon they'd buried their father, he told them that Zara was pregnant and that for the moment that news stayed within these walls.

"She hasn't even seen a doctor yet."

"But she's sure she's pregnant?" Tomas asked. "Those home tests can be—"

"She's sure. She's studying medicine. She knows the symptoms."

Tomas whistled. "A doctor. Nice."

Rafe grinned. "Seems big brother's been checking out her bedside manner."

Alex ignored his brothers' ribbing. He knew he should feel some measure of satisfaction. He'd fulfilled the terms of the will. He'd carried out Chas's last wish.

But even when Tomas unearthed his father's aged Glenfiddich to toast Alex's success, he felt no joy. When Rafe made a second toast to the first Carlisle grand-child—"I'm going to be an uncle!"—Alex's smile was forced.

And when he turned and saw his mother in the doorway, when he felt the shrewd sharpness of her eyes on his face, he knew she hadn't missed a thing.

"Rafe. Tomas." Mau's gaze didn't veer. "I would like to speak with Alexander in private."

They left without demur. When their mother used a name in full, they knew she meant business.

"You have some news to tell me?"

Mau hadn't been privy to the added clause in her hus-band's will and when she'd found out she'd been ropable. She looked no happier now as Alex repeated what he'd told his brothers. A bare-bones version of how she was to become a grandmother.

"If everything goes well. Zara's only eight weeks along."

"Zara." She seemed to weigh the name on her tongue, even as she weighed the story he'd told. Perhaps what he hadn't. "How do you feel about this? You don't look very happy."

"I'm…" He huffed out a breath. Looked away as he battled a heart-ripping surge of emotion. And when he looked back up, he knew he couldn't even try to hide all he felt from his mother's keen eyes. "She won't marry me. She's independent and stubborn and she thinks she's better off on her own. I've offered her everything. I don't know what else I can do."

"Have you told her you love her?" Mau asked.

"Why do you assume I love her?"

"I pray that you do, seeing as you seem so set on marrying her."

"She's having my child. Of course I'm set on marrying her."

Mau shook her head sadly. "You should know better than that, Alexander. What do you think would have happened if I'd married your father? Or Rafe's? I was too young and lost to know what I wanted then, but at least I knew enough not to marry for the wrong reason."

He looked away again. Studied his untouched whiskey. Saw Zara's eyes and heard her voice telling him about the right reasons. About love. "And if I do love her?"

"I suggest you tell her so."

"What if she doesn't feel the same way?"

"Oh, Alex." She put her hand on his arm. Squeezed gently. "I know you guard your emotions tightly and I think I know why. But you're nothing like him, you know."

His biological father. Alex didn't have to ask.

"He was wild, he had a temper, and he never had the will to try and control it. You're strong, like your grandfather and like the man Charles raised you to be. Sometimes I think you're too strong-willed. Too set on keeping everything inside." She squeezed his arm again. "Don't let that make you unhappy. If you love her, Alex, you need to tell her."

"And if she doesn't want to hear it?"

"If she's the right woman, that's all she'll want to hear."

By Sunday afternoon, Zara had had enough of sleeping and recuperating from exam stress. Not that all that lounging about didn't have its advantages. For example, she hadn't thrown up since Friday morning. But on the other side of the coin, not thinking about cytology and urology and hematology meant she had too much thinking space for Alex.

Unable to sit around doing nothing, yet not sure she wanted to push herself too hard—she could get used to this not-throwing-up thing very easily—she searched for her knitting bag, last used in the winter when she'd knocked off a scarf for Tim and another for Mr. Krakowski next door. Luckily they both supported the same football team so she could use the same colors and pattern. Black and white stripes were not that complicated.

She rummaged through her bits and pieces but nothing inspired her. Then it struck her. The baby. She could make…she didn't know what. She didn't know what babies needed and that struck her as a huge hole in her education. Up until this weekend she'd been too busy and too sick, but suddenly she wanted to know. Suddenly she had time to go to town to look through the shops. To educate herself.

Three hours later, she didn't feel educated so much as overwhelmed. Wandering back from her tram stop, she was a little excited, a little fearful, and incredibly thankful that she'd not been too proud to accept Alex's financial help. Raising a baby, she had learned today, was a very expensive exercise.

Turning the corner into her street, she started searching for her keys. She'd almost reached her house before she found them and when she straightened she saw him. Alex. Standing by her gate as if he'd been watching her approach.

Her heart thudded painfully hard as she came to a dead stop. Dimly she felt the key chain slipping through her fingers and when she heard the metallic jangle of keys hitting concrete, she tightened her grip on her tote bag. It felt like that might be the only thing she had a grip on.

"Hello, Zara." His voice sounded different. Thick. But perhaps that was her hearing. He took a step closer and she thought, for one breathless second, that he was going to kiss her. But then he ducked down and picked up her keys. "You dropped these."

Disappointment flooded her veins. "What are you doing here?"

"Waiting for you."

She was pretty sure they'd had this conversation before. It felt eerily familiar. Zara frowned. "Weren't you going to Kameruka Downs this weekend?"

"I've been. This morning I decided to fly down here instead of back to Sydney."

"The doctor's appointment isn't until Tuesday."

"I know."

"Oh." And she stood there in the quiet Sunday afternoon sunshine just looking at him. Her heart still beat too hard to be healthy. All she could think was *How could I miss him this much?*

His thick dark hair was slightly ruffled, as if he'd been raking his fingers through it. His blue-gray eyes swirled with some emotion she couldn't pin down. The grooves in his cheeks looked deeper but she didn't think it was from too much smiling. She wanted to reach up and trace them.

Wanted to touch him so badly she started to shake.

"Here. Let me take your shopping," he said, perhaps afraid she'd keel over.

There was that danger. Then he reached for her bag and their hands tangled and brushed and oh, the heat. The charge. The catch in her chest that had to be her heart standing still.

"I'll get the door for you," he said, and she followed him through her tiny gate and up the two steps to her door. He leaned down and picked up something from the stoop, and looked back over his shoulder at her. "When you didn't answer the door, I was going to leave this."

This, she realized was a pot of flowers. She didn't know what kind, only that they were bright and beautiful and shaking very badly when he put them into her hands. "Thank you," she managed to say even though her throat was thick with emotion. "They're gorgeous."

Then they were back to staring at each other again, except this time he smiled and touched her cheek with the back of his hand. "You're looking good, Zara. Rested."

"Not like hell?"

"The opposite, actually." His smile faded. "Please. Can I come in? There's something I have to say to you."

He looked so grave, so serious that Zara felt a belated jolt of apprehension. "Is something wrong? Is someone—"

His touch stilled her, silenced her. A hand on her shoulder. The stroke of his thumb against her collarbone. "No. It's nothing like that. I just…" He sucked in a breath and she realized that he also looked nervous. "Can we go inside?"

"Yes. Yes, of course." She nodded toward the keys in his hand. "It's the second key. The gold one."

Inside, she ushered him to the sitting room where he'd waited for her the last time. The day he'd got it all wrong. He put down her bag on the red sofa and when she fussed about making tea, he stopped her with a hand on her shoulder. This time he didn't let go. This time he turned her toward him and looked into her face.

"Unless you need that cup of tea desperately, I'd like you to stay. To listen." If he didn't say this now, they'd end up sidetracked and arguing. "I've been thinking about us. And about the last time I saw you. What I said and what I didn't say. I got it all wrong, Zara."

She moistened her lips. Said nothing. In her throat he could see the beat of her pulse and touched it with his thumb.

"What I should have said…what I wanted to say…what I think you needed me to say…"

"Yes?" she prompted.

And there was something hopeful in her tone. Something in the depths of those beautiful eyes that steadied the wild jangle of his nerves and gave him the words he needed. Gave him the confidence to do this right. His hand slid down her arm until he held her hand in his. Then he went down on one knee.

"Zara Lovett, I want you to be my wife. Not because you're going to be the mother of my baby. Not because I have this primal need to take care of you and it makes me crazy thinking that you're sick and I'm not here to help. Not because I want you in my bed every night or because you still have to teach me that smooth fishing cast."

His thumb stroked over her knuckles and he tightened his grip.

"I want you for my wife because I love you and want to spend the rest of my life with you. Will you marry me, Zara?"

For a long second she said nothing. She moistened her lips. She drew a breath that snagged in her throat, possibly because it felt like her heart was there. Crazy-dancing high in her chest.

Could she believe him? Oh, but she wanted to, so badly. He sounded sincere, but was this only to get his own way? Had he gone away and remembered what she'd told him about marriage? Is that why he'd gotten it so right—because she had supplied the lines?

"I'm on my knees here. Please, say yes."

He tugged on her hand, until she gave in and came down to his level. "How can this work, Alex? I don't know—"

"We can make it work," he said fiercely. "If we want it badly enough."

"There are things you don't know about me."

"You snore? Sweetheart, I know that. I've slept with you already."

She punched his shoulder lightly and he grabbed her fisted hand and kissed the knuckles, one by one. If she weren't already on her knees, that would have done the trick.

"Is this secret about Susannah?" he asked. "And your father?"

She sucked in a breath, her eyes wide. "You knew? How?"

"I didn't know for sure, until now."

"You guessed?" Her voice rose a semitone. "How?"

"An educated guess. I told you I'd like your sister." He smiled. "And I do. She introduced us, in a roundabout way."

Zara just stared, completely undone.

"And, please, don't say anything else about your mother

or your father or the scandal that might cause. If you marry me, you will be my wife. They can say what they like, it won't change the fact that I love you."

"I still want to finish my degree," she said.

"Of course you do. I can live wherever I like. Wherever *you* like."

"You would move?" she asked in hushed wonder. "To Melbourne?"

"If that's what you want."

Slowly she shook her head. "Why would you do that?"

"Because I love you. To be together."

She blinked rapidly, to ward off the emotion brimming in her eyes. And then she couldn't help herself. She had to put her hands on him, cupping his face. "You really do."

He smiled, and she leaned in and kissed him on that smile, drinking its happiness into her body. Feeling it wash through her in a wave of bliss. "I love you, too, Alex. I had no idea how much until right now."

His eyes closed for a second, and when they opened they were full of everything she was feeling. She touched her thumb to his mouth, traced the bow of his top lip. Kissed him again.

"Is that a yes?" he asked.

"Yes. That is definitely a yes."

Zara let that sink in a moment. The fact that she had just agreed to marry him. The fact that despite her happiness, the concept of marriage still scared her some. Then he smiled at her and that shadow of fear faded to black.

"I did you another disservice," she said.

"Oh?" His hands slid up her arms, then over her shoulders and down her back. As though he were learning her shape all over again.

"I thought I couldn't love you because you weren't a man I could have taken home to meet my mother."

He stopped with his hands on her waist, his expression slightly affronted. "I would have loved to meet your mother. And she would have loved me."

Zara raised her brows. "How do you figure that?"

"Because I'm going to love her daughter so well." His hands slid lower until they cupped her hips. "And spoil her rotten by giving her whatever she wants." He tugged her forward until their bodies touched. "And make her so damn satisfied she won't ever stop smiling."

She was smiling when he started to kiss her, and smiling even broader when he finished a long time later. Slowly her eyes drifted open and she snuggled against him, loving the feel of his body against hers. "Tell me about your house."

"What do you want to know?"

"Just…what it's like."

"It's like a house." Alex shrugged. "Walls, roof. Lots of rooms inside."

She laughed, amused and delighted by that answer. "Does it have a pool?"

"Two."

"Are you joshing me?"

"One outdoor, one indoor." Then perhaps misinterpreting why she'd gone still, he said, "We can fill one in if you think that's excessive."

"Does it have a gym?" she asked after another moment.

"It has a first-rate gym," he answered solemnly, and his hands slid under her shirt and peeled it from her body. "Now, is there anything else you want to know about my house? Because in about sixty seconds—" he unhooked her bra "—I'm not going to be able to talk."

"Oh, why's that?"

He pulled her bra off and tossed it. "My mouth is going to be otherwise occupied."

"So," she said some time later, when she'd regained her breath. They were in her bed, naked, sated. Happy. "How far is this house from Sydney University?"

Alex opened one eye. "Does this mean we're going to live in Sydney?"

"Possibly. Although I want you to know that this isn't to set a precedent. You will not always get your own way."

Alex just smiled and hugged her body close against his and started planning when he would next have his way with her.

Epilogue

Zara did move into Alex's Sydney home and she decided they would keep both pools. The gym was, indeed, first rate and Alex had his way with her several memorable times within its mirrored, equipment-packed walls.

He did not get his way over a quick wedding, however.

Zara refused to rush into marriage and insisted on a six-month cooling-down period. Things did not cool down and they were married in the courtyard of Kameruka Downs under the broad blue northern sky.

Rafe was Alex's best man, which gave him license to drop all kinds of lines about being the best man. Susannah returned from America in time to act as maid of honor, and although she remained quietly mysterious about her man she completed Zara's happiness by letting everyone know she was the bride's sister.

Angie, of course, organized the reception party for family and a small group of friends. Catriona was supposed to help her with the food except her delicate early-pregnancy stomach objected to the first whiff of seafood. Angie smiled and patted her mini-bulge and thanked whatever fates had made her so hale and hearty.

Maura Keane Carlisle sat in the front row for the ceremony, holding Tomas's hand tightly and smiling broadly despite the stream of tears coursing down her face.

And from up above "King" Carlisle looked down on them all and smiled. His beloved wife and his three boys, all happy, all smiling. His mission was accomplished.

* * * * *

NOCTURNE_INTRO

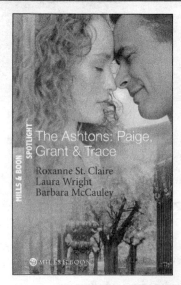

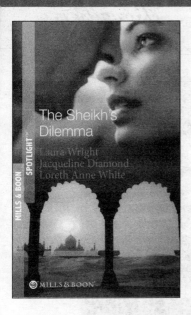

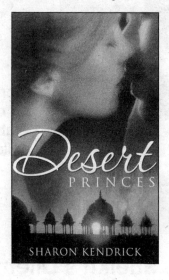

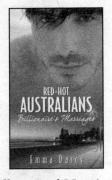

FREE ONLINE READ!

One Indian Summer

by Nicola Marsh

Don't miss this short story linked to
Nicola Marsh's novel in
Destination: Summer Weddings!

To read your free online story, just go to:

www.millsandboon.co.uk/oneindiansummer

www.millsandboon.co.uk

"You've been warned twice. Stop prying into Anne Trulane's death."

After someone comes to journalist Laurel Armand and claims her sister Anne was murdered, Laurel's determined to get the truth.

When a copperhead snake is left on her doorstep, Laurel realises that the warning means she's close to discovering an answer that someone doesn't want her to know...

Available 4th June 2010

www.millsandboon.co.uk

millsandboon.co.uk Community

Join Us!

he Community is the perfect place to meet and chat to
indred spirits who love books and reading as much as
ou do, but it's also the place to:

- **Get the inside scoop from authors about their latest books**
- **Learn how to write a romance book with advice from our editors**
- **Help us to continue publishing the best in women's fiction**
- **Share your thoughts on the books we publish**
- **Befriend other users**

orums: Interact with each other as well as authors, edi-
ors and a whole host of other users worldwide.

logs: Every registered community member has their
wn blog to tell the world what they're up to and what's
n their mind.

ook Challenge: We're aiming to read 5,000 books and
ave joined forces with The Reading Agency in our
augural Book Challenge.

rofile Page: Showcase yourself and keep a record of
our recent community activity.

ocial Networking: We've added buttons at the end of
very post to share via digg, Facebook, Google, Yahoo,
echnorati and de.licio.us.

www.millsandboon.co.uk